Nicholas House is a B... ...from the South of England. He t... ...nspired by the stories of Jules V...

Fascinated by the natural ... Geosciences at university. This afforded ... to travel and fuel his overactive imagination, allo... ...him to take inspiration from a vast array of varied sources.

He went on to merge his passion for writing and love for video production by creating scripted videos on YouTube which continues to let him experiment with a variety of writing styles.

Primarily writing Supernatural Fantasy and Science Fiction, Nicholas has also written numerous pieces of published poetry alongside short stories, e-books and scientific articles. With a mind so full of ideas and an ongoing literary passion he plans to continue writing about whatever inspires him long into the future.

Also by Nicholas House

Novellas
The Median
The Dark
Illumination

Collections
Abridged: A Short Collection of Short Stories

Chronicles of The Median

Nicholas House

Chronicles of The Median
(The Median, The Dark, Illumination)
Copyright© 2011, 2022 Nicholas House

All rights reserved. No part of this book may be reproduced or transmitted in any form or by any means, electronic or mechanical, including photocopying, recording, or any information storage and retrieval system, without prior written permission of the Author. Your support of author's rights is appreciated.

All characters in this work are fictitious. Any resemblance to actual persons, living or dead, is purely coincidental.

Contents

Book 1
Prologue – The City of Light
I-I – A Long Night
I-II – A Dark Past
I-III – VI of I
I-IV – Desert of Desolation
I-V – The Wretched
I-VI – The Other Side
I-VII – Necrosis

Book 2
Prologue – Nightfall
II-I – Noir
II-II – They Awake
II-III – The Horde
II-IV – Within Darkness
II-V – The Schism
II-VI – Obsidian

Book 3
Prologue – Dawn
III-I – No More Quiet Times
III-II – The Forgotten
III-III – Messiah
III-IV – Illuminatus
III-V – Static Tension
III-VI – Radiance

Book 1
The Median

Prologue - The City of Light

Then I saw a great white throne and him who was seated on it. Earth and sky fled from his presence and there was no place for them

-Revelations 21:11

M̲ankind's affliction with the physical and the spiritual has surpassed what anyone could have expected. Nations wage wars for the supposed 'Glory of God' in vain attempts to obtain their deity's grace. No-one ever supposes that they are fighting for the wrong side, plunging themselves ever deeper into the satanic flames.

Evil has always existed, not in the form of a devil or land of flaming brimstone but in people. People's greed and lust for power fuels deeds that shouldn't even be conceived of let alone carried out. An evil such as this can spread beyond life and if the will is strong enough, grow beyond control. Accepted should be the fact that it is futile to speculate about the next world. Is there an afterlife? Heaven? Hell? The true question is 'What lies between?' A ghost world? Some kind of nether plane, where the restless dead await their passage to the gleaming city of light, or await their trial and judgement. Nonetheless, no matter where, the evil of man will rule out and tyranny of the world's hate will consume.

There are those who know things. Things about the Earth and beyond that should never be known. Most of these few people refuse to believe it all to be real and the even fewer who do don't care to acknowledge it at all. Those few who do the truths are oppressed and dismissed by the masses and their 'righteous' religions as kooks and members of the occult. These people, though, are strong. Their abilities can place them in situations where reality can seem like a dream and dreams like nightmares. Still, the naive are at risk, the weak and the inexperienced. They can be seen as portals, unguarded gates by those longing to return from the Other Side, and are readily open to possession by powerful spirits with a long history in the Median world. However, instances of possession are rare and are dealt with as much due care as they deserve, sometimes hidden as extreme cases of Dissociative Personality Disorder.

Like they can travel to our world, we too are able to cross the silent borders that divide our planes. But only the most skilled of Medians may do this at will without fear of the shadows which stalk them. These instances, though, are even rarer than possessions and are not only looked upon by most with speculation but a great air of impossibility. It is unlikely that Medians can physically control the dearly departed; to do this would require a power far greater than anyone has ever possessed, rather they merely commune with them, ease their concerns about what comes next. Medians exist solely to guide the lonely dead to their spiritual destiny with as little disturbance to the world at large as possible. Maintaining the illusion that the unknown beyond remains exactly that. But on occasions restless souls will make themselves known and the Medians purpose is called upon for much more than its original intentions.

I-I - A Long Night

Absent in body, but present in spirit

-Corinthians 5:3

As a child I was never a large believer in anything other than what I knew to be true. As far as I was concerned, that was simply the world around me. There were dreams, though. Every child has nightmares but these were different; terrible visions of what I was sure couldn't be real. My parents always told me that I had an overactive imagination. How could they understand when they never even wanted to try? What's worse is that I believed them. At least up until that night.

I was only twelve. I had always been scared of driving in the rain. The noise. Not being able to see what was out there. But then our car was run off the road by a jack-knifing lorry and...No one should have to see that sort of thing, let alone a child when his parents are involved. There was only one thing that could have been worse and that was to live through it twice. In my dreams I had already seen it, every harrowing detail yet the very essence of what I had been taught told me not to accept it. For the next few months I lived with my aunt and every day wrestled to come to terms with everything that I had lived though, all the time experiencing more and more vivid visions. Amazing places constructed of what was almost pure light, shadowy figures and an ever-present feeling that I was not like the others. Eventually I accepted that I could no longer go on *denying that which was so obvious. I had something, a gift, and to deny it would bring something that wasn't even worth thinking about.*

Sure, I'd been christened...Haven't we all? But it's not as though I liked the religion, bunch of hypocrites if you ask me. It's safe to say that I try to keep as far away from any sort of church as I can. It must be some sort of cruel irony of fate, then, that those happen to be the first place they always think of heading.

The dull, sodium yellow of a flickering street lamp fell upon the single car parked beneath, its light doing nothing to warm the cold, wet street. Sat within, motionless, a dark figure watched shimmering silhouettes against the strained glass of the old stone chapel adjacent.

After a minute or two he abruptly opened the car door and swung a leg out into the drizzling rain. He paused and looked to the gloomy October sky, then back down and shook his head. He continued to exit the car and slammed the door, causing a torrent of water beads to run forward from the sunroof onto the windscreen. Pulling forward his leather jacket and adjusting the collar in a vain attempt to protect from the rain, he began to stride towards the chapel's large door.

He grabbed the iron handle and listened though the wood to what sounded like a scuffle, or at least a one-sided struggle. Eventually the doors were pushed open and he entered briskly, leaving a drizzly mist in his wake.

Inside, two youths were attempting to pull a poor box from the clenched arms of a clergyman.

"Hey!"

The youths quickly turned around and gritted their teeth, with one stepping forward and flicking his own collar up aggressively.

"Wha' do ya want!?" this was barked as though it were a command, despite there being no authority to command with.

"I would like you to leave..." the man looked them both up and down in turn, "right now," he began to walk forward, slowly sliding his hand inside his jacket.

A Long Night

"And 'ow ya gunna make us!?" the second youth snapped, squeezing the tip of his cap together and spitting on the ground.

"I said now." He smoothly drew a long barrelled six round revolver from a holster concealed under his glistening wet leather jacket and pointed it casually at the nearest youth. "I suggest you comply," he finished after a few seconds.

The youths shuffled uneasily and then started towards the door. The barrel of the gun tracked them out of the chapel and then began to fall as the door creaked to a close.

The priest stood, unsure whether to be pleased by the actions of this mysterious individual or appalled. Before he had a chance to speak, the chamber of the gun was quickly flicked open. Its sharp click made the cleric jump and a voice came from behind the still dripping leather as the revolver was brought into open view.

"Don't worry…It's not loaded," the chamber was flicked back into place and the weapon was replaced into its holster.

"Thank you, my child," the priest spoke at last and loosened his grip on the poor box as the stranger slowly turned around. "What is your name?"

"As if it matters…" he once again straightened his jacket and then looked directly at the priest "Weignright… My name is Richard Weignright," his voice discerned itself as soft yet with an oddly distant texture followed by a quality described only by that of an echo. His general appearance seemed to perfectly match his voice. He was clean shaven and his thick black hair fell loosely into whatever style it appeared to see fit with flecks of his fringe tumbling about his brow.

"Thank you, Richard," the priest reached a free hand forward in order to distribute a blessing but it was quickly pushed away.

"Don't think you can thank me yet," he looked around the chapel altar carefully. Two large candles burnt steadily; their light partially reflected by the polished brass cross at the centre of the arrangement. Suddenly the candles flicked violently in quick succession, right to left. Richard looked back to the clergyman. "You'd better leave me to it. It may get…" he sought for the correct word and eventually settled on something that was reasonably acceptable, "interesting."

The Median

He seemed largely taken aback by the proposal. "Leave you to what?" he didn't expect an answer but briefly waited for one nonetheless. "This is my chapel and if I didn't have those youngsters telling me what to do, I certainly will not have you doing so!" he breathed and seemed pleased with his sermon.

Richard quickly glanced to the heavens. "Fine. Suit yourself," he began to slowly walk towards the altar, the candles continuing to flick back and forth as he stepped up. The flickering abruptly ceased and became isolated to the left candle. He leant towards the flame, the flickering growing more aggressive as he did so, and felt an odd chill surround him. It took it upon itself to ignore any concept of flesh and bite directly at Richard's bone.

The priest craned his neck in an attempt to gain a concept of what kind of ritual was taking place. "What are you doing?" he finally inquired cautiously but was completely ignored.

Richard looked deeper into the fire, then abruptly closed his eyes. He whispered some inaudible verse before sharply blowing at the candle, extinguishing the dancing flame. He opened his eyes again and slowly swivelled them around. Gradually a breeze began to pick up and he nodded to himself, acknowledging the fact as though it had been spoken. The breeze only grew as he stepped down from the altar and took up a position in front of it.

The clergyman began to panic as a gust of wind swept in and extinguished the candles dotted around the building. The only light that was left was that of the misty moon and street lights outside. It filtered in streaks through the stained glass, tainting the church an eerie twilight blue.

The gust finally died down and the church was again silent for several moments. The priest stepped slowly towards Richard who remained concrete still. Just as he reached the corner of the altar an empty, tubular tone echoed around the rafters. It vibrated cobwebs from their century old hollows, startled dozens of bats and shook the very soul of the building. Still, Richard remained motionless.

Rather than fade, the lonely sound merely changed. It pitched in and out of audible range for some time but at last seemed to settle out into some kind of physical form. It was a slow-moving mist which billowed out from above the altar, wisps reaching out to

A Long Night

encircle both Richard and the priest. They explored and felt their presences before withdrawing in a slick motion accompanied by a sequence of low tones. They echoed among the relics and became apparent as distinct voices, wailing and bemoaning the fate of the eternally damned.

Suddenly a single voice became apparent among the drone. "Leave this place..." The voice was forceful but without aggression or malice. "Leave us."

All his life the priest had followed his faith with blind diligence and loyalty. But now, with all that he was witnessing he began to question whether he even believed what he had been preaching in the first place. He pushed the doubts to the back of his mind, trying to silence them with the story he had always been taught. As the voice spoke, he stumbled back and made a short spurt for his sacristy, fumbling the poor box to the ground and slamming the door behind himself, locking it tight.

Richard's eyes flicked open onto the altar and upon a much different world. The walls glowed as if the sun itself bore presence unto them. The air above the ground shimmered with a dark essence that now seemed to encompass the other worldly chapel. The candles that had shone so bright previously now burnt a quiet, almost black flame yet somehow still seemed to outline the solitary brass idols around them. A shivering atmosphere at Richards' feet grew in motion to mimic that of ocean mist rolling onto a dawn shore. It rose and encompassed the objects on the altar and eventually up to the pulpit. It moved as if attempting to prove all around it was insignificant when compared to its mere presence.

Suddenly the waves fell to the ground and broke on the stone slabs with no apparent reason or prompting. Still unphased, Richard began to move, casually reaching into an inner pocket and taking hold of a glass apothecary bottle. As he did, the darkness pressed up against his back, forcing him to pause his actions.

"Why are you here?" the voice of the darkness whispered in an almost surreal way. "Why do you not listen?"

Richard let go of the bottle, allowing it to slip neatly back into his pocket and withdrew his hand down to his side. Turning around he found the shadows had manifested themselves into a figure. A young boy, no older than fourteen, his complexion pale and virtually translucent.

"How are you here?" it added, mystified by the mortal before him.

Richard took a breath, at a loss of what to say. Before he had a chance to even think, a second presence drifted across his path. From the back of the chapel, it began to fade through the air, taller than the first, and started to take wavering steps towards Richard. It reached out and gently placed a hand on the boy's shoulder, looking squarely at Richard as its features became discernible. Both looked as though they had once, long ago, worked on the fields, sowing and ploughing. Beyond that he dared not think about how the pair had come to be here. "You know why I'm here?" he asked the taller spirit.

The farmer moved in front of his son and without any kind of concern gazed straight at Richard. "Are you a God fearing man, sir?" he continued to silently stare ahead for a few more seconds. "How could you live with yourself? You don't know how long we've looked for a way back. You have no idea how desolate, how empty it is there. What reason have you got to send us back?"

"I do know..." Richard replied simply, pausing in thought for a moment, "...and I'm sorry...I truly am."

The farmer only now broke his gaze and stepped back in line with his son. "So am I."

The priest, shaking with disbelief, opened his eyes and unclasped his praying hands. He inched around and found the door handle, grasping it loosely at first, only tightening his grip as confidence returned to him. He re-opened the door onto an empty church hall, lacking any trace of what had happened. He stepped from the doorway and lightly trod towards the altar. He looked up towards the dark shrine, the candles now extinguished, and up at the brass cross that, even now, still glinted in the gloom. He looked around and realised the absence of the discarded poor box. Without even searching for it, he knew that the stranger had taken it. Although, with everything he had seen that night, for all the priest cared, he could keep it.

A Long Night

The house was at most 35, maybe 40 years old yet it had a strange presence about it, one that made it feel far older. It encompassed the rooms and flowed through its residents, becoming the building's one defining feature. This sense of premature ageing was only reinforced by the ornately decorated skirting boards, antique figurines and bookcases brimming with texts on spirituality and other worldly planes.

Richard placed the poor box, much more gently than it had become accustomed to over the course of the night, on a small shelf next to the door. Placing his keys alongside it, he slipped off his dripping jacket and dropped it over a cloak stand. No sooner had he done that, from down the hall came the sound of the kitchen door swinging open and firm footsteps making their way up the polished wooden floor.

"Again?" came a young but raspy male voice belonging to the footsteps.

"It just seems such a waste," replied Richard, again placing a firm grasp on the poor box, this time only to toss it to his counterpart. "Take that round to Oxfam tomorrow, will you?"

"These charities..." he adjusted his grip on the box and held it to his side, "ninety percent of the money goes in the pocket of some fat cat."

"Mike, you see," he stepped forward and leant towards Michael, making him seem much shorter than he actually was, "it's better that at least some of the money, even if it *is* just ten percent, goes to whoever needs it rather than it all going in some cardinal's wallet." He stood straight up again, where it became apparent that both men in fact had much the same build.

Michael breathed out heavily as Richard turned into the lounge but seemed to remember something as he moved to sit down. "Oh yeah, you got a call while you were out. It was Chris. He sounded pretty messed up."

"Tell me, when *isn't* he messed up?" He took a seat and leant on his knees. "Did he say why he phoned or was it just his general brand of assorted doomsday messages?"

"He said he wanted to meet you. Tonight, in the alley next to Queens Square take away at 12 o'clock," Michael moved to the other side of the room and leant on the hearth while Richard seemingly fell deep into thought. "You've not had a proper break in days now. Is it something to do with Halloween being in a few days?"

Richard jolted his head up and looked Michael straight in the eye. "How long now? Three years? How many times do I have to tell you? Halloween has no special bearing on anything, it's just a few dumb shits on the Other Side think they have a better chance of getting through. Believe me, they don't so it's not my problem."

"I just thought-"

"Nothing! Alright?" he sunk back into the seat and breathed deeply. "Now, Queens Square, was it?"

"Yeah," Michael said cautiously, "the take away. I don't know what he wants."

There was silence for a few seconds as Richard contemplated the rest of the night. "I'd better check it out…You never know," he glanced at an ornate mahogany clock on the mantelpiece. "Half nine, now," there was silence for another few seconds before he smoothly pushed up out of the chair and headed for the hallway.

"Rich, where are you going?"

Richard grabbed his still dripping coat from the stand and slipped it on. "I need to stop off somewhere first," before anything more could be said he opened the front door and rushed out into the night.

"Hey!" Michael grabbed Richard's car keys from the shelf, "you forgot your keys!"

"I'll walk," came a voice from the rapidly shrinking silhouette.

"But it's still raining!"

There are not many people in this world who fully know what is going on. The purpose of life and other such related subjects. I never claimed to be one of them. I do take some pride in having a better idea than the majority of the populous, even if that idea is brought about by something I quite often wished I didn't have.

I know there's more than one plane of existence, far more. The living world, that of the dead and a lonely, desolate plane known only as the Median World. Fringing on each side of the Median World bridging the planes of the living and the dead are border worlds. Places where lost souls manifest themselves and occasionally break through to appear as ghosts and poltergeists. Where most can only catch glimpses of these or witness their paranormal activities, I can see them as clear as day, as though they were actually there, even when they were not supposed to be. It's considered by some that my duty, the duty of all Medians, is to move them on to the next world, even if it is not their desire to go. There's no duty really, for me it's just about trying to keep a little sanity in the world.

By the time Richard had reached Gateshead Cemetery the rain had finally eased but still lingered in the air with a cold odiousness. He stood at the chest high iron fence of the graveyard and gazed in, scanning the grounds as though he were expecting to find something. Eventually his eyes focused onto a point just off an old chestnut tree, its branches swaying lethargically in the gentle breeze. As misty night air began to clear, it became apparent that there was the figure of a man. He seemed to be casually raking leaves, without a shudder or care for the bitterly cold air.

Richard turned away from the fence and made his way to the rusty gate. Gently pressing it open, the gate moaned from decades of disuse and finally screeched to a contented silence. The figure did not turn as he approached, apparently unaware of his presence. "Albert."

The figure continued to rake the leafless soil for a few more seconds before it began to speak in a deep, empty tone that was almost lost to the open air. "Have you finally come to do it then, son?" His rake occasionally caught a drifting leaf which crackled loudly against the soothing breeze. "I suppose my time is somewhat..." he looked up and leaned against his rake. His face was old and as empty as his words, dark and faded to an empty mist almost as if he belonged to the night, "overdue."

"You know I'm not here for that," he paused and tried to gain some idea of Albert's expression, or whether he, indeed, even had one. "I've had quite a busy week. You wouldn't happen to know anything about that, would you?"

He stood up straight and clasped the rake firmly in his hand. "One sees only what they wish to see..." casually he began to move towards Richard, in the process walking through an age-old wheelbarrow that he had apparently been using at some point in time. "I wish only to see what it is my business to."

"I don't want to, but I'll do it if I have to."

"Of course, what I wish and what I see are not always one in the same," he turned away and headed back towards the large tree he was working under, this time having the forethought to walk around the wheelbarrow. "Souls are restless, then again they always are, but especially now. You know why. But this is different...They're scared, and not just of moving on. There's something out there, something you don't want coming here," he placed the rake gently against the tree and turned back to Richard. "I've learnt a lot in my time here, most I didn't think was possible. But I am too old to worry about such things now. That is the job of the young, your job," he took a step away from the rake and looked Richard straight in the eye. "Good luck Richard...And, please, take care of yourself." As his words drifted through the air his body began to fade into the night until all that was left was the eerie mist hovering above the graves.

Richard took a breath and looked down to the stone plaque at his feet:

HERE LIES:
ALBERT WEIGNRIGHT

BELOVED HUSBAND AND FATHER

1945-1988

WILL BE SORELY MISSED

"You too, dad," he turned and began to walk away from the grave as the rain started to fall again. He stopped at the rusted iron gate and looked back towards the large tree as it quickly became obscured by the night's mist. Turning quickly and once again flicking up his collar, he set off along the wet street.

A Long Night

For days the voices had haunted him, whispered omens in the back of his head, rumours of a dark shadow clouding everything just and good. Tonight was no different. With the quiet street it seemed as though the voices were screaming, and then there was the sudden realisation that they were. Richard was not the only one to hear them, though.

Chris wasn't someone many people liked, or even had anything much to do with. He had been diagnosed as mentally ill after several bouts of severe depression and from then onwards he had roamed homeless shelters with nowhere else to go, just another nameless face in the endless stream of human society. Appearances, it seemed, never told the full story for he was a Median, just like Richard.

After the death of his wife, he had all but given up on life and did something no Median should ever do. He left himself open to the spirits wanting to cross back to the living world; a vessel for as many souls as it could bear.

The square was deadly quiet. The neon light of a take away flickered but cast virtually no light upon the puddle ridden concrete.

Richard glanced at his watch, shielding it from the driving rain. Twelve exactly.

"Rick? Is that you?" a voice tentatively came from the dark alleyway.

"Don't trust him!"

"I have to, he's our friend."

"You have to tell him what we've seen."

"Yes, only he can help."

"Be careful, Chris."

"I still say don't trust him!"

Richard strained to look into the dark from where the babbled confusion of statements had come. "Chris? Don't be afraid. It's Richard."

"What do you take us for? We are not afraid," Chris strode out into the dull light of the square and looked Richard up and down. He was filthy, unshaven and wore a trench coat that looked as though it belonged in a museum.

"Yes, we are!" he recoiled back into the half darkness, his greasy and sodden blonde hair flicking over his face, "we are very afraid."

"Can I talk to Chris?" Richard asked as softly as he could, trying not to sound patronising.

Chris' head slowly emerged into the flickering neon light. "The world is changing, Rick. No-one's content on the Other Side-"

"As if they were in the first place," interrupted Chris to himself.

"-They can't do it, Rick, they can't…" he shook his head violently and began repeating his last two words over and over until he suddenly stopped and looked back up into the rain, "but if one could…"

Richard nodded shallowly. "Could what? Make it through to this side?" he breathed a sigh of frustration; it was clear this was not going to be easy. "What are you talking about, Chris?"

"The spirit can pass unnoticed but the physical can tip the balance," he stood up straight and looked Richard in the eye. "If he could…They all could…" Chris seemed to become transfixed by something and began watching the sky blankly, uncaring of the rain.

"He?" asked Richard irately. "Who? Who is He?!" his words flowed into the night and echoed in the ether. The whispered voices returned and scratched at the back of Richard's head, it was garbled and chaotic but they whispered a word over and over again. A name.

Chris looked back to Richard and spoke a single word more clearly and coherently than he ever had before. "Millaian."

As he spoke the word, the chaotic whispers ceased, apparently content that they had finally been heard. Richard nodded shallowly and repeated the name with a dark sense of knowing. "Millaian."

I-II - A Dark Past

For now we see through a glass, darkly

-Corinthians 13:12

He used to be my friend. The only one I could tell about everything I saw, everything I knew. Then it happened. He became a shadow of what he had been.
I hid the true nature of things from Michael for his own good...He shows great interest and, dare I say, promise but not yet the appreciation that the craft deserves. To know the truth would mean a risk beyond any that I am prepared to expose him to. One day he will want to know. One day he will need to know and, on that day, I will be there to give him the guidance he will surely need for what will lay ahead. For now, ignorance is a sweet bliss compared to the fate which may await him.

Richard pulled his finger roughly along the assorted volumes of spiritual encyclopaedia, through The Summoning texts and to a large, age-old book. He tapped the tome violently with his index finger before ripping it from the bookcase and slamming it onto the coffee table. The decade old hardback was at least three inches thick and had its name embossed in gold leaf down the spine; 'The History of Old London'.
Richard wiped his still dripping fringe from his face and descended upon the book, pulling it open at an already marked page.

His gaze flowed down the yellowing page and eventually settled upon a small sepia picture of a stately looking family. The caption simply read 'The Millaians.'

"You," whispered Richard to himself as he settled his finger over a specific figure in the centre of the photo. The figure stood tall and stern over the rest of the family, almost as though he had some sort of menace about him. The finger slid from the picture to a name just to the side and a short paragraph below it.

Joseph Millaian

Respected among his peers and feared by the workers in his factories, Joseph was the third generation of the industry owning Millaians to come to London. He owned lucrative properties in Manchester and Liverpool, topping off his enterprise with his purchase in 1884 of a textile facility in the centre of Birmingham. Reaching London in 1886, Joseph failed in an attempted bid to take over Thomas & Co. in the country's capital. Later that year he was reported missing, only to be declared dead by suicide, presumably from the immense stress of business. Yet to this day his body has never been recovered and it is unknown what truly happened to him.

Richard slowly stood back up, continuing to stare at the text, gritting his teeth with deep thought.

"Rich?" came a voice from the doorway.

He swung round, slamming the book closed as he did and settled his gaze towards Michael. "It's a little late for you, isn't it?"

"I could say the same for you," he looked him up and down. "You're dripping wet."

"I realise that," he leant flat palmed on the book as Michael began to move into the room. "Chris was…He was his usual self."

"Always is," he craned his head around Richard to look at the book. "What're you reading?"

"Nothing!" Richard snapped quickly, "…Just…Some family history."

"Alright, well-" he stood straight again and began to move back towards the door, "I'll see you tomorrow then."

Richard nodded and waited until Michael was completely gone before releasing his grip on the book. He gazed at it again and sighed heavily. "What's the connection?" He again sighed heavily and replaced the text to its appointed position.

As he retracted his hand, he glanced at the clock in the centre of the mantle and then slumped down into his armchair.

1:37am. It wasn't like those things in the night were anything new to Richard, far from it. Still, each second closer to the darkness he came, the more his concern grew. He never liked to sleep at this time of year, no-one in his position would, but then no-one is impervious to the will of their body, either.

As he sat, the whispers scratched at the back of his mind, repeating that same name over and over. Soon, though, their drone became but white noise and he began to sink into the dark sleep which forever left him vulnerable and consumed with fear.

"The night shall come…"

And so it did.

The dreams which dwelt within were filled with the shadows of untold figures. There was a numbing silence which pierced the very soul itself and the brightest light in the darkest of places. Then there were those who stood before it, each wanting a vessel as much as the next, so close yet just out of reach. Behind them stood a man, seemingly possessing no desire for a vessel or to return to the mortal plane.

Richard stepped towards the man with the gathered shadows around him parting like water. He reached forward for his shoulder but before he could grasp him, the figure turned and looked up sombrely.

"Chris?"

Sunlight washed in all about him and dissolved the darkness as quickly as it had manifested itself. Richard flinched and squinted his eyes as it became apparent that he was back in his own world.

The Median

"What happened last night?" Michael's voice came from the dazzling black.

Richard cracked open his eyes, barely managing to focus on him. "Last night?" he rolled his eyes over to the clock that he was certain he had only looked at moments ago. "Nine thirty?" he groaned and shook his head while growing more accustomed to the light.

"With Chris..." Michael took a deep breath. "I heard on the radio this morning...He's-"

"-Dead," he leant forward and cradled his head in his hands. "Don't ask me how I know."

He looked cautiously to Richard and began again. "He was found just outside Queens Square...They didn't say how he died," Michael's mind swelled with possibilities and finally one slipped out. "You didn't-?" his almost comment was met with quite possibly the sharpest gaze he'd ever experienced. "No, no...Of course you didn't," he looked away and spoke in tones he didn't intend to be heard. "It's just what with his condition...It would have been a release-"

"Listen!" Richard pushed himself from the chair, pulling himself upright, without even wavering. "Christopher was always my friend...He still is-" he breathed sombrely, "wherever he is." He relaxed slightly and rushed past Michael towards the staircase. There was no particular urgency but his step was one that was not to be stopped.

Michael watched Richard move swiftly up the stairs before turning away and whispering simply, "These things happen."

But they don't. Not like this. Something was wrong.

I could have stopped it. I was the last to see him. I am his last true friend, a lot of good that did him. In the end I abandoned him just like everyone else. For all the good I did I might as well have killed him myself...It couldn't have just been a coincidence, he knew something he wasn't supposed to and now so did I. The more I thought about it the more I knew it was better to keep Michael in the dark. I still wasn't sure how safe that would keep him though. Kids like that...They draw attention...

A Dark Past

Richard casually opened his bedroom door and let it drift gently shut as he passed through. The room was much like the rest of the house; rustic beyond its time and filled with bookcases stocked with assorted volumes on the afterlife.

Across from the foot of his bed was an oak desk littered with various scribbled scraps of paper and a single large, half burnt candle centred at the back of it. Around it stood an arrangement of small statuettes and precious looking rocks, each presumably with a significance all of their own.

He took a silver flick lighter from his inside pocket and lit the large candle before laying heavily down on the bed and flicking the lighter closed with a snap. Slowly his eyes drifted shut, compelled to close by the darkness of the room. The only thing that allowed him to cling onto the waking world was a small beam of dusty light which managed to find a gap between the still drawn curtains. In the murky darkness the air changed.

"Hello Rich," a voice said soothingly.

Richard lifted his eyelids gently, looking towards the desk and the lit candle. It still burned but now darkly, giving off no light, only an electrical blue aurora backed by an eerie black, absent of movement and warmth. He fully opened his eyes and peered carefully around the now grey and lifeless feeling room. His eyes settled on a shape standing against that lone beam of sunlight and without them even adjusting to the unusual brightness, he knew who he was looking at.

"You called...How could I refuse?" came the voice again, the figure stepping closer to Richards's bed and into a better light. He was now neat and tidy, with a sense of self unlike any he'd had in such a long time. "I'm free now."

"So it was you..." Richard sat up and turned, pushing himself up on the side of the bed. "Chris, I can save you...Bring you back-"

"No! I thought we had an agreement," Chris looked Richard in the eye, "I'm too close to her now...I can't leave."

"It could take years to find her."

"Fine, then, she's more than worth it," his voice was filled with love and joy at the thought of reuniting with his wife. "It's better for him as well. For the future...How is the boy, anyway? I take it you haven't told him yet?"

The Median

Richard shook his head with conviction. "No, he's just not ready for it. Maybe when he's more like his old man," he raised an eyebrow towards Chris. "Who else could pull me into the border world but you?"

"Listen, Rich, I wouldn't have done it if I had a choice but things are not exactly wonderful on this side. That name…It's not even the half of it," he breathed deeply. "I've brought you here to warn you. It's far worse than I thought," he suddenly became agitated and looked around as if someone was searching for him. "The night is coming, Rich. Everlasting night, like nothing we've ever seen before-"

He placed a hand firmly on Chris's shoulder to steady him and spoke harshly. "Chris! Who was it? Who killed you?"

"Not who-" he again looked deeply into Richard's eyes, "…I can't tell you much but believe nothing. All I know is that he is the tide…He brings the wave…"

"Who? Who!?" Richard shook him as he began to look around again, terror filling his eyes. "Millaian?"

"How do you know that name?" he gazed, stunned, at Richard for a second before something snatched away his attention. "He's here." Chris began to back into a corner, cowering from something apparently coming from the opposite wall. A thing Richard could not see, as much as he tried. Suddenly the blue candle began dancing and the curtains twitched violently.

The papers on Richard's desk blew up and started flying around the room as a deafening hiss filled his ears, forcing him to cover them and fall to his knees. He looked up at Chris, who had backed up against the wall and was continually mouthing a single word. Finally, his words overpowered the din enough for Richard to briefly hear. "Lancer!"

He knew this word. It was a name; one he knew well. Before his mind could comprehend what was taking place, a burst of dust shot from the wall Chris had been intently staring at. Finally, Richard could see what he had been so afraid of. From it materialised a tall man who reached down towards Richard's friend with a thin, almost bone like hand.

"I am your master now!" it stated in a raspy, commanding voice. It was about to grasp Chris' face when it suddenly turned towards Richard, a cloak of black sweeping behind it. He backed up against the bed as it began to approach. Its whole body was as thin as its hand, its face longer than any he had ever seen. Its eye sockets were sunken far into its skull and wrinkled, grey features were seemingly set directly onto the bone itself. It began to speak again as it now reached for Richard. "I am the master of all!"

As the hand fell towards him, he backed as far into the bed sheets as he could and, closing his eyes, screamed at the top of his lungs.

Then all was again silent. He gradually opened his eyes, breathing shallow and quick, still in sheer terror. Slowly coming back to his senses, he heard heavy footsteps beating up the stairs and finally the door burst open with a clatter.

"Rich! What happened?" asked Michael, moving around the room only to be met with a quick nod between the rapid breathing. "I just heard a thud and then you scream," he helped Richard up onto the bed and sat down next to him. "Are you alright?"

He breathed out slowly, regaining his composure and looked to the corner where Chris had been cowering. "I don't know."

"It's alright now, you're safe," Michael thought about the statement for a moment, knowing full well that Richard would never be this disturbed over nothing. Whatever had done this must be truly awful and wasn't about to just go away. It occurred to him that it might not be just Richard who was in danger. "I'll go and put the kettle on," he stood up and began to walk towards the door but stopped just short.

"Michael…" Richard pushed himself to his feet once more and wavered slightly before facing the door. "There are some things you should know," he thought about telling him everything, all the things he had tried to protect him from for so long. The truth of his past. A truth that could bring down the darkness. After what had just happened, he came close to telling him. He at least needed to know what was going on, Richard thought, for his own safety. He deserved that much at least. "I'm not even completely sure what, though…I think we should find out together."

The Median

Michael had become accustomed to how cryptic Richard could be and had learnt that it would all become apparent in time, so with that notion in mind he simply nodded, saying nothing.

"Get the car keys, we're going to the library."

If not for the drone of the engine, the car would have been silent. Richard had been moved by his recent ordeals and it preyed ever more upon his mind that Michael should know the truth about his father. He didn't know why, something just told him that the time was close. He idly slid his hands around the wheel and gripped it tight, deep in thought, barely concentrating on the road.

"What happened?" Michael had suddenly turned and was gazing at Richard timidly. "When you called out?"

Richard blinked and tightened his grip on the wheel again. That face had been embossed on his mind, the skeletal, horrifying malice in flesh. It had been clear for a long time that Michael knew what Richard was. He knew all about his work but he was never told any of the details, kept safe for all these years from the knowledge of a Median's true nature. His own true nature or at least what he would eventually become. The thought of telling him had consumed Richard for the longest time but, especially now with the memory of that spectre, he had decided he shouldn't. He couldn't.

"Nothing...", he replied at last, weakly. "I just had an uncooperative client, that's all."

Michael was about to question the reply but his tongue was held by a common sense he sometimes wished he didn't have.

"We're here," Richard stated flatly, pulling into the car park of a large, three storey building. As he got out, he looked over the roof of the car and stared at Michael blankly. "Don't concern yourself with this or it'll concern itself with you."

Michael nodded without much conviction and made his way into the library. He was unsure whether he had said something wrong or if Richard's attitude was simply for his own good. Lord knows he had known it both ways.

"Ahh, Richard!" an attendant called, waving him over. "Haven't seen you in here for quite a long while," he took Richard's hand,

A Dark Past

shaking it firmly, promptly moving on to Michael, "and is this the lad you've told me so much about?"

Richard croaked and swallowed awkwardly. "Yes…"

"I haven't the foggiest why you've never brought him in before. He reminds me of my lad," the elderly attendant seemed to reminisce from seeing Michael, momentarily drifting off. "Got kids of his own now, he has."

Richard smiled half heartedly. "Well, we're here to do some nineteenth century research. On a particular individual, in fact," he breathed heavily. "Joseph Millaian."

The attendant squinted and scratched his balding head. "Millaian, you say? Name sounds familiar but for the life of me I don't know where from," he thought some more before cheerfully looking up again and turning to his computer. "Oh well, it'll come back to me. For now, we'll just have to look him up, shall we?" he briefly glanced at Richard again with a large grin across his face. "Wonderful things, these computers, all I do is type in the name here, see?" he pressed each button with a single finger and waited for a second. "Ahh, there we go. It gives you a list of all the books he would've been in," he printed a copy of the reading list and handed it to Richard who nodded and smiled again.

The list had four primary titles, all local history books, with a number of censuses and other miscellaneous documents listed beneath. At the very bottom, marked in red as checked out, was a single title; 'Vessel' by Christophe Guillaume. It had a much later date of publication than its counterparts and was not a local history text but was simply categorised under non-fiction. Richard folded the slip of paper and slid it neatly into a side pocket before turning to Michael. "Well, we'd better get looking then."

No matter how he felt, books always managed to brighten Richards's mood, even if just for a while. It was partly why almost every wall of his house was lined with volume after volume of them. Of course, they were the only thing that had ever really comforted him as a child. Retreating into a world of words and dreams kept the voices away and the world from driving him to them.

The Median

The hours passed slowly, every one becoming more tiresome than the last. As they did, each of the four texts found themselves open on a narrow plywood table. Richard gazed over them intently leaving Michael to idly flick through the pages as each was tossed aside. For all their effort there was nothing more than the life and achievements of a simple Victorian entrepreneur. There was barely even anything on his disappearance although this, in itself, did seem to intrigue Richard more than anything else of the man's life.

He pushed back from the table and arched his back, realising how long he had been lent over the book. "This is useless."

"What are we actually looking for?" asked Michael, looking up from a page. "We've been at this for ages and you've still got me in the dark."

"Anything…" he rubbed his face and ran his hands through his hair with a sigh, "anything at all." As he spoke the attendant emerged from behind a pillar, grasping a small, scruffy looking notebook. He shuffled over to the table, prompting Michael to check his watch.

"I remembered," he exclaimed happily, waving a free finger loosely. "I was sure I'd heard that name before so I went searching in the archives and found this," he produced the notebook and handed it to Richard. "I'm not sure what it is, it's been down there for decades, I think. I can't read French but that name just stuck in my head, you know."

Richard picked through the pages gently, flicking past paragraphs of handwritten text and strange diagrams before slamming it shut in one hand and staring at the cover. It had a single word scrawled across it 'Navire.'

"French…" Richard reached into his pocket and pulled out the slip of paper. Unfolding it, he looked at the single absent book and then pointed it out to the attendant. "Do you remember who took this out?"

"I think so…" he thought for a second. "Yes…Now I remember. He didn't have a membership, just took it out on a short loan. Small man he was, about the same age as you," he waved his finger at Richard once again. "Untidy looking sort, though, very unsure of himself…Oh and that trench coat-"

27

Richard looked up quickly. "It wasn't him," he mumbled after a few seconds, "he didn't know I already knew that name," he turned to Michael abruptly, his eyes widening. "Navire…"

"Vessel," finished Michael, pleased he might have finally found a use for that French A-Level.

The attendant looked between the two of them and stepped back slightly. "I think you should take that…" he glanced cautiously at the notebook, "you'll probably understand it a lot better than me."

Richard looked back to the notebook and gripped the leather cover tightly as Michael thanked the attendant. After a moment he loosened his grip and ran a hand softly across it. "It was him," he spoke quietly and acted as if he'd much rather be somewhere else, "in my trance. It was this…Millaian. He's not what these books say he was," he tapped the closest open book firmly with the notebook before withdrawing it close to him, "not anymore. He's changed, corrupted somehow. But it's like nothing I've ever heard of."

"You said it wasn't him," Michael ventured. "Who wasn't?"

Richard exhaled heavily, finally conceding that there were some things he couldn't keep to himself. "Chris. When I went to see him last night, he told me about Millaian but…" he wasn't sure how to say it but tried to choke the words out regardless. "It wasn't Chris. I did see him in my trance, though…right before that bastard took him," he clenched his free fist, "this Millaian guy. But Chris… he was like I remembered him. He's not always been like you knew him. Once he was my best friend…" His fist unclenched and a small smile crept onto his lips but was quickly wiped away once he realised he was straying off topic. "He warned me about Millaian again and was surprised when I already knew the name. Michael, I think he's been in the border world for days already."

"How is that-?" he paused for a second. "Possession? Maybe Chris wasn't in there at all. He had multiple personalities, after all. Maybe he could have been dead for days and it was just the spirits inhabiting his body all along," he glanced at the book. "A vessel."

The smile returned to Richards's lips as he began to wonder why he had never let Michael in on his work before. "You're smart, kid, I'll give you that," he slipped the notebook into one of his many concealed pockets and was about to head to the door but abruptly turned back to Michael instead. "What's the next move, then?"

He thought and cautiously twitched his mouth, debating whether his idea was right. "Try and get to see the body? That could tell us a lot, I guess?"

Richard smiled once more. "Very smart."

I-III - VI of I

Forsake not an old friend; for the new is not comparable to him

-Ecclesiasticus 9:10

A *lifeless body wasn't something I particularly took pleasure in seeing usually but the thought of his like that turned my stomach in a different way. Then again, given how things had turned out I suppose I already had. I'll never understand why I hadn't seen it. Maybe I just didn't want to but his body was empty already when I had met him that night. Without the original soul the host will die within a matter of days, no matter how many parasites try to maintain it. There was something more, though, Chris was a bigger part of all of this than I thought and seeing him one more time may be the only way to know how. Getting in to see him, on the other hand, could prove to be more than a little testing.*

The day was getting late. Dusk was already beginning to create a haze over the horizon causing the low hanging sun to become orange in the sky.

Richard walked slowly to the hospital entrance and looked up at the building, shaking his head, then looked to Michael who followed at a distance.

"People die here..." he took a step back away from the hospital, "not good for me."

"You can feel them, can't you? Everyone who's crossing over in there?" said Michael raising his voice as Richard moved ever farther away.

Richard placed a hand firmly on the glass pane of a swing door and pushed it open harshly. "Yes." He followed the wide swing with a wide stride into a place where nothing was real to him.

The recently dead roamed the building, waiting for their time to move on, filling the silence of life with the chorus of death. It was subtle but near unbearable to those who could hear it.

"Getting to see him won't be a piece of cake, you do realise?" he stopped in the almost completely empty waiting room.

There was a receptionist sitting behind a waist high desk, slowly punching at her keyboard and a lone man waiting quietly, presumably for an appointment.

Michael hurried through the doors, trying to draw as little attention to himself as possible. "Can't you just go into your trance thing and go in without anyone seeing you?" he whispered loudly.

"No," Richard snapped, "my body still has a physical presence in this world. It's not like it makes me invisible or anything," he tried not to sound patronising but didn't succeed. "Anyway, I'm not about to do that in here, even if it did. They'd tear me apart."

Richard turned and began to walk towards a set of doors leading into the main hospital. As he did, he shot Michael a dark scowl, pressing home just how dangerous this could be for him. Even so, some part of him was pleased with how scared Michael looked with such little effort. At least now he might take the whole situation a little more seriously.

Richard had just about reached the doors when the receptionist jumped up from her chair and leaned over the desk.

"Sir, I'm afraid visiting hours end at 5 O'clock and we request that last entries are at four thirty," she hung over the desk for several more seconds until Richard backed away from the door at which point she returned to her seat and resumed typing.

"Well, that didn't work," Richard stated casually, walking back to Michael again.

"Really?" he replied sarcastically, "and there's me thinking they'd let you just waltz in."

Richard manoeuvred behind the rows of seats, making sure he was out of the receptionist's sight, and set about inspecting a wall mounted fire alarm.

"What are you doing?" Michael loudly whispered again, this time briefly drawing the attention of the single waiting patient.

"Just looking," he pulled the sleeve of his jacket across a clenched hand and quickly hit the alarm, breaking the glass and almost immediately setting off a loud buzzer.

The receptionist looked up abruptly and scanned across the room before hurrying through the door behind the desk.

"Problem solved, no-one will bother us now."

Michael looked around as Richard set off towards the doors again. "I can't believe you just did that! Do you know how much trouble you've just caused them?"

"Relax," Richard said, turning back for a moment, "they'll realise it's a false alarm in a few minutes and everything will be fine." He wondered briefly whether it would actually be that simple but decided that it wasn't worth thinking about. "Now come on, it's given us just enough time to get into the morgue."

"This isn't even a good plan," Michael mumbled, looking around in a panic one last time before rushing into the main hospital after Richard.

With the alarm blazing, assorted staff hurried around trying to find out what was happening whilst doctors fussed over their patient's safety. In the confusion the two interlopers were as good as invisible, slipping through the bustling corridors without so much as a second glance.

They arrived at the Morgue and slipped in just as the alarm ceased, causing Richard to look up and around.

"Damnit, thought it'd keep them busy a bit longer than that," he swung round, taking in the room as he did. "We need to hurry."

There were a number of stainless-steel tables, bodies led neatly on each with thin linen blankets draped across them. To the side of the room, under a large hanging light, was another table. This one with rolling tables scattered around it, filled with assorted medical tools.

The Median

Michael took a step forward to inspect closer, only to find that the table had another body led on it, this one already having been victim to the mercy of the pathologist.

"It's not Chris, is it?" asked Richard, making Michael start backwards in fright.

He took a shallow breath, realising how foul the air was as he did. "No...No, I don't think so," he shuddered and moved away from the autopsy, taking up a position next to the door as Richard started towards the covered bodies. "How come we found this place so fast, it's almost as though you knew where you were going."

Richard took hold of the sheet on the first table tentatively then threw it back, only to sigh when he found it was not Chris and move on to the next one. "Let's just say this isn't my first visit here," he grabbed hold of the second cover, more confidently this time, and again threw it back but was driven back by an invisible force, knocking the breath out of him.

After composing himself his gaze followed something across the room for a few seconds and then through the back wall. He shook his head and gritted his teeth. "Inconsiderate bastard," he quickly moved on to the next corpse, this time pulling the sheet off while keeping a distance. He peered at the body and smirked slightly. "Bingo!"

"You've found him?" Michael stepped up and examined the body. It was Chris alright. Unwashed, unshaven and still damp from the previous night. What colour that had been in his already pale complexion had now been sapped from his body, leaving only an empty grey husk.

"They've taken his coat," Richard stated suddenly, "check in the draws," he threw his arm back and pointed at a steel wall cabinet with several roller draws in its lower section. "He might've left something in his pockets," as he spoke, he inspected and searched the body, finding nothing but dirt and linen.

Michael opened the top draw and pulled out a long, stained trench coat which unfurled to full length as he held it and hung heavily to the ground. "Is this it?" he padded the pockets tentatively and removed a folded note from one of the side pockets.

"What did you find?" Richard took the piece of paper and flicked it open. The note was damp and the writing scrawled, the smeared ink barely legible against the wet paper. He read it and sighed deeply, gazing at the words sorely. "I'm sorry my friend," he laid a hand on the corpse's arm for a moment and then took the note with both hands. "The end is coming," he dictated, "they are all gone, except one. A powerful spirit who promises me release, promises me her. I don't believe him but I can't resist, I'm too weak. I hear him, hear his schemes. 'Seven of one and I shall be born again' he tells me. I am the one."

"What does it mean?" asked Michael. "Seven of one and I shall be born again?"

"Honestly, I don't know," he folded the note again and reached into his pocket, pulling out the strange book, "but it's got to have something to do with this," he waved the book loosely and leant against the table, placing it down.

"Richard," Michael said slowly, stepping backwards as his eyes widened. "It's moving," he pointed to Chris' arm as it raised, the fist clenching as it went.

Richard bolted upright and drew his gun, swinging around. The grey body sat up and looked around, examining the room and settled on the book Richard had left at the end of the table. "This has never happened before," he told himself, unsure whether to think any of this was real or not.

"The text has awoken me," the corpse said in an unsettlingly deep, grating voice while reaching for the book, "it has been too long."

Richard shuddered at his best friend being used like some puppet. "Freeze right there!" he shouted, pushing the gun forward as the zombie gripped the book, its dead hands seemingly able to move independently of the rest of its being. "Just what the hell are you?"

"Richard Weignright. I should thank you for waking me. I also appreciate you returning my text," it held up the book, grinning on half of its face. "But it is somewhat earlier than I had hoped."

"I said who are you?" he thought for a second and grimaced, "and how do you know who I am?"

"I know you, Rich…" it readjusted its wrist with a sharp snap, "I know everything this host knew," it peered back at Michael and saw

The Median

fear wash across Richard's face. Slowly its grin grew wider. "Does that concern you, my friend? And, oh yes, you know me. For a moment I had you within my grasp. Someone of your...talents... could be very useful to me but, alas, you slipped away."

"You can't be," he backed away slightly, putting up a free arm to try and protect Michael, "you were who he was talking about in that note. That's why you were after him in the border world."

"Yes. Control the mind, control the body. And as for that note, I really did try to stop him but his will was a great deal stronger than I had anticipated. Admirable, to be sure, but I still had to dispose of him, regardless."

"Son of a bitch!" Richard growled, "You killed my best friend!"

"Indeed," the embodiment of Millaian turned on the table and slid from it, grasping the notebook tightly, "I must thank you again, but just like your friend, I no longer have need for you." With slow, deliberate movements he removed a scalpel from a nearby tray.

"I said don't move!" he pushed the gun as far forward as he could while trying to back away from the psychopathic corpse. "I'm warning you!"

"Come now, we both know that it is empty," his words were calm and gentle as he started to move forward, knife in hand.

"Good point," Richard breathed quickly, lowering the weapon. "But this isn't!" he spun around, reaching into his coat with his free hand and pulled a vial from his inside pocket. In a single, smooth movement he popped the cork and threw the liquid at Millaian.

The substance splashed onto his face, immediately burning deeply into the tissue and, with a loud hiss, made him drop to his knees, screaming in agony.

Richard hustled Michael out of the door, running through corridors and crowds of bewildered medics until they arrived outside. By this time the sun was as good as down and twilight had firmly set in.

"That's it!" coughed Richard, gasping for breath. "We're getting to the bottom of this!" he growled, storming towards the car.

"What was that stuff you threw at him?" asked Michael, still cringing from what he had just seen.

"A mixture of extracts and oils. I normally use it to send spirits back to their rightful plane if they don't cooperate. Perfectly harmless to mortals," he paused for a moment in thought. "I'm just glad I didn't use it last night, it was my last bottle," he gave a slight chuckle amidst the anger and grasped the handle of the car door.

"How did you know it would work on him, then?" Michael already regretted asking the question, fearing the answer would be 'I didn't'.

"Best guess," he replied, shrugging slightly, "I figured he wasn't mortal anymore so something had to happen."

Michael rolled his eyes and leant on the roof of the car. "So where now then?"

"Chris' place, it's the only option. I did some-" he took a deep breath in, "-things for him there."

Michael looked suspiciously at him but eventually nodded, still trying to recover his composure. "Fine then, let's go," he rubbed his face and pushed his hair from his eyes. "I think I'm better off not asking any questions right now."

Richard nodded, "good choice."

Millaian, still on his knees, cradled his host's face. Pulling his hands away, he could see that seared, melted flesh now covered them and thick, dark blood began to drip between his fingers, pooling on the ground. He shook with a tormented combination of pain and rage and clenched his fists tightly, each bone in them cracking in succession.

Two doctors burst through the door only to be abruptly stopped in their tracks. "What on Earth happened here?" one asked, looking around the room while the second stared at the knelt body.

"I live," came Millaian's voice from the ground. As it did, he began to straighten up, unclenching his hands and reaching down to recover the notebook and scalpel.

"Get security," the second doctor whispered to the first, making him rush off again. "Don't worry; everything's going to be alright."

"No, it won't..." he turned his head and in the light the doctor saw his true appearance.

The Median

Nearly all of the skin on his face was missing and what remained was disfigured and burnt beyond recognition. His eyes bulged from their sockets and swivelled precariously on the bone. The holes in his face, covered only by a few surviving tendons, seeped a brown puss, the fetid coagulant of liquidised flesh and post mortem blood. He smiled a lipless grin and got to his feet.

"At least, not for you." Millaian lunged forward, forcing the razor-sharp blade forwards towards the doctor. A single, stifled scream rang out through the corridors and then there was silence once more.

I must have been crazy. Michael may have been scared but he just couldn't resist asking the questions he said he wouldn't. Questions I daren't answer but ones I couldn't just leave hanging.

He wanted to know about me and Chris, our history. That alone I may have been able to deal with but then he started asking about how a guy like Chris could hold down a flat. The truth was that I was the one who paid the rent. I had done so for all these long years and that wasn't something I could just explain away. I simply tried to avoid his questions and said barely enough to make sure he didn't think I was ignoring him.

What had happened tonight was almost incomprehensible to me. If it had been enough to knock me this much off balance then I can't even begin to imagine the impact it had on Michael. I wanted him out, away from all of this but it wasn't safe for him anymore. Millaian had made that much clear.

I needed answers and Chris was the only one who could give them to me. By the time we got to his place, though, I realised we were in for much more than I had bargained for.

Across Chris' door were various scores and marks, each tinted with a different colour, as though the wood had been treated in some way.

"Protection," Richard stated abruptly, reaching into a pocket for his bundle of keys. "The things I said I did for him," he waved his hand over the markings, "simple incantations and oils in the wood. Trickery basically, but they made him feel better. Something slightly more powerful inside, though," he spoke with particular self satisfaction about his work. He found the key and slid it into the lock, opening the door with the ease of a person who did it regularly. "And don't ask me why I have a key."

Michael put his hands up defensively and just let Richard talk, starting to understand that even if he got the answers he sought, he probably wouldn't like them.

He stepped in line with Richard as he passed over the threshold, noticing a trail of salt along the carpet just inside the doorway. "So, this more powerful thing?"

Richard moved into the living area and pointed to a table in the corner with a large section of amethyst perched centrally on it.

"Amethyst?" Michael said, clearly unimpressed. "Is that it? A nice table decoration?"

"Table decoration?" he snapped, turning harshly. "Do you realise how much those things cost?"

Michael placed his hands on his hips and stared at Richard. "A bloody lot I should think. They're rip offs, it's probably not even real quartz!"

"Look, it *is* real and if the people selling it knew just what it could do then it'd cost a whole lot more," he calmed down and breathed slowly. "It's a prison, of sorts. You could say it's naturally tuned to the wavelength of bad spirits, those who would want to inflict hurt on someone, especially someone in Chris' state, and it captures them," he looked back at Michael whose eyes had glazed over. He watched him for a few seconds longer before shaking his head and walking off into Chris's bedroom. "Forget it."

For a moment more Michael looked at the half geode in front of him, thinking about what Richard had said and took it upon himself to try and sound as though he actually understood any of it. "Yeah, well, I know what you mean. It's just that you can't be too careful these days. Everyone's trying to rip someone off," he began to move towards the bedroom when Richards' voice echoed loudly along the hall.

"Don't come in here, boy!" The door was slammed shut and a thud followed, almost like someone had fallen heavily against it.

Michael moved slowly along the hall, looking at the door with suspicion. "What's wrong? You're scaring me," he reached the door and moved a hand towards the knob but hurriedly withdrew it, instead tilting his head and placing an ear against the wood. As far as he could tell, the room was deathly silent, broken only by the throbbing of his uneasy heart. "Rich?" he finally breathed, pulling his head away from the door and looking around the hall.

Michael cocked his head and peered at the slightly ajar door of the bathroom at the end of the hall. Beginning to move again, he continued to gaze at the door with a growing sense that something wasn't right. Through the crack he could see that there were dark red flecks across the floor. Tentatively he reached a shaking hand forward and gently pressed against the door, leaning in as it slowly swung open to reveal smeared red streaks leading towards a large pool of drying blood standing out brightly against the white tiles. He held his breath, looking up and around the room at whitewashed walls coated in layer upon layer of blood, sprayed around in a manner almost beyond believability.

Eventually he was forced to breathe and as he did the putrid stench hit his nostrils, making him gag and cover his mouth with his sleeve. Panning around the horrific scene, he laid eyes on the worst of it all. In the bath lay the contorted body of a young man, his throat slit deep and his limbs bent in ways that were not naturally possible. He was wearing what looked like a suit, now stained beyond recognition with his own blood.

"He tried to escape," a voice came from behind Michael, startling him into swinging around. "The others didn't even make that far." Richard spoke in low tones, his voice quivering and his eyes becoming redder with every passing moment.

He'd never seen anything like this. He never thought he would or at least hoped beyond any reasonable hope that he never would. It was little wonder, then, when a tear finally broke from the corner of his eye and ran slowly down his cheek.

"Others?" Michael breathed, horrified at the idea that there may be more in this state.

Richard nodded, making Michael shudder violently. "Five more, all like him," he flicked his eyes vaguely to the bathtub. "I can't let you stay here-"

"I don't want to be," Michael cut Richard off abruptly, barging past him and rushing outside.

"Alright," Richard whispered to himself as he heard the front door slam shut.

He turned back to the bedroom and cautiously approached it again, preparing himself for the presence of at least one of the departed. Although he had been in the house for a while now and really should have felt something. There should have been a remaining spirit, even the after-presence of one but there was nothing there but that horrific stench, filling every breath with decay.

He pressed against the door which dragged against the thick bedroom carpet as it opened. Inside was humid and dark with the curtains completely drawn, forcing Richard's eyes to adjust to the gloom. As they did, several shapes on the ground came into focus. The shapes slowly gained structure and soon faces. Five more bodies were strewn about the ground, the carpet around them saturated with their blood, still fresh in some places. He closed his eyes for a moment, taking as deep a breath as he could without vomiting, before re-entering that wretched room.

Stepping over the bodies and treading lightly on the stained carpet, he made his way to a dresser in front of the darkened window, covered in scribbled notes and harbouring an assortment of books. They were spiritual texts, similar to those lining the walls of Richard's house, only these were bloodied and battered. Similarly, the dresser's mirror had been subjected to much the same fate with large cracks running its entire length and parts of it shattered entirely. Blood had also been spurted across its surface with the spatter making a clear reflection impossible to make out.

Around it were seven small pictures. They were of the victims now lifelessly sprawled around the room. Each had a thick black marker line across it, bar a single image of a woman on the right-hand side of the mirror. She looked near her thirties and had shoulder length, chestnut hair falling evenly around her face. Richard was caught for a second by her eyes, a strange dark blue that sparkled in a way he recognised. She wasn't like the others; he knew that much.

The Median

Looking around at the bodies he confirmed that she had not suffered the same fate as the others, at least not yet, and stared again at the picture. Beneath it, scrawled across the mirror in the same black marker that struck out the images and partially obscured by the dried blood spray, was a name; 'Hollie'.

Richard mouthed the name and abruptly began rooting through the assortment of notes on the dresser, no longer caring about the blood that was being smeared across his hands. Finally, he stopped and slowly lifted a small local newspaper cutting to what small amount of light there was.

The scrap mentioned one Hollie Michelle Reade, twenty-seven years of age, who had been rushed into hospital with a suspected drug overdose nearly a week ago only to pass away two days later.

Richard sighed and hung his head, tossing the slip of paper back onto the pile of scraps. His hand, as it began to fall back to his side, was suddenly diverted and grasped a thin book half emerging from the heap of paper. He carelessly removed the test, pulling the majority of the scraps onto the floor, and squinted at the cover. It had a renaissance style portrait depicting the devil's temptation of Adam and Eve in The Garden of Eden and above it in large, red, gothic letters read the title: 'VESSEL – Adapted by Christophe Guillaume'.

Richard swallowed heavily as he began to flick through the book, a chill creeping down his spine. Much of it contained the same drawings as Millaian's notebook, only much neater and in English. Flipping through a few more pages, he found one that had been marked and amongst the text a sentence highlighted. As he read, a cold dread filled his body and he began to shake.

'VI of I and I shall live : VII of I and I shall be born again'

Everything suddenly fell into place. Chris had been coerced in some way to kill those people and consume their essence so that the parasite inside him could take control of a new host.

Richard had never known anything like it. There had been myths of such things but never had it really happened. It was becoming clearer now that he knew what VI of I meant. Millaian still needed this Hollie for something although he dreaded knowing what it would be. Still, she was dead now, had been for a good few days, more than enough time to cross over…Unless…And then it hit him.

That sparkle in her eyes. She wasn't just anyone, she had a power that none of the others had, a power Millaian needed, and someone like that never goes quietly to the Other Side.

Richard knew exactly where he could find her, that much was easy enough to deduce. Getting to her, on the other hand, would be a challenge all to itself for she was in the Desert of Desolation. The Median World.

He slammed shut the book, cursing softly to himself, and slid it clumsily into a side pocket of his jacket. Looking back at the picture of Hollie, he quickly ripped from the mirror before rushing out the room and into the fresh night air. Taking a deep breath to clear his lungs of the putrid stench, he glanced sideways to Michael.

"I know that look, Rich, but we have to call the police about this," Michael stated soberly. "This isn't exactly an everyday occurrence."

"Nothing's ever an everyday occurrence for me, you should know that," he looked carefully at the small picture of Hollie and touched the mysterious book before thinking for a second.

"I think you might want to wash your hands, whatever you do," Michael casually offered, noticing the smears of blood on Richards's hands. "You should have really left things alone. You do know that's evidence tampering, right?"

Richard looked up abruptly. "Evidence? Evidence for what? The police couldn't make heads nor tails of what's going on here. What're they going to do when they find out the guy who did all this is technically dead but just happens to be wandering the streets with half a face! *I* don't even know what it all means," he closed his eyes and gritted his teeth. "What I do know is that Chris didn't do this, not willingly. At least…I don't want anyone thinking that he did!"

"There's no way around it," Michael quietly said. "If he was anything like you and it meant protecting what you do then I think he would have wanted you to call it in. The police will deal with it in their own way but the people who matter will know he's innocent. At the end of the day, that's all that matters."

Richard raised his head and looked at Michael remorsefully. "Do it," he closed the door and looked at the picture of Hollie again as Michael began to dial. "They need to do what they need to do... and so do I."

I-IV - Desert of Desolation

The wise man's eyes are in his head; but the fool walketh in darkness...

-Ecclesiastes 2:14

The Border World was one thing. When falling asleep most people slip in and out of it and never even realise. Those moments just before you lose consciousness, when the world slows down and nothing feels as it should. The only difference is that Medians can go there at will.
The Desert was something else, though. Few had ever willingly gone there. Even fewer had come back. It's a stopping place for spirits with unfinished business, those who want to try and get back to our world. None of them spend any more than a few minutes there, they either find a way back to the Border World or are sent to the Other Side.
The only exceptions are us. Medians never go easily to the Other Side and this would be no different if I was right about Hollie. But there was only one way I was about to find out, I would have to do something every fibre of my being told me not to. I would have to die.

The moon rose high in the night sky, casting a thin veil of light across the quiet side street. On the corner opposite to Chris'

The Median

apartment two dark outlines lingered in the shade, seemingly waiting.

"What time is it?" Richard asked faintly, breaking the distant droning of the bypass. "They should have been here by now."

Michael pulled back his sleeve and quickly looked at his watch. "Twenty past ten," he dropped his arm and sighed. "Maybe we shouldn't wait around like this. You must know how suspicious this looks."

"Twenty past ten…Just under twenty-six hours," Michael squinted slightly at him and opened his mouth to say something but quickly closed it again and turned away. "I just feel I should be here for this," he paused again and looked out across the street. "Things have changed, Mike… I guess you need to know a few things," he rubbed his face and tried to think of the best way to proceed. "You remember me telling you that Halloween was nothing?" he grimaced slightly. "I lied. It's a time when the lines between worlds blur and spirits can cross over easier than usual. What I do-"

"I know," stated Michael abruptly. "I know everything you do, how deep you get yourself. I even know why you tried to hide it from me. It's because I'm like you, isn't it? I'm a Median…Or will eventually be one, at least," he looked into Richards eyes through the haze of night and felt somehow vindicated that there was no response.

"We'll see," Richard finally said as a police car pulled up on the other side of the street. "There are things *they* understand," he tilted his head in the direction of the Police exiting their squad car, "and there are things we understand. But some things that nobody can understand. Just remember that," he craned his head into the street and watched the authorities enter Chris' apartment block.

Michael sank down to the ground, his back against the wall. He was becoming convinced that Richard was toying with him, that nothing would ever please him, that everything would be forever scrutinised and that he would never be accepted as an equal.

"Come on, we're leaving," Richard said quickly, helping Michael up from the ground, pulling him closer for a second. "Just remember something else. I am proud of you. Don't you ever think I'm not," he hurried off down the street, making certain to keep to the shadows as Michael smiled gently before following.

Twenty-six hours. Something told me that if Millaian was going to do something, he was going to do it on All Hallows. If he managed to get his hands on the last victim by then, there would be no stopping him. Twenty-six hours was the longest amount of 'safe' time I had left. Even so, that scarcely made me feel any better, especially with what I was about to do.

I hadn't seen Lancer in years and although I knew Chris wanted me to visit him, something had been stopping me, pushing it to the back of my mind to forget. But I had no choice now.

They hadn't walked for long before Richard abruptly stopped and looked across the street at a boarded up and decrepit church. He gestured his hand towards it, forcing Michael to turn sharply and rush back towards Richard, having breezed past him in his hurry.

Apart from the boarded windows the building was half covered with scaffolding. The only parts of the sandstone walls not covered with thick moss and ivy were crumbling away, if not missing at all, replaced by shoddy bricking.

"This place?" Michael asked dismissively, grimacing at the building, "but...It's-"

"I appreciate the irony. Apparently, so does Lancer," he looked up at the precarious steeple which was missing the majority of its tiles and threatened to collapse at any time. "At least, that's what he used to say."

Michael looked sharply at Richard. "Lancer? That's who we're going to see?" Richard nodded quickly. "I didn't think he really existed"

Richard tore his gaze away from the chapel, his face awash with bewilderment. His mouth hung half open as words developed in the back of his throat. "You know about Lancer?"

"Only rumours. They're more myths really. About him being a Seer and all," Michael began to stammer under that scrutinising gaze before coughing awkwardly. "Just stories though."

The Median

Richard was quietly impressed yet ever so slightly disturbed. How had Michael found all this out on his own, even when Richard had tried so hard to prevent him from doing so? It all made him wonder just what else he knew.

"You could call him a Seer," he answered finally, "to the extent he can see beyond this world into the Median plane, yes. Apart from that he's just another guy," he paused for a few seconds before sighing and shaking his head slightly. "Though he does dabble in fields I wouldn't dream of. He's rather eccentric, you see, so keep your wits about you," he looked back up at the old chapel. "This is it, though," added Richard flatly, "not much to look at, I realise, but that's how he likes it. Always did," he finished quietly before striding towards a doorway obscured by a loose, graffiti strewn plank of chipboard.

He pried away the board, sheering loose sand grains from the wall which drifted down through the dust filled air. Leaning against the board when he was done, Richard looked back at Michael. "So, are you coming?" he turned back to the chapel again and disappeared into the dark opening.

Michael smiled briefly and raced towards the doorway while Richard pushed open a second, much more stable, iron gate into a reasonably well-lit chapel hall. The hall was gutted of everything that would have once defined it as any type of church. The pews, organ, pulpit; they had all been ripped out, leaving a much larger space than the building should have presented. The walls were lined with lamps and bright spotlights stood over piles of crates, making the chapel resemble more a warehouse than a place of worship. At the far end, atop the alter step, was a high-backed wooden seat, a lone silhouette seated silently.

Michael stepped forward quickly, peering at the figure but was harshly pushed back. "Why is he just sitting there?"

"He doesn't sleep, just spends the whole night wandering," replied Richard quietly.

"But he's just sitting there," he stepped back, realising that even here he may be in danger.

Richard slowly began to approach Lancer, his arms slightly outstretched as though he were feeling for something ahead of him.

"Just because he isn't moving doesn't mean he's not off somewhere else," he turned back to Michael for a second and smirked, knowing full well that he had thoroughly confused him. "Problem is that he doesn't much like being disturbed," he edged closer to the altar step, waving his arms all the way until his fingers suddenly sparked and ghostly waves drifted away from them. "Watch yourself," he waved his arm back towards Michael with his other still pointing towards the chair, "he's not the most agreeable person in the world." In the chair Lancers eyes flicked towards Richard and two of the ghostly forms drifted down to his sides.

"Your back," the thick, dark, German accent quickly drew Richard's attention back to the altar step, his eyes wide open, "I didn't think you'd ever return."

"Well, you know," Richard began as Michael approached cautiously, "not even you could ever predict me."

Lancer looked to Richards' side and to the scared lad coming up behind him. He squinted at him before looking back. "This much I know to be true."

The ghosts drifted forwards and seemed to examine the interlopers briefly, forcing Michael to become rigidly still, before drifting away silently.

"Come, Richard...And the prodigy," he looked down to Richard's side again. "After all, what else could he possibly be for you to bring him here, of all places," Lancer flicked his eyes around the building and then down at Richard and Michaels still figures. "Don't be afraid, Rich. I suspect that anything I could do to you cannot possibly be as bad as whatever it is you actually want from me."

Richard reached forward and through where the ghostly barrier had been, then took a tentative step up. He breathed a quiet sigh and continued several, more confident, steps towards Lancer. "Maybe I had you wrong. Maybe you can predict me."

"What is it you want, Richard?" he opened out his hands welcomingly. "Such a long time, it must be something important for you to finally come back."

"I need to go there, Lancer. I need to go to The Desert," Richard stated quickly, despite how much he wanted not to.

The Median

Lancer grinned and pushed himself from the chair, starting to walk slowly forwards. "I never thought I would hear those words from you, not again. You do realise what it entails, do you not?" he carried on knowing full well what the answer would be.

"Yes, I remember. This is something that needs to be done, though," he stared straight at Lancer who gazed back casually but then suddenly flicked his eyes towards Michael.

"The boy doesn't know," Lancer began to walk to Richards' side and tried to reach out but his arm was grabbed and pulled away sharply.

"He knows enough," Richard threw the seized arm aside and took a step in front of Michael.

"Perhaps but I feel he fails to understand the gravity of what he would involve himself in," Lancer rubbed his aged hands together and turned back to Richard. "Do you, for that matter?"

"I know exactly what I need to."

"I know the only thing you could possibly find there is absence. An emptiness and loneliness beyond compare…Unless…" he turned around and started to walk back towards his chair, "…it is not? Are you hoping to find something there, my friend? Someone?" he chuckled faintly as Richard stepped forward and opened his mouth but was silenced by Lancer's arm being thrown up. "I know of this individual…In such desolation I feel any slightest disturbance," he breathed in heavily and seemed to savour the thought of the 'disturbance.' "And this was…" he closed his eyes and breathed deeply again, "so powerful."

Michael slowly placed a hand on Richards' shoulder prompting him to turn quickly. "What does he mean, he can feel it?"

Richard spoke as quietly as he dared, not knowing exactly why but clearing possessing a deep fear of Lancer. "Seers. They're the guardians of the Median World. They can see all who pass through it. I thought you said you knew this!"

"I said, just stories!"

"Indeed, we *can* see all!" stated Lancer loudly, swinging around. "A whole world at our fingertips. Such a wonderful thing you may think. It is truly not," he rushed back down towards the pair again, right up to stare Michael in the eye. "A world so full of emptiness, scratching at your senses every hour of every day-" he quickly turned to Richard, grasping his arms tightly. "You Medians have it easy! For me every second is a lifetime's insanity, the endless void pouring through my mind, dominating my sleepless nights!" He seemed to regain control of himself and let go of Richard's arms, removing them as though he didn't know how they had gotten there. "Then again, you are aware of this...You've been there."

"And I need to go again," Richard replied tentatively, "you said yourself she's there. I need to bring her back."

Lancer shook his head and rubbed his face. "*She* is something else. You know I can't even be sure about bringing you back, let alone two of you," he looked to the ground and shook his head again. "And even if I could, I'm not sure if I should. It is different, Richard...*She* is different."

Richard suddenly saw something glint in Lancers eyes and stepped towards him, looking closer. "You've felt it haven't you? The presence in the Border World."

"That is your jurisdiction, my friend," he replied firmly, gritting his yellowed teeth, "it has nothing to do with me."

"But you know. You've felt him. He crossed the desert, didn't he?" He thought for a second, "and you knew I'd come...For her..." he pointed an accusing finger sharply at Lancer. "Come on! You're not stupid, far from it! You know she's in danger and it doesn't matter whether she's here or the Other Side, the worst possible place she could be is the desert!"

Lancer hung his head, wiping his face. "This presence you speak of. It is nothing like I've ever felt. Such pure power and raw hatred; there's not a Seer that couldn't have felt it," he raised his head and flicked his eyes between the two. "I heard him, Richard. I heard his thoughts as though they were my own...Such darkness..." A tear began to drip from his face as he spoke. "The void filled with hatred and a haze of malice. He spoke of Christopher and the poles of balance. Cause and effect, yin and yang, good and evil. He spoke of his opposite. Of you."

Richard looked deep into Lancers eyes and saw something in them he had never seen from a Seer. He saw an unmitigated, unrelenting fear which ran so deep that he could never possibly begin to understand it. If Millaian could do this to a Seer then he dared not think about what else he could do. "It's alright," he ventured.

"It's alright to be scared, even for you." He quickly looked back to Michael, now so petrified that his eyes had become bloodshot.

"I'm ok," Michael whispered, nodding reassuringly before looking back to Lancer.

"You have to help me bring her back, "Richard continued. "He's out there, Lancer. He's out there right now with Chris' body and she might be our only chance to stop him before he ends up doing god only knows what."

There was silence for some time as the old man considered Richard's words. Eventually Lancer stood up straight again, wiping the tears from his face and breathing in deeply. "Of course," he stated flatly, casually raising an eyebrow and chuckling shortly to himself. "I would be only too glad to oblige," he finished as he began to walk off towards a shadowed door at the side of the chapel hall.

Richard put his hand on Michael's shoulder lightly and patted gently. "I have every faith in you. I know you'll be able to do whatever you have to," he patted his shoulder again and started following Lancer but was quickly stopped again.

"Wait, do what? What do you expect me to do?"

"You'll know, don't worry. For now, I think it would be better for you to stay out here. Don't be afraid, Lancer's got this place pretty well protected. I think they should know you're trustworthy enough by now," he smiled and looked to the rafters before continuing on to the side door.

Michael slowly gazed upwards to the roof and couldn't believe his eyes. The entire roof space was aglow with a brilliant white from ghostly spectres drifting around the supporting beams. He remembered reading about these things; the protectors of the precious living. "Guardians?" laughed Michael in awe of the wonderful sight, "I'd say they were more like angels."

Lancer forced aside a rusted bolt on the old wooden door and pushed it open, making its thick iron supports clang on the stone wall.

"I can't say I've missed this thing," said Richard sombrely, stepping into the room ahead of Lancer.

Before him was a half-blackened steel table with leather straps and harnesses, positioned for the restraint of a person's limbs. Beside the table was a strange looking device sat atop an old medical cabinet with several thick cables and coloured wires looping around it. Within it was housed a number of old car batteries, dirtied from years of use and dried battery acid encrusting their seals.

"Could have at least cleaned it up a bit," Richard casually offered, continuing to examine the room.

Around the dingy cell were low shelves full of strange vials and implements he cared not to know the purpose of.

"I think you should just lie down," Lancer answered flatly, taking a jaw ended wire from the knotted jumble and clamping it firmly to a pylon on the underside of the table. "You'll want to relax during the process. Sudden separation can be a little-" he clamped another wire onto a second pylon and moved to Richards's side.

"I get the idea," Richard finished, doing as he was instructed. "It's not like you forget these things," he took a deep breath and clenched his fists nervously as Lancer reached for the restraints. "Are those really necessary, though?"

"I'm afraid so," he strapped an arm tightly into the leather bond and moved on to his feet, securing them as harshly as he had the arm. "Trust me, it's for your own safety."

"Safe? I don't think there could be a less operative word for what you're about to do then 'safe,'"

Lancer briefly acknowledged this as he fastened the last restraint in place and moved back to the machine.

"Sure, they're tight enough?" Richard added, tugging at the straps. "Don't want me getting loose, do we?"

"Just relax," Lancer stated again, flipping several switches on the contraption, causing it to emit a low-pitched buzz, "this might hurt a little."

"Says the master of the understatement," Richard breathed in deeply and clenched his teeth as Lancer took hold of two rubber handled paddles from the device. He quickly touched them together,

The Median

creating a bright spark, before placing them just short of Richards temples.

"Any last words?" Lancer asked, chuckling lightly and quickly pressing the cold metal against Richards's skin before he could respond.

Immediately he started to convulse against the restraints, writhing against the electricity now surging through his body. He continued to thrash against the leather bounds for some time, eventually throwing his head back against the metal slab with a sickly crack. After a split second of blissful calm Richard's body was suddenly lifted, contorted, into the air by a final pulse of static and he let loose a harrowing scream to rival that of a rabid wolverine.

Outside, the haunting wail pierced Michael to his very core. Without a second thought it made him race towards its origin, barely allowing his mind a chance to process the terrible sensation.

He threw open the door just as the screaming ceased only to see Richard's body fall limp and Lancer slowly withdrew the paddles.

"What the hell have you done?!" Michael yelled, grabbing Lancer by the shoulder and throwing him harshly against the cabinet with a clatter. "You've killed him!"

"I would prefer not to hurt you, boy," he replied calmly, trying to hold the still buzzing conductors away from them both, "so if you would allow me to-"

Michael snatched at one of Lancers hands and pushed the paddle close to his face while holding the other away. "Why did you do it?" he growled, resisting his urge to complete the circuit using Lancer's face. "Tell me!" he shouted finally.

"The current will do nothing to me," he casually pushed away Michael's grip with the least amount of effort and forced him to the ground. "Trust me, I've tried," he quickly turned and flicked the machines switches back to their 'Off' positions and sighed gently, placing the paddles down. "This is distressing, I realise, and for this I forgive you your abrupt actions but you have to understand that you have been entrusted with a great responsibility. You must ensure the protection of the body."

"You what?" Michael stated in disgust. "After what you just did, you talk about 'protection?'"

Desert of Desolation

"Not *his* body. There is another whom you must retrieve."

"This is some kind of nightmare, it has to be," Michael said quickly, grabbing his head wildly

"It is not," replied Lancer flatly. "Be aware this was Richards choosing. In order to pass into the desert, the body must not anchor the spirit to this world."

Michael stumbled to his feet again, thinking for a second and suddenly came to a realisation. "You mean the Median World? I didn't think it was possible to *really* go there. I thought it was a metaphor... Or something." Michael's brow narrowed as he tried to understand everything that was going on.

"Oh, it is quite possible. It is in returning that difficulties arise," he walked to the large steel slab and began to undo the restraints that held Richard.

"'And for the ones who live astride the worlds; the sore silence prevails before peace,'" quoted Michael. "I read that once. It means Medians can stay there longer than most, doesn't it?"

"Smart boy. I see why he let you come here," Lancer smiled shallowly and unhooked the last leather bond. "It is a great power when seeking that which is hidden...Or lost"

"So that's who he's looking for? He thinks she's like us? A Median."

"Like you, my boy, like you," Lancer placed a hand firmly on Michael's shoulder. "I wouldn't have let him do this if she wasn't there. You see, Richard isn't the only one who can step between the worlds. Let's just say that if some adversity were to get to her first then..." he shook his head, trying to repress the feeling. "Such evil was never meant to exist."

"That zombie...that thing Chris turned into?"

"Millaian...He has found his host but will not remain there, he cannot. Soon, if we cannot stop him, his plan will come to pass. I do not wish to experience what will happen if it does."

Michael paused fearfully for a second. "So where is Richard now?" he asked tentatively, changing the topic.

"Right next to you," Lancer looked just to the side of Michael and grinned, making him glance around wildly. "You won't be able to see him. Only I have that pleasure. It's the-" he thought for a second if to use the word 'Gift' or 'Curse' but came to the conclusion that neither was suitable, "-Bequest of the Seers, to see the unseen, for those lost in torment. To forever witness The Desert."

Michael sighed heavily, growing tired of Lancers exposition. "Yeah, that's all very well and good but was electrocution *really* the best way? Wouldn't, say, Nitrous Oxide have been much more appropriate? You know, a painless method?"

"The spirit must be driven from the body quickly if we are to stop this evil in time. A shock of great intensity is the only way to do so without physically harming his body." He looked to Michael's side again and seemed to listen for a moment or two. "We must hurry. Richard has tasked you with a vital objective," he began to rush around the room, inspecting seemingly random bottles until he came to a small vial containing an off yellow serum. Quickly he turned back to Michael, grabbing a sealed syringe as he went and rushed forward, forcing the items into Michael's hands.

"Wait!" he barked, stopping Lancer in his tracks. "What does all this mean?"

Lancer looked to Michael's side again and sighed solemnly, nodding slightly. "You have to bring her back. This serum-" he pointed firmly to the vial now poised clumsily in Michaels hands, "-will reanimate her body, reverse any rigour mortis and prepare her for the merging. Richard will find her spirit. If he is right, and to go to the desert he must be pretty damn sure, he'll be able to sense her and bring her here…I'm afraid so must you. I can then re-merge her body and spirit and, for lack of a better way to describe it…" he thought for a second whether he really wanted to say it in such a clumsy fashion but finally relented. "Bring her back to life."

Michael stared, wide eyed at him, not fully sure he wanted to participate any longer. "So just find the body, inject her with this stuff and bring her back?" he reiterated simply.

"Basically, yes," replied Lancer, now thinking the simple approach would have probably been better in the first place. He started to usher Michael out of the small room, all the time fumbling with the items he had been given. "Do you think he can handle this task?" he asked, turning back to where Michael had been standing.

Desert of Desolation

Across the border world and through the astral boundaries Richard stood. To Lancer, he was as a shadowy aura against a dark and desolate reality inhabited now by fear and a deep, empty loneliness.

"He can do it," came Richards' faded echo of a voice, "it might just take him a while to get used to it." He looked around the place, a washed-out world with the air tinted a depressed shade of brown from an eternity of neglect and no real purpose in the cosmos. "I could never get used to this place, you know," he sighed quietly. "But I guess no-one could, that's the point."

"You won't be there for long," replied Lancer firmly, "either way about it."

Richard adjusted his jacket casually and tried to take a deep breath but getting nothing but void. "I had better be off then," he finished, giving Lancer a meaningful nod before exiting hurriedly.

Lancer lowered his head slightly, possibly the only one who was fully aware of how pressing the situation really was and let two near silent words drift from his lips. "Good Luck."

In the desert, nothing felt real and nothing existed as it should have in the real world. The gutted chapel had a harrowing absence of any sound. A deathly silence that chilled to the bone. The guardians no longer drifted about the rafters, their absence depriving the space of that warm sense of safety that could only be truly appreciated now it was gone.

Richard strode with conviction towards the door, trying to block out the overwhelming desolation calling out from every inch of this place. It was no help, though, for even his thoughts were empty. The encroaching voices of a thousand lost souls that constantly tormented him had fallen silent, unable or unwilling to pursue him back across the void, closer to whence they had come.

He carefully pressed his fingers against the iron portal to the outside. It was ice cold to the touch and made him shiver, forcing him to withdraw his hand. Finally, he heaved open the doorway and stepped out into a gloomy daylight. Richard hated how, in this place, it was never truly night. He looked to the sky but there was no sun, and no night to come. There was only a thick sprawl of dusky clouds emitting their dull, sickly glare.

The Median

Trying to put this all out of his mind, Richard closed his eyes and, in the emptiness, searched for her. As he did, he couldn't help but think that on some level this place was where he, and all Medians alike, were strongest. They were free from the endless threat of spirits from the Other Side, free to think clearly, and sense things through the eternity of silence that they never could in the din of the real world.

He slowly opened his eyes and realised what he had been thinking, cursing himself for it. Neither he nor any Median ever wanted to be in that place but it was an undeniable fact that it had a power over them, one so strong it could change even their deepest thoughts. It was their celestial home, the true place of the Medians, the root of what they were and all that they knew. It allowed for Richard not only to know that Hollie was there but exactly where and what she was.

He looked up and down the dull, deserted street hoping that she was, indeed, as important as they thought her to be. Eventually he set off down the street as fast as he could walk, knowing what this place could do to him and how much danger they could both be in.

I-V - The Wretched

For I know that thou wilt bring me to death, and to the house appointed for all living

-Job 30:20

F*or every being of true goodness and light in the universe, there must be something of equal evil and darkness. This was most apparent in everyday life. For every old woman helped across the road there would be one whose bag was stolen. It was also true of the shadowy worlds which separate reality, with whispered beings lurking in the dark regions of the emptiest desert of them all. Few had observed these things first hand and fewer had returned to tell of them. They were corrupted spirits of the long past trapped between the walls of this world and the next, driven insane by their torturous plights. Many despised them, feared them, but I pitied them; the Wretched condemned and damned.*

A dark cloud dragged slowly across the bright, not quite full moon and trailed off into the night sky. It obscured even the stars able to pierce the city's yellow haze, making the night seem that much darker. Michael looked down from the sky and sat back heavily in the car seat, thinking about what he was about to do. Looking across at the hospital again, he could only consider what would happen if he was caught.

Body snatching was a high crime, not to mention an utterly despicable action unto itself. He tried to remind himself that it was for a greater good and that lives could be saved by going through with it. It hardly did anything to ease his mind, however, by now he'd seen enough dead bodies get up and start walking around for one lifetime and wasn't keen to see another. Come to that, Millaian was still out there. Michael just prayed that he was far away by now. Better still would be if he was back in the land of the dead but then, he supposed, zombies weren't known for being the easiest beings to put back down.

Eventually swallowing his fear, he opened the car door and stepped cautiously into a yellow pool of light cast by the street lamps overhead and looked over at the hospital, sighing. It was no longer just himself he needed to fear for but all those who would suffer if Millaian were able to succeed in his plan.

He closed the door and, with the anxiety rising in his chest, he began to walk towards the building.

Thoughts raced through his mind of how he was going to go about getting into the place. He doubted very much that Richard's fire alarm trick would work a second time and he simply did not have the mindset needed to break into anywhere, let alone a hospital.

As he neared the A&E entrance it started to become apparent that a distraction may not even be required. Panicked people were rushing around, some with large, clotted gashes across their arms and clothes smeared with blood. Getting closer he could see a body sprawled limply over a gurney. His throat was slit and he seemed to have several deep stab marks through his chest. Michael turned away, covering his mouth, and nearly walked into one of the nurses rushing by.

"You alright?" she said hurriedly. "He didn't get you, did he?"

Michael looked at her sideways, slowly removing his hand from his mouth, shaking uncontrollably. "What? ...Uh, no," he thought for a second and looked at her properly, remembering that there were more important questions to be asked. "Who? What happened here?"

"A guy went psycho with a scalpel in there, don't know how many people he killed in the end but he managed to mess up the chem lab

The Wretched

before he escaped. Whole ward's a biohazard now!" She looked about suspiciously and came to an otherwise obvious conclusion. "Wait, you're not a patient!"

"I have family in there," spurted Michael quickly. "I came as soon as I heard something had happened," he paused for a second to assess if the nurse had believed him. To his surprise she apparently had. "Where did he go?" he ventured. "This psycho guy?"

"I don't know. The police reckon they have a trace on him. Not that you could miss him, he's supposedly got half his face missing, although I didn't see him myself," she looked around again but this time quickly rushed off to help with a patient.

Michael was left with a chill creeping up his spine. Part of him had hoped this was all a bad dream or a figment of his imagination but now that hope was gone. This was Millaian's wrath and it was going to continue until he was stopped once and for all.

He worked his way as silently as he could between the crowd of distressed patients and doctors alike and slipped into the deserted reception area. The swing doors to the ward were now crisscrossed with yellow tape emblazoned with biohazard symbols. Beyond, hazard suit clad figures shimmered behind the tinted glass. He looked carefully behind the reception desk. There was an un-taped and most likely overlooked plywood door back there. Michael knew very well that the door was probably locked tight and left him no recourse but to break in. On reflection, he concluded that, given the gravity of the situation, a level of civil disobedience may have been acceptable. Besides, it was nothing compared to the intended act of body snatching.

Michael swiftly clambered over the reception desk and tried the door which was, as he had expected, locked firmly. Without a second thought, he looked around for something to force the door with. He scrambled through drawers and filing cabinets but found nothing but clipboards and flimsy folders. Eventually he stopped and looked carefully at the door, then down at his feet. Bracing himself against the side wall, he threw a foot as hard as he could towards the latch. Immediately the lock splintered and flew off, leaving the door to swing open wildly into the opposite plaster wall, digging a considerable hole in the weak partition. Realising that this hadn't been the quietest and that someone would no doubt investigate any second, Michael started off along the staff corridor as fast as he dared.

Michael had never wanted to return to that or any other morgue, having neglected to note how to get there. As it was then, his less than subtle mode of entry had ultimately been fortuitous. Signs lined the staff corridors directing to places the public were never meant to visit, including the morgue.

Hurrying along the corridors, following the signs the best he could, Michael could hear the muffled voices of suited inspectors growing ever closer.

Instead of trying to flee their approach, he decided to duck behind a nearby partition and tried to control his anxious breathing. As much as he had tried to put it out of his mind, the fear of those spilt toxins had consumed his thoughts. He had to know just how dangerous they were and whether he, himself, would be long for this world if he stumbled upon them. Without a more reasonable option, his only choice was to find out from the only source available, a source that could also bring his task to a premature end.

Footsteps grew closer until voices were discernible. "…over the place. We were lucky this time; sectors 3 through 7 are clean. Looks like the toxic stuff was contained to the lab." There was a short burst of static and a blip the words were directed into a radio, most likely to the Police or Hazard Control Agency operatives stationed outside.

"Roger. Continue with recon and keep us apprised. Cleanup crew are inbound," the mostly garbled response came across the radio before another blast of static and a bleep.

"Oh well, looks like we're all done here," said a different voice.

"I should bloody well hope so too, supposed to be at home with the wife and kids too…" the voice faded away as they continued on down the corridor, out of earshot again.

Michael slumped against the wall and breathed a sigh of relief before carrying on towards the morgue. As he went, it became apparent that the lights were becoming dimmer and eventually ceased to work altogether, the corridor lit only by the glow from offices and adjacent rooms.

The Wretched

Although his better sense was screaming for him to turn back, he pushed forward until he finally rounded a corner to his destination. Almost immediately he was halted by the visage of a person standing halfway down the next hall. Retreating back around the corner, Michael stood for a few moments, pressed flat against the wall, hoping that he hadn't been seen. He stood in silence for several more seconds, his heart pounding so hard against his chest that he felt it may give him away. The seconds continued to tick by, slow enough to be eternities unto themselves, until a word drifted gently around the corner to Michael's ringing ears.

"Hello?" The voice seemed scared, lost almost, but with a relief that came only with the breaking of solitude. "I know you're there...Please come out," the voice began to tremble with fear. "There's something dark here...And it's coming back to get me...To get all of us."

"I'm here," stated Michael softly, without thinking. He didn't know why but he stepped from the shadows and began walking towards the figure. All the time it remained motionless, silhouetted against the still functioning lights at the end of the hall.

"Help me! Please God, help me!" the man pleaded in terror as Michael continued to approach. "He will complete himself and then return for us all!"

"Who?" The question was asked even though the answer was known but still there came no response.

As what little light there was drew across the man's face it became apparent that he was a young doctor although his features had become long and drained of all colour. His white coat was now dulled a dirty brown and had streaks of blood across it, the result of three deep stab wounds through his chest. This had been Millaian's work. Soon a sickening realisation dawned upon Michael. This had been the first doctor who had found him. The first of what would soon to be many victims.

He composed himself and turned slowly to the door of the morgue, taking hold of the handle firmly and, breathing a deep, fear-fraught breath, opened it. Just inside lay the body of the young doctor, his coat dyed red with his own blood and his face twisted into a vision of horror.

"Is that me?" asked the doctor quietly, unsure what was transpiring.

Michael faced him head on and knew what he had to do. There was no doubt anymore, he had taken the final steps towards being a true Median and knew instinctively what to do.

"It's time to let go," he finally replied calmly, no longer afraid of the shadowy dreams or apparitions in the night, for he now knew that there were much worse things to be afraid of. "Once you do, you'll be safe," he went to place a reassuring hand on the man's shoulder but thought better of it once remembering that he wasn't entirely there. "Trust me, there's nothing to worry about on the Other Side."

After a moment's contemplation, the doctor nodded shallowly and closed his eyes, his shape rippling and beginning to drift away. His being was scattered, taken like dust in the wind, leaving a faint echoed voice in the air which came back to Michael and whispered simply, "thank you."

Smiling slightly, Michael at last entered the morgue, carefully stepping over the body, and headed for a specific door in the freezer cabinet. He stopped for a second before pulling open the small door, unsure of how he knew which one Hollie was in with such certainty.

Stepping back, he looked carefully at the whole wall of metal doors but still came to that same one. He could sense it was her. Some residual trace of her past life had left a dull imprint on his newly horizoned mind. He quickly pulled at the handle, forcing the door open and allowing the cold, metal body-plate inside to slip quickly out.

On it laid a black body bag, apparently unaffected by the freezing temperatures but still cold to the touch. He grabbed the zip and, after a moment more of hesitation, pulled it some way down, revealing the body concealed inside. It was indeed a woman, her skin frosty and turned a faint shade of blue by the sub-zero temperatures.

Michael scrambled in his coat to find the picture Richard had taken from Chris' apartment and held it up to her face. Apart from the distinct colour change of the corpse and lack of any identifiable expression, it was her. He, once again, began to search his coat for the syringe and vial of serum with which he would attempt to revive her. Once found, he clumsily managed to draw the liquid into the syringe and, after pausing again to assess the best way he should go about doing it, pinched the sterile needle into her frozen arm, injecting its contents.

Richard came to a halt at the crossroads of what, in the real world, would have been a busy street, even as late in the day as it was. He grinned briefly at the idea that he was standing in the middle of a busy intersection and wasn't causing all out chaos. Better yet, he wasn't even at any risk of being run over and killed. It wasn't simply that there weren't any cars to endanger him here but, in all the ways that mattered, he was already dead, immune from that which had already occurred. His grin fell away as he realised that there was a good chance he was going to stay that way if he didn't speed up his efforts and his thoughts turned quickly back to the matter at hand. He looked about the empty street with the cold air of absence weighing increasingly upon him.

Buildings stood here only as a testament to man's echoed legacy. It was something that, like all things, would eventually wither and crumble. The only reminder that it lived still was the occasional shimmer of a car, static in place for several days, having imprinted itself upon the fabric of this reality.

Richard had never fully understood how this could happen. How long did standing fixtures of the living world need in order to press through to this plane? How was it even achieved in the first place? Nonetheless, despite its apparent impossibility, it was. Buildings, roads, even furniture providing it had been there long enough, they all eventually left their mark, the ghosts of life.

He continued to gaze about the street. She was here somewhere but now too close to pinpoint exactly where. Ahead of him, a figure appeared in the middle of the street but before it could know where it was, it faded away again. It was just another soul passing through on its way to the Other Side, not able to know or even acknowledge where it was before being sped on again across the existential planes.

Richard continued to stare at the buildings, not knowing where to start but acutely aware that he didn't have time to systematically search them all. Closing his eyes, his thoughts drifted out into the void of emotion. He knew there was a good chance that it wouldn't work but a long time ago he had been taught that in the absence of all else, the smallest echo could be deafening to a well-trained ear. Having no idea what this had meant until his first trip to the Median World, he quickly came to realise that all Medians are natural Empaths. Empathy was the root of their ability to commune with the Other Side, the understanding of those who had come from there and it was just another one of the traits this place happened to enhance.

Richard's mind drifted around the street, probing into every storey of the buildings around him, finding only an increasing sense of harrowing emptiness. The tormenting feeling grew within him, attacking his primal fears and was about to force him to stop when suddenly something hit him. An overwhelming sense of sorrow traced through his body and convulsed him into weeping.

Upon composing himself, he turned sharply to the street he had just walked down and ran towards the second building along from the intersection. He forced his way through the main door, shattering its imprinted image on this world, and rushed up a set of stairs, knowing exactly which apartment to head to. Only stopping once he reached an apartment on the third floor, Richard paused, panting heavily, and inspected the door carefully.

The feeling was stronger than ever here but, despite being one of the deepest miseries he had ever felt, it was somehow comforting for it meant that he was not alone in this place.

He moved to take the door handle and thought back to something Chris had once told him. 'The worst feeling is better than no feeling at all'. He nodded to himself and slowly opened the door, stepping into the apartment.

From the far end of the entrance hall came the sound of sobbing which Richard quickly followed into the living room, finding Hollie huddled in the far corner. She was mumbling incoherently amongst her sniffled sobs and holding her knees so tight that her hands had turned white. She did, indeed, resemble her picture, only now looking as if she had been through hell and back. For a moment Richard reflected that, to some extent, she had.

The Wretched

He stepped closer to her and reached out a hand carefully. "It's alright, Hollie, you're not alone anymore."

"No!" she snapped abruptly. "You're not real! Just another one of them!" she began to rock back and forth repeating the words 'not real' over and over.

He thought about who 'they' may be but decided that getting her away was his main priority. "I assure you I am as real as I possibly can be," he stopped for a second and considered what he had just said, "in this place at least," he added quietly. "I'm here to help you, take you back."

"They say they want to help me too…They lie!" she raised her head towards Richard and tilted it slightly, wiping a tear from her face. "But…you don't look like them…You look normal."

Richard stepped closer to her and gently placed a hand on her shoulder. "You're in danger here, I'm going to take you home." What she had spoken of had certainly piqued his curiosity but, for the moment, he managed to sway his attention back to the more pressing issues.

"No!" She squirmed back from him, against the wall. "That's where they were. I thought I could escape them but they followed me, I don't know how." She calmed and looked at Richard carefully. "You're not one of them, though, are you?"

"Who are 'They?'" he finally asked. "*What* are they?"

She turned her head and gazed into the open room. "They are the starless night…The plague of the void…" she spoke slowly, transfixed upon something in the room and raised a shaking arm, finger outstretched. "They are his dark minions."

Richard spun round and backed into the corner as he laid eyes on something he never truly believed existed. A myth of the underworld and what he had hoped never to face. "Reavers!"

Reavers were a mythical demon of the border worlds, twisted amalgamations of outcast spirits, formed into horrific visions of the void between life and death. Stories told of them prowling silently through the borders, seeking lost souls to corrupt and make theirs.

Three stood hooded and silent, near motionless other than slightly swaying in a haunting, simultaneous fashion. Each looked different, their spirits merged in different ways but all were a sickening, charred red, as though their flesh had been stripped and burnt.

One stood with a single twin jointed leg aside a normal one. Sharpened elongate bones protruded from its elbows and a third limb reached out from inside its half-exposed rib cage.

The other two had otherwise normal limbs, only with their finger tips sharpened to needle points. One even seemed to have faces pressing up against the inside of its chest. None of the creature's faces were distinguishable, only dull yellow glows emitting from beneath their hoods.

Hollie gradually opened her hand out and waved across each one in turn, leaning forward slightly as Richard tried to pull her away. "Seeker..." she stated across the most human of them. "Carrier..." she waved across the second most human and gazed at the faces in its chest sorely before moving on to the last one. She grimaced at this abomination of a creature and darkened her voice, "...Hunter."

Richard stared at her for a second, hardly able to believe she knew so much about their hierarchy but eventually pulled her back and managed to manoeuvre himself in front of her. He was unsure if this would make any kind of difference if they attacked but at least it was something.

"From what I know of these things they can only take willing souls," warned Richard harshly. "Don't give into them!"

A hissed breath drew from the Seeker and it took a step forward, its near skeletal feet clicking hideously on the wood panelled floor. "You will...come...with us," its chilling hissed voice was abrupt and disjointed, intended to invoke fear into everything it met. "You have...no choice."

"I think we do," Richard replied aggressively, "if you want us, you'll have to take us by force...But you can't do that, can you?"

The Seeker glanced back and forth between them. "*We* do not...desire you..." it turned to Hollie sharply, "*he* does," its reply came in low, malignant tones. "You will...be taken..."

The Hunter stepped in line with The Seeker and turned slowly back towards Richard, stretching its long, sharp fingers. "You will...perish."

The Wretched

Hollie stood up quickly and moved in front of Richard. "Maybe it is time," she took a step forward. "I will go with you, but he must go free," she pointed backwards toward Richard.

"No!" he stood up shouting and tried to pull Hollie back again but was shrugged off.

"You have no need for him. He's just a guy," without turning she pressed Richard back, keeping him silent. "Do we have an agreement?"

"You can't do this," Richard growled finally. "I'm here to *help* you! You don't realise what's at stake. You can't go with them!"

"I know who you are," she whispered to him, "they will kill you and take me anyway..." She turned around and looked at Richard meaningfully. With the presence of another like her, Hollie's solitude induced madness was beginning to and her true sight re-established itself. "I don't know what's happening to me but I know that this is not where you save me... You will, just not here."

Richard didn't know what to think but slowly took a step back regardless, concluding there wasn't any other choice.

"So, do we?" Hollie asked the Reavers as sternly as she could muster, completely terrified of what she was doing.

The Reavers were completely silent for a few more seconds until The Seeker reached up with jerked, deliberate movements, about to pull the hood from its head but stopped short and lowered the clawed hand. "Your...proposal has been...accepted."

The Carrier looked at Hollie expectantly, forcing her to begrudgingly step towards it. As she did The Hunter quickly struck out towards Richard, gripping him tightly around the neck and carrying him to the nearest window.

"No!" Hollie screamed, squirming against The Carrier as it grabbed hold of her. "You said he'd be spared!"

"He will not...be harmed..." The Seeker stated in the least reassuring way.

The Hunter raised Richard up, tightening its grip as its eyes glowed a brighter yellow. "...much," it added slyly to its counterpart's statement before throwing Richard as hard as it could. It shattered the window's image on the world and left Richard to fall helplessly to the concrete street two floors below.

The Median

The Seeker looked to Hollie, its pinpoint eyes standing out against the harrowing darkness in its cowl. Eventually low hissed words slithered from the tattered hood and struck a cold, primal fear into her heart. It simply said, "you are his."

I-VI - The Other Side

For many are called, but few are chosen

-Matthew 22:14

Hurriedly pushing the gurney down the corridor, it dawned on Michael that all he had done so far had been the easy part. The challenge of getting Hollie's body out of the hospital unnoticed still stood before him. He abruptly stopped and looked at the black body bag, trying not to think too much about what was inside. It was still cool to the touch and the sight of it made him agonise over whether he had carried out the procedure correctly. How hard could a simple injection be, anyway? He breathed heavily, knowing he had never actually given one before and considered again if he would really be able to get her out.

As if without thinking, he flicked up his arm and pushed back his sleeve in one smooth motion to look at his watch. It was closing in on two in the morning and he tried to reassure himself that at this hour it should be easy enough to go unnoticed once he was out of the hospital. Then again, he wasn't out yet and the small hours hardly meant anything to a perpetually bustling hospital. He nodded to himself slightly and started pushing the gurney again.

Knowing that he would never get out the way he had entered, he was already following signs directing to the service exit. He presumed it was where undertakers picked up their bodies so there should have been room for the gurney. At least this was the hope for, in truth, he genuinely had no idea. Either way, he wasn't leaving without that trolley for, in his mind, wheeling a body from a hospital was one thing. Carrying one out was something entirely, and much more disturbingly, different.

The gurney's wheels squeaked faintly down the polished corridor as distant sounds could be heard of staff re-entering the building, forcing Michael to pick up his pace. Eventually, having managed to keep ahead of the sprawl of staff and patients approaching, he came out onto a much wider corridor lined with several more gurneys. Some stood empty but most held body bags, occupied by those awaiting their final journey. He shuddered and cautiously continued on towards a pair of wide double doors leading to the dark car park beyond.

As he approached them, he was overcome with a sense that being caught for body snatching may yet be the least of his worries for he felt as though something foul stalked him. Suddenly, the feeling became all too real and he stopped again, staring at the floor ahead.

Droplets of fresh blood trailed down the corridor, becoming more apparent as his eyes followed them towards the night. The pools soon turned to smears across the smooth surface as if a dead animal had been dragged away. The trail continued for some time and eventually led to a single leg protruding from behind one of the stationary beds.

Despite fearing the worst, all Michael could do was press on, pretending as if he had seen nothing, but as he took a tentative step forward the fluorescent lights overhead began to flicker and failed altogether with a sharp buzz.

The sudden loss of light left him in a complete, unceasing blackness, his eyes taking far longer than he was comfortable with to acclimatise to the light spilling in through the far doors. As they did a silhouette became outlined against the sickly yellow light, its slumped and stiff appearance giving little hope of this being anyone of kind intentions.

Michael watched the lone figure for longer than he felt reasonable until it abruptly spoke in a piercing, gravelly tone. "How does it feel, my boy?"

"I know that voice," Michael mouthed, shaking steadily with fear. "It's you."

Millaian walked forward slowly, withdrawing a scalpel from the pocket of his bloodied trousers. "Yes, of course you do...But in more ways than you care to accept."

"I'll never let you have her!" he shouted, stepping in front of the gurney. "Not as long as I'm still breathing!"

Millaian laughed quietly and stopped his slow advance. "Although I would relish the opportunity to take you up on your offer, I do not need her shell. It is of no importance to me." In the darkness, a grin cut across what was left of his lips and he started to stagger towards Michael again. "I have her essence and that is all I require...No, it is not her I desire...It is you."

Michael was startled back into the gurney, making it clatter loudly. "Why?" he managed, shaking uncontrollably.

"Of course, you do not know, he would have kept it from you...To keep you weak...And now his weakness has led to his death," he pointed the scalpel accusingly at Michael, grimacing and gritting his decaying teeth. "This host felt much for you. You see, there was a bond between you, my boy...Or should I say," he took a long, wheezed breath in, truly enjoying toying with him, "my son," he finished slowly, pleased with the effect his words would bring.

Michael ran the statement through his head, trying to wrap his mind around its meaning whilst Millaian's haunting grin beamed darkly through the night.

"Wait..." Michael whispered, realising that some part of him had known all along. "It's true, isn't it?" he breathed quietly, moving towards the faceless being. "He *is* my father. Richard knew it...and so did I..."

"No..." growled Millaian, backing off slightly. "You could not know, you are weak. Give up your delusions and submit or you will die."

Michael stepped up to Millaian and smiled. "No, I won't," he cocked his head and grimaced. "That's what you've wanted, isn't it? A lackey...A minion..." he looked straight back at him as it became clear. "An apprentice...You wanted someone to corrupt. Someone to make just like you..." He grew bold in his new found confidence and simply asked, "why?"

"I need not explain myself to the likes of you!" he struck out a blood smeared arm and grabbed Michael around the throat, raising him from the ground. "You will taste death for your insolence..." he tightened his grip before throwing him into the wall so hard that the plaster cracked. "For this I pity you for there is no peace on the Other Side." He once again took Michael by the throat, pressing him against the ground and raised the scalpel high, the bloodied blade glinting in what light there was. He hesitated for a second and leaned in close to Michael. The congealed rot oozed from his face, tendons in his exposed jaw tensing as he gritted his teeth.

"Why wait," Michael croaked finally, unafraid of the monster looming over him, instead seeing something in Millaian, a strength that he did not control. Michael pressed against the grip, leaning towards the blade. "Do it!" he added, knowing that he would not.

The dull light of the other world failed to even make Richard squint as he opened his eyes onto the glowing sky of the desert. The window high above shimmered indecisively, unsure whether it was still in phase with the living world or not. He sat bolt upright in the empty street as he recalled the Reavers and what they had wanted. There was little chance that she was still there, he couldn't even feel her anymore. Even so, he jumped to his feet and rushed back into the building, pounding up the flights of stairs and burst into the apartment to find that it was completely deserted. He hung his head mournfully and wiped his face, not knowing how next to proceed.

Suddenly, he looked up again, only now realising that he was still in the Median World. He had no idea how long he had been unconscious and it might have been too late already. Still, he wouldn't be any use to anyone if he stayed dead this time and had to at least try to save himself.

Turning sharply, Richard rushed from the building and ran along the street towards Lancers chapel. As he did, he could feel the strength leaving him as the last of his proverbial sands trickled away into the abyss. He could feel the Other Side clutching at him, trying to pull him away, through to the land of the eternally dead.

The Other Side

Still, he continued on, fighting against a rising wind and the cold air of the world darkening around him until, at last, he fell upon the great door to Lancer's sanctuary. With the last of his strength, he managed to heave open the massive door and, covered with a thick layer of frost which chilled him to the bone, he collapsed before the dull and distant silhouette of Lancer. As he laid there, Lancers' shape drifted ever further away, fading into the depths of an unknown reality while the land of death tugged at Richard's very soul.

With one last effort, he managed to look up through the snow laden gales that tore at his flesh, blistering it to a burning rawness. A dull glow approached slowly through the blizzard and stood over Richard motionlessly until three words drifted gently through the turmoil, settling softly on his ears.

"Not your time," they stated calmly before Richards' grip on the world was lost and he slipped into darkness.

There was an absence of everything. Light, sound, even the unbearable sense of solitude was gone. It was a place of absolute absence, the incarnation of nothing; the Void of Souls.

Supposedly this was the true afterlife, a place where time and space did not exist. A place where even those within did not truly exist to experience it. There *was* something, though, Richard could feel it. Some thread of his being that still clung to the world of the living and refused to let go.

Suddenly streaks of scattered light washed across his vision. They moved so slowly that he could see the particles merge and divide, some sweeping majestically as their very structure changed and twisted whilst others swarmed, shattering the fragile waves of their counterparts. Then, just as the particles tried to drift into a veil of impenetrable light, they were pulled away, drawn into an everlasting abyss and, once again, there was nothing.

Richard's eyes flickered open and burned as the buzzing fluorescent light overhead bore down on him. He writhed uncomfortably, clenching his eyelids from the glare. Soon a brightly outlined shadow leant over him, blocking the light to an extent.

The Median

"Thought I lost you for a minute there," came Lancers' Germanic accent softly, "but that's the last time you're going there, for sure."

Richard sat up uneasily and cradled his spinning head delicately. "I know what you're going to say," he croaked, bodily functions still re-establishing themselves after several hours of being out of use, "I knew the risks after being there so long last time."

"A Median can exist there much longer than anyone else, yes. But the time of every visit is added to the last. Parts of your spirit fall to the Other Side every time-"

"I know!" snapped Richard, sliding himself off the table. "Eventually we all run out of time..." he rubbed his face and steadied himself. "Thank you, though. If you hadn't-"

Lancer turned and put his hand up. "Forget it, you're the one who made it back...What the hell happened out there, anyway?"

Richard paused for a moment and shook his head, barely even believing what he had seen with his own eyes. "Reavers," he managed to state weakly. "They took her and left me for dead. I don't know how long I was out but obviously not as long as they'd hoped."

"No, they don't just leave people. They either take them or kill them outright," he said firmly, rubbing his face in thought. "But that's not the important thing now," he waved his hand dismissively, "we don't know where they have taken her or how to stop Millaian...Or even where to find him for that matter."

Richard reached into his seemingly bottomless pocket and slowly withdrew a half-tattered book, streaks of dried blood across its cover. "This is some sort of an adaptation of a notebook he carries around. Don't ask me why but it seems to be really important to him. I don't know why it was made but I'm pretty sure its content is virtually identical," he waved the book around gently. "I think it's somehow got the answer to all this."

"I believed this text to be a myth," Lancer reached for the book and held it carefully, caressing its pages, "and for there to be a copy?" he breathed slowly, gazing at the pages. "I know not how this could have slipped us by," he shook his head and then came to a much more startling enlightenment. "It could not be true that he is the one...The Observer?"

The Other Side

"You mean the madman who went to see the Other Side..." Richard asked coyly, aware of the level of Seer legend they were dealing with, "and come back from it? The one true greatest Seer of all time?" his words were spoken mockingly but not without some degree of reverence.

Lancer nodded shallowly. "Indeed, this is who I speak of. We are told that the unnamed one accomplished many things thought to be impossible for both Seer and Median." Lancer brushed his hand across the cover. "It is said that to achieve these feats he utilised a supposedly magical text named 'Navire.'"

"Vessel," whispered Richard, becoming unsettled by the revelations. "It's possible he isn't. Millaian might be using the Observer's work for his own ends..." He stepped out into the open chapel and looked up to the Guardians as if for an answer.

Lancer followed him and pressed his temple, again shaking his head in disbelief. "Matter still stands, if he wasn't then how did he manage to cross over in the first place?" he sighed a breath of begrudging acceptance. "It is him. But no matter what we think of this myth. No matter what other worldly forces or incantations he may wield, Millaian is still just the embodiment of a human based evil, nothing more. The ideal of The Observer remains an inspiration to us all. That we can respect the Other Side and learn to coexist with its spiritual nature," he grinned, reassured of his convictions, even if he was the only one.

"The Other Side..." stated Richard bluntly, still staring at the swirling spectacle of Guardians above. "That's it! That's the answer!" He turned and looked directly at Lancer; his eyes wide open. "You see, we don't even need to confront him. If Millaian is who we think he is and he came back from the Other Side using a ritual in that book," he pointed accusingly at the book in Lancer's hand, "then there has to be one that he used to get there in the first place!" He looked away for a few seconds and thought through the idea. "If someone goes and tells on him then," he waved his hands about," whoever is over there might just be able to pull him back. I doubt they're very keen on people escaping."

"No!" Lancer shouted harshly, grabbing Richard by the arm. "There's no way you're going to try this! You have no idea whether there's any help there or if 'there' even exists, for that matter! You've spent too much time in the desert as it is. This could be a one-way trip for anyone, let alone you!"

Richard smiled and eased Lancer's arm away. "Just as well I've got you here to bring me back then, isn't it?" he smiled again as Lancer lowered his arm and hung his head slightly.

"There never was any stopping you, was there?" he conceded reluctantly, only to be met with another brief smile from Richard. "There is a way...A rite which all Seers know of but for good reason do not know how to conduct," he sighed solemnly for a moment. "We know of it so that if this very text was ever found to be real then it could be destroyed. Such a dangerous power is not meant for anyone of mortal blood lest they fall to the same fate as The Observer," he sighed again heavily, unsure if this was the right course of action. He was, however, acutely aware that it could be their only chance to stop Millaian before he unleashed whatever hell he had planned for the world. "It's called The Rite of à L'autre...It translates roughly as 'To the Other,'" he handed the book back to Richard carefully, who immediately began rifling through the pages, searching for the incantation. "I have done a terrible thing this day...I have broken the oath of all Seers, what ones that are left anyway. For over a century I have followed my path diligently only for it to come to this."

Richard stopped searching and looked up at Lancer. "I don't believe that...This could have been your path all along...And, if you'll excuse the cliché, you could have just saved all our eternal souls," he went back to searching the book until arriving on one of the last pages. "I think this is it..." he flicked quickly through the book again and returned to the same page. "The Rite of à L'autre et Reconstituer...Looks like it was one of the last he ever used."

Lancer carefully took the book back and gazed at the ritual instructions. "I am not familiar with Reconstituer although I believe it stands to reason that it is a natural part of the ritual that allows the traveller to return to the living world. A part, I feel, that Millaian was unable to use, hence his incarceration in the other world," he rubbed his head briefly in thought. "But how was he able to return at all without this knowledge-?"

The Other Side

"I don't really care," snapped Richard, snatching the book from Lancers hands and quickly reading through the incantation. "We have a chance to stop him without any more bloodshed and that'll do just fine for me," he held up the book and pointed to it firmly. "Do it. Send me to the Other Side."

Lancer opened his mouth loosely, about to reiterate how dangerous the idea was but came to the conclusion that it would be pointless and reluctantly took back the text. "For all it's worth, if you don't come back then I hope you find peace out there somewhere," he spoke the words as softly as he could but only received a simple nod of acknowledgement from Richard.

There was an extended pause before Lancer could bring himself to begin the rite but at last lowered his head and read through the ritual.

"Fire is the key…A doorway, like any element to the many planes of existence." He squinted with effort for a second and waved his hand around a single point in the air. He moved his fingers together into a point and twisted them quickly to spark a small flame that burnt motionless just above his finger tips. "Like the transition between this world and the border, the element must be engaged with. It must be allowed to encompass you and the very essence of what you are. Only then will you have sufficient understanding to proceed…Now, focus on the flame, let it take you away…"

As Richard stared ever deeper into the flame, he could begin to see the true nature of it, the essence that lies beyond normal perception. Slowly his eyes closed with the whispered words flowing from Lancer's breath, becoming ever more distant until they were all but gone. His eyes suddenly flicked open again to see a darkened outline of Lancer before him. He still held the flame aloft but now it burnt with an empty shade of blue, its heart darker than the deepest pit. He was back in the border world he knew so well.

"It was so simple…" stated Lancer flatly, "in front of us the entire time…The flame born by the earth, sustained by the air and doused by water. It holds all elementals within its grasp; Birth, life and death," he gazed into the dark flame and smiled. "It's a portal within a portal. The Other Side has always been here, within the flame. The gateway is only our own capacity to see it as such," his voice was

The Median

full of a fearful glee, as though he were a child toying with something forbidden. "Concentrate again, my friend, and you will see the truth..." Lancer spread his fingers, allowing the flame to move across his palm and waved it before Richard. "Fire is the gateway, the endless portal to the unseen world..." he pressed his palm forward and allowed the dark core to embrace Richard. The world began to fade, eternal night drawing close and just before the starless eternity took him, he heard Lancers final whispered words. "L'eau pour renvoyer la vie...Water to return the life..."

"Can you feel that...? It's the sense of death."
All around there was nothing but darkness and a terrible, chilling cold. Slowly a soft texture took hold, still as cold as before but with a comforting edge that didn't afford the chance to feel alone. It swelled and spread all around, along with it coming a harsh, abrasive wind.

Richard gradually opened his eyes to find himself laid in deep snow with drifts that continued on as far as the eye could see. The blizzard which raged around him, however, ensured that this would not be far at all. Despite this, when he looked skywards, the air was crystal clear allowing him to see a dazzling galactic arc, single stars glittering prominently along its edge.

Richard staggered to his feet, struggling to gain a footing in the soft snow as the gale tried to push him back to the ground. He turned around a few times, trying to see some kind of life or purpose in the windswept tundra but all he found were the faint outlines of twisted, icy forms in the distance, no doubt shaped by centuries of wind and snow. Regardless of the endless stretches of ice and a cold which could freeze a man solid, Richard did not feel the deathly stab of solitude and desperation that he did in the Median World. That voice was with him, even now, the itch of it still in the back of his mind.

"Your time grows short in this place..." it whispered again, "you don't belong here."

Richard swung around and squinted into the snow. "Where are you!?" he shouted at the top of his lungs. "Somehow I don't think this is the Other Side," he added quietly to himself.

"This is true," the whisper seemed to move close and then away as the words were spoken.

"Show yourself," Richard said more calmly, looking up to the celestial horizon again, "I know you're here."

"Our form is beyond your comprehension," it stated one more time, "but we will accommodate if it pleases you."

There were several seconds of complete silence with even the wind seeming to fall quiet while still gusting as strong as it ever had. Soon another outline became apparent in the blizzard, striding closer from the land of ice. It appeared to elevate higher and higher until its shape was far above Richard, positioned atop an icy overhang.

Richard looked around again and now found himself to be surrounded on one side by a sheer glacier wall with nothing behind him but the storm that raged on.

"What is this?" he shouted to the figure with no reply. "Where is this place?"

"You could not be allowed to continue," a deep, gravelly voice eventually came from the overhang, "you would condemn both our worlds."

"This is the Far Side, isn't it? The border world to the Afterlife?" he asked, not quite believing that the place was real.

"You are intelligent yet far from wise. Your incursion on us has damaged the membrane between our worlds. None must travel between worlds unless it is their time!"

"That's why I'm here-" Richard tried unsuccessfully.

"We know why you are here. The one you call Millaian has already breached the membrane. You only weaken it further!" The figure seemed to point accusingly at Richard and then withdraw its arm carefully. "But your intentions are true. You wish to return him to us. I only wish to do the same for you... but I fear you both are now one in the same," he raised an arm as though he was about to swing it.

"Wait!" Richard screamed, raising his hands, submitting. "I only want you to bring him back, stop him from harming my world."

The arm was again lowered, this time more reluctantly. "It is not our place to deal with the matters of your plane, and he is now exactly that." The figure fell silent for a few seconds before crouching and leaning closer, still obscured by the snowy air. "Though we have watched and seen...His ties are of your world, the ones he controls. Separate them and he shall return," he stood again, bolt upright and looked down the cliff. "And so now must you." Quickly he raised and swept his arm harshly in front of Richard calling up a whirlwind which threw him into the night. He managed to look up to the brilliant sky one last time to see the stars streak back into obscurity before otherworldly colours blurred before his eyes. Quickly, he was overcome with a disorientating spinning, a sensation of falling which eventually came to its end with an abrupt jerk.

Slowly Richard opened his eyes and found himself gazing up towards the mass of Guardians swirling around the rafters of Lancers chapel. He gave a gentle sigh of relief and looked about the space. Lancer had placed him on an old mattress in the corner of the main hall. Around him, he realised, were lit candles and burning incense, making the air thick with flavoured smoke. It hung like a fine veil, gently distorting the dull orange light that crept through the stained-glass windows.

He sat up, shaking his head at the arrangement. Of course, he knew what it was and grimaced at the idea of Lancer having so little faith in him. It was a ritual Seers carried out for those who had passed on, to ease their spirit on its journey to peace.

Richard got to his feet quickly, slightly unsteady after his experience, and strode towards one of the side rooms following the sound of distant voices. As he got closer, he found them to be the raised voices of Lancer and Michael, apparently arguing.

"...It is too dangerous! We cannot-!"

"I don't care, it's the only option now!" shouted Michael, cutting off Lancer.

"Do you want all we have accomplished to be for nothing!?" Lancer growled back sternly. "Because without a way to send him back that's exactly what it would all be for."

The Other Side

There was a harsh bang as Michael slammed his hand on a table in frustration. "And if we do nothing then all is lost! We have to confront Millaian and at least try!"

Suddenly the door swung open to reveal Richard standing against the misty air which quickly began spilling into the room. "He's right...We have to confront him now." He smiled at Michael then turned to Lancer seriously, "and I know how to do it," he smiled lightly to himself and stepped further into the room. "We have to exorcise him."

Lancer stared at Richard for quite some time, becoming ever more unsure as the seconds passed. "You're awfully chatty for a dead man."

"Dead?" Richard chuckled. "What makes you think that? I must have only been away an hour, maximum. I mean it's only just dawn now," he waved a hand back at the glow coming through the windows.

Michael and Lancer looked at each other, cautious of how they should proceed. "Rich...I don't know how to tell you this but it's dusk...You've been gone for over 17 hours..." Michael ventured tentatively.

"You see..." Lancer carried on, "after half an hour you still hadn't awoken so I tried the return ritual...It...didn't work," he breathed heavily and shook his head slightly. "I tried it over and over for hours until Michael returned-"

"Which, by the way, is another story entirely," Michael interjected loudly.

"With his information we had a chance but not without you...We tried everything we could Richard, I promise you...But with time running out until All Hallows we finally had to commit ourselves to the idea that you were... gone."

Richard said nothing, trying to comprehend how so much time had passed in this world. The only explanation, he thought, was that considering the time frame of the Median Worlds never seemed to line up with the living world, there must have been a similar effect in the Other Side. The same must have been true for its border world, only much more pronounced. He considered venturing into why this was, what the significance of it had to be but decided he would have to leave the academics for another time. "That doesn't matter now," he tried to convince himself. "What matters is if we have a real chance at stopping him," he looked between the two, each of them still clearly shocked that he was alive. "Now, Michael, what's this information you have?"

"Erm..." he started unsurely, "he found me, Millaian...But I- I managed to get away and found out where he's going," Michael stuttered, thinking it was better he didn't go into what had really happened.

"He's at the Ansen Memorial...The dome at the centre of the cemetery in town-"

"I know the one," assured Richard quickly, "we should get going now, before it's too late."

"We should take the body, " Lancer stated flatly. "I don't know how much longer she will survive over there. I need to remerge the spirit as soon as possible."

Richard nodded quickly to Michael, prompting him to head outside before turning back to Lancer's stone-like features. "Something on your mind?"

"What do you mean by exorcism?" he asked finally after Michael was out of earshot. "Not only is it impossible but the mere idea has been decreed to be forbidden... This whole thing about permanently severing a person from their eternal soul," he clenched his fists and gritted his teeth. "It was never supposed to be done."

"Listen," said Richard firmly, "I never got to the Other Side. I think it was the Far Side border world. Wherever it was, I encountered what I think was their version of a Median. He told me that the only way to defeat Millaian was to separate him from his power...The spirits he controls. The only way to do that is an exorcism. If he won't do it willingly then we have to separate them from him by force," he took a deep, sullen breath. "I don't see there to be any other way."

"There's always another way. Exorcism is wrong-" Lancer tried.

"No!" spat Richard harshly. "The body he controls is not his! He has violated seven people, one of them I consider to be family, and he intends to do it to another before doing God only knows what to everyone else!" He turned away angrily for a few seconds before turning back and pointing a finger accusingly at Lancer. "Your kind! If you had never pushed the boundaries then we would never have been in this goddamn situation!" he breathed heavily, trying to control his temper and eventually lowered his finger. "All you're 'rules'. They don't apply anymore. This is different! Do something right, Lancer. Help me save these people and give them peace."

Lancer stared, furious at Richards outburst before quietly conceding with a gentle sigh. "The process is considered impossible but I suppose you have a way to overturn this assumption, yes?"

"If it's considered so bad, scares Seers so much and has such a strong rule against it then it has to be more than just a theory. Someone must have succeeded in doing it at some point...and I guarantee there's something about it in Millaian's book," he looked meaningfully at Lancer, placing a hand on his shoulder. "We chase the extreme, make sure everyone's where they're meant to be but, really, nothing's ever just black and white. Sometimes some evil must be done to maintain the greater good."

"That's what I told you, many years ago...It is strange what the student ultimately becomes... and how grateful I am for it," he nodded gently once more and took a deep breath. "Alright, let's do it."

I-VII - Necrosis

The last enemy that shall be destroyed is death

-Corinthians 15:26

I can't deny that I was scared, more so than I had been in a very long time. If Millaian managed to take Hollie before Midnight then, when the worlds aligned, his true form would return with all the power of the Other Side. I had seen this form. Decades of attempts to return to this world had changed him into a skeletal apparition of twisted humanity. Any sense of the man which had once been was gone. What was left was a creature driven only by a hunger for power, unshackled from what the rest of us would call morality. Yes, I was scared, we all were, but even if I was doing this just to give Chris the peace he deserved then it would have been worth it a thousand times over.

As the veil of the chilled night fell, so did the boundaries between worlds. The planes of the living and dead moved so close that they were capable of imprinting upon each other, going so far as to open fragile portals between them. Usually, it was a joyous time for both spirits and the living alike, where reconciliation across the void was possible. A time when long lost relatives could return to their families for a single night.

Tonight was silent, however, for a dark mist hung over both worlds, each knowing that something was coming, one who would defile the sacred time and exploit it as his own.

A car jerked to a halt outside the cemetery gates, mounting the kerb as it did. Quickly, the doors were thrown open and Richard stepped from the driver's side, rushing to assist Michael. Carefully they slid Hollie's body from the back seat with Lancer guiding her exit from inside. She had been robed and some colour had returned to her skin although, to anyone looking on, it was clear that she was still dead.

"What time is it?" snapped Richard. "We can't wait any longer."

"Half nine," replied Michael promptly.

"Michael, take her," Lancer passed Hollie into his arms gently and gave Richard a slanted glance. "I'm going to need my hands free if we're going to do this."

Richard glanced back and then at Michael before taking a deep breath and starting towards the large domed building at the centre of the yard. There was a small opening to the crypt, covered with a slightly ajar wooden door. Richard looked back at the others and slowly pressed it open into the damp gloom of the age-old tomb.

All around were shadowed alcoves with skeletons lying therein, each with an engraved plaque above. They lined the walls row upon row atop each other and in the centre stood a raised platform where Millaian crouched, eyes closed, chanting quietly to himself.

The repeated, incoherent words were enough to strike a chill through Richards nerves. Even so, he slowly stepped towards the platform, looking closer at his seemingly unaware foe.

"Can't be that easy," he whispered to himself, gazing at Millaian's figure hunched in the hazed darkness. He turned back and waved Lancer towards him, speaking in low tones as to try and avoid drawing attention to themselves. "I guess now's as good a time as any."

"I'm sure it is," Lancer quipped back, walking gingerly up the shallow steps of the circular platform. Coming within a few feet of Millaian, he drew a deep breath and took his final step forward, rigidly reaching out an open and shaking hand.

The Median

Lowering his head and closing his eyes he placed his hand within half an inch of the decomposing skull and started to mumble repeated words in Latin. His words slowly began to overpower Millaian's continued chant and a dull, ultraviolet glow began to creep from beneath his hand. Starting to smile with his success, Lancer stated the words over and over with ever growing confidence. As he did, the glow continued to spill over Millaian, creating a pool of almost unseen light on the ground around them.

Suddenly the light vanished, along with Lancer's sense of nearing victory, as Millaian's eyes flicked open and his teeth began to grit against his exposed jaw.

Lancer removed his hand, clenching it tightly as Millaian rose before him. "Oh no," he whispered gently just as he was thrown back down the steps.

Millaian raised his arms, calling forth a shimmering wave which rippled through the air, knocking everyone before him to the ground and illuminating the crypt with a brilliant light.

Slowly the light began to fade and Richard looked about, blinking, eyes stinging as his sight returned to him. At first, he thought it to be his eyes adjusting but as he was assured they had returned to normal, it became apparent that the entire crypt was lit with an otherworldly glow. It was not just as if a light were now shining but every wall, every surface now shined with a pale, sickly radiance. He looked around again for Michael and Lancer but they were gone. The only one who remained was Millaian's true, twisted form atop the platform, glowing brighter than the rest of the crypt.

There was silence for several seconds as Millaian stood motionless, the atmosphere around him appearing to drift like an early morning mist. "Such ignorance," he stated in a hollow, terror-inducing tone, "your failure shows your weakness..." He leaned forward, every part of his tall, lean body moving distinctly to the next, giving his movement a serpentine quality. "It is futile to use my own incantations against me...for I am immune." He straightened back up again and grinned a terrible, toothy grin, the sight juxtaposed awkwardly against his washed out, withered face. "You have not the intelligence to devise something original. This you have already proven."

"I demand you give her back to this world and return to your own!" shouted Richard, getting to his feet. "I know what you are and you cannot remain here anymore!"

Millaian grimaced slightly, almost grinning at Richards's statement. "That's exactly what he said…Just as he let me slip away into that hell. You know nothing about me!" He stepped off of the platform, his tattered cloak flowing weightless behind him, and slowly began to move towards Richard. "I do know much about you, however, and for that reason I have already triumphed," he grinned again, turning around and heading back to the platform.

Richard watched the hollow being for a while and then decided to take a bold step. "Christophe Guillaume…" he stated flatly, making Millaian stop abruptly and swing around. "He was the one, wasn't he? The one who couldn't let you do those things anymore. He knew this would happen so after you were gone he took your notebook and published it so that there was at least a chance to stop you."

"That book is nothing…Just words. Mine has innate power, merged to my very being. It awoke me and at last I could be rid of that wretched text." He stared sternly but something in his face gave away a humanity that still resided deep within him. Merely hearing Christophe's name had invoked a pain inside of him. Richard imagined that having to use the published work to conduct his deeds, the very thing intended to betray him, hurt more than any hell he spoke of. "You remind me of him," Millaian said softly at last, "that is why I brought you here…I wished you to be the first I destroy when I reclaim my dominion."

"Reclaim your dominion?" repeated Richard disapprovingly. "You never had one in the first place! By all accounts you died. Committed suicide because life got too much for you."

"Exactly what I intended the weak minded to think," he straightened up to his full height and began to laugh hauntingly. "I could not go on living a normal life, constantly seeing these things! After my supposed death I travelled to France and spent years working with the best Median I could find trying to discover the truth of life and existence itself…"

"Christophe," Richard said gently.

"Yes. But I eventually came to realise there is nothing! Nothing at all...Only power. Power the strong should take and the weak should obey! My old friend... He did not see it as such. He lied to me each and every day, gained my trust and, when we were so close to the end, betrayed me!" Millaian threw his arm down in disgust and growled darkly. "Never again. This time my victory will be complete." There was a shimmer in the air beside him and a shape began to form. It wavered and rippled until it was all but discernible.

"Hollie!" Richard tried to rush forward but was stopped as more figures started to appear all around him. Somehow, they were Reavers. He tried to take in the situation for a moment, then made a stark realisation. "This is a Merge, isn't it? A point between the worlds that become one in the same? But only for tonight? "

Millaian nodded and opened a bony hand towards Hollie. "Blood is thicker than water, as they say. Her blood is very thick indeed. It shall be my conduit to this world..." He turned his head towards her with a crack and gazed down on her with deep set eyes. "My lineage is strong in you."

"No," said Hollie softly, "I can't be." Her lip began to tremble and her breath grew rapid with morbid terror.

"Millaian!" shouted Richard again, past the Reavers. "I'm giving you one last chance! Stop this and return to the Other Side!"

He laughed again with the Reavers looking back, as if surprised he could do such a thing. "You have no way to command me...I do as I please."

Richard chuckled lightly as there was a change in the air. "Then you should have killed me sooner," he said quietly. "Lancer only began the process. Now the worlds have merged, I can finish it." He looked up at Hollie, "only I'm not leaving without her."

Millaian looked down upon him, bewildered at what he saw as a mere insect, as Richard bowed his head and closed his eyes.

"*Libertas tua est, amici mei.*" The words echoed around the building and fell gently upon all who heard it like a fresh spring rain until it faltered and finally drifted away to nothing.

"That's it?" said Millaian harshly. "Latin?"

Richard lifted his head again, opening his eyes. "I command you..." he raised his hand to the sprawling crowd of Reavers before him. "Leave this place." The words moved forward with no force or malice, only the pure assurance of a clear mind capable of directing the spirits that walked his world.

As each comprehended the meaning of the words, they turned and vanished into the ether. "You choose to bring this to my plane and so I will use the power I have on this night alone to command all who would infringe on the living. On this night I decree..." he started walking towards Millaian as the last remnants of the Reavers vanished into mist, "freedom is yours."

There was silence for a few seconds and Millaian was about to belittle Richards' attempts at grandeur. He was stopped when Hollie too gasped and vanished into a mist which drifted towards the door where her body had been dropped.

As she went, a single word echoed back through the air, "life."

Milliaian went to open his dried lips to speak again but instead slowly looked around to six pale and translucent figures standing behind him. As he looked from one to the next, each began to dissolve away in turn, leaving only a fading imprint in the air.

"Your power has gone, you have no choice anymore," Richard continued softly. "Leave this place."

While Richard spoke, Millaian fell to his knees, gritting his teeth as he tried to hold on to the world but with every passing second another part of his spirit slipped away.

"I cannot be destroyed," he managed to say, his gravelly voice broken by laboured gasps. "I will have my triumph!" he growled finally before clutching his chest and exploding outwards into a dark powder that drifted to the ground, fizzling as it did.

Richard took a deep sigh and rubbed his face, hardly able to believe that it may just be over.

"Thank you," came a gentle feminine voice from the platform, making Richard look up again. It was one of the spirits who Millaian had enslaved, still standing in place where the rest had left. "For everything you have done, we wish to give you this," she smiled brightly before lowering her head and vanishing like the others leaving the distorted but solid shape of Chris behind her.

"It can't be..." Richard walked, unfaltering towards him, "are you-"

"Real?" finished Chris, his shape becoming truer as the spirits imprint faded. "As real as I can be," he looked around at the building, its walls beginning to fade back to their normal colour. "They pulled you over to the border but I still don't have long. The worlds are already beginning to move apart and we are on different sides of a *vast* divide." He nodded towards the doorway, calling Richard's attention to Michael and Lancers faint, ghostly figures tending to Hollie as she started to sit up. They turned and looked at Chris' mangled body lying just at the feet of Richard's astral figure, unable to believe it was done.

"So much to say…" tried Richard. "Stay with us."

"I can't," he looked down at his feet and the mutilated body of his real self, "but you can join me. Your time in the mortal realm has been honourable but now it is time to leave," he reached forward a hand. "Come and you will see a world beyond your imagination."

Richard looked down, thinking for a second and slowly began to raise his arm, stretching it out to take Chris's hand.

Behind him, Hollie watched Richard's spectre begin to fade and quickly pushed Michael and Lancer away, getting up to rush towards him. Distraught, she tried to reach for him but soon stopped and took a deep breath, realising why everything had happened to her. Just as Michael had, she took the final step of understanding and embraced what she truly was. As she did, she stepped across the divide, becoming as much a phantom as those before her.

"Richard," she spoke as though she had known him for years and reached for his shoulder, causing him to withdraw his hand from Chris. "You can't do this. I know now that the world still needs you…They need you," she waved her hand back towards the other two and looked around unsurely, "and I think I'll need you…Please, don't leave us."

Something told Richard that he should listen to her. Now, after all these years of feeling alone, he realised he always had people all along, people who cared for him and could understand everything he went through. He looked mournfully to the fading figure of Chris and shook his head gently. "I'm sorry, I have to stay."

Chris said nothing but merely gave a shallow nod and a gentle smile.

"I hope you find her..." Richard added finally.

Chris' image had almost dwindled away to nothing but just before he vanished completely, whispered words drifted across the divide. They simply stated, "look after him."

With the living world returning to normal around them, Richard looked to Hollie and smiled. She barely knew these people but somehow felt everything had changed. Instead of saying anything she merely smiled back as Michael and Lancer finally joined them.

The sun slowly rose over a world oblivious to how close it had come to anarchy, Richard, Michael and Hollie walked along a damp street as the lights overhead flicked off from another night of illuminating the shadows.

Hollie looked down at the robe she was still wearing. "I should really get some clothes if I'm going to be alive again, you know," she stopped and thought for a second. "Come to think of it, what's going to happen to me? Everyone thinks I'm dead."

"Don't worry," said Richard reassuringly, "I have some contacts. They can make it look like a clerical error in hospital paperwork, everyone else will just dismiss it. I've found people have short memories. Now the Reavers are gone, everything will be back to normal for you in no time."

"Oh, I don't think things will ever be normal again after this," she chuckled brightly and moved closer to him. "Honestly, I don't think I'd have it any other way."

"Question is..." started Richard suspiciously, "how did Michael get away from Millaian?"

Michael stopped, sighing and turned to Richard. "My father," he said, startling Richard somewhat. "I know it was Chris... When Millaian had me pinned, I think he took control somehow, stopping him from killing me. Instead, he just knocked me out," he clutched his head and shook it briefly. Gave me one hell of a headache, but I'm alive, at least."

"Family's a powerful thing," Hollie offered reassuringly.

"As for the cemetery, don't ask me how I know he'd be there. When I woke up, I just knew where he was going to be... like I just knew that I was a Median..."

The Median

Richard nodded uneasily. "Family's a powerful thing..."

I wasn't about to question what he had said. I had always known just to respect the old ways and this latest incident had driven that home all too well. I'm glad he knew about Chris now. He was a good man who succumbed to the pressure of too many worlds on his shoulders, the fate of all too many good Medians. I think Lancer learnt a thing or two about his kin as well, although it surprises me to think that a century old Seer could still be so deeply shaken by new revelations. It just goes to prove that no matter what we think we know, there will always be more to this universe than meets the eye. It was something Michael would come to learn very soon for the true meaning of what it meant to be a Median ran far deeper than even I could possibly understand. One thing was sure, though, Hollie was right when she said that things wouldn't go back to normal. Something tells me that, after all this, nothing will be the same again... for any of us.

Book 2
The Dark

Prologue - Nightfall

I have put before you today, life and good, and death and evil

-Deuteronomy 30:15

Centuries trapped in the endless abyss, nothing but the ongoing silence and abject passage of time slipping away moment by moment, never to feel the embracing freedom of death. Our hunger grows stronger, the craving for blood, the sweet taste of flesh on our lips. At last, we feel the time is near. Our imprisonment in a world of unceasing nothing and the everlasting knowledge of our fate weighs heavy on our very being but knowing our persistence will present our reward maintains us. Soon may we be released and allowed to feed forever. Our life in this world grows short for we feel the outside, taste its sweet freedom and crave for when our kind may spread across their existence with nothing to stop us. With this sentiment of triumph over the weak and the enslavement of the innocent, we wait…and rise…

Source: "Navire – Voices in the Dark"
For the longest time I believed not what I had seen in those empty nights. Hours of the lone experience looking for answers in the great abyss, the nothing that divides the worlds. Many have thought these places to be a myth, a mere condition of unknowing between the states of consciousness but I have seen. Through coming to realise the truth, I can comprehend the meaning of this world and beyond.

Nightfall

To see the world behind the world. The truth that there is no empty space, no void between the unseen planes, only another place where the rules of reality do not apply but bend to accommodate its occupants. In my dreams I hear their voices and see their being, the world in which the living dwell while their minds wander in the peaceful drifts of sleep. The place which holds those terrible beings who fed on the world for so long in the aeons before time itself, now imprisoned for the good of all humanity in that cell which, in their whispered murmurs, they refer to only as 'The Abyss'.
-J.M.

Source: "Navire – Nights VI-VII, X, XIII"

VI – *These spoken words taunt me this night. Like all Seers and Medians before me I am burdened by the endless drone of a thousand passed scratching at my mind, trying to take back their place in the world they came to love. These were different, though, much fewer but more tormenting than before, speaking in unison of a dark future they believed to be the past. I fear these to be a result of my most recent experiment. I do not wish to experience them again, as such I am ceasing my investigation into the worldly divides. [28.01.1901]*

VII – *Experiment ceased. I have still experienced the voices in my sleep, this time more prominent. They still speak of the same future they believe to be their history. I feel them to be lingering remnants of the experiment. I will employ amethyst this night in an attempt to block these beings from entering my dreams. [29.01.1901]*
Update – I believe the crystals to have worked for I have not experienced any more visitations this night. [30.01.1901]

X – *Why must they return to me when I have been free for so many nights? They return to me, speaking of the demise of man, clearer, stronger than before. I fear now for my sanity as they claim they shall return and I will become their conduit into this world. A single, united voice of thousands spoke true to me as clearly as any day. They proclaimed, "yours shall become ours." I cannot sleep any longer for I fear they will only find me once again. I will not* *close my eyes upon this reality until they have left me and allow me peace once more. [02.02.1901]*

XIII – *I failed. I slipped into a dark, haunted sleep this day and, as promised, they returned to me. I feel relieved, however, for something within me tells me they have finally abandoned their chase upon me. Although their words were, again, clear to me. They spoke of the coming times and for the century of this day, on the new centenary of millennia they will rise and consume the worlds before them. I saw only a glimpse of what they see but it is neigh unimaginable. A mighty civilisation beyond anything I could imagine crumbling into decay and running red with the blood of the innocent. Before they left me, they said only one last thing, "theirs will fall, The Abyss shall be free...and you will be our means." Their words concern me but at this time I am merely glad to be rid of them. [05.02.1901]*

II-I - Noir

(…) I commanded them: Obey Me and (…) you will be My people

-Jeremiah 7:22-23

*I*t was quiet.
Even the whispered voices that forever reminded me of the caste to which I belong were unusually subtle lately. Ever since she had come into my life those few months ago. Maybe that whole situation had caused a disturbance in the fabric of our reality, making any ambitious spirits trying to get back from the border think again. Although I liked to think it was because I now had a companion in my trials, someone to ease the burden of life as a Median. Of course, that wasn't the only reason I liked having her around. Still, even if the world seemed as good as it could, considering my line of work, I couldn't help but think this was only the calm before a much larger storm. It causes me to continue walking the streets, watching and waiting, hoping that sickly feeling to be only a lone sense of caution, one that would drift away amongst the time I now hold so precious…Yet I fear I am wrong.

    The street laid dry and the air still, every breath taken of it like ice. A fine fog slowly drifted from a nearby vent, lit up by the absent, amber glow of an overhead streetlight. In the far distance the roar of the motorway was soothed into the ether, now but an echo on the light breeze that hushed through the allies. A footstep on the cobblestone broke the gentle silence, followed by another as they came to an abrupt stop. The warm mist swept around a figure standing just inside a large arch leading to an alley criss-crossed with rusted gantries and assorted telephone cables.

Richard finally took another step forward, out of the mist and into the dank gloom of the grubby alley. He looked down the shadowy walkway cautiously, seemingly waiting for something. Suddenly there was a clatter and he started forward, turning sharply towards a rubbish pile in front of several trash cans. He waited for a few seconds before edging along the wall closest to him until the cans clattered again causing him to freeze. With a sharp jump, a small black cat emerged from behind one of the cans with a final clatter and rushed off past Richard with a low chirp that made him relax. He backed away from the alleyway casually and continued off down the street.

High up in the gantry something looked down at where Richard had stood, watching curiously. Then with a silent, almost unnoticeable movement, it fled off into the cold winter night.

The low tones of distant civilisation forever carried on, softened into the dull drone that everyone had become accustomed to over the years. Against that silent din, the only noticeable sound was that of Richards' soft footsteps on the brick pavement. He contemplated just how empty it all was now, part of him missing the single thing that had been there for his whole life. The whispers in the wind which grabbed at his senses and guided him to the lowly souls he was ultimately born to help. Yet, despite this, for the first time he felt content with what he was.

He continued to walk for some time, through the cold new year air, until he eventually reached his house, still presenting an age far beyond its years. In the drive, beside his own, was parked Hollie's small car. Its simple presence made him smile lightly before he proceeded towards the door. As he turned the latch and stepped inside, he was confronted by Hollie, grimacing slightly.

"Again?"

"It's what I do," replied Richard easily, placing his jacket carefully on the coat rack.

"It's what I do as well, you have to remember," she put a hand on her hip and cocked her head slightly. "You don't see me obsessing about it."

Richard walked into the front lounge, followed by Hollie, and slumped down into his armchair with a slight sigh. "I'm not obsessing, I'm just being thorough."

"We haven't heard hide nor hair of anything for months now."

"That's what concerns me. This quiet isn't going to last forever and I don't want us to be caught off guard..." He got up and took a step towards Hollie, placing a hand softly on her arm. "Any of us."

"I can't win with you, can I?" She placed her arms around his shoulders and kissed him tenderly. "Just try and ease up on it a bit otherwise you'll burn yourself out for nothing."

"Trust me..." a voice came from the doorway, followed by Michael wandering in and falling loosely onto the sofa. "This is nothing compared to what he used to be like."

She chuckled slightly and looked at Michael sideways. "You mean he could be worse?"

"Alright, that's enough of that," Richard put his arms up and moved to lean on the mantelpiece. "How about we forget all that for now and go out for a nice meal?"

"I would," stated Michael after Hollie nodded quickly, smiling widely, "but I've got some things to see to." He got up and grabbed his coat from the back of the desk chair, slipping it on quickly. "I'll just leave you two love birds to your lonesome," he sniggered and walked out hurriedly, the front door slamming behind him.

"So..." asked Hollie, moving towards Richard again, smiling brightly. "How about that meal?"

Michael hurried along the dark streets for some time, occasionally passing by a boy racer or late worker, finally on their way home for the night. A strange sense of anticipation hung in the air, as if the ether were waiting for something. It drifted in and out of the empty buildings, through the dank alleyways and made even the busiest streets, with their bright, fluorescent light spilling from closed shop windows, seem almost desolate.

The Dark

He continued on, trying to shrug off the feeling, until he came to a small door. Once it had been some sort of blue but was now covered with graffiti. Just to the side was a faded and grimy copper plaque with several barely discernible words on it.

ENTER NOT THOSE WHO REFUSE TO SEE

Hardly even glancing at it, Michael proceeded to hammer on the door several times. His clenched fist produced a hollow, metallic clank that permeated into the bricks the door was bolted into, shaking a small cloud of dust clear. After a short pause the door was opened barely an inch and a curious, glowing eye appeared at the crack. "What do you want?" stated a raspy, Cajun voice looking Michael up and down, "Median…"

"Just a drink," he replied, "I don't want any trouble."

The door was opened slightly more to allow Michael in before being slammed shut and sealed with a large deadbolt.

"That's what they all say but there have been…incidents."

"You really need to work on your people skills," said Michael softly, walking down a darkened corridor into the rest of the building.

He emerged into a large, lavishly decorated room with multi-coloured strobe lighting illuminating the walls, a heavy bassline throbbing through the air. Scattered around the room, sprawled on wine coloured velvet sofas were groups of what could almost be defined as people. Some had distant gazes, apparently staring at something that wasn't there, occasionally stating something as though replying to someone. Some had glowing eyes like the doorman and were engaging in indiscrete sexual acts while the rest of the group watched. Others simply sat alone, looking around shiftily and apparently talking to themselves. Some were even translucent, drifting around the place with no real sense of where they truly were.

Michael pressed through a crowd of dancers, towards a neon lit bar, as they casually swayed in the flickering light, the beat thumping through the dance floor viscerally. He eventually managed to fall at the bar clumsily, making two leather clad women adorned with spiked neck braces look at him disapprovingly.

"Smooth, kid," stated the Barman casually, "a knock out with the cats I see."

Michael nodded back and forth, squinting accusingly. "New doorman?" he adjusted his footing and managed to take a seat on one of the chrome bar stools. "What's with his eyes?"

"He's a Vesper..." The bartender looked at Michael steadily for a second or two to try and gauge if he had any idea what he was talking about, quickly concluding that he didn't. "It means 'evening', less of a cliché on the whole 'Children of the night' thing." He casually pointed to a small group of Vespers on the dance floor, slowly grinding their bodies on one another. "They're special...Their very being repels the other side. It doesn't want them and they don't want it. As a result, they're sort of-" he watched the small group again for a moment, "outgoing..."

"They're immortals?" stated Michael simply.

The Barman grinned and nodded quickly. "You got it, kid. Immortal...Every last one of the lucky bastards. Usually make up the regulars around here but they're only just coming back now. Most of them did the shuffle when your mate, Weignright, had that little scuffle with the Other Side." He anticipated Michael's reaction and raised his hand stopping him, open mouthed, "and yes, I know about that...There ain't one among us who don't. Go doing shit like that people are going to notice."

Michael sighed, gently lowering his head to the bar then raising it again quickly after a moment or two. "Trance been in?"

He laughed shortly and leaned over the bar, placing his hand on Michael's shoulder. "Women like that...They don't stick around for long," he patted his shoulder and turned around, picking up a cloth. "Forget her, move on."

Michael sighed again and was about to lower his head to the bar once more when a pair of hands were placed on his arms from behind and ran around across his chest.

"Sometimes they don't," came a soft but commanding voice with something of an abrasive quality to it, "and I'm not just any woman," she finished, taking a stool to his side. She was thin with fairly pale skin and short, dark yet almost iridescent hair which bobbed around her shoulders as she moved.

Michael couldn't help but stare at her tight, deep blue jeans as she sat, moving up to a short leather jacket covering a black halter neck top. "Like what you see?" she asked playfully as a deep red drink, softened only by a single ice cube floating at its surface, was placed firmly in front of her.

"Same thing every time," said Michael casually, breezing over her last comment, "are you ever going to tell me what you drink?" he asked as she raised the glass to her lips.

"Hmm," she said, lowering the glass and gesturing a finger for him to move closer, which he quickly did, "it's blood," she whispered in his ear, making him pull back, startled as she smiled at him.

"Sure," he replied incredulously while she continued to smile sweetly at him.

The hours began to pass with various types entering and leaving the bar but for the whole evening Michael and Trance remained, talking casually and occasionally exchanging suggestive gestures to each other until she abruptly got up from her stool and looked around. "I have to go," she said shortly.

Michael followed her lead and rose from his stool, glancing around the room with slight concern. The place was all but empty, only a few stragglers left lounging around on the sofas. "Well, err…" stuttered Michael for a second, "when can I see you next?" he finally managed to cough out, catching the bartender's attention in the process.

Trance shook her head gently. "I…don't know if you can," she breathed solemnly, "but it was fun," she added happily, turning away.

"Can I at least know your real name?" asked Michael, raising his voice slightly and stopping her in mid movement.

She hovered, motionless for what seemed to both of them much longer than it truly was before she turned around, lightning fast and grabbed the back of Michaels head, pulling him to her. "No," she whispered, stroking his hair soothingly, "you can't." She kissed his cheek and quickly rushed around the bar to the back exit.

"I hate to say I told you so, kid," stated the Barman dryly, turning to Michael as he slumped back down onto his stool, "but I don't think it'd help too much if I did."

Michael sat silently for some time, staring at the polished black bar blankly while the Bartender continued to buff a glass absently.

"Women..." said the Bartender flatly, at last, "who really understands them?" he turned his back and placed the glass gingerly upon a shelf, "but I suppose that's what makes them so provocative, the mys-" he turned back around and found nothing but an empty stool "-tery," he finished soberly to himself before going back to attending to another glass.

Michael pushed open the back exit of the bar harshly and stumbled out into a grimy back street with only a dull glow from the main road filtering down this far. He held out little hope that Trance would still be around but chose to look around nonetheless.

Pacing up and down the damp street, barely a few metres from the door, he found nothing but an overflowing skip and the rats therein. He shook his head ruefully and was about to head for the reassuring light of the main road when there was a sudden crash from far into the darkness. He turned and looked cautiously into the gloom, straining his neck slightly to try and get a glimpse at what was down there. It was too big to be a rat or even a cat, he conceded, pausing before taking another curious step forward.

Without thinking, Michael edged closer until he was well out of reach of the streetlight and as his eyes needed to grow accustomed to the darkness. As they did, an outline started to grow against the haze. It was hunched to the ground, moving only slightly in short, sharp jerks and there was a sickly snorting, a repugnant grunting unlike any he had ever heard. Slowly Michael leaned closer, entirely unsure what this person could be doing until a second figure gradually became apparent. It was slumped against the ground in front of the first, completely motionless. Michael gasped, starting back as a sudden realisation hit him.

Backing off quickly, he wrestled with his own mind about whether what he had just seen was real. As he did the first figure, now alerted to his presence, began to rise and turn towards him with slow, steady movements until it was at full height. With calculated, creeping movements, it gradually emerged into a dull pool of light cast between the buildings by the bright moon. His short hair was greasy and covered in grime. His gaunt face was almost ghost-like, bar the still fresh smearing of blood around his mouth which gathered on his chin and dripped down onto his once white shirt. Michael searched for the words to stem the approach as he backed away, the cannibalistic assailant following his every move intently. He thought about turning and running but feared he would be struck down from behind.

Finally, the man raised his arms, his hands curled around like talons, and opened his mouth, growling. Astride his bloodstained teeth were two large fangs and Michael rapidly came to the realisation that this was no cannibal but something much worse and far more impossible. He backed off again, faster this time, as the creature moved ever closer to him. It had a savage purpose about it, its eyes dilating more than should have been possible. Across its pupils, a strange, white substance spread like webbing, highlighting every blood vessel in his eye. As the creature was about to pounce, Michael turned to run but was caught by a side on tackle, forcing him into the wall.

"What the hell are you doing here!?" screamed Trance, pressing him into the wall before quickly moving off towards the creature which approached for another attack.

It leapt at her but she kicked it harshly in the gut and grabbed it by the throat, throwing it into the side of a dumpster, leaving a large dent in its metal frame.

She approached the still body on the ground and looked it over, slowly reaching into her jacket. From her pocket she withdrew a long, ornate dagger which, even in the darkness, seemed to glint like the pure sun were shining on its blade. She raised it high and was about to plunge it towards the creature's chest when it suddenly jumped up, pushing her back down the alley. It snarled and turned back to Michael who pushed himself into the wall, trying to find a way out.

The creature raised its arms again and brandished its razor-like teeth, about to sink them into his neck, when the glinting blade was heaved through its chest from behind, coating Michael in a gushing fountain of blood. The blade was quickly withdrawn to allow the creature to fall lifelessly to the ground.

Behind it was not Trance, as Michael had expected, but a finely dressed man who might have been considered of a higher class, setting aside the fact that he had just impaled someone.

"State friend!" the man growled at Michael, flicking the blade to within an inch of his face.

"Friend, *friend*!" Michael shouted, distraughtly trying to pull back as far against the wall as he could. "I swear to god, I'd rather be your friend than anything else at this point," he gazed, terrified at the ornate short sword, still dripping blood from its tip.

Trace stepped up behind the man, staggering slightly, and placed a hand softly on his shoulder. "Diego...It's alright, he tells the truth."

Diego relaxed his arm but kept the sword pointed oppressively at Michael. "You know this...Human?"

Trance looked to the blood smeared visage of Michael, who had now cowered to the ground, and hesitantly nodded. "Yes...I do."

Diego threw down the sword to his side, narrowly missing both Michaels face and his own leg. "You have been warned! Just because of your position doesn't mean you can blatantly defy our ways!" he breathed for a second and composed himself, lowering his voice. "How much does he know?" he raised the blade slightly again, almost as though he were poised to use it at a moment's notice.

"Nothing," stated Trance firmly, "only what has transpired tonight." She began to consider that, after all of this, he might actually know a little more than nothing.

Diego gestured his sword towards Michael, casually flicking a few drops of blood at him and turned back to Trance. "I sense you feel for this one," he stepped towards her and placed a hand on her face gently, "they must not know." He removed his hand and turned sharply, walking silently out of sight, leaving Trance standing solemnly by herself.

There was silence for a few seconds as Trance stood motionlessly over the fallen beast.

"What's going on?" Michael ventured tentatively.

The Dark

"They must not know," Trance repeated after a few more moments of silence, "it's best for all of us." She took a deep breath in and turned to look down at Michael, slowly crouching down to him. "Close your eyes, my love," she stroked his bloodied hair soothingly and looked deeply into his eyes, "please."

Without thinking he complied, letting his eyelids fall softly shut. For a while there was nothing and then the tender press of Trance's lips on his. Almost without him noticing, she pulled away and, after a few moments, he opened his eyes again but found nothing but the dank alley and the filthy, cannibalistic creature fallen next to him. He quickly got to his feet and looked up and down the alley but found only the chilly night that bit at his senses. He looked down at the body again and then at his blood-stained clothes. They had left him alive for reason and, as he considered what had occurred, he began to fear that it may have been better if he had perished after all.

"We see you..." came a voice from an empty place beyond sight and sense. "This place claws at our being...This dark tears at my eyes. But the time is soon... and you shall be ours."

Richard abruptly sat bolt upright in his bed, sweat dripping from his brow. He slowly reached up and wiped his face, sighing heavily as he did.

"Can't do this," he whispered to himself.

They kept haunting him. The voices were returning as the worlds drifted back into their rightful places, the dead once again becoming complacent. These were different, though. Deathly, overpowering like nothing he had felt before.

He pulled his hand away, staring at it for a few seconds, knowing that he couldn't let Hollie go on thinking that nothing was wrong. He reached for a mobile phone sat silently on the bedside cabinet, catching a glimpse of the glowing red numbers on the clock: 02:17. As he pressed the button a message popped up on the screen, time stamped from just after he had fallen asleep.

Thanks for a wonderful night, Richard, the meal was lovely. See you soon. Hol xxx

He finished reading the message and hung his head, dropping the phone to clatter loudly back onto the cabinet. He couldn't tell her. She needed to know things were going back to how they were before Millaian. But what if they didn't? What if he lost her? He couldn't bear to consider that. For the longest time he had shut people out, even Michael, doing only what he needed to keep him safe. Things were different now and he was happier than he had been in years but he couldn't just ignore what was out there, what had always been there. The very reason he was who he was.

He sat for a few seconds, silently contemplating what his life had become and what may still remain in the future. Suddenly he threw the bed covers back and swung his legs over the side of the bed to stand up. Grabbing his clothes from the back of a chair, he quickly put them on and hurried from his room onto the landing, about to step down the stairs but paused and curiously looked back at Michael's ajar door. He crept towards it and gently pushed it so that it swung slowly open.

Peering round, he found that the curtains had been left open and the bed was made. He sighed heavily before turning and rushing off down the stairs. In one fell movement, he swept his coat from its hook, opening the front door as he went, and drifted out into the night, slamming it shut behind him.

Richard looked about at the freezing night and shuddered as something drifted across his path. No doubt a spirit thinking they could get away with murder, he thought begrudgingly. He decided to leave it alone for the moment, and began to walk through the still air. He had no idea where he was going or even why he was going there but a fierce wanderlust had driven him out into the night. Part of him felt as though he should just turn around and go home, ignore the voice that pushed him into the unknown. Despite the reservations, he was confident it would lead him somewhere, a place that may have answers.

Even though he walked with no great sense of urgency, the time passed and places came and went, taking him ever further from what he knew to be safe. Eventually he stopped and looked around sharply. There was nothing there but an empty, silent street, isolated to the point where even the usually comforting glow of the street

The Dark

lamps had abandoned him. He surveyed as far as he could see in the thick darkness and only barely recognised where he was. It was a bad idea to come to this part of town during the day, and here he was in the middle of the night. He shuddered as the biting cold began to sink in and finally decided that the journey had been utterly futile. Not only that but it was becoming increasingly risky for every second he lingered longer than he needed to. Around here he knew that just about anything may emerge from the gloom.

Quickly he turned and started to march back the way he had come but was promptly halted by the faint sound of footsteps. It might already be too late, he considered, swinging around and briefly catching the outline of a person fleeing into the night. He strained to see beyond the darkness and once more saw the figure dash across the street. With a knot of fear starting to well up inside him, Richard started to back off along the road, ready to start running, but abruptly stopped as his skin prickled and he felt a distinct presence behind him.

"You could not resist," came a whispered hiss, forcing Richard to jolt forward, turning around once more to face a dark silhouette. "Just like the others."

Then it was upon him, a washed-out face covered with horrific sores leaping from the night. It brandished meticulously sharpened teeth; two long, razor sharp fangs framing them at each corner of its mouth. The creature wailed as it struck forth and then there was nothing as Richard felt the tight embrace of unconsciousness, falling mercy to the creature's whims.

II-II – They Awake

Let us make a man with our image and resemblance

-Genesis 1:26

*E*ven *with what I had seen, everything I had experienced, nothing could have prepared me for what was to come. As that foul beast leapt towards me, I felt nothing could help me. Nothing would be able to save me from a fate I had managed to avoid too long already. Falling to the ground, I felt entranced somehow by the end of my own existence, compelled not to resist that which was long overdue. Yet, as the void called to me, there was something else. I didn't know if it were real or some phantom dream but I heard footsteps quickly approaching and stopping for a moment. While I felt the presence of my attacker growing uncomfortably close, the steps moved around my head and then were gone, pulled away in a second. Before I slipped completely from consciousness, I heard only a few faint words spoken in a tone that was as dark as the winter night is long.*

"Wait...This one is special..."

Richard lazily blinked his eyes open against a dust filled gloom. Faint streaks of light crisscrossed a stone clad room, glinting off the flecks drifting through the air, making them shine against the shadows. He tried to move his arms but found them bound tightly to either side of the chair he had been placed on. Glancing down, he found that his legs had also been tautly roped together, rendering any form of movement an impossibility. Richard coughed on the thick, damp air and looked about the room for any hint on how he had come to be here. In the corner stood a tall, thin shade just about outlined by one of the beams coming through a small, barred opening high up in the wall.

"I see you are back with us," came the familiar, gravelly voice. "I apologise for my counterpart's behaviour of late. He clearly cannot tell when he is in the presence of such…" he breathed in shrilly and let the breath drift from his mouth, "greatness."

"What do you want with me?" asked Richard, pulling fruitlessly at the bonds, his voice quivering. "I'm no one."

The figure stepped silently from the shadows, the beam of light now illuminating his face. It was gaunt and pale, appearing as though any colour had been washed away, contrasting his raven black hair. Conversely, his features were in perfect precision to his bone structure, making it difficult to imagine he should look any other way. "I want so many things," he replied cryptically, "and you are far from no-one, we know that for sure…We have followed your progress with interest and, might I say," he chuckled slightly at what he alone found to be amusing, "we could not have expected so much out of those so weak…For that we thank you."

"For what?" asked Richard flatly, ceasing to struggle at the bonds for a second.

"Oh, that should be obvious, my friend," he took a step closer to the chair and leaned in close to Richard. "You helped to free us from our eternal slumber…The very few of us that there are." He leant closer still, nearly enough so that Richard could feel his hot breath drift onto his neck. "You will free the rest. Our brethren shall rise for we are the night and we will take back what has been lost to us for so long…The Dark."

Richard breathed heavily, the hairs on his neck prickling as the breath lingered on his neck. "What are you?" He said eventually, imbuing his voice with as much dominance as he could muster.

The man pulled away and stood bolt upright for a moment before raising an eyebrow and casually reaching out a hand. "Come now," he grinned widely, revealing a pair of razor-sharp fangs at the corners of his mouth. "What do you think we are?"

"Vampires!" Michael growled harshly. "Goddamn Vampires!" He slammed his fist on the bar and grabbed the small glass of whisky, downing it straight and leaving a half-dried smear of blood across the glass.

"They don't tend to like that term, Mike," stated the Bartender calmly, "they can be quite touchy about it."

"I don't care!" he growled again, looking around at the almost empty bar before continuing. "They're trying to frame me for murder!" he calmed slightly and lowered his voice. "Come to that, I can't believe you knew all along what she was!"

"It's not like that, you have to understand," The Bartender attempted. "They're a secretive bunch, they can't have just anyone knowing they exist. Trance was breaking the rules big time by just being here."

"Shit...That *was* blood you gave her, wasn't it?" He quickly ran his hands through his hair, not even caring where the blood went. "What the hell am I supposed to do now?"

The Bartender sighed and refilled the glass. "They left you alive, doesn't that prove they don't want to hurt anyone?" He placed the whiskey bottle back behind the bar as Michael quickly picked up the glass, again downing its contents in one. "Look, I can't in good humour tell you this is the first time something like this has happened. As such we have...methods of dealing with these situations. There'd be no end of crap for me and everyone who came here if the mortals were to find out about this place. So, it's generally in our best interests to make these incidents..." he made a vague flicking gesture with his hand, "disappear"

Michael looked blankly at him for a few seconds. "Somehow that doesn't really make me feel any better," he sighed heavily. "For one, that thing out there tried to kill me- No! *Eat* me! Then some vampiric cult tries to frame me?" He calmed slightly and sombrely sunk towards the bar, "and she was part of it all along."

"I tried to warn you, son," said the Bartender simply, "but if I were you I'd just try and forget about it all now...You need to forget about her."

Michael rubbed his face and slowly looked back up at the Bartender. "I can't," he replied quietly. "I can't leave this. It's too big for me to just ignore...That thing was *eating* somebody for crying out loud!"

"I realise it's not something anyone would be able to ignore, I do. But what if it's *too* big for you? What if it's just better for you to stay out of it?" It seemed that The Barman was merely trying to emphasise how it was in Michael's best interests to stay away but it was more than that. His eyes betrayed a meaning to his words.

"You know something," stated Michael quickly, "don't act like you don't. Even if I couldn't feel it from you, clear as day, it's still pretty obvious. You're a horrible liar."

"Fine," The Bartender said bluntly, snapping his towel onto the counter. "I do, but only as much as it benefits them. I do a few things here and there. I give them information, tell them who's been in the bar. Word on the street type stuff." He stared at Michael who grimaced back menacingly. "I don't know where they go or anything though, I swear."

"But you can meet with them..." mused Michael, "and then I'll do the rest." A plan was visibly developing in his mind, expressed on the contours of his face. "All I need you to do is get one out in the open."

The Bartender seriously considered flatly refusing to do as Michael asked. He knew that going along with the plan could result in issues he wasn't prepared to deal with. As he opened his mouth, however, he came to a realisation. For whatever reason, be it fear or some misguided sense of duty, he had been blindly assisting these mysterious visitors for some time now and knew far too little of them. Every time he had tried to ask something of them, he had been met with either a thinly veiled threat or ignored outright. Regardless of the problems that may arise, to learn more of these strangers was certainly a tantalising prospect.

Finally closing his mouth, The Bartender breathed out gently, silently conceding to the plan before moving to speak once again.

They Awake

"Alright...But if we're going to do this then you can't be going around looking like that," he pointed to Michaels blood-soaked clothes. "People are gonna ask questions."

"Speaking of questions, there are a few I should probably ask an old acquaintance," he leaded over the counter and drew The Bartender closer. "I assure you; I will be back and then we are both going to see this through."

"Fine, whatever," The Barman spoke dismissively, waving a hand at Michael. "Just get a change of clothes, alright?"

"We were not always like this," said Richards's captor simply, "confined to the shadows, never to see the light of day. Once this entire world was ours...And then you came," he finished, gritting his teeth and turning his back to Richard.

Richard looked around, shaking his head. "Humans drove you from your home?" he asked, hoping to grasp any semblance of understanding.

The vampire turned around again and stared at Richard, about to raise his voice at him but stopped, coming to understand the level of obliviousness before him. "In a way," he finally permitted, "but you don't appreciate the full picture. Your race, your evolutionary strain tried to force us from mere existence!" He stepped closer to Richard again, filling the ether with that sense of discomfort again. "We were forced to change our very being just to survive in your new world!" He seemed to relax and placed two fingers on his temple, pressing firmly in an attempt to temper his anger. "You took so much but it was never enough. You wished to take more and when there was no more to take, you sent us to that hellish place. You know of where I speak, a place where you cannot breathe or feel and where every vacuous second feels as an eternity. Whole galaxies might rise and fall in the space of a single blink of the eye... and yet time is nothing there...An endless void of nothing!" He dropped his arm and looked up at the small, barred opening in the wall. "But soon all that will change. Our brethren will be free and we shall once again feel the air of a world rightfully ours...As for you, my friend. You will lead us there."

The Dark

Richard unclenching his hands, relaxing from his futile straining at the ropes. He thought about making any number of statements in order to demonstrate his resistance but was instead compelled to ask a question which troubled him above everything else.

"Why me?" he asked calmly, "I don't believe for one minute that I was just some random Median unlucky enough to have a run in with you guys."

"You are very perceptive, Richard," he ran his fingers gently along his chin without breaking his gaze. "I feel you are by no means as weak as the rest on this plane. A trait such as this demands my respect."

Richard looked blankly at him for a moment or two then tilted his head. "I have your respect, yet I don't seem to have your name," he ended expectantly.

The Vampire considered the humans request and reluctantly decided to humour him. "Costin," he stated flatly, "if you must know."

Richard nodded shallowly, feeling that he had somehow gained ground with the creature. "So...Costin," he said carefully, trying to say the name right, "why is it me you want?" he asked again, hoping to get a genuine answer this time.

Costin smiled and took Richard's shoulder. "Because you are the only one..." he breathed deeply, seemingly savouring the statement. "The only one who has seen the Other Side and returned." He paused, waiting for Richard to say something but was met only with a vague uncertainty upon his face. "You see, you hold within your blood-" he leaned in and took a deep, unnerving smell of Richards neck, "-such sweet blood-" he pulled back again and grinned darkly, "a power never meant for this realm...A power to warp the very fabric of this world. To open a gateway to forgotten planes beyond your comprehension. It is this power with which the sleeping beast shall be awoken and the Horde will be freed from their eternal shackle."

Richard waited for a few seconds to make sure Costin had finished before giving a sudden stunted laugh, making the vampire start back in surprise. "I'm sorry to disappoint you, but I've never been to the Other Side." As he spoke, an unsettling thought occurred to him. If they came to realise that he was worthless to them then his life was as good as forfeit. Thinking it better to die in defiance, he decided to continue on regardless. "I almost made it there once but it didn't quite go as I planned."

"We know," Costin stated flatly, "the power is from another...One whom we had watched for a long time. In that place we saw all of time, glimpses of the future and past pressed together so that every second flowed into one everlasting moment...It was then we saw him and the return of his true form to this world. A single point in eternity where we could see our impending freedom through his will. We had not expected you, though...You rose up and took a part of that power..."

Richard stared at Costin, slowly realising that he was not only a creature of the night but of that place. The abyss of which he spoke had obviously driven both him and his brethren insane but at the same time it had granted an insight beyond even the Seers. "What do you intend to do with me?" he asked tentatively, unsure if he needed to know the answer.

"Of course, we shall free that power so that my brothers shall be given back what is rightfully theirs...the right to walk upon this land." He placed his cold, pale hand softly on Richard's face and ran it round to his chin. "Your name will be revered among our people...You will be the father of the new age... The destroyer of mankind...I promise that your noble sacrifice will ensure this," he grinned again before whipping his hand away and hurrying back into the shadows. His exit was closely followed by the screech of metal on stone and the harsh slam of a large door swinging into place. All was soon silent and Richard was again alone.

There had always been a strange quiet to this street. Cars were lined up along the curbs and the rows of narrow terraces seemed to be occupied but there was still a bizarre absence of life about the place. Of course, it was getting on for 4am, Michael thought distractedly, but even in daylight that feeling persisted, almost as though the whole street had been abandoned long ago. It had even crossed his mind that the place may be entirely illusory, like it wasn't even there.

He stopped just in front of the dilapidated chapel and looked at its crumbling walls, still unsure of why its occupant had chosen such a place to take refuge. Looking about uneasily, Michael quickly pulled at the graffiti strewn plywood board and slipped behind it, heaving at the heavy metal door as he did. Squeezing through the small gap he had formed from the outside world, Michael stumbled onto the grubby, tiled floor and looked around, not entirely sure what to think of the scene before him.

"What have you done, Lancer?" he whispered to himself.

Several of the large industrial lamps were led helplessly across the ground, their light now focussed into a bright beam which burned into the tiles. Most of the others still standing were broken, cloaking portions of the chapel into almost complete darkness. Many of the crates had been knocked from their stacks, smashing upon the ground, scattering polystyrene and broken pieces of priceless artefacts across the ground to smoulder in the beams of light.

Michael looked up to the rafters in anticipation of the Guardians gracefully circling the building but found none. He started to walk between the broken crates and general chaos Lancer's home had become. Upon reaching the altar step, Michael found that the ornate chair had been overturned and three words had been scrawled across the bare stone wall in a substance he could only hope wasn't blood. It simply stated 'we are wrong'.

"Lancer!" Michael shouted, "where the hell are you?" He waited for a few seconds for a reply but none came. "You'd better not be dead you old bastard," he mumbled firmly to himself, taking a step up to the wall and running his hand across the cold stone. He hung his head and shook it sombrely, clenching his fists as scenarios of what had happened raced through his mind. "Why? Why did you do this?"

"Because we are wrong..." a voice said quietly from behind, forcing Michael to turn around. "Everything we ever did... What gave us the right for any of it? Seers should have never been allowed to walk the Earth!" Lancer looked a shadow of how Michael knew him. His clothes were torn and dirty, his hair long and uncontrolled and his voice conveyed a disbelief in his own existence. Most of all his features, wrinkled and dishevelled, now betrayed his true, considerable age. "Richard...My friend. He made me realise this."

"Lancer," Michael started, unsure how to react to his appearance, "what the hell happened to you? Where are the Guardians?" He stepped back down from the altar and placed a hand on Lancer's arm, looking him up and down then around the chapel. "Why all this?"

"I dwelled on what I had learnt...About my kind," he turned away and looked mournfully at the mess strewn across the chapel floor. "We went too far...*He* went too far and now all Seers bear the burden of his deeds." He slowly looked back around to Michael and rubbed his face. "We are all born knowing what we see, what we are capable of...All of it...It's a curse. But now..." he closed his eyes tightly as if trying to shake the thoughts from his mind, "now it is a punishment."

Michael sighed. "You can't blame yourself. It was one man, one terrible person that was responsible and you helped to send him back to where he belongs."

"You don't understand," Lancer snapped abruptly, "one Seer, all Seers. There's no difference. If he was capable of it then any of us could be. We are all one in the same. They knew that," he pointed to the rafters where the Guardians had once swum through the air so majestically. "When I came back that morning they were gone. I waited for them, I tried to summon them but they did not return," he clenched his eyelids shut again and cradled his head in his hand. "That's when I knew. My kind has been walking a fine line for a very long time. What happened simply pushed things over the edge." He chuckled slightly, almost manically at the sheer bleakness of it all, "you could say we've finally fallen from grace."

"You can still do good; be the person I know you are." Michael placed his hand back on Lancer's arm again gently, "be the person Richard knows you to be. You can still make a difference. Please...I need your help. I need guidance from my Seer," Michael bowed his head subtly before continuing. "I honestly thought I'd never say anything like this but..." he paused and tried to find the best words he could. "I need to know everything you know about...Vampires."

The Dark

He felt awkward using the term, still feeling as though he might have imagined the whole event.

Despite Michaels embarrassment at asking such a thing, Lancer froze and slowly leaned towards him. "Strigoi..." he breathed gently. He thought for a few seconds before starting to grit his teeth agitatedly, "Upir' likhyi...They didn't touch you, did they? Foul creatures!" he growled, throwing his arm down firmly. "Don't trust any of them! They're not like us!" he gazed at Michael, his withered features stern and serious.

"So, you know about them, then?" asked Michael eagerly

"More to my pity, yes," he started, wishing for no more troubles than those he already had. "Seer legends...Isn't it always? But a warning like that can't just be ignored. It was set in place and kept for all that time for a very good reason."

Michael raised his eyebrows and stared at Lancer expectantly. "And that is?"

"Because they are evil," Lancer breathed quietly. "They were imprisoned in a world of nothing, between the fabric of the astral planes themselves because they could not be stopped. To allow them to remain would mean the end of mankind...It was vowed that if they were ever to escape then they would finish their work and ruthlessly sweep away all that stood against them."

Michael shook his head and laughed lightly, much to Lancer's surprise. "You really do have a flare for the melodramatic, don't you?"

"Listen!" Lancer snapped loudly, causing the slight grin to drop from Michael's face. "Don't you understand how bad things could get if they are back!?" He turned away with a grunt and began mumbling to himself as he paced back and forth aimlessly. At last, he stopped abruptly and fell silent for a second. "I was afraid this would happen...But it seemed like the only way," he sighed and rubbed his face once more, pulling his fingers through his greasy hair. "No-one's supposed to force their way between worlds. When Richard travelled to the Far Side he must have opened a rift...Punched a hole in the unseen walls of this world just long enough for a few of their kind step through."

"It's not like Richard was the first to do it, though," Michael replied, bewildered as to how an act could have such large ramifications.

"No," Lancer replied simply, considering the words carefully. "It was *him* ...The one who started all of this," he looked around solemnly at the mess his home had become. "Either way the result would have been much the same... We only made it worse." He paused for a minute and eyed Michael knowingly then turned sharply and punched at the air. "Scheiße!" he shouted abruptly, turning back to Michael with purpose. "You want to face them, don't you? ...Goddamn it boy, this is how you get yourself killed..." He thought for a moment more, his eyes wildly darting around, before eventually continuing, his voice now gentler. "What other choice do we have?" he nodded knowingly and looked sideways at Michael. "Come with me." Lancer began walking towards one of the building's many side rooms, the gaps around one wooden door in particular still illuminated by a surviving lamp. "There is a lot you need to know," he took the handle of the door and pressed it open.

As the door swung open, Michael was amazed to see the room completely unscathed where the rest of the place had been turned upside down. In fact, the room and its contents seemed even more pristine than the rest of the chapel had ever been.

The space itself was relatively small with a simple wooden bookcase bolted firmly to one of the bare stone walls and three shelves attached to the one opposite. They were all filled with books, new and old, that seemed to hold special reverence to Lancer as well as a variety of bound documents and folders. Upon the ground at the back of the room sat only a small wooden chest adorned with red and gold trim.

"What is this place?" asked Michael, transfixed by the small room.

"It is my repository," replied Lancer calmly. "It holds only my most important texts and sacred artefacts," he stepped lightly into the room and crouched to the chest. "You see, the warning was taken so seriously that, throughout the generations, the Seers would bestow a weapon to be used against the Strigoi upon a Median within their realm." He unlocked the chest in a way that was obscured to Michael and carefully opened it, reaching inside. "I did so with Richard and, although I am not the man I was, I can still do this much for you." He lifted out a small, ornately decorated wooden box and passed it gently to Michael. "Be vigilant for their death will fly on assorted wings…"

Michael stared at the box briefly before running his hand over the top and opening it carefully. Taking up most of the space inside was a glinting, short barrelled revolver. Within the chamber were placed six silver bullets and another six to its side. Around it were a number of other items including a dried branch of Hawthorn, a small bag of salt and a highly polished mirror. Along the top of the box was a solid wooden stake inset with bands of engraved silver running its length, capped with another piece of solid silver.

"…As can ours," Lancer finished, grinning slightly. He craned and looked into the box. "They are not as they once were and as such have weaknesses we can exploit…" he began pointing to the objects sequentially. "A piece of nature, its prick poison to the unworthy. Salt; a barrier which they dare never cross. A surface to channel the truest light for their form may not stand the sun…Ah, yes," he picked up the stake and held it firmly by the end. "'Plunge deep into the heart of thee, and it shall set me free'. They spoke the truth in the old times. As time goes on, however, we must adapt to what is available hence…this," he placed down the stake and gently picked up the gun, pressing out the chamber with a click. "Just as they could not withstand the silver blades of old, neither can they survive a silver bullet. Treat it with care, my friend." Lancer looked at Michael meaningfully and placed the pistol back into the box, closing it as he did.

"I thought silver was for Werewolves?"

Lancer grinned slightly and shook his head. "You watch too many movies, my boy."

"So, I guess that's why Richard has a gun," mused Michael quietly. "I always wondered but never dared to ask."

Lancer placed a hand on Michael's back and guided him from the room, closing the door. "As it was once his duty to watch for their return, so it is now yours and, in this time, I fear that much more shall be required of you." He hung his head for a moment and closed his eyes before looking up again. "So go, my friend. Go to what is to be…Go and be safe." He turned and walked back towards another room, leaving Michael stood, silently gazing at the box in his hands.

Michael had come here for advice but could never have expected this. He felt as though he should not be prepared for this moment, that nothing could possibly have made him ready and yet something inside him told him that he was. It told him that he always had been.

It scared me to see Lancer like that. I didn't know him nearly as well as Richard did so I didn't expect him to give even half a damn about me. I'm still in two minds whether he actually does or if it's all part of his greater good. Still, even though I don't really know who he is, I feel like I know what he is, or rather what he isn't. He wasn't like the other Seers who were constantly obsessed with finding the eternal secret of life and death. He would have given up everything for a Median in need and, in many ways, he did. I think that's why I trusted him when he put his faith in me to do what anyone else would have seen as madness…But there was something that had to be done. Richard needed to know and for some reason that scared me more than facing these vampires alone. I had learnt to accomplish a great many things by myself in a very short time but to follow this through to the end… No. He had to know everything.

By the time Michael had walked back to Richard's house, the sun was beginning to crest over the rooftops, the thick warming light filtering between aerials and chimneys.

Michael opened the door as silently as he could and looked around the hall curiously. Stepping in, he noticed Richard's jacket missing from the coat rack. He never puts that jacket anywhere else, Michael thought, his mind uneasy with thoughts of what Lancer had told him.

Quickly he ran up the stairs, caring no longer to be quiet as he pressed open Richard's door only to find the bed unmade and his phone placed clumsily on the bedside cabinet. Michael thought for a second of the places where he could be…Hollies? No, he would have his phone…Chris' grave? His dads?

All of his tame thoughts were quickly subdued and were replaced with any number of the worst cases his mind could dream up. He could sense that nothing was right anymore. No matter how he denied it, things had felt ever so slightly off since the incident at the bar. Then it dawned on him what Lancer had really been speaking about. Richard had created a rift in the worlds, letting the first through and now…He shuddered at the idea as it became clearer by the second…Doing something like that has to change a person, leave something with them. What if they thought he held some kind of power now? A power very few had ever possessed, one that connects to the empty spaces between worlds. What if he was the only one within their reach?

There was no time left to lose. Michael thought anxiously as he turned to leave but instead of hurrying down the stairs he paused, only to re-enter the room and approach Richard's dresser. Whether or not he had been aware, for years Michael had known this to be where he kept his most prized items. Even so, Michael was still astounded by the content as he pulled open the draw into the dull orange light of dawn.

There were assorted crystals, talismans and notebooks, including the one text that should really have been destroyed already. He soon saw the item he was looking for, however; Richard's short barrelled revolver, identical to that which Lancer had given to Michael. He snatched it from the drawer and slid it halfway into the back of his trousers, alongside where he had placed his own with the stake and bullets concealed within the inside pocket of his jacket. Nervously he took a breath, looking around the room uneasily and started back towards the door feeling that he may have to go it alone after all.

Even in the dawn light the dungeon remained embraced in a dark gloom, lifted only by a gentle haze lying in the air. As the sun continued to rise, Richards' hopes began to fall. No-one knew where he was and by the time they realised he was missing it may have been too late. All he could do was hope his captors would not return until somebody managed to track him down. His hopes were soon shattered as the bolt was once again thrown aside and the door ground open. Costin slowly strolled in and stopped briefly to look at the lit grate in the wall.

"Sometimes I mourn for the life we have lost," he stated casually, "we found the light so beautiful once." He reached a hand out into a single beam of sunlight where it began to smoke before it was wrenched back. "Now it would kill us…But not for much longer," he gestured a hand forward and two unseen assailants rushed towards Richard, roughly cutting his bonds and restraining him as he tried to struggle.

"What the hell are you going to do to me?" growled Richard, trying to stall for as much time as he could.

"Why, my friend," Costin walked closer and placed a hand softly on Richard's stubbled face. "I would merely awaken those who have not had our fortune to feel again. To smell the sweet air… Or to see the accursed daylight," he snatched his hand away and looked deep into Richard's eyes. "My brethren, you see…They just want one precious little thing from you… They want your blood," a menacing grin crept onto his face and he casually signalled to his minions.

"No!" screamed Richard, struggling against the creatures pulling him away, "you can't do this! You hear me!?"

Costin's grin widened as Richards' voice began to fade away down the corridor.

"No! You bastard! You can't!"

II-III – The Horde

For they are My slaves whom I took (...); they may not become the property of another

-Leviticus, 25:42

Michael stepped up to the graffiti covered door of the club he had spent most of the previous night and looked around cautiously. As the sun crept ever higher in the sky, people had started to swell into the street. Each and every one of them followed the routine they had for years, completely unknowing of what had transpired the past evening and the many others before it.

Michael knew better than to try to get in during the day, especially via the street entrance, yet he couldn't face walking down that alley again, not after what had happened. He leaned to the side and strained to see down its murky length. Even in the growing daylight, the overhanging gantries and water trickling down the walls gave it an unsettlingly dark and gloomy atmosphere. Eventually taking a deep breath in, he took a step to the opening, his heart racing and started to walk into the narrow, dank entry.

As he moved further into the hazy gloom, a fear welled up from his stomach and pushed at his throat, forcing him to swallow just to keep it from choking him. Yet still he continued, on through the seemingly endless passage until he caught sight of the skip bin where it had occurred and stopped dead. His heart throbbed uncomfortably against his chest, driving the air from his lungs and forcing him to catch his breath in the thick, warm miasma. He waited for a few seconds and glanced at the bar's back door, almost hidden in the shadows. Nodding shallowly and trying to put the previous night out of his mind, he again stepped towards the doorway.

Moving to knock, he abruptly stopped and looked around at the ground where the bodies had been, finding only a suspiciously clean patch of concrete. He lowered his arm, crouching to the ground as he did, and reached out to touch the clean patch. Suddenly the door was cracked open making Michael reach for one of the pistols concealed under his coat.

"I knew it was you," said the Barman, peering out of the doorway. "You need to learn to conceal yourself better, you never know who'll sense you." He grabbed Michael's arm and pulled him in as he slammed the door shut.

Michael looked about in bewilderment and loosely raised his arm back towards the door, vaguely indicating outside. "Wha- How?"

"I told you we took care of things around here," stated the Barman firmly. "The less attention the better, remember?" he looked expectantly at Michael for acknowledgement and was eventually given a vague nod. "Now I have a meeting with one of them at two in the high street, they-"

"Wait!" snapped Michael, turning to the Barman with a renewed confidence. "Two? In the afternoon?" he queried suspiciously. "What about the whole burning thing?"

The Barman sniggered slightly. "That's why they do it during the day. It throws people off," he slowly tilted his head to the side and breathed in through his teeth, making a shrill hissing sound. "As for the burning thing, these vamps are clever. It's not like they spontaneously burst into flames as soon as the light touches their skin. Don't get me wrong, they can't stay out in it for too long but so long as they cover themselves up well enough they can survive alright," he tilted his head back and forth, squinting with slight thought. "Of course, if you ask me, someone going around covered head to foot is going to look a bit suspicious whatever time of the day. Just like me, attention is the last thing they want. But then…they have their ways."

The Dark

Michael looked blankly at him for a few seconds before rolling his eyes and turning away. "I'm just going to have to trust you and go along with this," he said, casually taking a seat at the bar. "At this point, there's not much else I can do... Other than wait, I guess." He placed his head in his hands, rubbing it firmly. "The least you could do is get me a drink"

This was all getting too much. Too real, too quickly. I was so far out of my league that I couldn't even feel what I thought was right anymore. Richard was gone, I dared not think where. I especially dared not think about what may have happened to him. He was gone, that was all I knew. Lancer was counting on me to do...something. I didn't even know what it was I was aiming for but whatever it was I knew that she was the key. If what Lancer had said was true then Trance and her night dwelling friends had a lot to answer for and I wasn't about to let them slip away... Ultimately though, all I really wanted was Richard back...

The hours passed slowly and with each one that slipped by Michael's mind was drawn ever deeper into that hazing darkness where a person's purpose is lost, replaced only with a world now alien and strange. The bartender spent the time recalling days of past exploits, dealings he had been part of, some of which strained the fabric of belief. None of it worked to ease Michaels deep unease of what was to come, however. Eventually the Bartender fell quiet for some time, apparently realising Michael's disinterest and set about arranging various bottles and glasses for the coming night. Soon a neon clock above the bar shelves fell into place at two and he leant forward towards Michael who was hunched over the bar, his head placed deeply into his crossed arms.

"It's time," said the Bartender gently.

A muffled sigh came from the bar and Michael sat up slowly. "Then we must go," he replied sombrely. "If it needs to be done, it needs to be done," he stood up slowly and stretched from his time on the cramped stool before walking slowly to the back door

The bartender had a hand placed firmly on the door but did not make any effort to push it open. Rather he stood, staring at Michael meaningfully. "Now you have to understand, these…people," he hesitated at the word and grimaced, "whatever you want to call them, they're not like us. They will know if something's amiss so, for both our sakes, don't do anything stupid!" He gazed sternly at Michael, silent for a few seconds. "Understand?" he added, not especially expecting a reply. "They said I'd be met under the bridge across the way from here so I'll go meet them and you stay in the alley. Watch carefully but, for god's sake, make sure you stay out of sight! You don't realise how keen these bastards are."

Michael nodded quickly and was about to ask what would happen if he were to be seen but decided he'd much rather not know.

"They'll be watching me so even when I come back you need to stay in the shadows and whatever you do don't acknowledge me. I'll make sure you know who my guy is and then you're on your own." He stared at him again and raised an eyebrow, this time expecting an answer. "Alright?"

Michael tried to catch his voice, becoming increasingly nervous about what was about to happen and finally gave another nod. "Yes," he stuttered out.

"Good," The Barman stated finally, pulling his apron off and throwing it back towards the bar. "We should leave," he finally pressed open the door and stepped out into the alley, followed closely by Michael vigilantly looking around as he stepped tentatively onto the overly clean concrete. "Remember, stay out of sight." The Bartender held a spread palm in front of Michael, halting him where he stood before rushing towards the misty daylight at the end of the passage.

Michael watched him for a few seconds until he became nothing but a hazy figure against the bright day before cautiously following him. Upon approaching the opening, Michael hurriedly moved towards the side wall, clinging to it as he peered out across the street towards the bridge. At first he saw nothing and the panic began to rise again in his chest as he supposed he had been deceived in some way. Then he caught a glimpse of the Barman standing in the distance, looking around in bewilderment.

With a start he looked down at a homeless person wrapped entirely in rags and blankets with a thick hood draped loosely over his head. The Barman cocked his head and crouched down to him, reaching into a pocket for some loose change.

"Could I give you some help, my friend," said the Barman gently, reaching out his hand into a solitary sunbeam penetrating the bridge. Suddenly a pale hand was struck forward, grasping his wrist tightly and turning it over, forcing The Barman to open his clenched fist to reveal a palm full of coins.

After a moment, small wisps of fine smoke began to rise from the hand around The Barman's wrist accompanied by a quiet hiss. Quickly its owner unclasped its grip and withdrew from the light with a short groan.

"You would patronise us?" came a shallow, grating voice from under the pile of blankets. "We would end you."

"I meant no disrespect, I'm sure," The Barman stated quickly, starting back in an effort to ensure the creature could not reach him. "I merely wished to make sure it was you," he added quietly, trying not to draw attention from passing bystanders.

Slowly the blankets began to move and the cloak rose up, revealing the lower half of a washed out face still covered with shadow. The creature grimaced, briefly unveiling the razor tipped fangs at each corner of its mouth until the hood was adjusted, obscuring them again.

"Enough with this talk. You have been summoned for a reason." The vampire growled slightly as it mused on the idea of having anyone assist them. "You must obtain our supplies and deliver them with haste. This is important so listen well, mortal."

Michael continued to watch as The Barman listened to the creature's instructions. After a while he shuffled away from the mass of blankets and started back towards the alley. As he neared, Michael threw himself back, bolt upright, flat against the wall.

The Barman, without hesitating, walked straight into the shadows of the alley and down towards the back door of the bar. He did not acknowledge Michael in any substantial way, instead only whispering simply "good luck" as he passed.

Peering back out from the alley once the Barman had re-entered the bar, Michael could see that the Vampire was still there, covered over by several layers of thick blankets. He considered that it may soon attempt to leave now its business was complete. Then he feared that he may instead end up waiting for quite some time. These things were patient, they had to be. In a world advancing so fast around them patience was one of the advantages such an ancient race still possessed.

Where the sun had risen and shone so brightly beyond those damp walls, Richard's cell remained as dark as it always had, saturated with the fear and solitude of a thousand captive souls before him.
Slowly he awoke to find himself staring into a pair of spotlights positioned over his face. As consciousness once more took its hold over him, Richard was confronted with the horrid realisation that all of this was real. The gentle hope of it all being an illusion, a lucid nightmare, shattered against the bright, incandescent lights burning against his skin. He gradually managed to turn his head to one side but stopped abruptly as an intense stabbing sensation shot through the side of his neck. He dared not move again, fearful of greater pain yet to come.
Just behind him he could hear lowered voices. One was clearly recognisable as Costin but the other spoke in low, eerily subtle tones, forming the impression that even the sum of all the world's evils would not be capable of disturbing him.
"...I find his strength admirable," remarked Costin's accomplice. "I would have seen many others die by this point."
"I would expect as much from him," replied Costin, seeming to shift closer to the table Richard was strapped to, "and I should expect no less from you, Savant. He needs to be alive for this. If he is not then..." There was a sharp intake of breath and Costin lowered his voice further, "let's just say it all depends on whether you enjoy your head remaining on your shoulders."
"Of course," chuckled Savant back, surprisingly brightly considering the threat he had just been issued with.
There were several seconds of silence and Richard again tried to move his head only to be met with the same sharp stab of agony, this time forcing a short groan from him. Suddenly Costin appeared over him, blocking out one of the bright lights.

The Dark

"It's good to see you are back with us," he said warmly, grinning down at Richard. "Although I wouldn't do that if I were you, things could get a little…messy," he nodded shortly down towards Richard's body and raised his eyebrows. "It'd be better for us both if it didn't."

Richard slowly managed to strain his neck to see what they had done to him. His mind could barely accept what he saw and tried to make him convulse in a vain attempt to escape it but was overpowered by the knowledge that he would likely not survive any such movement.

At points all across his arms and torso were large syringes driven deep into major arteries and, as far as he could gather, various organs. Attached to the spikes were metal hoppers with a slit of translucent glass along the side, each filled to differing extents with blood.

"What the hell have you done to me?" growled Richard, his voice shaking.

"We merely wish to gather the essence of a power which now resides inside you. The power of the Other Side. You see, each of these devices," he caressed one of the syringes protruding from the side of Richard's chest, the slightest movement making him flinch in pain. "They now contain the key to a gateway through which my brethren will flood upon this Earth once more," he slid his hand around the hopper and firmly gripped it causing Richard to grit his teeth, "and it will all start…right here."

Costin grinned again menacingly, staring deep into Richard's eyes before ripping the device from his chest making him scream in agony and spattering blood across the floor and nearest wall. Suddenly he turned on Savant, grabbing him by the collar of his filthy lab coat and plunged the metal stake through his chest and deep into his heart. Releasing a valve on the side, Costin drained Richard's blood into its new host before allowing him to fall to the ground. Within moments, Savant's eyes glazed over and his head hit the tiled floor with a sickly crack.

Costin looked back to Richard and stepped over to his side, rubbing the warm blood between his fingers, smiling widely. "The

The Horde

power of the Other Side will now call to any who have our blood ... and they will come."

He looked back down at Savant's body, his own thick blood mixing with Richards. It welled up around the syringe still protruding from his chest and spilled out across the ground, seeping out across the ceramic.

"Do not fear, my old friend. You shall be remembered in the new world for the newborn will carry the name of the one who bore them. In your honour they shall be dubbed 'The Savant' and they shall burn a great legacy across this land."

The blood ran along the grooves in the tiles, creeping across the whole room, spreading far more than any wound should allow. As it did, it darkened a sickly black and eventually drained away into a grate under the table Richard was laid upon.

"You're insane!" Richard managed to spit through the searing pain.

"Am I?" Costin asked casually. "We shall see," he turned to look down at the pool of blood spreading across the ground, now seeming almost like tar. Regardless of the gaping wound in his chest, Richard felt compelled to watch as well for this was something unlike anyone had witnessed before.

Upon encompassing a large enough portion of the room, the pool began to ripple. It was gentle at first, then with more vigour before eventually beginning to move as if it had a life of its own. Finally, from out of the pool raised three thin, tar coated fingers which hovered for a second or two before slowly gripping the floor tiles, bringing with them a deep sense of unease.

Costin grinned menacingly once again, the smirk only growing larger as the arm continued to rise from the pool. "The Horde has awakened."

The short winter day began to fade quickly, the feeble light replaced by a heavy rolling mist that ushered in the dark evening. Michael had never been particularly concerned about the dark but with the sinking sun, a thick shadow fell across the streets, forcing a primal fear to rise in his chest. As a child Richard had confidently assured him that there was nothing in the darkness any worse than

The Dark

what was in the light. As the chill of the cold night breeze drifted over him, Michael shuddered and reconsidered the validity of those words. Maybe the night *was* worse.

He continued to watch the covered creature, barely visible under the bridge, with a growing concern about its motives now that the sun was all but gone. Still, it remained motionless with the occasional commuter walking by, entirely unaware of its existence. Michael shifted uneasily as the temperature continued to fall, the wind whistling through the alley and biting viciously at his extremities. For a moment he considered that he had been lied to, led on a wild goose chase while the Barman had gone off to make who only knew what kind of deal with the Vampires.

Just as he was about to turn heel and march back towards the club there was finally movement under the blankets. For a moment he thought that it may have just been nothing, a twitch or casual repositioning. Then again, why would it have remained perfectly still, refusing to shift from its concealment for the past few hours only to arbitrarily adjust its position now?

Michael backed up against the wall, making sure he could not be seen amongst the shadows and peered around the corner. Beneath the bridge, the creature began to rise up, shedding it many layers as it did and gazed around cautiously. Michael remembered what he had been told about how keen these things were and knew that any false move could end in a way he didn't want to consider. The thought alone made him want to turn and run as fast he could although they would no doubt be on him in seconds and it would be over.

The creature backed up to the edge of the tunnel, glancing around again and Michael was forced to retreat around the corner, standing as flat as he could against the wall. His heart pumped so hard in his chest that he could barely endure it without gasping for breath. After a few seconds he carefully leant around the corner again only to find that the vampire was gone, leaving the pile of cloth and assorted change it had accumulated during the day scattered across the ground.

In a single moment Michaels mind raced, deciding on what course of action to take. Should he run to the bridge, risking that it was still there or should he stay for a while longer and potentially lose the only lead he had back to Trance. By the time he realised his decision, his legs were already carrying him as fast as they could across the street. He knew that if he was going to do this then he didn't have time to think, everything had to be judged on bare instinct alone, even if that meant risking his life.

Michael stopped abruptly, just short of running into the wall head on and hugged against it, looking around the weathered stonework to see his target hurrying around the corner at the far end of the overpass. Quickly he swung around the edge and ran after the vampire. Once more he caught a glimpse of it further along the road as it ducked away, heading towards a derelict house. Continuing to blindly follow his mark, Michael marched towards the building, feeling as if his efforts were finally paying off. Only once he was far too close did he begin to sense that something may have been amiss, as though he were being watched.

Since learning of his creed, Michael had experienced so much more than he ever could have believed, maybe more than he was ready for. It was as though simply being open to the worlds beyond made him susceptible to their influence and their problems. He was beginning to accept that it was the curse all Medians must bear yet this felt different. It was nothing like the apparitions of restless dead that naturally haunt Medians thoughts. Rather there was an overwhelming sensation of displacement, almost like the air around him didn't belong. Richard had told him that he would experience sensations that were otherwise inexplicable. He had urged Michael that he shouldn't fight them but instead trust and let them guide him. Only now did it become apparent that this feeling of scrutiny had been with him for far longer than he had realised. Ever since the night he had first met Trance it had been there, guiding him and moulding his fate. Where before it had been subtle, insidious enough for him not to even notice it, now the sensation was like a great wave washing over him, the leading edge of a storm that would be released upon the whole world. He couldn't deny that the feeling scared him but as he neared the house there was something which told him to look past the assault on his senses and not to be afraid.

The Dark

Michael stood in front of the house for a moment and looked it up and down. At one time it would have been rather impressive but time had obviously left it long behind. Looking closer he noticed that the door had been left ajar, like the creature wanted to be followed. More than willing to oblige, Michael took a step past the large broken fence encircling the garden and shuddered briefly. The sense that they were close almost overtook his resolve but he continued on regardless, determined to follow through with his plan. He walked slowly towards the deep shadow of the overhanging porch, aware that he could be being watched from any angle. If he were being watched, Michael noted to himself, then curiosity may at least be something, however little, that they had in common with humans. The thought comforted him for a second before the sense that he could meet his end any moment reasserted itself. Then again, if they had wanted him dead then they could have done it by now. While it was still a distinct possibility that they would grow bored of toying with him and take his life, somehow Michael knew that they would not.

He stepped up onto the rotting wooden porch, which creaked unnervingly under his weight, forcing him to stop for a second. Once the wood settled, he ventured onwards, causing it to squeak yet again as he pressed open the door. The inside was even more decayed than the exterior. The walls were stripped of their plaster, exposing the supporting beams with some going so far as to have whole panels of insulation removed. The wooden floor was scuffed and splintered with entire boards missing in places, creating a warren of precarious hollows to avoid. Scattered across it was an assortment of detritus ranging from torn wallpaper to fragments of plasterboard and a variety of litter left by squatters.

Michael uneasily looked up the stairs directly in front of him and then to the doorless frames either side of him, leading to what would have once been the lounge and dining room. Something whispered to him from the twilight atop the old, broken stairs and he was again drawn towards them, stepping up each one like it was made of glass. They creaked and moaned ominously and thick veils of dust were shaken from their underside after years of neglect.

The Horde

The top landing was bathed in an inky halo that grew ever darker as it stretched back into the house. The large window at the top of the stairs had apparently been painted over long ago, now only allowing a hint of the evenings dull ambience to seep through the cracked paint around the edge. Even so, Michael was compelled to step into the black, ensuring to tread gently upon the age-old rafters. Suddenly something caught his eye at the end of the landing as it struck across his view.

The hall was all but pitch black now, only a sparse scattering of hazy light pools softening the intolerable darkness. A floorboard cracked sharply in one of the side rooms and Michael turned abruptly, peering into the grim emptiness. Slowly he took a tentative start into the room and looked around but was barely even able to see his own hand in front of his face. Without notice, the door was harshly slammed shut, forcing Michael to swing around, only to find himself now in perpetual blackness. Even those faint spatters of dull evening glow were gone, depriving him of even the smallest sense of comfort. He dared not move for he now knew for sure that he was not alone.

To his eyes, the room was deathly still but, in the darkness, Michael could feel the presence moving silently around him, sizing him up, judging his purpose, assessing his weaknesses. Eventually he heard a low growling from just behind him and a warm, moist breath drifted across his neck. Still, he refused to turn around, frozen in terror to the spot as his heart started to beat as though it were trying to escape his chest again.

"Welcome," came a low, hiss-like voice at his ear, stretching the syllables long and tainting them with a soul chillingly malevolent tone, "we've been waiting for you."

I had never expected any of this. I always knew life wouldn't be perfect but this? For the briefest of times, I had a chance at normality and for that time I was happy. But now, lying on that slab, the very essence of my own existence seeping away as those abominations rose up around me, I knew I was still tied to the old ways and I had squandered that time. They took my blood, my dignity. They destroyed all the good I believed I had ever done and

The Dark

finally they desired to take my life. All I could think of through the pain and fading consciousness was Hollie. She was the only light left in my fading illusion of life...Then, as I fell into the abyss that I had risen from so many times, I heard their plans...In my mind I saw...They were coming for her...

Hollie stepped from the street, the tarmac starting to glisten with the early evening frost, onto the driveway of Richard's large, eloquent house. Suddenly a shiver shot up her spine as the normally warming aura of the house turned deathly cold, feeling as though it were resisting her very presence. Something was wrong, she knew it, she could feel it. No contact, no trace of either Richard or Michael and now with the house itself trying to warn her against whatever was going on she knew she should turn and run but she couldn't. Every step closer to the building yielded only a deathly prickling of her skin and a deep sickness reaching to her stomach. Eventually Hollie reached the front door, only to find it slightly ajar with the step scuffed and a smear of blood on the doorframe. She pushed the door gently and stepped into the freezing corridor. No lights were on yet a small yellow glow emanated from the top of the stairs. She glanced quickly into the rooms either side of her and, barely aware of what she was doing, stepped up the stairs. Slowly she crept up the soft carpet, trying her best to avoid the unavoidable creak of the stairs. Inevitably there came a loud groan from the wood and she froze, staring fixedly into the partial darkness.

At that moment a realisation flashed before her eyes. Everything had changed so much in so little time. Four months ago, she couldn't have even imagined the things she had seen, the things she had come to learn. One of the first things Richard had done was to take her to the border. Suddenly, there in the world of lost life she was changed, like all other Medians had been. Her mind had been flooded by the sea of souls screaming for freedom from their endless slumber and like all those others, it had terrified her.

"You learnt though, didn't you?" came a softly spoken voice down the staircase.

The Horde

"Who is it?" she snapped, starting backwards, almost losing her footing on the carpet. "What are you?" she added quietly, feeling there was something not quite human about the presence.

The glow slowly drifted from Richard's room, becoming apparent as a small oil lantern held by a smartly dressed man. His features were not old by any means yet they still conveyed the rigors of time. So too a large scar across his throat told Hollie that he was not a stranger to bloodshed.

"You learnt you could be much more than you ever thought," he stated casually, "but I'm afraid you may not be able to reach that potential."

Hollie backed down a step, away from the warm glow of the oil lamp. "How did you get in here?"

The strange man raised his free hand and gazed at it distractedly before gently turning it to face her, revealing a deep cut across his palm. "In a place protected such as this, a certain sacrifice must be made…In order to show willing, you understand." He moved forward slightly towards Hollie, forcing her further backwards.

"I'll give you one chance," Hollie started harshly, finally deciding to stand her ground. "Who are you and what are you doing here?"

The man grinned menacingly and bent down into the light. "For now, you need not know, but everything will soon become clear…Now I must insist that you accompany me…"

"I don't think so," she quickly replied, clenching her fists and gritting her teeth. "Now I don't even care who you are anymore, just get the hell out of this house! …Before something happens that you will regret."

The man sighed and shook his head, standing back to full height again. "I fear if you do not comply then I shall have to take you by force." From the shade of Richard's room, two pale individuals stepped out to either side of the staircase and each growled subtly, revealing the fangs at the sides of their mouth. "Now…" added the smartly dressed vampire, "what will it be?"

II-IV – Within Darkness

And you are to be holy to me; for (...) I have separated you from the nations to be Mine

-Leviticus, 20:26

The damp breath lingered against Michael's neck for a while, making the fine hairs along it prickle with a fearful knowing. At any moment he could feel the stabbing agony of those fangs sinking into his neck. Instead, the breath was suddenly gone, in a moment replacing a paralysing fear with the bewildering sense of security. Maybe it was a trick of the mind after the abrupt relief of such fear but he knew that of all situations to feel in any way safe, this was not it.

Remaining motionless in the pitch black, Michael tried to convince himself that he was not nearly as secure as his gut was implying. He sensed arms slowly moving up either side of his face and then felt as a cloth was abruptly pulled across his eyes and fastened tightly around the back of his head. The arms were quickly withdrawn and for a few seconds he stood, seemingly alone. Even with the blindfold now securely tied around his head, he had the growing temptation to gaze around the darkness for some semblance of shape, lest his mind produce ones for him.

Before he had a chance to move, a large hand was firmly placed against his back, pressing him forward with a start. Thoughts raced through Michael's head as the creature pushed him onwards. Where were they taking him? Was this only a brief reprieve before a much worse fate? Nothing, however, none of the hundreds of suspicions coursing through his mind could have prepared him for the truth.

After being guided back along the creaking landing and down the rickety staircase to the entrance hall, he was turned into one of the side rooms before being guided forward and turned again only to step headlong into nothing. Almost falling, his coat was grabbed quickly by the vampire behind him who carefully guided him down yet another staircase. These steps were much firmer to walk on than the first and Michael sighed with a relief that he wasn't entirely sure he had earned considering his predicament.

"Careful," the vampire behind him growled in low, subtle tones, "they wouldn't like you damaged."

Michael shivered at the voice being so close to his ear but was mildly reassured that the weapons beneath his jacket had remained concealed during the altercation.

Guided remarkably gently down the remaining steps, Michael was pressed with less force now for a fair way before being abruptly stopped while it sounded as though his chauffeur attended to something. There was a great deal of metallic clanks followed by the slam of a large, thick door which made him jump forward slightly. Soft footsteps approached from ahead and a hand was placed firmly but not maliciously on his shoulder.

"I had a feeling about this one," came a voice which Michael vaguely knew although couldn't quite place. The hand was withdrawn and he heard a thoughtful sigh. "Bring him." The footsteps disappeared back off along the corridor then he was once again pushed forward for a way until the blindfold was suddenly pulled away.

For a moment, Michael was dazzled by the blinding glare but soon enough it faded to present a stone walled room filled with people he could only presume to be vampiric in nature. Each was clad in various forms of attire but all had a motif of leather and chains. To his side, large brutes stared down at him, holding tightly to the leashes of strange coyote-like animals. They snarled at him before leaping forwards with a hissed bark, only to be pulled back by their masters. Through their large patches of horrid mange, it was apparent that they had sickly grey skin and from their snouts sliced huge fangs, largely blackening with decay. Their eyes were the most haunting aspect to Michael, though. They were fixed, always staring at him and seemed to glow red when the light caught them.

"They are the Gwyllgi," came the voice which had been guiding him around. "Dogs of the Night." His escort bent down and took one of the dogs firmly by the snout, looking it dead in the eye causing it to cease its barking. He grinned, rubbing the animal's head and patting it firmly on the side. "This one is domestic, though... I assure you..."

He was a broad, dark vampire dressed in only a fur waistcoat and leather chaps yet had an air about him which told Michael that, despite his imposing stature, he should not be feared. Even so, he still did. Michael feared everything in this place and backed slowly away from the brutes, looking about at the many vampires who now started to observe him warily.

Michael breathed heavily, withdrawing slowly into a corner as the creatures gathered around him. "Screw this," he exclaimed quickly to himself and whipped the pistols from beneath his jacket, pointing them aggressively at the crowd. The gathered mass responded with a chorus of hisses and growls, causing the dogs to start barking again. "Back the fuck off!" he screamed only to be responded to with even more hissing. "Now!"

The vampire who had brought him to this place sighed gently and turned around. "You really don't think I knew you had them?" He stepped forward and instantly had a weapon pointed at his chest. "How many of us do you seriously think you can kill with those? I wanted to give you a chance."

"A chance? Is that what you gave those people you butcher?" Michael shouted back. "And I'm pretty sure I can kill enough of you! ...Enough to slow you down at least."

"You don't understand-"

Michael laughed shortly, cutting the vampire off. "I understand well enough. The way you brutally kill people and take their blood to continue your own sickening existence!"

"Human!" a familiar voice called from the crowd. "Stop this!" The smartly dressed vampire pushed his way to the front of the bustling mass of his brethren and pointed a finger at Michael only to have a gun pointed right back at him. "Stop this now."

"I know you," Michael said softly, "you framed me...You tried to pin those murders on me! You and Trance, if that's really her name."

The vampire lowered his arm and shook his head. "At first...yes, but then you became something else in our arrangements, an asset. *She* convinced me of that. That's why I had you come here...And why I was forced to bring Hollie-"

"What the hell have you done with her!?" Michael screamed again, forcing the pistol forwards. "So help me god-"

"Nothing," another voice came from the crowd, this one feminine and one Michael recognised right away. "You have to put the guns down, Michael," Hollie pressed her way through the throng and stepped in front of the vampires. "You really have to try and understand what's happening here."

"What?" Michael whispered to himself, allowing the barrels to fall slightly as he tried to decipher the situation. In an instant they were raised again and flicked wildly from person to person. "What kind of trick is this? What have you done to her? Brainwashing?" he grimaced and pointed a pistol accusingly at the vampires behind Hollie.

"Please, Michael, if they had wanted to kill us they could have done it long before now..." Hollie briefly looked down at the guns tightly gripped in Michaels hands. "These mean nothing. Even now if they wanted to take your life they could without hesitation."

"She's right," a voice softly sounded from behind, forcing him to swing around only to catch a glimpse of Trance bearing down on him, the heel of her palm outstretched.

Michael was thrown heavily to one side from the force of the blow to his cheek and fell hard onto the stone floor, releasing his grip on the pistols as he went.

"You didn't have to do that!" spat Hollie, taking a step forward. "I was getting through to him, for god's sake!"

Trance crouched down and gently stroked where her palm had struck Michael's face before kicking the guns away from his hands and quickly retrieving them. "He isn't hurt...Might have a sore jaw but apart from that..." she smiled sweetly and walked towards the dispersing crowd.

The smartly dressed vampire tilted his head and looked disapprovingly at Trance. "Subtle isn't your forte, is it?" He walked slowly towards Michael's limp body as he twitched slightly, futilely attempting to get up again. Bending down, sweeping the tails of his lavish jacket away as he went, he leaned towards Michael's ear. "My name is Diego, for you will come to know me well." He quickly got back to his feet again and turned to Michaels former escort. "Baeloe. Take our... guest to the central chamber. I wish to discuss many a topic with him." Diego turned to Hollie but stopped and sighed. "And please be careful, he is but a delicate boy," he smiled slightly at Hollie before gesturing that she follow him back into the den.

The voices were stronger here, each calling out in fear like something unnatural walked amongst them. Yet their screams told of something greater, something impure. An arriving fate newly born unto this world.

In the drifting state of unconsciousness, Michael's mind dwelled on the people he had met all too briefly. The ones who had, in their own way, invited him into their existence when they could have remained hidden, a myth as they had always been. The potential reasons he was brought into their lair coursed through his mind, the most sinister of them naturally held above the rest. The one fact he couldn't ignore, however, was that whatever else this place could be, it was the one place an enemy would never be taken. It was their home.

Michael's thoughts drifted to the people here...they were just people. Of course, they were different but not unlike anyone else who had fought their entire lives just for mere survival. At last, he began to make the realisation that these people were not some new scourge upon humanity. They were outcasts, content only with hiding and protecting their own from the real monsters who came to roam the streets. Those who had stolen the sunlight from them long ago.

Michael flicked his eyes open with a start and quickly looked around. He had been laid on an old sofa which looked to have been discarded as rubbish by its original owner. Gazing up at the strange surroundings, all he could see were four pillars supporting an arch carved from solid rock. It had subtle patterns embedded into it, running its whole length to the ground on either side. At the limits of his vision, Michaels eyes met a number of figures sitting on other tatty and stained settees. As he panned around the room, still with his senses providing a disturbing lack of clarity, he became aware of indistinct images framed upon the stone walls and a low murmuring from the seated parties. Suddenly a sharp cold took hold of him and he saw a clouded gasp of breath billow upwards, escaping from his body and dissipating in the chilly air. He heard movement to his side and turned to investigate, a swollen numbness inside his head following his every move.

As if out of nowhere, Hollie appeared over him, her face slowly fading into focus as he managed to regain some level of control over his senses. She silently moved her mouth, sound only reaching his ears seconds after the words were spoken. She spoke again, screwing her face into a contorted expression of anxious confusion as her words fell upon Michaels ears only as a distorted murmuring.

"Are you alright?" she repeated once more, the words still distorted but at least discernible this time, "she hit you pretty hard." Her voice became clearer as she took Michael's arm and pulled him into an upright position, making his head spin unbearably.

"Well, he was going crazy," stated trance firmly, strolling through an entrance to the side of the chamber and placing her hands on her hips. "Talking about shooting us all..." she looked sideways at Michael and raised an eyebrow, "that's not okay."

"Enough of this!" Another voice exclaimed from behind Michael, making him turn around sharply. Diego stood above the sofa with Baeloe towering over to his side. "We brought you both here for a reason-"

Hollie took a quick gasp in, "Richard," she sputtered.

"Yes...But I'm afraid he is not our primary concern; he is but their conduit-"

The Dark

"Not your primary-!?" started Hollie forcefully, cut off by Diego throwing up a hand and hissing sharply.

"If you would mind!" he snapped fiercely, brandishing his teeth at her threateningly. "We are very short on time and if you ever want to see him again, dead or alive, then there are things that you both must know...So if I would continue..." he raised an eyebrow and lowered his hand, giving one last quiet snarl before turning back to Michael. "Now, my son, there is a lot you clearly do not know of our kind. For centuries we have been looked upon in something of a darker light... possibly for good reason too as our past is far from untainted." He took a deep breath in and sighed heavily, strolling slowly across the cold stone of the chamber floor. "We come from an ancient time, a time many of your practitioners consider a myth. It was a time before the earliest of men, before the reptiles rose up and claimed dominance over this world," he stopped and threw up a finger as if to emphasise his point. "Before even the unification of the very lands we stand upon. It was a time when we could still stand in the open day and bask in the light of the sun." He sighed again and hung his head, turning it slowly towards Michael. "We were all too different then, a form which you would find alien, one that would change time and time again. As we evolved and hunted and fed upon the creatures around us, our abilities grew, eclipsing anything that roamed this Earth. To be outmatched was merely a game for us, something to overcome and inevitably take for ourselves."

Michael's lips fell apart and his face contoured, unable to believe what he was hearing. "Are you trying to tell me that your kind became the dominant species by... stealing the abilities of the animals you hunted?" The words spilling from his own mouth did not feel real, as if they made no sense. "That's-" he tried to think of an appropriate term for what he was feeling but had to settle for denial, "it's impossible."

"Do not think it some sinister ploy, it is but how we evolved. Some of our older followers believe us to be divinely created to watch over existence itself. Quite literally at one with the creatures that surrounded us. It was thought we existed only to keep balance within nature...But then you came..." He gritted his teeth and quickly closed his eyes, reminding himself that the humans in front of him were not to blame. "Your kind was unlike anything we had encountered. You were a true rival to our dominance, willing to exploit the land and its animals to your own needs. That was all bad enough but then you brought the wars that would destroy everything in their path. Of course, your simple ignorance would become the least of our worries." Diego rubbed his face and leaned against one of the pillars under the archway. "Like we did with any other threat throughout history, we tried to consume your essence, add it to our own... but you were different," he gestured casually between Michael and Hollie. "An evolutionary process that usually took generations to take effect occurred within individuals in a matter of years. We began to change, our form becoming like you." He trailed off for a second, as if lost in through before snapping back with a start. "In a twist of fate, though, the process apparently worked both ways because everyone who was fortunate enough..." he turned the words over in his mind before shaking his head gently. "All those who remained alive after being fed upon began to take our traits. They became the first true forms, the ancestors of who you see here today. They were quite different, however. Bloated, mindless, their skin horrifically bruised from the blood running too thickly in their veins. They were the ones you first called Vampir. Although that was not the only name you gave us, not by a long way." Diego strolled slowly towards Michael and took a seat next to him. "After thousands of years of this, our original form had all but vanished, replaced in part by the barely sentient creatures Humans would hunt with such fervour. The rest were like us. We were capable of fitting into your society easily enough... just so long as we didn't smile too much," he chuckled gently and shook his head at the fact he should find such a thing humorous.

"Fascinating story," Michael quipped shortly, "but what has this got to do with anything? Richard? The deaths?"

"It has everything to do with them," Diego threw himself up and tossed his arms into the air. "To understand what has happened to your friend, you must fully understand the nature of my people." Diego clenched his jaw, his patience for Michael's attitude waning.

"Fine," stated Michael flatly, "please continue to enlighten me."

Diego gazed at Michael as if trying to burn him into him then huffed and turned away. "In the time known to your culture as the Dark Ages, three brothers rose in the land now named Romania. They sought to bring order to the chaos that had ensued for millennia in our society. Of the brothers there was Dragoş, one who would unite with the humans, to co-exist and Dracul who merely desired to wipe your race from the face of the planet, believing it rightfully belonged to our kind alone."

"And the third?" Michael ventured after a moment's silence.

"Dragomir," Diego stated, almost mournfully. "He wished neither peace nor destruction but for our people to live silently, unknown to the humans and continue to watch over creation as we once had. He would be the one who supposedly tempered his brothers and kept us true to our form, staving off war for centuries."

There was another pause and Hollie looked between Michael and Diego. "I imagine it...didn't last?" she asked carefully, unsure if she should press the story on.

"The third brother was found dead. All knew it to be Dragoş but still the brothers blamed each other, blinded by their own rivalries and soon the clans descended into violence. Of course, there was no victor, just death and a silence that fell over our people. Dracul was believed to have fled into exile while Dragoş remained to help the survivors yet he constantly feared his brother's return. He went so far as to place agents within the Serbian court of King Offleson as knights of the realm in an attempt to protect the humans caught in the crossfire."

Michael chuckled shortly with genuine surprise. "There were vampire knights?"

"Indeed," Diego stated with pride, "I, myself was honoured to be counted as a member of that legion," his bright demeanour faded quickly. "Although Dracul did soon return, but not in a way we had ever expected. He brought forth an army of mindless hybrids who he had culled and conditioned into creatures whose purpose was to kill. Rather than attacking our clans outright, he trained them directly on the court at which I stood guard. I was there as they overran the defences, ripping the humans apart in front of my eyes and gorging themselves on their broken bodies," he shuddered at the memory which still haunted him after so many centuries. "Villages and entire towns were overtaken as though they were nothing and my clan were forced into the hills. We watched as the peoples of Europe marched in retaliation against Draculs horde, breaking over and over on his feral creatures. The humans just kept coming, though, a horde unto themselves until Dracul and his beasts were routed." Diego nodded between Michael and Hollie, something approximating admiration in his eyes. "In the face of annihilation, your kind never stopped fighting. Europe would be saved... and yet the dead?" His thoughts were thrown into the past again and his brow rippled as he seemed to relive the memories. "That amount of blood would not again be spilled for another thousand years."

So..." Michael attempted, holding up his hands expectantly. "What then? The world is saved, this Dracul is dead..."

Diego shook his head firmly. "We made the mistake of thinking that for far too long. We don't have a clue how he managed it but somehow Dracul opened a rift between this world and the next. He let it envelop The Horde, trapping them in the void between. It's a place I believe Medians are familiar with; The Abyss." He stared off absently with the gaze of a man who had clearly been through more than any human would have been able to survive.

Hollie and Michael eyed each other, both as bewildered as the other. "Honestly," Michael started sheepishly, "we're both still quite new at this."

"Really?" Diego remarked flatly, snapping his gaze back to them. "Well, I assure you your friend certainly knows of what I speak," Diego waited for any reaction his words may elicit but to his surprise there was none."

"Looks like you guys are gonna get a crash course in a lot of this stuff then," Baeloe finally added, breaking the tension a little.

Hollie squinted for a second in thought then seemed to come to a realisation. "You don't think this Dracul is coming back, do you?"

"He's not just trying."

"That thing in the alley," whispered Michael, "they're already here."

"Not all of them, not by a long shot," Diego spoke the words as though they were some solemn guarantee, "but there's going to be more on their way."

"So, you get it now?" Baeloe looked down imposingly over Michael as though a simple answer would not suffice. "They're the real threat, not us!"

"He knows we won't hurt them," Trance stepped from beside one of the pillars and moved over to the sofa, slowly sitting down next to Michael and placing a hand softly on his arm. "There's no need to be scared of me, at least..." She caressed the bruise on his face and winked. "You should know that," she ended softly, whispering into Michael's ear and making Diego roll his eyes.

"The Horde *do* have your friend," Diego finally confirmed, trying to get back onto topic. "They need him for something, a power we haven't seen in a very long time."

"What kind of power?" Hollie asked bluntly.

Diego floundered to find the right word, shaking his head. "A... connection, a tether, something linking him to the Abyss."

Hollie scowled and took a breath. "Care to elaborate?"

"I can't tell you what I don't fully understand. The important thing is that we've been watching them ever since they first broke back through to this plane. We were able to keep tabs on them but we never had the means to move against them...until now, that is," he stared back and forth between Michael and Hollie, grinning slightly.

"What the hell's so important about us?" Hollie demanded, getting to her feet.

Trance smiled up at her and took a refreshing breath in, placing her arm casually around Michael. "You two are Medians, conduits to the Other Side...The bridges of worlds over the Abyss..." she stopped and thought about going on but decided not to waste her breath, instead raising her free hand loosely. "You're our bait..."

The car rolled up quietly onto the pavement and the chugging engine fell silent. Diego slumped back into the driver's seat and grimaced at the crumbling yet still imposing building down the street.

"Is that the place?" asked Hollie quietly from the back seat.

Diego nodded slowly without a word and turned his head to Trance. "It's not too late to back out, you know..."

Trance laughed slightly and shook her head. "It'll be fine. As long as someone keeps his cool and doesn't go pointing guns at everyone," she leant around her seat and grinned at Michael.

Michael sighed and looked firmly at Trance. "Why? Don't you trust me?"

Trance smiled again slyly before turning to Hollie, her face immediately dropping. "Are *you* going to be ok?"

Hollie thought about what she was getting herself into and peered at the building. "Going to have to be, aren't I?" Without a second thought she opened her door and stepped out of the car.

Michael watched her fearfully as she gently closed the door and moved out in front of the car.

"Don't worry, we won't let anything happen to her," Trance patted the seat firmly as if to convey a conviction she did not fully possess and turned back around to watch Hollie walk into the darkness.

The road was largely disused, without houses or even street lamps, seemingly there only for the benefit of that large, otherwise abandoned building.

"What is that place?" Michael queried after a while in an effort to sooth his nerves. "The building. What was it used for?"

"Old workhouse," Diego replied flatly. "Asbestos, child labour, that sort of thing."

"We've been watching the place for a while," started Trance quickly, "they weren't exactly subtle about where they hang out."

Michael looked between them both, bemused. "So why haven't you done anything yet?"

"We didn't have an in," stated Diego abruptly before Trance could reply.

"'An in?' Is that all she is to you? What if they just kill her here and now?"

"They won't," Trance tried to sound reassuring but her own reservations couldn't help but slip into her voice. "She's too important to them."

Michael signed and looked out at Hollie again. "She's important to us."

As he watched her a pair of cloaked figures appeared as if from the night itself and grabbed at Hollie, trying to pull her into the shadows. Just as suddenly as they had appeared, each was apparently struck with something and fell to the ground, leaving Hollie looking around wildly.

"Ok you two," Diego reached for the door with an urgency he had not displayed before, "we're up."

"Soon all this will be over...Our swarm shall engulf the world and we will have our redemption," Cosin hovered over Richard's limp body, still strapped to the blood-stained slab.

He drifted in and out of consciousness, his eyes flicking open only to fall shut again as he tried to cling to the last remnants of his lucidity.

"I fear you will not live to see our final victory...In fact I am all but certain of this. That is why I would have you see them...They are the first. Savant gave his life so that they may be born. His blood gave them life. A piece of him is imprinted on each and every one of them...As is a piece of you..."

Suddenly Richard managed to gasp and forced his eyelids open, just to see a thin apparition with skin like ash stood behind Costin. "...No," he breathed, exhaustedly, "I don't believe it."

The creature raised its hand, its fingers ending in talon-like tips. Growling in low tones, it tried to move forward but was waved back by Costin who took the step himself. "But these are your children, Richard...They are your legacy... and we thank you. Soon others will be chosen to bear the seed of the next but you, my friend, you are the one who made it all possible. You are the one who lives in each and every one of the newborn. Father of the Horde....You shall be remembered as such for all time-"

"I'd rather die," Richard coughed out, trying to lean forward only to have the devices tear at his skin.

Costin laughed quietly and stooped down to Richards' side. "That time will come, rest assured...Just not quite yet," he stood up straight and chuckled again. "Enjoy your stay," he turned and ushered his prodigy from the room, slamming the large iron door of Richard's chamber behind him.

The creature of ash growled and bore its teeth, looming threateningly towards Costin.

"Soon, Anak-Savant. It will not be long before our work is complete. Then a new age will rise across this land and we will once more be dominant," he grinned and started to walk along the damp, crumbling corridor, followed by the newborn. "Only we will not idly stand by 'protecting' this world as our ancestors did. If there's anything I've learnt from these humans, it is that anything is possible if you use even a little initiative. Just imagine it, a revolution of industry; forging steel from the Earth's own core, the sun blotted out with the choke of our toils, bringing with it an endless night. We will exploit that which we have so long overlooked and only then will we achieve our true purpose." He grinned subtly to himself again, only for it to fall away as he glanced back at his counterpart. "I sense you do not share my confidence, brother."

Anak-Savant growled quietly and cracked its sharp fingers. "The cult concerns me," it hissed at last in a hollow, gravelly voice. "I was the first to arise from our host, I retained his memories, his consciousness. I am by all accounts the one you knew as Savant. Only I possess the essence of The Horde, their strength and it is my honour to lead them, but I am not but the sum of my creators. Savant feared they would come. Dragoș was a powerful leader and taught his cult well. They may yet be bolder than even you would suspect."

"Indeed, but if you truly are Savant then you would have faith in The Master and in the power of the Horde... your own brood," Costin stopped and turned to Savant, taking it by a leathery arm. "Do not fear, the end grows close."

"I fear nothing, for although I exist to lead, I was born to serve and bred to kill," it grinned a sharp fanged grin and cracked its fingers again.

"Quite," Costin said quietly and started walking again until he came to another rusted iron door. "Even so, if the Cult were so, what was it, bold as you claim, then would they have allowed such a valuable commodity to fall into our hands?" He took the steel handle and forced it up, pressing open the door to reveal Hollie gagged and tied to a chair. She had been bound in the same fashion as they had held Richard not so long ago only this time two hooded guards stood watch either side of her.

"She is a Median," Savant stated firmly, holding his ground as Costin entered the room and started circling Hollie.

"Indeed, she is, but not any Median…Do you feel it? It's not quite there yet…but soon. Soon she will become the gateway for those who would remain in the abyss."

"I feel nothing of this power. She has not touched the Other Side," Savant snapped aggressively, growing weary of Costin's riddles.

"Not yet…I feel she never truly will," Costin continued cryptically, "yet it will touch her…in such a profound way."

"Silence, impure one!" Savant barked. "How dare you bring one of these here!? Already I can feel her in my thoughts," it shuddered as it looked Hollie deep in the eye. "I will kill her now!" It started forward, brandishing its teeth and raising a sharp claw to her face, only to be swiped away by Costin.

"No, you fool!" he pushed Savant back who growled again, holding its talon to Costin's face. "If nothing else it will lead the remnants of the Cult here so we can truly finish them."

The talon was slowly lowered with a grunt. "She will lead them here and then I will take the pleasure of killing their leader myself," Savant said, relishing the thought of slowing slitting Diego's throat while Costin nodded slowly.

"Well, you've one thing right," a voice came softly from the dark corner, "but I don't think you'll be killing anyone today." Diego stepped forward out of the shadows and raised a small crossbow, pointing it directly at Costin's head. As he did, the guards on either side of Hollie threw down their hoods revealing Michael and Trance, themselves each pulling a Median pistol on Costin and Savant.

"What is the meaning of this!?" Savant growled jerking forwards only to be pressed backward by Diego taking aim.

Costin sighed. "It is true then; you are Savant's spawn. At least you have his awareness," he ended spitefully as Michael moved to untie Hollie. "I, on the other hand, have felt *him* all along," he indicated towards Michael, slowly stepping forward and immediately becoming everyone's target.

"Save it, asshole," snapped Hollie, throwing a loose rope to the ground, "where the hell is Richard?"

Costin took a casual breath and opened his arms, loosely shrugging.

"She asked where is he?" growled Michael, pushing his gun into Costin's face.

"Michael," Diego said softly, shaking his head.

Michael grimaced and withdrew the weapon, ushering Costin and Savant into the far corner of the room as the four of them sidled around towards the door.

"So, is this what the cult has come to?" Costin asked as they exited the room. "Rats and cowards, cavorting with humans. You see, Savant, really they are far weaker than we had thought."

As they were about to close the door, Diego stopped and re-entered the room, lowering the crossbow.

"What are you doing!?" Trance hissed, grabbing at his arm.

"Savant?" Diego whispered, looking to the newborn. "This is what they've done to you?" He shook uncontrollably and glanced to Costin, a fire in his eyes. "I'm so sorry. It should have never come to this. Do you understand? We did what we could but..." He abruptly turned his back on them and stormed towards the door again without another word.

"You knew what would happen, Diego. You knew all too well," whispered Costin as the door was pushed closed and locked from the outside. "You missed out, my friend," Costin's voice echoed through the thick door hauntingly, "you truly missed out."

"I take it we're going to discuss what just happened later, then?" Michael asked agitatedly while Diego caught his breath, shaking gently.

"Let's finish this," Diego eventually stated, heading down the corridor, "the rest of them will be here any second."

The others quickly followed behind, watching over their shoulders for the inevitable resistance that they would encounter.

Passing several large blast doors along the way, Diego ignored every one, continuing on as though the exact one Richard was behind.

"Workhouse, eh?" Michael mused sceptically, gazing at the doors.

"I'm not going to lie; things could be pretty messed up back then." Diego stopped abruptly and pressed his face against the cold, rusted iron of an apparently arbitrary door. "He's in here."

"How can you be so sure?" queried Hollie, barely giving him a moment to finish. "We can't waste time guessing!"

Diego pulled the handle up and forced open the door. "We can sense your kind, remember?" He stepped into the room and quickly stopped at the sight of Richard.

"Oh my god!" Hollie gasped, rushing to his side and gazing in despair at the devices implanted all over him.

"What the hell have they done to you?" asked Michael quietly.

"They're harvesting him," answered Diego flatly. "Trance. Get those... things out of him and we might be able to avoid dying today." As Diego took up a defensive position, watching down the hallway.

Trance took hold of one of the hoppers and pulled gently, making Richard groan as the pain reached into his unconsciousness, causing Hollie to grab her hand, forcing her to stop. She turned and looked into Hollie's eyes. She said nothing but eventually the hand was removed causing Trance to nod shortly.

"Michael...Talk to him, keep him calm," she continued to slide the steel stake from his body leaving a surprisingly bloodless hole in the side of his chest before moving on to the next.

Diego stepped out of the doorway and listened carefully to the distant sound of dozens of footsteps rushing along the corridor. "Shit...Hurry up or we're going to have a real problem."

Trance jarred another stake from Richard's body, making him flinch. "I've only got a few left," she replied nervously, taking hold of another device. Suddenly she stopped and looked up at Hollie who held Richard's hand firmly, staring in horror at his barely breathing form. "Could you?" she asked gently, gesturing to the vial closest to her. She was responded to with a short look of anguish before a quick nod as they both moved to work.

The footsteps continued to grow closer and Diego moved back into the room, closing the door tightly as he did. "That's it, we're out of time. It's now or never!"

Trance pulled at a vial just as Hollie placed hers down on the surgical table next to her. "Last one," Trance breathed, removing the device with a jerk and throwing it down to her side where it smashed on the stone floor, spilling the blood across the uneven slabs.

"Then let's go," stated Diego, pointing at Michael to help Richard up off of the slab.

Suddenly there was a harsh slam at the door, making every one of them jump.

Michael eased Richard's limp body into Hollie's grip and moved up in line with Diego. "This better bloody work," he said quietly to himself as another loud clang echoed through the metal door.

Slowly the door was pried away from the wall and thrown back into its open position revealing Savant, his large fangs clear to see and his clawed fists clenched as his deep black eyes watched Diego with a seething hatred. Next to him stood Costin, looking relatively composed considering the attempt to rescue Richard. Behind them the air shifted uneasily and dozens of dark eyes belonging to the newborns glinted in the low light.

"So, you wish to have him back?" Costin mused calmly. "I'm afraid I just cannot allow that. Neither can I allow you to leave this place."

Michael stepped forward and stared at Costin. "You'll get your way when I'm dead," he gritted his teeth, terrified but determined to stand his ground.

Costin smiled malignantly and slowly turned his head to look straight at Michael. "That, my child, was the idea," he muttered the words quietly yet more than clear enough to make his point. Turning away, he disappeared into the dark columns of The Horde, allowing Savant to step into his place. The beast looked at Diego with a purpose and cracked its dark grey knuckles sickeningly.

"Michael…" said Diego quietly.

"Yes?" replied Michael, not looking away from the terror hovering in front of them.

The Dark

"We're in trouble."

Suddenly Savant struck forward, teeth brandished and claws outstretched. Diego tried to pull his crossbow but knew it was already too late and that any second he would feel the creature tearing his throat out. Just as Savant's claws were about to slash at Diego's face, Michael tackled it to the ground and rolled away giving Diego the chance to take a shot only to be struck by one of the New Borns now flooding into the room. Firing almost blindly into the doorway, Trance shot as many as she could with Hollie throwing Richard to the ground and holding him tightly in a futile attempt to protect him.

No matter how many were felled, more continued to pour into the room, slowly overwhelming them. In the chaos Diego caught a glimpse of Savant holding Michael down to the ground and baring its huge, razor-like fangs down onto him. Powerless to resist, Diego watched as they sank into Michael's neck, causing a small fountain of blood to spray across the near wall as the flesh was torn from his throat. Diego screamed at Savant and turned back to see the others rapidly fall to the young brood just before he was forced to the ground himself.

As the creatures tried to tear at his skin there was a large, muffled smash and a crash like glass hitting the ground before the sound of rapid gunfire and a deep voice shouting various obscenities.

"How'd you like me now, bitches!?"

The voice alone seemed to force away the savage horde, allowing Diego to gaze up at a series of blacked out skylights high in the roof. One had been smashed through and held Baeloe's large outline silhouetted against the night, an assault rifle clutched in each hand.

"Diego! Trance! ...You alright down there?"

Diego watched as The Horde retreated back through the large door and rolled over quickly to see several bullets impacting Savant in the back, spattering more blood across the walls. The Horde Guardian turned, its face covered with Michael's blood, and hissed at Baeloe only to receive three more shots in the torso before it could shamble off away from danger.

"Baeloe!" Diego shouted up, "took your bloody time! Throw down the ropes, we've got wounded." He moved over to Michaels body, inspecting the deep bite mark in his still bleeding neck and held his blood-spattered face gently. "I'm sorry," he whispered, his voice shaking. "I am so very sorry."

II-V – The Schism

So you shall remove the evil from the midst of you

-Deuteronomy 13:5

So close to death, I didn't even care anymore. I had all but given up any hope of ever escaping and was willing to finally give myself to The Other Side. The voices of the beckoning night had fallen silent and, for the first time in my life, I was alone. Not even the border world invited me into its numbing embrace. I felt weak, helpless... I felt human. And then they came. In the fading lights I caught glimpses of Hollie and Michael with people who I did not know and I believed it to be a delusion, a symptom of my mind's last stand against the unknowability of death. My last memory was the unbearable screaming of a thousand feral creatures in my head and Hollie throwing herself on me as darkened glass fell from the sky. Then all was dark, no thoughts, no meaning...nothing. I felt only death...yet it was not mine.

"Is he alive…?"
"Barely…He's not what he was."
"…No! He can't be! I won't…You can't…Michael, come back to me…I…"
The voices came and left Michael as though they were merely whispers upon the wind and were quickly replaced by innumerable

muted voices calling to him. Soon enough a single tone of pure shadow overpowered the rest, drawing him closer.

"Give in...You are one of us now..."

Diego watched as Trace knelt down to the ground next to the smashed window, staring at Michaels expressionless face, her hands spread wide across his chest. Slowly she leant down, pressing her face against his, holding him tightly as his blood smeared across her skin. Diego looked back to Baeloe hauling Richard onto the roof, slinging him limply over his shoulder as Hollie gazed distantly back at him.

"It won't take them long to get up here," Diego finally said, bending down to Trance, "we have to keep moving if we're going to get out of this."

Trance raised her head and looked distraughtly at Diego, a tear running from her pale blue eyes, washing through the stained blood on her face as it ran down her cheek. She was about to speak back at him but knew he was right. Instead, she simply closed her eyes, submitting to his guidance and stood up, stepping away reluctantly.

Bending down, Diego scooped Michael from the ground and dropped him over his shoulder, far more carefully than Baeloe had with Richard. Suddenly a terrible, haunting scream echoed out across the city.

"He's freed them..." Diego murmured as The Horde was finally released out into the world.

For now, there was no time to address the development further and all the group could do was retreat into the shadows.

The hours passed slowly but even in that short time The Horde managed to destroy so much. Driven by Savant's fury they tore across the city, taking people's lives as they wished, demolishing their souls from the inside. For all the damage they would cause, though, the only trace anyone would see of them would be a mere shade illuminated by the fires spurred by their presence. Where the lucky ones would meet a swift death, ignorant of their fate, the rest who encountered the Horde could have only dreamt of such fortune.

Trance stood in front of the old house disguising the entrance to her lair and watched out over the city as the dull glow of fires silently flickered on the horizon. In the air rang the faint sounds of a civilization calling out for mercy, knowing there was none to come. A gentle warmth hung in the ether, accompanied by the sharp stench of smoke and fetid, burning flesh reminding her that the turmoil was not as far away as it seemed.

She turned abruptly and started back into the lair, unable to stand the idea that the one thing her kind had protected for so long could be wiped out in one fell swoop. As she stepped back down into the damp tunnel to the hollowed-out cavern, she thought about how safe they were down there. The Horde didn't even know of their presence there, let alone able to get in. This was no way to live, her thoughts continued, living underground, away from the real world, away from all that they should have been able to embrace. Once she had considered her immortality a gift. A chance to see the future and what it would bring for mankind, to watch them shrug off their petty, animalistic urges for conflict and see them develop to achieve their true potential. But now, she considered, it was far less of a gift, feeling more of an unending trail of will. All she saw was the planet decline into madness while her kinds dwindling numbers continued to flee until that inevitable day when they would be caught.

She stepped past the half-risen portcullis and silently raised her hand to a guard who quickly turned and pulled a lever making it lower back into place. She slowly continued into the main chamber, unable to stop herself from dwelling on what was going on outside. Startling her from the melancholic musings, Diego quickly stepped out in front of her, stopping Trance in her tracks.

"Well?" asked Diego sternly, concerned about the nature of the situation outside.

"It's chaos in the inner city," replied Trance, her voice gently trembling, "but they haven't quite reached out here yet," she finished, almost preferring that they had rather than waiting for the end to come.

"Good," said Diego harshly, "then we still have time."

Trance stopped and looked at him in shock "Time? ...Time for what? They're still coming."

The Schism

"Let them. By the time they reach us they'll be nothing but a disorganised rabble...No threat whatsoever," he spoke quickly and confidently as though the war was over before it had even begun. "I realise what you are thinking," he placed a hand firmly on Trance's shoulder, "but the humans...Their sacrifice will allow our survival," he saw Trance about to speak and cut her off abruptly. "Look! There are millions of them, billions even...But very few of us. We protect them in ways they can't begin to imagine. If some of them must perish for that ultimate greater good then so be it," he looked Trance in the eye until she reluctantly nodded in agreement. "Come" he breathed finally, leading her across the auditorium.

The chamber was empty and completely silent now, the quiet only broken by the occasional rustle of a bat in the high cave walls. He led her down a small corridor filtering off from the large den hollow, passing several openings just big enough for a person to fit through, some with rudimentary doors or beads covering the entrance. Suddenly he stopped at an opening with nothing but a fine silk veil across it.

"This is the greater good, my daughter. They will continue rampaging over the Earth until they find him and when they do, it will all be over," he gestured to Trance to look through the veil at Richard laid peacefully on a cushioned slab of rock, his wounds treated and bandaged. "As long as we keep our heads and follow through with our plan, we may just survive this..."

Trance turned away and looked straight at Diego. "Plan? What plan?" she asked hurriedly, shocked that he may have kept information from her.

Diego took a breath but said nothing, rather ushering her onwards down the corridor to another veiled opening, this time with Michael on a slab of bare rock. He twitched unnaturally, as if something were trying to take control of him. "...I fear, though, he will not."

"Michael," said Trance quickly, laying eyes on him in a much worse state than he had been. "Why have you let him get like this?" she snapped as Diego pulled back the veil and strolled in.

"There's nothing we could do," Hollie answered softly, standing up from a chair concealed in the shadowy corner. "Richard will live...Thank god," she muttered quietly, "but the blood of The

Horde is flowing through his veins now, corrupting him..." she gestured to Michael.

"Like they did Costin," came a sudden voice weakly from the entrance, making the rest turn around sharply in surprise, "isn't that right?"

Diego took a deep sigh and shook his head. "It's a dark secret only few of my kind know...Cosin, Savant...The others like him not of The Horde...They were like us once," he turned to Trance and stroked her face. "I've kept so much from you, my dear... Our history is not what it seems." Diego half turned to Richard; his head lowered almost in shame. "I trust you know..."

"Yeah," Richard weakly grunted, attempting to stumble further into the room only to be caught by Hollie and lowered into the chair she had been sitting in. "I had that pleasure when that Savant guy was killed. A part of me...my blood, merged with them, a connection was made. They learnt everything I know... and I mean *everything*," he mulled on the disturbing fact for a moment. "Lucky me, though, it was a two-way thing," he grabbed at a bandage on his side as a sharp pain shot through his chest, slowly dulling to nothing. "They weren't just *like* you...They *were* you."

"The powers of Median and Seer alike were far greater back then. Given a reason, they could tear a rent in the world to the abyss itself... Dracul did not give them that reason...I did... I gave them my blood..."

The cloaked old man stared at Diego as if gazing into his soul. "You understand what this entails, do you not?"

"My foe has been routed but I cannot say they are defeated," Diego spoke in such a way as to almost plead with the old man. "My people dare not risk the return of such evil."

The Seer was robed in white and was flanked by a pair of Medians, barely visible in the light of the moon. "Such power would consume this Earth and all upon it. The gods must have focus lest they convey us all to the hereafter."

"A target..." Diego mused, looking between the Medians for approval.

"A thing common to all those you wish to cleanse, yes."

The Schism

Diego took a weary breath and glanced about. "The blood which flows in my veins is as that of my enemy... but it is also that of my people."

The Seer nodded slowly in thought. "Take leave of this place. Travel beyond the mountains and foothills of yonder and your kin may yet survive."

Reaching a shaking hand forward, Diego looked into the Seer's empty eyes. "I do as I must..."

The old Seer flicked a finger forward and the two Medians each took a sharp step forward, grabbing hold of Diego and forcing him to his knees. "Your sacrifice is an honourable one..."

The Seer retrieved an ornate athame from his robes and placed it against Diego's neck, slowly pulling it from one side to another. Wiping the blade clean and returning it to his robe, the Seer gestured to the Medians again and they released Diego, allowing him to fall onto his hands. Stooping down, the Seer placed his hands below Diego's throat, coating them in the blood gushing from him. Rubbing the blood between his palms, the Seer muttered an incantation of some kind as the Medians raised their hands to the dark sky.

The air thrummed as the Seers' indistinct words grew louder with each passing second and then suddenly fell utterly silent, a faint ripple passing through the air as Diego collapsed to the ground.

"Fly with haste, my friend," the Seers' final words came. "Your time grows short."

The next Diego knew he was opening his eyes on the dawn threatening to spill over the horizon. The Seer and his Medians were gone but as Diego touched a hand to his open throat, he knew that their work was complete.

Clawing his way from the ritualistic plateau, Diego served up all of his remaining strength to return to his people, practically falling from the summit and dragging himself to the safety of the caverns with the encroaching light of sunrise ever biting at his heels.

"Your encounter with the enchanter bade poorly, I presume?" Costin spoke calmly as Diego stumbled in from the virgin sunlight, smouldering faintly and fell against the sheer rock wall.

"Quite the opposite," croaked Diego, blood still dripping from his throat. "The curse has been bound but we must, all of us, leave and go far away from here." He pushed himself from the ground and fell against the cave entrance. "The curse will seek us all lest we flee."

Costin pursed his lips and thought on what it all meant before finally snapping his fingers. "We must be ready to depart by nightfall," he stated to an attendant appearing next to him, "our continued existence demands nothing less."

Diego nodded to Costin and slumped against the wall, gripping his neck again. He would heal, there was no doubt in his mind about that for it was far more difficult to dispatch one such as him than it was a mere human. Even so, he would require time to rest if he were to fully recover and yet this was a luxury he would not have.

while Diego's people busied themselves with preparations for the journey ahead, night fell and from it something terrible would approach.

"How did he find out?" growled Diego, grabbing his sword and storming through the bustling crowd to the cave entrance.

Costin followed behind, as composed as he had ever been. "I would think their demise was not as sudden as we would have hoped."

"So, he's coming here. He knows he's damned and he wants us to be as well." Diego stared for a moment as the stars warped upon the horizon, like they were being dragged towards something. "Ensure our people make it from this place. I will take my guard and do what we can."

Costin bowed his head and set to assisting those left within the cave while Diego and his small force of soldiers mounted horses and began riding hard towards a rift to the beyond and those who it would consume.

It wasn't long before the warping stars gave way to a crimson storm rimming a sphere of total nothing. Before it raced the remnants of the Horde and at their head was Dracul, wanting nothing more than to see the children of Dragoş consumed by the void along with him. Defiant of the harrowing sight, Diego commanded his force to engage the Horde and in the shadow of the earthbound abyss they battled one last time. It was not for victory or even retribution. What Diego battled for was not even his own survival but that of his people. He hoped that if he could hold Dracul and his Horde at bay for long enough then their blood may satiate the abyssal rift, sealing them all away forevermore.

At last, the fighting slowed, warriors on both sides knowing that to continue would be futile for the rift grew close and each became transfixed on the eye of nothingness, coming to accept their fate. Then there was a sound, the beating of hooves and Costin screaming for Diego and his men to turn back. He cried that there was yet a chance for them but Diego knew the truth of it and desperately waved Costin away. In a moment as the screaming void closed over them, Diego saw the Horde vanish into the eye, then his own men and finally Costin. Then he was alone.

Looking about the plane, Diego gazed upon the far-off mountains as if for the first time. The rift had been closed and, somehow, he had survived. Slumping down to the ground, Diego reached for his throat, the pain suddenly becoming all too real again, and made a realisation. The rift had sought the blood of vampires, something he had given all too much of during the ritual. A sacrifice, he considered, which had ultimately saved him. Diego did not feel saved, though, for he dwelled on the fate of his men and that of Costin, the torment they would face and cursed himself for not having been taken with them.

Indeed, where the abyss was eternal torment for some, for those already twisted and lost it was not but time with which to weave a future triumph. Within the void, Cosin, Savant and all of those that Diego had lost on that day were slowly corrupted, polluted with the ideals of Dracul, willing to do anything if it meant escape from their hell.

Over the centuries, the Horde clawed at the abyss in a bid for freedom and from time to time one would succeed in falling through cracks back to the world of the living. Isolated on their own, these stragglers, mindless, opportunistic and without the guiding hand of Dracul, would not survive. Those who remained in the void continued to wait and watch and eventually their patience was rewarded when they saw one possessing the great power of the

Other Side break through to the living world. It would not be Dracul to formulate a plan for the Hordes' salvation but Costin. He planned to use this beacon within the living world as a conduit but just as he moved to act on his machinations, the beacon was gone. Instead, he saw the boundaries between worlds fractured and another who had touched the Other Side. He saw Richard.

Diego sighed with remorse for what had happened all those centuries ago.
"When I travelled to the Far Side, I cracked the borders and Costin saw a chance he couldn't pass up. I don't know how many got through the cracks but it was enough to start all of this," Richard waved around his arms the best he could. "I touched the Other Side, it's in my blood now...a gateway to the beyond."
"Oh god," gasped Hollie, unable to fully grasp the scope of the tale. "If I knew this would have happened when we- I wouldn't have-"
Richard took Hollie's hand and looked her in the eye. "This was my fault, there's nothing you could have done."
"No," said Diego abruptly, "this all started with me. If I had never made that damn pact then this never would have happened," he turned back to Trance. "I'm so very sorry for all of this."
"I don't care about any of that," stated Trance quickly, "you all did what you thought was best, it can't be changed now," she slowly turned her gaze to Michael. He was sweating profusely and shaking with hauntingly stunted movements. "All I care about is him now," she nodded to Michael and moved to his side.
"There's nothing we can do," Diego tried to make the tone of his voice reassuring it was to no avail as Trance sank to her knees, resting her head on the cold slab. "If he can't fight this off himself then I'm afraid we will have to put him to rest ourselves," he rested one hand on her arm and the other on Michael's forehead, the action apparently soothing him slightly. "That's our only option."
"No," replied Trance quickly, raising her head, "there has to be a way..." She looked around in a daze as though something would reveal itself to her. Abruptly stopping, she fixed her eyes on a pair of faint scars upon her wrist. "There *is* another chance," she got

The Schism

back to her feet, running her hand along Michael's arm and looked to Richard softly, "but you will have to allow it... and there's no guarantee."

Diego narrowed his eyes at Trance then in an instant of stark realisation grabbed her arm and pulled her around to him. "No!" Diego snapped, "I cannot allow what you are contemplating," he stared at her hard and raised his top lip slightly to give just a glimpse of his fangs. "Do you realise how dangerous it is? Not to mention we have never taken anyone against their will!"

"He's dying, father. Soon all that he is will be gone and he will become one of them, the very creatures we fight against. What will be lost from trying?" she stared back at Diego, gazing deep into his vibrantly green eyes until he turned away, unable to bear his child's gaze any longer. "Was it so different with me?"

"What exactly are we talking about?" interrupted Richard, getting to his feet again with more ease this time. "What do I have to allow?"

Diego took a solemn breath and looked to Trance one more time before stepping forward. "It is the Schism...The rarest and most dangerous form of The Schimba," he finished only to silent, bewildered faces.

"It means The Turning in our old tongue," came Trance's voice as she turned back to the waiting faces. "The Schimba Schism is when one has been taken by The Horde but is then given the breath of our own cult. The separate strains then war inside the infected body until one becomes dominant. Only then will we know which was stronger and where their allegiance lies...Few have been saved in this way. Their will must be strong and true..." she lowered her head slightly and thought for a second before raising it again. "Like me."

"No," snapped Diego, turning to her again only to be ushered back by a raised hand.

"It's alright, they should know. It's the least they deserve." Trance looked to Richard and then to Michael, still convulsing gently on the slab. "A very long time ago, when I was a child, I lived on a farm not far from here. One night one of the rogue Horde attacked us..." she stopped and shook her head, the memory far more difficult to relive than she had expected. "I was...too young for that..."

"I had been tracking it for days," Diego continued, placing a reassuring arm around Trance, "but when I arrived, I found her parents being fed upon by the beast. When I finally slew the creature I discovered a child, bitten but alive and I had a singular choice. I could end her short life right there or allow it to continue forever." Diego looked over Trance as if she was still that scared child and his eyes crept towards the faint bite mark on her wrist. "In the end I could not bring myself to end the life of one so innocent, even if it was for her own good. I had no idea if she was already too far gone but I had to try," he seemed to lament his actions, the guilt of choosing for her forever with him. "I watched for what seemed like days until she finally awoke as the person you see now. As my daughter."

"I understand if you do not wish this life for him," said Trance, her eyes turning to Richard, red with the vivid memory of that terrible night, "but the alternative..."

"I only ever wanted the best for him," Richard murmured, his voice filled with regret, wishing they had never come to save him. "He had so much life ahead of him...He should have a chance to live it in any way he can," he lightly brushed a hand against the slab and looked Michael up and down. "Do it."

Trance turned to Diego who opened his mouth to speak, his eyes full of conflict but eventually remained silent, giving only a single submissive nod. Glancing mournfully at Michael, Diego started towards the opening; unable to watch his progeny give in to what he considered the same weakness he had all that time ago.

Trance stepped up to Michael again and leaned over him. She placed a hand softly around his face and bowed her head towards his for a few seconds. "Please...let him live," she whispered to herself, continuing to lean in further.

At last, she opened her mouth, unsheathing her long fangs and sank them gently into the undamaged side of Michael's neck. A small trickle of blood spilled from the wounds, running around his throat and dripped silently onto the cushion. After a few seconds

Trace withdrew her fangs, allowing a little more blood to well up from his neck, and raised her head, her mouth-stained red.

"Please," she whispered before finally standing up straight again and turning back to Richard. Try as she might to act as though she was unaffected by her actions, her eyes were distant and her lips trembled, eventually managing to form a few words. "It is done."

The hours crawled evermore into a night that seemed without end and the lair lay eerily silent as the terror continued on the surface above. Richard had returned to his cell to rest and Michael had fallen motionless as Trance and Hollie continued to keep a wordless watch over him.

"He saved my life once," Hollie said suddenly, breaking the silence, "or rather gave it back to me," she added, still not quite understanding how they had brought her back from the dead. "I can see you like him," she continued, failing to gain Trances attention, "maybe more than like-"

"I can't," Trance started abruptly, "even if I did…I just couldn't. I should have never…He was just some dumb mortal I met in a bar," she wrestled with her feelings, trying to convince herself of a lie. "I could never think like that because I am ageless. I would have to watch him grow old and die while I never changed by a day." Trance took a shaky breath, the words she spoke without conviction or belief. "That's all he ever was…Just a mortal."

"But he's not anymore," mused Hollie, "if this works then he will be every bit as ageless as you…He'll be scared. It'll be a whole new life for him. He's going to need you," she threw a hand up and leaned forward meaningfully. "I saw the way he looked at you-" she stopped, feeling she might be pushing her boundaries, especially given what Trance was capable of. "Just think about it, alright?"

Trance kept staring at Michael, unblinking for several long seconds before she thought to respond. "We'll see." She did not turn her head or even flit her eyes, continuing only to stare forward as if entranced. "He's going to attack them, you know," said Trance, abruptly breaking the silence again, only now turning her head to look at Hollie. "My father. He tries to protect me with secrets and half-truths but I know him…Sometimes I think too well," she looked back at Michael sombrely and sighed deeply. "He's going to have us attack The Horde. Not those roaming the streets, no. He's going to attack Costin and Savant, and end what they started centuries ago. Without them The Horde will fall apart."

"Makes sense..." ventured Hollie, unsure where Trance was going.

"My father is blind," growled Trance, digging her fingers into her palms. "He doesn't show it but now I know how personal this is for him. I know he'll want vengeance and I'm scared. I'm scared he'll lead us all to ruin and condemn this world."

Hollie didn't know how to respond. She struggled for words of reassurance but none came. Eventually she conceded and simply spoke her mind. "What if this is the only chance, though? To end it for good so that none of you need be fearful of them ever returning again."

"Time will tell..." Trance responded coldly.

"Time has told," snapped Diego, marching into the cell without notice. "You are right, my child, I am not without the lust for revenge but I still know what is best for our cult. Every Strigoi stands ready to move on our foe but to truly end this Costin needs to die. Without him no more will be reborn. Other than doing it myself there is only one person I would trust with such a task... I just need to know if you are with me?" he was met with silence from Trance who continued to gaze fixedly at Michael. "Please... I do this for you...For all of those who have had to live in fear their entire lives."

Trance slowly looked up. "For us all?" she asked cautiously, turning her eyes to him.

Diego nodded firmly, as if his life relied on it. "It's the only reason I've been able to live in this world for so long."

"Then I have no choice but to stand with you," she stood up and took Diego's arm firmly, shaking it hard, "as I always have."

Diego smiled softly, that guilt of choosing Trance's fate for her eased by his pride in her.

"Thank you," Trance said quietly, partially turning back to Hollie as Diego left the cell. "I can see why you Medians get called guides."

"Go...Do what's right," Hollie looked to Michael who appeared more peaceful than he had for a long time. "I'll stay and keep an eye on him, don't worry."

Trance flashed a brief smile and started quickly from the room, hurrying past Richard's cell without noticing him getting up from his makeshift bed.

"Where do you all think you're going without me?" he growled, limping slightly towards the opening of his chamber.

Trance swiftly came to a halt and looked back at Richard. He had managed to pull his stabbed and bloodied shirt over his wraps but was still struggling to slip a second arm into his jacket. "You can't be up!" she started, pointing a finger at him, "you're in no shape to-"

"Look!" Richard Barked, stepping up to Trance, "if something's going down then I want to be part of it. You know what they did to me..." he tailed off, looking away then barged past her, trying his hardest not to show his limp. "Just remember you're not the only ones with a grudge against these bastards anymore!"

Trance quickly caught up with Richard as the corridor opened out into the auditorium, revealing dozens of vampires, regimentally facing the main entrance where Diego stood proudly atop a large wooden crate.

"It's started," breathed Trance quietly, asking herself if this was really the right thing to do. Should they risk death today for a chance to prevail or was it better to keep running and live only to be hunted down along the line?

"You guys can really get organised when you want..." Richard turned his head and looked calmly at Trance. "I could be scared of you. Your kind tortured me after all..."

Trance snapped her head to him and grimaced at the words.

"...but you *did* save me," Richard bobbed his head back and forth. "Hollie and Michael clearly trust you... who am I to question their judgement?" he looked back to the crowd in front of him and peered over their heads, trying to see just how many there were. "Truth be told, I'm damn glad you're the good guys cos..." he sucked in his breath and shook his head, "I really wouldn't want to get on your bad side."

Trance thought for a second on what Richard had said. How after being tortured, defiled and finding himself in a bizarre place surrounded by those who looked like the ones who had hurt him, he was still willing to trust. "Maybe some things *are* worth dying for..." she sighed gently and placed a hand on Richard's arm and peered through the crowd.

"Friends!" came a harsh voice from the front of the crowd, "this is an historic night! For centuries we have lived in fear of the time when The Horde would return. When they would hunt humans like animals and seek to eradicate us... As you already know, this time is now upon us." Diego looked across his gathered kin as they muttered to each other. "By the end of this night, by the rise of the new sun, only one will remain...If we are to die and the light of our kind extinguished forever then I say we should give them hell first."

Diego's words were growled, almost primal in their tone, riling up those gathered below him causing the mass of bodies to writhe restlessly. Gradually their murmurs grew louder into cries and cheers of support.

"Who is with me!?" Diego finally screamed at the top of his lungs making the chamber roar with the fury of a thousand generations, each pledging their allegiance solely to Diego's cause.

With what weapons they had raised high in the air, the children of Dragoș charged out into the night, anxious to fight the oncoming enemy. As the lair cleared, Diego laid eyes on Trance and Richard still stood at the back. Trance bowed gently and reached into a concealed holster on her back, pulling from it a razor-edged dagger, punching it into the air.

Glancing at what Trance had done and feeling he should accommodate them in some way, Richard took as much of a bow as he could, keeping his eyes locked on Diego the entire time. "I'm going to get my gun back, right?"

With a slick, almost imperceptible motion, Trance swung her blade around and returned it to its holster then much more carefully pulled the pistol from her jeans and whipped it around, offering the grip to Richard.

He inspected the weapon and straightened up with a stifled groan. At last, taking hold of his gun, he flicked open the chamber to find it filled with silver bullets. Looking back up at Trance as she raised her eyebrows, he slowly clicked the chamber back into place and couldn't help but allow a grin to creep onto his face.

II-VI – Obsidian

For they have sown the wind, and they shall reap the whirlwind

-Hosea 8:7

Like the night pressing ever onwards towards the dawn, The Horde closed in on its prey. They were unrelenting in their dissection of mankind's empire and yet it paled in their search for the Cult of Dragos. Above the city, the clouded sky was tainted by an eerie orange hue from the fires raging below, the air thick with searing ash.

Tentatively stepping across the soot laden tarmac of the inner city, Richard could hear the distant screams of The Horde and their victims ringing out through the glowing night. Diego had sent his soldiers all over the city in an attempt to quell The Horde in any way they could but it didn't help the thought of what people were going through out there. Richard tried to focus, putting the screams out of his mind but couldn't help but be taken back to the times his aunt would proselytise to him, the night seeming to him not unlike the depictions of hell she would obsessively go on about.

"Isn't there anything we can do for them?" asked Trance, haunted by the never-ending sound of suffering.

"We are doing something," replied Diego, waving away the two vampires accompanying him, "the only thing we *can* do..."

The two guards shuffled up behind a wall and peered around it carefully, quickly falling back against it as they signalled that they had seen something. Immediately Diego, Trance and Richard dropped to the ground.

"Let me take a look," whispered Diego, pushing himself into a crouch and slowly venturing out into the open.

Hiding behind any cover he could find, he eventually came to a concrete crash barrier and glanced around it at a single minion tearing at the flesh of a dead body. He checked all around to make sure the creature was alone then silently vaulted over the barrier and slowly moved up behind it. When he was close enough, he quietly drew his silver short sword and grabbed the minion around the neck, making it thrash at him. Before it could make too much of a sound Diego brought the blade against its throat and carved a deep, gushing swath across it.

Once its struggling ceased, Diego allowed the body to tumble to the ground, its deep red blood spilling out across the soft, grey ash. He looked at the fallen, a scowl of disgust rippling across his face, and raised the dripping blade up, wiping along its length with a cloth hanging from his belt. Turning away from the minion, Diego began to signal the rest but as they started to move, he was jerked forward by a crossbow bolt catching him in the shoulder, making him topple to the ground in a cloud of dust.

"Down!" cried Richard, falling against the crash barrier with a laboured groan.

Trance shuffled up to the barrier, frantically waving for the guards to stay back. "Diego! Can you hear me?" She sank low to the ground and tried to catch a glimpse of him. "What happened?"

There was a flurry of ash as Diego tried to claw his way back to Trance. "He's here..." he gasped, his rasped breathing fast and shallow. "I can feel him..."

Sitting upright against the barrier, Trance looked wildly about as if she were being stalked. "This is bad," she said quickly, her tone betraying just how panicked she was.

"Worse than you know," echoed a voice loudly around the buildings. "You should have run...at least then I would have something to hunt." The voice seemed to shift around, refusing to remain in any one place long enough to identify. "I wouldn't worry about your sentries either..."

Just as the words came there were a pair of muted chokes and Diego's guards fell into the open, their hearts having been speared through.

"Savant!" screamed Diego at the bare walls, clutching at the arrowhead through his chest. "Show yourself!"

"As you wish." Savant's voice lowered to barely a whisper which echoed incessantly around the walls. Almost on cue with his voice fading from the air, a cloud of ash was kicked up next to the fallen minion as though someone had landed next to it. "I don't appreciate you killing my brethren, old friend... That is now what they are to me, after all," Savant took a hissed breath and almost chuckled. "But still, Diego, this is too easy. I would have expected far more of you."

At last, the dust began to settle, unveiling Savant's full shape, his grey, leathery skin streaked with the blood of any who had encountered him. Slowly he stepped towards Diego, prompting him to wave his blade wildly while trying to get to his feet.

"You don't need to do this!" Diego shouted, backing across the street. "You still have a choice," he pleaded quietly.

"But you don't seem to understand," Savant bent down to inspect the half-eaten corpse, running his long, talon-like fingers along it, "I *want* to do this." He stabbed the bladelike digits through the body and tore a chunk of flesh from its bones, savouring the viscera as though it were some delicacy.

Diego stumbled to maintain his gait and raised his wavering sword again with Trance and Richard watching on, powerless to help him.

"Be mindful of your actions," Savant growled, unceremoniously dumping the butchered flesh to the ground. "Clearly I am not dull witted enough to face you alone," he eyed the bolt through Diego's shoulder then gazed absently around the buildings.

Diego grimaced and grit his teeth, taking hold of the crossbow bolt and breaking it in half, tearing the remaining stump from his body with barely a groan. "You leave me no choice," he stated simply and took a sure footing, directing his blade steadily at Savant.

Before Savant could acknowledge what was going on, Diego was already leaping towards him, the silver blade cleanly cutting through the air, slicing the haze of ash as though it were silk, and finally striking Savant in the chest. Diego drove the sword deep into

Savant's sternum, piercing his tough hide and plunging it deep into the cavity beyond.

Roaring out in pain, Savant was forced to the ground, almost pinned to the tarmac by the ferocity of the attack and for a moment Diego watched his fallen friend with a despairing triumph. It wasn't that he had neglected to acknowledge the snipers no doubt lining their shots up on him, but merely did not care for only now had it truly dawned on him what they had been subjected to in the void.

"For god's sake, get down!" shouted Richard, manically waving at Diego as another crossbow bolt whistled through the air, just barely missing his head.

Jerked from this daze, Diego scrambled behind the crash barrier, ducking in tightly as bolts occasionally ricocheted off the other side.

"There's only one of them," stated Trance confidently.

"You sure?" asked Richard, receiving a firm nod in response.

Diego grinned and absently clutched his shoulder. "We can deal with that."

The thuds of bolts striking the barrier suddenly stopped with the clatter of one last arrow falling to the ground.

"Think he's out?" Richard wondered, considering if to take a look over the street.

Diego was about to speak again but was stopped by a strained growl from just beyond their cover. "Shit," he mouthed quietly, shaking his head.

Still laying where Diego had struck him down, Savant shifted as if trying to regain control over his limbs. His razor-sharp teeth gritted in agony while he slowly pushed himself up and back to his feet. Snarling at the empty street, he reached for the sword still protruding from his chest and began to pull it free, screaming out a harrowing cry as the blade was slowly ripped away, having just barely missed his heart.

"You'll have to do better than that, Diego!" Savant tossed the sword to the ground with a clang and spread his arms wide, turning his gaze to the sky and letting out another howl, this one much more primal. The scream was quickly joined by any number of other, more distant responses and Savant grinned menacingly, bathing in the cacophony.

"You need to go," whispered Diego urgently, pulling a dagger from beneath his once lavish coat, "I'll take care of him."

"What?" Trance almost shouted the word, nearly giving them away. "We're not leaving you here! We fight together!"

Diego grimaced again at her. "They're coming and someone still needs to finish this, even if I can't," he pointed firmly at the way they had come. "You run and you don't stop, alright?" he did not wait for agreement, instead turning straight to Richard. "Look after her..." he looked him up and down, almost forgetting about what he had been through, "and yourself. I want to see her safe when I get away from here."

"We'll be alright," Richard assured him, gently pulling at Trance's reluctant shoulder.

Diego nodded and looked into his daughter's eyes one more time then, in a single motion, got to his feet and strutted into the middle of the street. "We are not finished here, Savant!"

Trance felt her heart leap as she watched him through the falling ash but had no time to process what was going on as she was pulled up by Richard. He forced her to run as fast as she could while crossbow bolts began to rain down on them again, whistling past their heads until they managed to duck away into the night.

Savant abruptly raised his arm, preventing the sniper from turning their attention to Diego and turned around slowly. "Not fleeing like your coward of a child, I see..." Savant smirked slightly, an expression not meant for a face such as his. "That's the Diego I know."

"Let her go," Diego demanded firmly, watching several figures moving in the smoky haze behind Savant. "You don't need to go after them."

"No..." Savant inspected the wound in his chest, running a talon across the bloody lesion, "*I* don't," he flicked a finger to the waiting minions behind him, prompting them to move up to his side. "Find them..." he commanded with a gravelly, haunting tone, "bring me the daughters head."

Diego stepped forward, raising his dagger but was stopped by the flurry of minions racing past him. As quick as they had descended on him, they were gone and even though they could have torn him apart, Diego had remained unharmed. Quickly regaining his focus, Diego flicked his dagger back towards Savant who alone remained in the gently falling ash.

"You sick bastard," Diego forced the words between gritted teeth. "Is this some kind of game to you?"

Savant grinned. "Why shouldn't it be? Why shouldn't we be free to indulge ourselves after an eternity of imprisonment?"

"I know how that place changed you, twisted your mind..." Diego shook his head. "Once we fought side by side as friends.... as brothers..."

"And I was weak then," Savant spat, staring down at Diego with the void filling his eyes. "That place showed me the truth...about everything. It taught me that life is nothing but the respite of the vile and the wretched," he stepped closer and swung his claws through the air. "I have seen the Other Side and it is nothing but a warped, infested abyss! Our true domain must be staged here! We must cleanse this world and give only those who are worthy eternal existence."

"The Abyss is not the afterlife, Savant! It's a crack in existence, the space between planes, nothing more. The Horde were imprisoned there to stop them bringing the same destruction they wreak now!"

"Enough!" Savant screamed, stepping forward and barely stopping himself tearing Diego's head off. "You speak of us as though we are not one in the same...I *am* The Horde and nothing you can say will change that," he began circling around Diego, slowly waving his talons through the air, choosing the right opportunity to strike. "We will complete what was started all that time ago...The destruction of you and your pathetic cult."

Savant clenched his fist and leapt forward towards Diego, throwing his arm forward in an effort to stab Diego clean through the chest but was deflected and thrown to the side. Without a breath he again sprang towards Diego, this time slicing a deep wound across his side, and shredding his long coat. Managing to parry him away before he could do any more, Diego quickly turned, his blade cutting smoothly through the air, and caught Savant as he moved away, gouging a gash across his arm making him recoil in pain.

The Dark

Clutching the gushing wound, Savant grimaced at Diego who stood resolute, trying not to betray how hurt he really was. As if fuelled by the blow he had suffered, Savant dove forward once more, both arms outstretched, seemingly a primal assault rather than a calculated strike. Just as Savant's claws were about to drive into Diego's skull, he ducked and rolled out of the way, scooping his sword from the ground as he went. In one quick motion Diego brought his blade up firmly, cleanly slicing through the tough hide of Savants lower arm, breaking the bone in half and finally severing the limb entirely. Swiftly raising the blade back up, Diego drew an arc of thick red blood through the falling ash and sliced back down again, slashing a deep cut along Savant's back.

"I don't want to do this," screamed Diego, turning back to Savant crouched on the ground cradling what was left of his arm, grinding his teeth in the agony, "call them back and I will spare you."

Savant breathed heavily, cursing under his breath at how quickly things had turned against him then abruptly fell silent. He looked up meaningfully at Diego without showing any hint of pain. "Never!"

Savant stood to his full height and started once more towards Diego, swiping at him with his single remaining claw. The attack was easily deflected, however, and Diego again plunged the blade deep into Savant's chest, this time impaling him squarely through the heart.

"I'm sorry," whispered Diego at last as Savant came to a sudden halt upon his blade and grasped limply at its hilt. Eventually he ripped the sword away and let his defeated foe fall lifelessly to the ground. After a few seconds he kissed his half-clenched fist and offered it forward to the heaped body. "You have my respect for you did not ask for this. I fear who you truly were died long ago..." he returned his blade to its scabbard and bowed his head. "Rest in peace, old friend." Diego briefly reached for his wounds in pain and glanced around, awaiting the sniper's attack but none came. Diego concluded it must have joined the rest of the rabble, assuming that Savant would prevail. Finally, he took a deep breath and started off, praying he could catch up with the others before The Horde did.

"I never thought I'd come back to this place," Richard mused quietly as they approached the decaying old workhouse, "especially not by choice..." He looked distractedly around, and realised that the city had suddenly fallen into a strange veil of silence, only broken by the crackle of distant flames and the soft whistle of the ash filled breeze.

"You don't have to do this," Trance reassured softly, "you can still go back," she turned and nodded into the night, the prospect of travelling back to the hideout unappealing but far better than the alternative.

"No," he stated firmly, shaking his head as if to jostle the idea loose, "I have to do this...Besides, what kind of person would I be if I let you go alone?"

"Smart?" Trance chuckled and sidled up to a pair of wooden cellar doors hidden at the base of the workhouses' imposing walls. She looked around quickly then heaved open the doors with a laboured creak. "Last chance..."

Richard glanced at Trance, for a moment considering the option but quickly stepped down onto the cold, worn steps into the murky cellar. Behind him the trapdoor was allowed to close with a heavy bang leaving them in a thick, muggy blackness. Along the corridor there was a faint scuffling, almost inaudible against the sound of their own breath.

"This was too easy," Richard murmured, lingering just long enough for Trance to catch up with him. "Where are they? You'd think after you broke in here to get me they'd be more alert."

"Most of them are out wreaking havoc," Trance lamented, peering uneasily into the gloom, "they probably didn't think we'd come right to them again."

"Maybe it's a trap," Richard considered bluntly. "How *did* you know the way in here?"

Trance stopped and scowled at Richard's outline. "You think we haven't done the legwork? Hunted down century old schematics, mapped out every inch of this place?"

"Just a thought," Richard ended simply, unable to shed his pangs of doubt.

The Dark

Beginning to walk down the dark, tight corridor again, the scuffling grew louder until it sounded as though it was right in front of them. Stretching out a hand across him, Trance stopped Richard in mid step and pulled a lighter from her pocket, sparking it alight and casting a dull orange glow across the corridors haze. Slowly she lowered it to the ground and then back up, eventually catching the shadow of something shaking on the ground. She approached cautiously and lowered the flame again, stretching it out across the dank stone floor and revealing a minion of The Horde. It convulsed helplessly on the ground, its dark grey skin prickled and shivering.

"Diego..." said Trance quietly, staring at the creature and beginning to wonder why she had ever been so scared of such a fragile being, "he must have slain Savant and severed his control over the newborns. Without his command they are without purpose." She withdrew the silver blade from her hidden holster and quickly lunged it forward into the minion's chest, making it shudder one more time before limply collapsing. "Rest now. Once you were like us and maybe now you can be free once again." Trance spoke a few more words of blessing under her breath while slowly removing the blade and stood up again. "We have to use this to our advantage," she started, her words spoken with purpose. "The Horde are disorientated but they won't stay that way for long. Either they'll go feral or Costin will summon another overlord to take control of them," she paced back and forth, wrestling with the wretched choice. "Between the two," she started again, stopping abruptly, "I'd rather those things not have a leader."

Richard nodded gently, inspecting the corpse in front of them. "We need to get to Costin."

"We need to *kill* Costin," Trance corrected, quickly taking to her heels again and running off along the corridor.

Following her as quickly as his battered body would allow, Richard eventually caught up with Trance as she struggled to prise open the rusted lock of a heavy metal door.

"Are you sure this is it?"

"How could it not be?" Trance grunted back, forcing the lock open and allowing the door to swing ajar. "Trust me, he's here."

Trance pressed the door open and stepped into a long dark room lined with metal tables, stretching on as far as the gloom allowed them to see. Beside each one were counters each containing an assortment of blood filled vials and implements like the one which had been used on Richard. Along with them were an array of items which would not have gone amiss in Lancer's possession.

With Trance continuing to tread carefully onwards, Richard finally ventured into the room, the unsettling sense falling over him that danger may not be as far away as he would have hoped. He drifted over to one of the tables and out of a pure morbid curiosity began inspecting the devices which had brought him so much pain. Without warning, the large metal door slammed loudly shut, making Richard start back towards it.

"Leave it," Trance barked shortly, "it's only forwards from now on." She continued on between the tables and with each step felt ever more that they were being watched.

"I didn't think I'd be seeing you so soon, my friend," Costin's voice echoed hauntingly around the room, its source hidden in shadow. "I know what fate befell Savant...Such a shame," a raspy laugh choked around the walls for a second then abruptly ceased. "No matter...Where one falls, others shall rise."

"I'll be damned if you're getting your hands on me again, you bastard!" shouted Richard to the heavy air, his teeth grinding with a seething hatred for what they had done to him.

"Who said I need to?" Costin replied calmly, his voice shifting to the far end of the room, prompting Trance to swing around towards it. "I already have what I need from you."

Trance waved towards Richard, pointing out where the voice was coming from and started to silently run towards the far wall, partially hidden in the dusty blackness.

"Therefore, you no longer serve a purpose," Costin continued unperturbed by Trance's advance, "but I can hardly have you roaming around this place."

Just as Trance reached the end of the room, a door was swung open and three of Costin's men jumped through. They were not minions but rather each of them looked to have once been part of

Diego's own cult, only they had been just as twisted by The Abyss as Costin.

"This is goodbye I'm afraid," Costin's voice trailed off as he moved off again, leaving his men to finish the job.

Trance breathed heavily, grimacing at her new adversaries and reached for her pistol. "We really don't have time for this," she stated quickly, whipping the weapon out and firing off two shots as the closest henchman flew towards her.

Catching a bullet in his side, the first of Costin's men fell to the ground, grasping at his wound in pain while Trance quickly ducked back to dodge another attack, narrowly avoiding being caught across the throat.

Reaching for his own pistol, Richard drew it directly at the head of the second henchman and pulled the trigger without hesitation. Before he could recover for another attempt at Trance the force of the bullet shattered his skull, leaving his body to slump to the ground.

Following through on the momentum of her dodge, Trance swung back, drawing her sword on the final henchman and impaled him through the heart. Before she could withdraw the blade, the first she had wounded started forward, barging her to the side and knocking the weapon from Richard's hand as he tried to raise it. Quickly overpowering him, the last of Costin's men bore down on Richard, its teeth primed to bite, but instead of blood, all it tasted was another bullet, this time to the back of the head, sending it back to the ground again, this time permanently.

Richard turned quickly, unable to fathom how fast everything had happened, catching sight of Trance, arm outstretched clutching a slightly smoking pistol. Casually she let her other arm slowly fall, allowing the second vampire to slide from her blade, tumbling uncomfortably to the ground.

"I told you we didn't have time for this," she said simply, brushing some loose hair from her face with her bloodied sword hand before moving towards the far doorway.

"Wait..." Richard said shortly, starting forward and grabbing Trance's shoulder, much to her distaste. "That weapon," he said softly, reaching for the pistol only for it to be quickly pulled away. "There's only one type of weapon that has those markings."

Trance raised the pistol up again and looked to the set of stark engravings, painstakingly etched along the barrel. They were written partially in an ancient, indecipherable language mixed with lavish pictograms.

"That's a Median's weapon," Richard stated firmly at last, "how did you get it?"

She paused for a few seconds, trying to decide if she should tell him the truth but quickly concluded that she was hardly in a position to beat around the bush if they were ever going to catch Costin. "Michael," she breathed gently, turning her head away. "Before we came to get you, he gave me his to use," she glanced back at Richard, unsure if to say anything more. "He didn't want me to use yours..." she ventured at last. "Out of respect."

"Michael," repeated Richard, considering him in possession of such a thing and slowly realising what he had become. All of those years looking after him, he had never realised that the son he had never had was now his own man. Grown up and capable of anything he put his mind to. "I suppose he had to one day... Lancer must have thought he was ready... I just never thought it would happen like this."

Trance looked at the pistol and slowly offered it to Richard who looked down at it for a second only to press it back to her.

"It's not my place. If he entrusted it to you then..." he looked sideways at Trance and smiled gently. "He's as much yours as he is his own now."

Trance nodded and smiled back, taking another moment to think of Michael and what had happened to him, almost oblivious to the task at hand. Before Richard had the chance to usher her on, however, she suddenly turned and rushed through the opening as if nothing had happened.

Beyond the doorway lay a more squared off room, a gantry running around the upper level and the roof lined with skylights arranged into a pyramid which stabbed into the night. Unlike the others dotted around the building which had been blacked out, these were completely clear. They allowed the bright light of a full moon to spill into the chamber, cutting through a thick smoke that hung in the air.

"I fail to understand the reasoning behind your continued survival," growled Costin, appearing at the edge of the gantry ahead of Richard and Trance. "I must admit this turn of events does aggravate me..." he continued, showing more emotion than they had seen from him before, "but I am not defeated yet-"

There was a metallic clang from the corner of the gantry and slow clinking footsteps across it as a figure appeared from the shadows. "You are wrong, old friend," the moon's light drifted across the figure as it moved across the walkway, slowly creeping across his face. "Give it up Costin, your puppet's dead and your minions are useless now," Diego stopped, his outline bathed in moonlight and looked to Costin, earnest and exhausted. "Face it. It's over."

"Is that what you think of me, *old friend*? That I would resign myself to failure at your whim?" He slowly reached behind his back and started to withdraw a large syringe containing a vial of blood. Richard's blood. "You should have destroyed them all while you had the chance..." Costin gazed at the syringe, a remorse in his eyes. "His time had not yet come... but you leave me no choice," he raised the syringe up high in front of him and turned it to inject himself. "I shall be reborn more powerful than you can possibly imagine."

"Enough with the clichés, Costin!" screamed Richard, losing all patience with his theatrics, "It's done, you've lost!"

"Don't do this!" Diego started forward again but immediately came to an abrupt stop, fearing Costin would do something stupid. "We can help you..."

"I'm beyond help," Costin replied calmly, a hint of fear in his voice, before plunging the syringe deep into his own heart.

He gritted his teeth and ripped the empty vial from his chest, throwing it to the ground. For a few seconds he stood, breathing heavily, as Diego slowly approached him. Suddenly he took a ragged breath in and convulsed forward, falling onto the gantry rail. For a time, he lay limply over the metal bar before he started shaking violently making Diego step back quickly.

Glimpsed between his thrashing limbs Diego could see Costin's skin begin to crack with small tendrils whipping from the new wounds and diving back into his body. Costin's arms stretched out and bent backwards as the forearms snapped into a second elbow.

Pushing himself back to his feet, what had once been Costin let out a haunting scream and turned to Diego. His face had cracked open, having swollen on one side into a bulbous red growth. Tendrils pierced through his abdomen, feeling out into the world like new limbs.

His gaze abruptly snapped down to Richard and Trance and his bisected jaw quivered at them, blood trickling down the side of it. Finally, he looked down at himself, stretching out his duel jointed arms and screamed again, this time more out of distress than pain.

"I wasn't expecting this," mouthed Trance quietly as she backed away from the creature above them.

"I don't think anyone was." Richard wanted to back away as well but something stopped him. He wasn't sure if it was some morbid curiosity that kept him there or a kind of twisted satisfaction to see this happen to the one who had caused him so much pain.

"Why?" the creature gargled, turning once again to Diego, "what is this form?" As it tried to claw its way to Diego, a fissure ruptured on its back into another bulbous growth.

"I know what you are," Diego replied, moving away from its grasp. "It didn't work. There wasn't enough power to draw you through...Your true form... had it become so twisted there that this world now rejects it completely?" he stopped moving back and looked down at the abomination. "Look at you...What you are now, just because of their corruption...You no longer deserve your true name," he lent down to the creature which salivated through the grating of the gantry. "Dracul!" he growled.

Dracul pressed itself up and looked at Diego through bloodshot eyes. "I know you...You were there. You condemned us!" it tried to swipe at Diego and instead fell under its own bulk, barely managing to catch itself again. The creature tried to laugh but ended up coughing harshly. "I may be weak now but my power will grow. I shall pull myself from that Abyss and return to this, the world of our ancestors."

"I don't think so," Diego said casually, pulling his sword from its scabbard and pointing it at Dracul's deformed head.

Suddenly Dracul struck forward again, this time catching Diego's leg and gripping it tightly. "I feel them...They are with me," he said with a heavy whisper as howls went up from all over the city, The Horde pledging allegiance to their new master.

"Shit!" Trance quickly turned and pointed her pistol towards the door. "Just kill him already!"

Diego inspected the wretched form in front of him and raised his sword, ready to put it out of its misery. Just as he began to strike, a window above shattered, showering Diego with shards of glass followed by a Minion falling through one of the skylights, catching him as it fell past the gantry and pulling him over the railing. As he impacted the ground Diego rolled and stepped back up to his feet, slashing across the Minion, cleanly severing its head as he turned to instantly look back up to Dracul.

At that point the rest of Dracul's Horde smashed through the skylights and poured into the room, gunshots from Trance and Richard lighting up the dingy space. No matter how many rounds were fired, ever more flooded in until all their ammunition was spent. Slowly the Minions closed in on the three of them, surrounding them, savouring the moment before the kill. Before they had the chance to strike, Dracul painfully pushed himself to his feet, stopping The Horde in their tracks eagerly awaiting his direction.

A minute or two passed, a lifetime to those hemmed in by The Horde, until Dracul began to chortle with a sickly, deranged rasp. "I feel a new presence among us," he said finally, beginning to regain strength for each second he remained in the living realm. "It is strong...But tainted by the touch of Dragoş," he raised his head to the air and sniffed as if he were trying to seek this one out. "Come to me, my new child. Come and join our blessed coven..."

As Dracul spoke, The Horde closest to the doorway started to part and a silhouette stepped calmly between them.

"Michael!" breathed Trance in disbelief.

"No!" screamed Richard trying to run towards him only to be held back by Diego.

"Don't Richard. He's one of them now..." Diego held Richard tightly and looked solemnly to Michael. "There's nothing we can do."

Dracul laughed hauntingly again. "Yes...He belongs to me now... You have failed, all of you," he fixed his attention on Michael. "Who do you serve?"

Michael glanced around at the distressed faces of his friends and then around at the terrible mass of The Horde. Finally, he fixed his gaze on Dracul. "I serve you, my master. My pleasure to be of The Horde."

"Now..." started Dracul again, "kill them"

Michael nodded in compliance and walked towards Richard, grabbing him firmly around the throat.

Richard looked into Michael's pale, vampiric eyes at first in fear, not for himself but for what Michael had become. Then he saw something, something he recognised.

"You were right when you said this wouldn't be easy," Michael whispered, making Trance and Diego turn to him in shock. "Thanks for everything."

Michael released his grip and leapt up to the gantry, pulling the silver tipped stake from the back of his jacket as he went. Landing directly on Dracul and knocking him over, Michael stabbed the stake forward as hard as he could and pressed it hard into Dracul's heart, making him scream out in agony. At the same moment The Horde below screamed along with him and started to flee in any way they could as if to get away from Dracul's cries.

"You have broken the bond," Dracul managed between his groans, "but it will take more to kill me then a stake to the heart," he pushed against the stake, pressing it deeper as he leaned towards Michael. "I am pure in my origin and span across the realms of existence."

"But your host doesn't," stated Michael flatly.

Dracul breathed deeply in one last time and faded away, his spirit falling back into the abyss, relinquishing the body back to Costin. For a few moments he raggedly sucked in breath, his lungs filled more with blood than air. Eventually he spoke two single words before allowing himself to let go of life.

"Michael..." said Richard as he jumped down from Costin's deformed corpse, "that was one hell of a bluff...Is Hollie ok?"

"She's fine," Michael answered absently, looking at his hands, red with blood. "She's safe in the lair."

The Dark

Diego slapped a hand firmly on Michael's shoulder and smiled widely. "What you have done... You can't begin to understand what this means for us."

"He said something," Michael started weakly, trying to avoid Diego's eyes. "He said he was... sorry."

Diego nodded his head knowingly. "He is finally at peace now. Dracul had haunted him for so long but now he's free and Dracul is back in the Abyss... hopefully for good this time."

"What about those things running about out there?" asked Richard, throwing his thumb vaguely towards the door. "You know, completely out of control?"

"We'll take care of them, don't worry," answered Trance quickly. "Now that their leaders are gone, we shouldn't have any trouble finishing off the stragglers."

"What about anyone they hurt in the meantime?"

"Well then there's no time to waste, is there?" Diego prompted with Trance giving an affirming nod before starting towards the doorway with him.

"Michael?" said Trance, turning back.

Michael raised a hand and lowered his head. "Just...Give me a minute."

Trances' eyes flicked to Richard and she stifled a gasp of realisation then, without another word, followed Diego out of the chamber.

"...This," Michael started after a hesitant pause. "I never could have imagined this...Hollie told me you had to make a choice but..." he searched for the words but wasn't sure how to proceed. "This is too much. I'm immortal now, aren't I?... I'm supposed to live off of blood? And never see the sun again?" he sighed hard and went to carry on but couldn't.

"You can make a difference like this as well...I'm pretty sure you're the first Median Vampire..." Richard placed a hand on Michael's arm and squeezed gently. "You'll be ok. This Trance of yours, she'll look after you."

"I...I can't come back, you know. I know I have to stay with them...I guess they're my kind now... They-" Michael was cut off by

Richard moving his hand over his shoulder and pulling him in, hugging him tightly.

"You'll always be like a son to me... And no matter what I will always be here for you." Richard tightened his grip and, terrified of what was to come, Michael embraced him back, cherishing the moment for as long as he could.

I never wanted this.

It was a mistake that saved my life and now I have to get used to this whole new world I live in. Richard went back to his old life chasing lost souls only with a new appreciation for the things he should hold dear. He has Hollie now, someone to guide him through the trying times like I never could. As for me, blood is an acquired taste and I sometimes wonder if the abattoir gets curious where all the pig blood goes. But Richard was right, I can *make a difference like this. Our kind has as much right to be on this Earth as any other animal and hopefully I can help to rebuild a culture that was lost when The Horde first washed across the land. I'm still scared, still the outsider to a lot of kin but, like Richard said, I have Trance to watch my back...*

A dark figure darted along an alleyway followed high above by two cloaked figures, silhouetted on the rooftops against the clear and starry night. The figure below stopped and set down, thinking it had lost its pursuers.

"How many is this one then?" asked Trance, leaning over the guttering, watching the unaware Minion below.

"Sixth one this week already," replied Michael looking across to her, smiling gently. "I'm not sure if I'm ever going to get used to these teeth," he said, reaching for the new set of fangs growing under his top lip, "they don't exactly suit me."

"I dunno," Trance said playfully, "they're growing on me," she smiled brightly at him and tilted her head. "I'm glad you're with us now, Michael...I'm glad you're with me..." she added coyly.

Michael smiled back. "There's no one I'd rather be doing this with..." he looked down again at the oblivious Minion. "Ok, let's finish this," he stated at last, turning to Trance before they both

The Dark

jumped from the roof, their coats trailing behind them like a swarm of bats, into what they hoped to be a brighter future.

Dawn

Book 3
Illumination

Prologue – Dawn

(...) they took usury, though they were forbidden; and that they devoured men's substance wrongfully

-An-Nisaa 4:161

The fires continued to rage below and the screams of a dying caste rang out across the city. Patches of sky cracked open to reveal the bright glow of a full moon piercing through the orange, smoke filled clouds. High above the turmoil of the streets, a stern silhouette stood out against the night. Behind him a tall steeple reached into the sky, harbouring a secret that would go unnoticed in the chaos of the hell below.

The clouds continued to shift, scattering broken beams across the figure picking out parts of his features and attire. He wore a long white gown, trimmed with delicate gold edges and a cowl that hid the majority of his white hair. Beneath it his face was wrinkled and blemished, beyond an age his stature would suggest. Only the array of liver spots truly betrayed the truth of his age but even these seemed misplaced against his distinct, self-assured voice.

"Can you see them?" he asked, as another white robed figure stepped up behind him. "Their forms inhabit this world but their shadows roam the next..."

"Such a creature," the second man started, elderly but still younger than the first, "it would pollute the sacred gulf-"

"The Median World is no longer our concern..." for the first time his demeanour wavered but was swiftly composed. "Not since they abandoned us," he took a deep breath and looked down at the fiery haze below. "What news have you?"

"The connection, my lord, has been lost...the creature no longer adheres to our methods," he bowed slightly, fearing that his superior would be displeased.

"The bond is broken," he replied calmly, "their master has been slain and they are now not but mindless beasts," he thought for a second and turned around slowly. "Fear not, we have what we desire. The Abyss has spoken of the one who would lead our destiny, show us our true calling...For too long we have existed in the shadow of our lesser brethren but now we shall rise above them...And it will be glorious..."

"Indeed, Sire..." the subordinate stepped forward eagerly, "when would you have us make our move?"

"Patience..." the old man snapped quickly. "It is patience which is our greatest virtue. The Abyss is an existence of considerable extent. Within its grasp lies all of time and we must be wise to heed times will. For now, we must remain aside from its flow until what we have foreseen comes to pass...For that is how we exist and how we have existed for millennia," he placed an old hand on the younger man's shoulder, the long arm of his robe hanging loosely as he did. "Our time shall come, rest assured," he withdrew his hand and turned back to the open night.

"And what of the creature?" the second man asked as its cries grew louder from within the steeple.

The old man turned his head down slightly and sighed harshly. "It is no longer of any use to us...Kill it."

The old man returned to watching the clouds parting across the deep blue, moon filled sky, the deathly cries raging on behind him until suddenly they were cut short, replaced by an empty, cold silence.

Illumination

III-I – No more quiet times

(...) did they feel secure against its coming in broad daylight (...)?
-Al-A'raf 7:98

*W*ho knew so much could happen in three years...It felt like yesterday that I could have simply ended it and stepped through to The Other Side. It's funny what holds you back from these things. I could see all eternity pass before me but more than anything I saw her. I saw all that she was and what we could be. She was more than the woman I loved, she was my potential and my conscience.

I had made too many mistakes in the past, sabotaged my own life for what I believed to be a greater good. Too many Medians think they can do more by pushing others away, by being unrestrained but really, they are just throwing away everything they could have been.

For now, I was content, I was happy...Normal.

The voices that had been with me all my life had faded to barely a whisper. Sometimes I even managed to fool myself into believing they had never been there at all. It wasn't until I stopped actually seeing them, the unsanctified dead, that I began to realise I was leaving it all behind. What's more was that I didn't even care. After a lifetime of struggle and torment, forever feeling the clawing spirits grasping at one last slither of a life, I felt an absolution which I thought I deserved, a reward for my long service. I would soon come to see that some destinies, however, cannot be avoided, only to be shirked at your own cost... and the ones you love...

No More Quiet Times

Through the warm sunlit haze of the bright spring morning a car pulled up alongside the short railings of the cemetery and sat for a few seconds until the engine was abruptly cut off. The door was carefully opened over the pavement and from it stepped a pair of well-polished shoes. They were the feet of a smartly dressed man adorned in pleated black trousers and a crisp, clean white shirt. He turned and reached back into the car, withdrawing a small bunch of flowers containing no more than four stems.

Softly closing the door behind him, Richard straightened his shirt and momentarily took in the peaceful morning. His trimmed hair was styled neatly and a distinct shade of stubble spread across his face, framing a well-maintained goatee. He took a breath and held it for a second before sighing slowly and starting towards the rusted gate.

Even bathed in bright sunlight, the place had a potent air of foreboding about it, as though it had been forgotten by the living altogether and forsaken by the dead. Richard trod carefully between the cracked and fallen gravestones until he came to one particular plaque embedded in the ground. Kneeling down, he gently placed the small bouquet on the moss-covered slab and bowed his head.

"I'd finally make you proud, dad," Richard uttered softly to the empty, silent yard, "settling down... Normal life and all that...Giving up all of this..." he thought for a second about how his father had spoken of his claims when he was alive, "voodoo. I barely even hear them anymore. It's quiet now, even lonely sometimes, I suppose," he chuckled and sighed again at the thought of what he was prepared to leave behind. "It's just the way it has to be, the way it should have always been...The way it would have made you happy," he raised his head and stood up but couldn't help but look back sombrely at the grave.

"You don't know what I want," a voice said suddenly from behind Richard, making him swing around with a start. "You never used to scare that easily either." He raised a translucent hand to the sun and glanced through it before giving a short humph at how futile the act had been.

"What are you doing here?" Richard asked quickly, sternly stepping forward and pointing a finger accusingly.

Illumination

"Can't a father see his only son?" he asked shortly, receiving only with a fierce grimace "Ok, fine. You need me-" he saw the look of disapproval across Richard's face and raised his own finger as Richards was dropped, "-and before you say anything this isn't a pep talk. I just don't want to see you lose yourself. I still don't get this whole other worldly crap but it's who you are and without it you're just another one of them," he threw his arm back towards the row of houses across the road. "A small person with small dreams, whiling away their life. Please don't be that…"

Richard gritted his teeth and put his hands firmly on his hips. "You've changed your tune! When I was a kid, it was all 'pagan' this and 'occult' that-"

"Look, I was wrong, is that what you want to hear?" Albert breathed and calmed down before carrying on. "I was wrong. Dying can change your perspective on a few things. I didn't understand what you were back then… still don't, really but I know it's important. The point is I was scared and all I wanted to do was help you. I just never realised I was giving you the wrong kind of help," he extended his arm, offering an ethereal hand to Richard, "…the girl. She's like you. You don't need to hide what you are, or try to be normal. Be what you are together."

Richard turned away and shook his head. "It's too late. I've already made my choice. I can feel it fading and, to be honest, I've never been happier. The things I've been through…I still have scars, trust me, but now I have a chance to leave it behind. I can finally have a normal life and be who I was always meant to be."

"*This* is who you were meant to be," Albert tried one final time. "Please, just think about it. Without it you'll lose me," he added quietly as Richard turned back and started walking back through the graveyard towards the street.

Stopping abruptly, Richard glanced around to see his ghostly father stood like a mirage in the middle of the cemetery. "Goodbye, Dad," he said simply and started again towards his car.

Albert sniffed and swallowed hard, raising his head in an effort to fight the fear welling up inside of him.

"Goodbye son." As he spoke a soft mist started to rise up from the ground. It slowly enveloped him and carried him away in the breeze so that he may reside another day in restless undeath.

Arriving back to his large, hallowed home, Richard's thoughts still lingered on what his father had said. He had always made a point to never listen to what his father had to say. Not in life when he had feared and despised his child's gifts and not even now when he had finally accepted what Richard was. Maybe it was because he had been so close minded that it had taken him literally dying to see things differently. Maybe it had only ever been resentment on Richard's part but for whatever reason, this time had been different. Over and over Richard ran the words through his mind, haunting him with their meaning.
"This is who you were meant to be..."
In the past, when he had needed to hear it the most, Richard would have wholeheartedly believed the sentiment yet it was one he never heard. Now he could have done without it, the words resonated with him more than ever, as if calling him back.
Richard had never *wanted* to be a Median, no one ever did, but a part of him had always somehow *needed* to be one. That part of him was silent now so what was it which kept calling to him?
He slowly ascended the steps towards the front door, reaching into his pocket and pulling out his keys loosely, letting them jangle against each other. Stopping mid step, he looked around at Hollie's car parked in the driveway. She didn't need him dwelling on such things, thought Richards, hovering in front of the door. She shouldn't have the needless turmoil of his mind imposed on her.
Richard breathed in deeply and nodded, convincing himself that it shouldn't concern him. What will be will be, he decided and confidently slid the key into the lock, opening the door.
"What did he say?" Hollie quickly asked, waiting at the foot of the stairs, "and don't just say 'nothing.'"
Richard opened his mouth to contest her but knew from far too much experience that it was futile. "Can't I hide anything from you?" he replied at last, swinging the door closed behind him.

"You shouldn't have to," Hollie replied firmly. "I know what you're going through and you shouldn't have to hide it from me." She watched Richard pass her into the lounge, eventually following when he didn't come back out. "You can talk to me, you know that."

Without responding, Richard idly picked out a book from the bookshelf and flicked through it absently before returning it and retrieving another.

"Was I always meant to be this?" Richard asked at last, turning abruptly with the book still open in his hand. "I didn't ask to be a Median and now when I have the chance to leave it behind..." he closed the book and placed it softly on the coffee table. "...I can't," he choked finally.

"It's not whether you can or should or want to...It's simply whether or not it happens," replied Hollie, trying not to sound condescending. "I can't claim to know what it's like for you. You embraced the sight in a way I never did. You gave yourself to it and opened up to all who have passed on...I ran from it... I ran for so long that it cost me my life," she closed her eyes and thought back to what had happened those short years ago. "You saved me... *because* of this gift," she sighed heavily and stepped towards Richard, placing a hand softly on his chest, looking him in the eyes. "My point is that you can't control these things and you shouldn't have to try. If you do then I'm afraid you could risk more than you're willing to lose."

Richard took Hollie's hand gently. "I don't want to be like this anymore," he stated simply. "Normally I wouldn't have thought otherwise but it's fading... The voices...I can barely hear them anymore," he let go of her hand and walked to the window, looking out at the bright day. "I want to live a normal life, Hollie. No sight, no Median World, no spirit incursions. Just you and me and a life free of haunted dreams. Is that too much to ask?"

"No," she murmured quietly, "but I've been down this path and I don't want you making my mistakes... They always come back."

Richard turned round and looked back at Hollie. She was staring at the floor, a sorrow filling her eyes. "I know they're leaving you as well-"

"They always come back, Richard!" she snapped, this time spitting the words. "I don't trust for one minute that they will ever leave me alone," she lowered her voice to barely a whisper as she remembered back to her old life. Back when the voices and the visions tormented her without end.

Richard quickly stepped back to her and without a second thought wrapped his arms tightly around her. "We'll get through it…Together."

Hollie nodded against Richard's arm and put her arms around him. "I hope so…Because I don't want anything to spoil this."

Almost imperceptibly, the short summer night began to fall, its gentle veil of deep blue softening the lush green of the trees. Out from them crept the long shadows which shimmered with deviant motion. From the cover of shade struck three figures, darting along the road lit only by the dull yellow streetlights. Eventually they ducked beneath the large, elaborate door arch of New Street Mosque, each of them briefly illuminated by the bright spotlight upon its wall. Two of them were apparently local youths, each dressed in a scruffy tracksuit, their faces half covered by hoodies. The third was a reasonably well-dressed man, considerably older than his companions, who wore a smart pinstriped suit with a striking burgundy tie. His attire was all but covered by a long white robe, golden trim lining its edge and a cowl which covered his face just like the hoodies.

After a few seconds of checking the road, one of the youths withdrew a short crowbar from under his shirt and set about prying the lock from the door while the other bounced around him excitedly. While they worked, the older man stood motionlessly, just out of reach of the spotlight. Finally, after a minute or two of effort, the lock flew off with a prang and the youths heaved the door open with their shoulders. The first youth turned and nodded to his counterpart as he concealed the crowbar again before approaching the robed man, cracking his knuckles as he went.

"'Ight, so…" he muttered forcefully, spitting when he paused, "we cracked the door, where's our money?"

Illumination

"Yea!" stated the other youth firmly, punching forward as he spoke.

Slowly the older man reached into his robe and pulled a wad of rolled up bank notes, dropping them casually at the youths' feet. The two Hoodies looked around, bewildered at how much the man was paying them and quickly checked the streets for police cars, fearing some sort of setup. Eventually the second of the two started forward and grabbed the wad of money, fleeing off into the night, quickly followed by the second.

The man breathed out slightly and shook his head under the cowl. "So materialistic," he murmured before approaching the broken door and casually pushing it open.

Before having a chance to enter, he spotted a figure approaching along the road. It was an older man, appearing older even than the robed man, his clothes ragged and filthy and his face half covered with an unruly beard.

"'Scuse me, squire..." The homeless man croaked, sidling up to the robed man before realising what was going on. He looked the splintered door up and down then glanced at the robed man, withdrawing as calmly as he could. "I won't tell no-one. All I wants is a light, governor..." he raised a short, dirty dog end to his lips and gestured for a lighter in front of it.

The robed man chuckled slightly and scrutinised the homeless man from beneath his hood. "Well, I'm afraid, you see..." he started simply, smiling at the man, "we are the light." In one smooth, quick motion, he pulled a dagger from under his robe and stabbed the homeless man deep into the abdomen. "Rest now, my friend," he added, twisting the knife and ripping it away again.

Wiping it clean, he casually replaced the blade into his robe as his victim fell limply to the ground. He raised an eyebrow approvingly at his work and turned to finally enter the Mosque.

Stepping through the doorway, he was confronted by pillars lining an open space, arches bridging the gaps between them and an ornately decorated mosaic floor that seemed to shine even in the partial darkness. The only illumination came from the dark blue sky of the summer evening flooding in through the patterned windows.

At the far end of the space was a golden sceptre placed into an alcove in the wall.

"The worship of false idols," murmured the robed man, "they may not be as false as they believe," he finished, striding towards the alcove.

"Ne yapıyorsun? Sen kimsin?" shouted a man in Turkish, wearing a turban and long ceremonial robe. "Sen kimsin?!" he shouted again, stopping the trespasser in his tracks. "Who are you?" he repeated finally in English.

The hooded man slowly turned away from the alcove and looked carefully at the Imam. "I see you…" he started to walk towards him slowly, making the Imam stop abruptly. "I know what you are…You are like us," he reached forward a hand, extending it from the folds of his robe. "Seer," he stepped forward slightly, making the Imam start back. "Our calling is the same but your eyes remain closed to the truth… Mine have been opened to what we could be if our shackles were thrown down, if we revealed ourselves to this world."

The Imam took another step back and raised his hands. "And I know what you are, Darkling…I feel the void in you."

The robed interloper gritted his teeth and turned his head stiffly. "Do you fear the dawning of a new age so much? Are we so repugnant that you must resort to such childish slurs?"

"It's more than you deserve," the Imam spat, disgusted at the mere thought of his presence. "We were wrong to stay our hand. We spared who we could because we thought your ideals to be dead. The very idea of your kind tainting my house tells me we should have done far more…"

"You must know we are patient," he opened his arms, palms laid out flat, facing the ceiling, "we have waited a long time and would be willing to wait longer still… but our time has come. Now is when we shall take our rightful place where we can elevate this plane above all."

"Rightful!?" shouted the cleric, throwing his arm down harshly, "piç! Lanetli piçler, her biriniz!" he breathed heavily, staring at the blasphemer before him. "You claim it to be your rightful place!? You're legacy? I'll tell you what your legacy is! It's death and chaos, the destruction of us all!"

Illumination

"Enough!" screamed the robed man, sharply stepping forward. "We will not make that mistake again...The unfaithful were large in number and their blind arrogance was our undoing. Now, though, you are weak. You have no choice but to listen when we speak, for *they* have abandoned you. Left you alone in the cold darkness of your own sin." From under the hood a faint grin struck out, catching the Imam off guard and forcing a cold shiver up his spine. "The souls of this world will come to us, their desperation fuelling our cause and swelling our ranks..." he stepped forward again, this time slowly shuffling towards the Imam. "As for all those who would remain devoted to the old ways... well, I fear their dissonance cannot be tolerated in the new world and any who would not conform must be removed."

The robed man grinned again and started to reach out a hand but stopped in mid-motion as the Imam looked up to the high ceiling and uttered a few inaudible words. Almost immediately, a gust of wind rushed in through the open door and whipped around the mosque. With it came the unsettling sense that the Imam and robed man were no longer alone.

"I see," the interloper began shortly. "So, they have not abandoned all of you, after all," he tilted his head and gazed upwards to see dozens of bright, translucent shadows streaking around the ornate pillars.

"The Guardians would never abandon the truly righteous!" the Iman shouted at last. "You have nowhere to go so tell me, why do you dishonour these hallowed halls with your sacrilege?"

"Sacrilege?" he asked calmly, a low thrum drifting down from the enraged Guardians above. "Is that what you would call it?" he took a step against a rising gale and reached up, taking the edges of his hood and pulling them down around his neck. Under the hood was an old, wrinkled face, topped by a head of white, wire-like hair. "I am here merely to retrieve what was ours in the beginning."

He raised a hand against the gusts as the Guardians swooped down and began swirling around him, darting in and out attempting to intimidate the stranger. Suddenly he clenched his fist tight and the Guardians were thrown back as the air shimmered and abruptly fell still.

No More Quiet Times

"You have no idea of the power you deny yourselves," he added simply, looking directly at the Imam trying to scramble back to safety.

"Who are you?" the Imam pleaded, falling backwards to the floor while the dazed Guardians swirled around in a futile effort to protect him.

The old man grinned and raised an eyebrow, starting towards the sceptre again. "I am your future," he said without looking back, "I am the one all will bow to." He stopped in front of the sceptre and took a deep, stifled breath, grinning again. "My name... It is Earnest Franklin...A name all shall come to know and fear."

He reached out towards the relic and, for a moment, the Guardians tried to compose themselves, striking out towards him. As Earnest took hold of the golden rod, though, they were thrown silently to the ground, shimmering gently as if a carpet of pure light. Earnest looked about at the subdued Guardians and then at the sceptre approvingly.

"I'm glad to see it still works..." he said, stepping down from the alcove and gazing over the relics' jewelled head. "Lucky for you," he added darkly, glancing at the Imam before striding off towards the doorway.

"You cannot!" screamed the Imam from behind. "To control the Guardians, it is-"

"Sacrilege?" asked Earnest without stopping. He began to laugh loudly at the notion and dropped the pommel of the sceptre loudly to the ground. The sharp echo rang out through the mosque, prompting the subservient Guardians to rise up and begin following Earnest. "The time will come, my friend, rest assured," Earnest shouted back as both he and the Guardians moved out into the night. "The time will come..."

A stillness fell across the night as a pair of pale moons passed through the heavens, twisting the air and altering the very nature of the night itself. In the lucid darkness, shapes shifted and morphed, watching the skyward bodies with reverence. Slowly they would become aware of another, one who did not belong and, in turn, curiously rushed up to investigate this new arrival before hurrying away back to the safety of the shadows. The sight here was overwhelming, not meant for mortal minds, but to avoid its gaze was to not see the darkness behind closed eyes. It was everything, at the same time enlightenment but also the most terrible of burdens. To glimpse beyond the veil of life and death was as fantastical as it was absurd. An incomparable feat for the uninitiated but for those who remained it would be not but a blight on a scarred psyche.

From the dark clouds a shape began to form, its presence sapping the light of the moons from the sky. The shadowy mists swirled in the sky, slowly defining a swaying, skeletal figure which loomed overhead, sending the roiling mass of shapes below into a panicked frenzy. It sank from the void and inspected the newcomer, its sunken eyeballs barely visible against their shaded sockets and its thin cheek bones seeming to cut through and the tissue of its face. Suddenly it pulled back sharply and grinned a broad, toothy grin.

"I knew this day would come..." it breathed, the substanceless words more imagined rather than spoken. It slowly leaned in again, the grin still fixed upon its emaciated lips. As it did, a portion of its cheek began to melt away, followed by the entire side of its face. It dripped down into the nothingness, leaving only bare bone and a pitch-black liquid oozing slowly from the wound. "Welcome home."

As the words were spoken, their tone changed from an empty breath to a haunting growl and finally a manic, roared laughter, echoing into the distance.

Richard sat bolt upright in bed, breathing heavily and with sweat dripping from his brow. "Please no," he whispered to himself absently.

"What's wrong?" asked Hollie vaguely as she sat up next to him, trying to wake herself up. "Are you alright?"

Richard tried to find the words to tell her but couldn't bring himself to think back to the nightmare and what it could have meant.

Hollie placed a hand gently on his arm, making him jerk slightly. "It's ok, Rich. It's over."

"...No," he replied eventually, managing to catch his breath. "It's not, that's the problem..." he thought for a few more seconds. "It was him...I don't know how but it was. I'm trying to let go of all this and he doesn't want me to," Richard gritted his teeth and wiped the sweat roughly from his face. "He still needs me," he finished fiercely, spitting the words.

Hollie tightened her grip on his arm and turned to face him. "It was just a dream. You have a lot on your mind and you're bound to get a few night terrors…It doesn't mean anything, it's just a dream."

Richard opened his mouth to debate her but decided that she was probably right. It bothered him that despite being convinced that he wanted to give it all up, the voices and visions, it still had this kind of hold over him. He had never wanted any part of this world in the first place but where he had always felt as if he had been pushed along, now he had a reason to fight against it. She sat there in the dull light, hair twisted out of shape, skin pale from sleep but he couldn't help but think she was the most beautiful thing he had ever seen. More than that, she was redemption to him, she was life. Yet, no matter how he fought, something inside him couldn't let go. The smallest part of him needed it for something, promising to give up his 'gifts' would mean losing something far greater in the long run.

"I need to take a walk," said Richard simply, slipping out of bed and beginning to get dressed. "I need to think."

Hollie sat up further and rubbed her eyes, turning to the clock on the bedside table. "At this time? It's…It's half three in the morning!" She got out of bed and rushed around to stop Richard.

"I'm sorry…I'll be back soon," he leaned forward and kissed her lightly on the lips. "Promise."

"You'd better be," she added, running her hands over his bare chest, lightly touching the healed scars across his body, "I don't want anything happening to you."

He sighed and nodded gently. "It won't, don't worry. I'll be back before morning," he kissed her again and stepped out of the room, grabbing his shirt from the back of a chair as he went.

Hollie slumped down on the bed and rubbed her face as she heard the front door open and close. "Be careful."

A fond sense of familiarity hit Richard as stepped out into the chilly night air. He had done this so many times before but never for the sake of simply walking. No matter what it had ever led to, whether it was an exorcism or trip to the border world, the night had

Illumination

always managed to clear his head. It had allowed him to think straight when nothing else had and now, he hoped, it could again, if even just this one last time. Allowing his mind to wander, Richard began walking with no particular idea of where he was heading. Occasionally a car would rush by and break his entranced state but he would always keep walking.

After a while he abruptly stopped, taking a few seconds to realise he had done so. Looking, bewildered, at the street around him, Richard could see it was a long, regular enough looking street with terrace housing lining the road on either side of it. Barely half the street lights were working and, for a moment, a sense of apprehension hit him, feeling a distinct familiarity about this place. He had not planned to come here, with it being so long it hadn't even crossed his mind, yet something inside must have driven him here for a reason. He turned and looked up solemnly at the dilapidated chapel and rubbed his hands together nervously. Things had changed so much and Richard wasn't even sure he was welcome anymore but if this is where he was meant to be then he had no choice but to accept it. Taking a deep breath, Richard finally stepped towards the chapel, unprepared to meet an old friend.

III-II – The Forgotten

(...) those who reject (...) Our Signs, they shall be companions of the Fire; they shall abide therein

-Al-Bagara 2:39

Pushing open the rusted door, just like he remembered doing so many times in the distant past, Richard's thoughts dwelled on whether it had been a good idea to come here. Everything had changed and they were both different people now. Regardless, he kept pushing at the metal door, scraping it past the bare sandstone wall and showering himself with the sand he was sheering free.

Finally, the door clanged open against its shallow groove in the grubby floor tiles, causing Richard to stumble back a little. Once he caught his balance, Richard finally looked up and absently gazed around at the chapel. It was far from what he remembered, now dark and empty, stripped of the eclectic array of furniture he had been accustomed to. There was something more missing, however, almost as if the soul had been drained from the building, leaving only a dry husk behind. Only a pair of spotlights remained pointed towards the far end of the building, illuminating the altar step. Suddenly it dawned on Richard just how different the man who lived here was to who he used to know...

"I haven't changed that much, you know..." a thick, dark voice echoed across the hall, "but you can't expect me to be entirely the man you knew, especially after all that's happened."

His footsteps echoed around Richard, concealing his location until he appeared at his side, starling Richard back towards the door.

"Don't be surprised, my friend," chuckled the old man with a rasp, "you know I've always been inside your head."

Richard stepped forward again but stopped abruptly as the figure moved out of the shadows. "I don't know what's happened here…I don't know who you are anymore…" Richard tried, unsure how to treat the man before him.

"It's been a long time, Richard…" replied Lancer softly, his features becoming clearer as he moved. His face was ragged, much more so than it had ever been before, and was covered with a thick beard which reached towards his chest. "You never came again, not even after The Horde. I saw more of the boy then I did of you…You just left me."

"I had no idea how you'd react to any of this…" Richard raised his voice knowing in his heart that anything he said would be an empty excuse. "After I found out what was happening…I didn't dare come back. They were angry."

"They were angry!?" Lancer shouted, his voice booming around the entire chapel. "They abandoned us! Just left because of something we had no control over…I tried to stop him and *still* they left!" Lancer shifted back into the shadows, seemingly uneasy about being seen. "This punishment was meant for all of us, Richard. All Seers bar those they needed to do their bidding. The 'truly devout,'" he threw his arms about, mocking the sentiment. "The Guardians. They are our conduit, our sight... our protection. Without them our powers are meaningless. They mean to punish us. They mean to keep us in line, stop our power from growing too far. Why? It's because they're scared."

Richard opened his mouth to speak but choked on the words, unable to believe that what he thought to be benevolent beings could be so ruthless and spiteful. "They can't just control you like puppets-"

"They can and they will," Lancer stated shortly, not willing to hear Richard out. "It's complicated…Suffice to say we did what we had to do. I saw what any one of us could turn into if we were left unchecked." Lancer hung his head and leant on his knees. "I don't like it but I've come to realise that they did it for the greater good. Deep down I always knew what needed to happen... I don't blame you, Richard. You got it all out in the open but there are many who do. 'Why does a Median have the right?' They ask."

Richard started towards Lancer and carefully reached out a hand. "I'm sorry for leaving you... I never meant for any of this. After everything... Everything I had done and seen, I-"

Lancer grabbed Richard's arm firmly from the shadows. "You couldn't go through with it anymore...I understand but you have to realise what you are saying. I know you are trying to give up everything you are, everything you have, but are you really so willing to leave yourself defenceless?" Lancer leaned into a pool of light and gazed at Richard, the whites of his eyes burning like the sun. "They're not just going to give up on you. They'll hunt you even as a regular mortal...And kill you if necessary."

"Hunt? Kill?!" Richard asked, confused. "The other Seers, you mean? It's been three years, why would they suddenly want to now?"

Lancer sighed. "There's a lot I should tell you," he released Richard's arm and gestured to one of the side doors. "Come."

Richard complied and walked briskly towards one of the old oak doors lining the side of the chapel, cautiously eying his surroundings as he went.

"What's this all about, Lancer?" Richard asked, striding through the arch into the sparsely decorated room.

Lancer stopped behind him and closed the door gently. "Please take a seat," he added without looking around. "We get old so quickly. My strength is not what it once was," he turned around to see Richard still standing rigidly before him. "Please..." he waved his hand towards one of the two wooden stools to the side of the room, "I really would prefer it." He reached out and took one of the stools, placing it firmly in the middle of the small room as Richard gingerly lowered himself onto another.

"Lancer-" Richard tried and failed once again.

"There's balance to everything, my friend," Lancer started cryptically. "Even us," he added the words as if he was purposely trying to deepen Richards' confusion. "Have you ever heard of the

Illumous? Most people call them Dark Seers, a sect who broke away from my forbearers thousands of years ago. They believed that sight alone wasn't enough. All it took was a glimpse of the Other Side and ever since their only goal has been to capture it, manipulate it for themselves..." he gazed at Richard who glanced back with a vague disinterest.

"Why are you telling me this, Lancer?" Richard asked at last with an exhausted huff, "I don't have time for your legends-"

"Why did you come here?" Lancer replied calmly, stopping Richard mid-sentence.

The question made him think for a minute but no reasonable answer came to him. Instead, he simply gave a sigh and shrugged.

"*You* may not know, but *I* do. After these long years, why would you return at this time? You're trying to forget about everything you've learnt, live like a 'normal' person. Work, marriage, children... That's not who you are and, in your heart, you know that. This is what brought you here tonight. You were drawn by the need for something greater," he looked squarely at Richard again and reached forward, placing a hand on his arm. "She is worthy of your effort but I can only help you if you help yourself."

Richard lowered his head in thought for a few seconds and then shook it gently. "I can't very well go around living a nine to five life if I've got rogue Seers on my back or whatever," he said, his voice muffled. Eventually he looked back up to his old friend, his eyes almost pleading. "...So?"

Lancer smiled shortly and patted Richard's arm. "They were banished centuries ago, thought to be gone. But all who are wise see both the good and evil among us...They are far from gone, lost only in obscurity but now, with this turmoil in our ranks, they are returning. Already they turn the weak and destroy those in their way. They will hunt you because their minds have been poisoned against the true path," Lancer ended abruptly, leaning back perilously on the stool.

"Illumous," repeated Richard quietly, peaking Lancer's interest. "I had a dream...A haunting dream...By any chance was-" he tried only to be cut off but Lancer snapping back at him.

The Forgotten

"No," the words were barked back quickly, "he was different, an anomaly. But surely the Illumous are aware of his work and will be, shall we say... grateful for his contributions."

"How do we even know whether they're a valid threat?" asked Richard eventually, finding the whole situation hard to believe. "A whole sect of Dark Seers with an aim to... what? Take over the afterlife? It doesn't just go unnoticed by the powers that be," he flicked his eyes upwards subtly.

"They are cunning and patient. Believe me they are a threat like none you have ever seen," he stared Richard down, silencing his argument before it was even voiced. "Two nights ago, an item was stolen..." he turned and started rummaging around in his pocket, pulling out a tattered piece of newspaper. Opening it up, the page revealed a large image of the stolen sceptre beneath a bold headline stating 'Middle Eastern Treasure comes to Britain'.

Richard took the page and shook it out straight, looking carefully at the dull and yellowed parchment. "So, I'm guessing it's not just some old Arabic artefact?"

"No," Lancer answered in earnest and stared deeply at Richard, his annoyance with him growing. "I've got to say, Richard, I'm disappointed by your lack of concern. I can see that you are not taking this remotely seriously," he added after pausing for a few moments, continuing to grimace at him. "I would have expected more."

"Look! You're right!" started Richard, throwing his hands out. "I don't really care what's been stolen or what crazy cult is roaming around. As far as I'm concerned, the police will take care of any nutcases out there. The only reason I'm still here is because it's *you* who needs my help. Anyone else and I'd be out but I'll go along with it one more time because you've always had my back... I owe you at least that," he sighed and looked Lancer in the eyes. "But you have to understand that this isn't my life anymore."

Lancer sat silently for a few seconds then gently shook his head. "Disappointing..." he reiterated, lowering his head and rubbing his face. "You'll come to see what truly matters," he muttered under his breath, "eventually."

Illumination

Richard opened his mouth but Lancer had already started again before he could speak.

"It's a staff of power," he stated firmly, lifting his head back up and tapping the old paper as roughly as he dared. "An ancient and sacred item bestowed unto my kind in the time of lost history. One of five items empowered by those on high..." he flailed his hand around absently, unable to accurately state where this power had come from. "From the great beyond, if you believe in that kind of thing. The point is that they were given to us as a show of good faith. A way to say that we could make our own determination, free of *them*," Lancer waved his hand around again absently. "With an artefact like this, any one of us could control the Guardians themselves. The power to bend their will is the first step to gaining unlimited majesty over the astral planes," Lancer sighed again and seemed honestly distraught by the thought of the items' theft.

"Where are the others, then? Why this one in particular?" asked Richard, not able to contain his curiosity.

"Lost, hidden, destroyed. Anything could have happened over the millennia but as far as I know, this is the only one that remains, passed from Sultans to Kings to Royal families and private collectors. They were never meant to be used, though, merely exist as a reminder to us that all things were indeed equal. A symbol of trust. But now the Illumous seek to break that trust. No doubt they plan to build an army with it, rally all the lost Seers out there to their cause. What's worse is that they'll go, all of them, simply because they have nothing else left."

"Wait," Richard said putting up a hand, "how do you even know it's them, it could be-"

"It's them," Lancer answered shortly, "I can't explain but we see the worlds differently to you. I can feel them. Even though my Guardians have been gone for a long time now, I can still sense their presence out there. Their fear...It's the Illumous, trust me," he bobbed his head back and forth shortly, debating if to concede something which could pull back his veil of mysticism. "Of course, if you need something a bit more solid, I did get a call last night. A Seer who was deemed not to have strayed from the path like the rest of us. If you ask me, the only reason he kept favour with the

The Forgotten

Guardians is because he's the keeper of the Staff." Lancer subtly rolled his eyes and took a restrained breath. "Anyway, suffice to say he and I...worked... together some time ago. As such, we have a certain trust between us," he stopped and looked Richard squarely in the eyes. "I knew you would return when the time was right. The power of a Median comes from his own heart. Therein lies your strength... but our weakness. You see, Seers may be able to see across the worlds yet we are only capable of perceiving what is in front of us. You must go to him, the keeper, and find out as much as you can. See what I cannot and maybe we can stop this before it begins."

"But surely you can-" Richard tried to ask but was quickly stopped by Lancer's piercing gaze which told him everything he needed to know. "Ok, I get it," Richard said at last, reluctant to admit he had been convinced to go. "See past what's right in front of me."

"All Seers are threatened by the power the Illumous now posses-"

"Even you," finished Richard, leaving Lancer to slowly nod. "You can't risk placing yourself in that position," he folded the newspaper snippet and forced it into his pocket, turning to the door. "You do realise you're going to have to find someone else to do this kind of thing, right?"

Lancer smiled and chuckled to himself. "Not if all goes to plan," he mumbled under his breath, only raising his voice again as Richard moved towards the door. "It was good to see you again, Rich."

Richard stopped and slightly turned his head back towards Lancer. "You too," he offered indifferently then hurriedly slipped from the room.

Before he reached the quiet of night, Richard stopped and looked back to the small wooden door, quietly repeating the words to himself, this time as though they genuinely meant something.

"You too..."

Stumbled footsteps echoed through the dank, narrow tunnel. No matter how many times he walked the path he could never find his way, the slippery walls and damp ground always hindering his progress. Soon the darkness gave way to a bright arch of light,

Illumination

brilliant compared to the sickly gloom of the tunnel. Slowly he emerged into a dim lamp light produced by wall mounted oil burners each side of the tunnel opening.

He was a Dark Seer, young but nonetheless initiated into The Brethren as one of their newest members. He cautiously stepped into a large auditorium, a high domed roof reaching above him and incredibly detailed artwork adorning the lavish walls. Around the room were perfectly sculpted statues of figures in various contoured positions, too excellent to be crafted by any mortal hand. Positioned around the edge of the domed chamber were watchful sentinels, each rigidly stood at attention. Every one of them tightly gripped halberds to their sides and were cloaked in the same white gowns favoured by The Brethren, only with an extra black trim embellishing the seams.

The Dark Seer looked up towards the side of the chamber to see a large, meticulously painted mural depicting the world but rather than oceans and continents, it portrayed interpretations of the astral planes. The Mortal realm merging through into the Median World and on to the Other Side. It showed a single horizon with several subjects walking through the seamlessly interconnected worlds. Contrary to the reality of it, each of the figures passed through the worlds with no apparent struggle or effort, from the bustling world of the living to the darkness of the unknown which lies beyond.

"Do you like it, boy?" came the gruff, distinctive voice of Earnest, head of the Dark Seer sect. "It represents our vision," he continued as the young heretic flicked his eyes beneath the painting, searching for the voice. "Although I am sure you knew that..."

Just below the mural, seated upon a golden throne was Earnests' robed silhouette. Around him, strewn across shabby tables were assorted trinkets and artefacts, apparently trivial enough to be cast aside. In his left hand was the stolen sceptre, its base held firmly against the ground, resistant to any who would dare take it from his possession.

"The Other Side belongs to us all," the Dark Seer stated firmly in an effort to curry favour. "There is no barrier between greatness and power,"

The Forgotten

"Very good," Earnest replied simply. "We think not of these worlds as separate entities but as one in the same. A great fabric which is not crossed but moved through as if we are at one with it," he grinned slightly under the hood and raised from his seat, maintaining a tight grip on the sceptre. "Come closer, my son," he said kindly, groaning with the effort of ascending while his subject complied. "First time in the great hall?" he asked, moving towards the young man as he nodded gently. "A lot of power resides here, you realise? You should be humbled."

"I am, my lord. Truly I am," the young Seer responded weakly, afraid of what may happen if he hesitated.

Earnest grinned again and chuckled, placing an old and frail hand on the lad's shoulder. "What is your name?"

"Aaron, sire," he replied again quickly.

"Aaron!" he gripped his shoulder firmly and released it as he started strolling across the chamber, banging the staff on the polished floor as he went. "You are one of the newest, are you not?" he asked without expecting an answer. "You see, you are but one of many who would flock to us. Already I feel them coming, lost without meaning...I shall give them the purpose which they seek...Give them the reason that they always desired," he stopped and turned back to Aaron, smiling as he pulled the hood from his head with his free hand. "I am proud of you... Aaron. You joined us out of true behest, something we see so rarely now. But willing or not they will come."

"If I may be so bold...Lord," said Aaron quietly, his voice quivering. "What is it you intend to do once the others have joined us?"

"In the grand scheme they are not as important as they would have themselves believe... Merely the seeds of our new civilisation," Earnest turned and sauntered back towards his throne, "and that, I fear, will be nothing without the right leadership."

"You do not intend to lead us?" asked Aaron, forgetting himself for a moment.

Earnest sighed and sat back down. "However long I may have guided our movement through the dark times, I am far too old to hold provenance over an entire reality. No, to bridge the gap between worlds, we must seek one with the power of the Other Side. One who has it coursing through their veins. One who could lead us to our divine vision and finally erase the gulf humanity has placed in our way."

"Sire, my apologies but what you speak of is not possible for I know of only one who has touched the Other Side and lived." Aaron instinctively recoiled back, fearing the repercussions of his words.

For several seconds Earnest stared at Aaron, his vision boring into his skull before he finally relented and sat back calmly.

"I respect your honesty but know that doubting me is hardly something I would advise..." He scowled briefly and breathed in deeply. "Not that it matters," he added quietly to himself, "but there is indeed another, unknown to all but I and the blood beast. The creature witnessed their coming centuries ago in a void beyond time... the impressionable mind of one who would lead us to our destiny."

Earnest lifted the sceptre and struck it against the ground, the impact echoing around the auditorium. It rang out against the walls, awaking the mass of captured Guardians which flooded out around them as if from nowhere. They were greater in number than any single person had ever witnessed, swirling around the domed room in an endless ethereal wave.

"Yes, my friend. Our time has come," Earnest stated, his grin full of malice as he bathed in the radiance of the Guardians. "Our future is laid out before us, ready to be taken without pause or second thought..." Earnest raised his voice above the deafening sound of the thousands of spirits rushing around him, obscuring him from Aarons sight. "And that future..."

Earnest slammed the sceptre against the ground again, making the storm of Guardians rise up above him, merging it into a single cloud-like entity. It hung over the chamber like a mighty storm, sparking with the immense power contained within it.

Transfixed by the sight, Aaron nervously tried to pull his gaze away, only to find Earnest rapidly approaching him.

"...That future begins with you," Earnest finished calmly as all other sound drained from the room, leaving his echoing, hollow voice to fill the void.

The Forgotten

"Sire?" Aaron asked nervously while Earnest stepped closer to him, extending an arm, his hand stretched open, fingers like claws extended for the kill.

Earnest grinned maniacally. "It will all be clear soon," he said finally with a haunting calm.

The old man struck out with starling speed, denying Aaron any chance to dodge before he felt a firm grip tightening around his head. Earnest's palm pressed into Aaron's forehead, fingers digging painfully into his skull with far more force than someone of his age should have been capable of.

"Now kneel before me!" Earnest commanded through gritted teeth, pressing firmly down and giving Aaron no choice but to cooperate.

Earnest dug his fingers deeper into Aaron's scalp until blood began to well up between them, trickling down the young man's face as he began to whimper and eventually cry out with the pain.

"Such energy..." Earnest stated, throwing his head back. "Such youth!" he finally exclaimed, digging ever deeper into Aaron's flesh.

With a final despairing scream, Earnest's fingers pierced Aaron's skull and dug into his brain. The old man's eyes flashed blood red and a dark hue crept across his body, encircling him and flicking about it as though a parasite, roaming free about its host. Finally, the ghostly shape manifested as a black, wispy mist which spiralled around his outstretched arm, cascading down towards the agonised vision of Aaron. It coated his head, its inky tendrils searching his countenance until it drained along Earnest's fingers, burrowing into the young Seers skull. With a violent jerk, Aaron began to writhe as his features sank and drooped with the rapid onset of age. Before Earnest's eyes, Aaron's years were drained away as the shade rampaged through his body, stealing the very life from his veins.

In a final, haggard gasp, Aarons eyes glazed over with a milky substance which crept out across his face and coated his entire body, making it hard as stone. At last, Earnest gave one last squeeze, crushing Aaron's skull into shards of white obsidian which scattered across the ground, releasing the entity into the air. The smoky shadow hung above Aarons statued form for a second, its tendrils scrutinising the space around it, then struck towards Earnest. It covered his body and soaked into him, making his eyes glow that same red again as he breathed deeply, seeming to enjoy the experience. In a single moment the skin on Earnests' face tightened, making many of his wrinkles vanish. The numerous liver spots about his temples faded and a subtle blonde tint returned to his hair. He didn't grow young by any great stretch of time yet the reversion of Earnests appearance to that of someone not yet out of their sixties was nothing short of astounding.

As the last of the dark mist vanished back into his body, Earnest sighed contentedly and lowered his arm, relaxing his much younger hand.

"It has been so long," he said, his voice no longer old and withered but now with a returned energy.

He looked down at the headless statue and then at the fragments scattered across the polished floor before looking to the others lined along the room.

"I'm obviously out of practice," he looked at his new hand and smiled. "That will soon change."

Richard walked slowly along New Street, squinting against the glare of the bright, early morning sunlight. It was warm but not so much that the shade of a rogue cloud could not make him shiver. Each time it did, he questioned why he should carry on. Why he shouldn't just turn away now and go home, back to the warmth he would never feel out here. Richard knew that he would never be free if he kept on doing this. Favours begat favours and Lancer would never let go of him if he had a choice. No matter how much he thought it through, as the fresh dawn air chilled his face, it still felt like the most natural thing in the world.

Richard slowed to barely a crawl and began merely placing one foot slightly ahead of the other, exaggerating the movement to make himself feel as though he were actually in motion. Eventually he fell to a dead stop, trying desperately to convince himself that simply visiting Lancer was a step in the wrong direction, let alone entertaining his requests.

The Forgotten

While he stood, ridged in the middle of the street, a sudden, sharp breeze drifted across him, chilling his senses and distracting him from the conflicted thoughts that plagued his mind. The cold air drew him forward again, faster this time, pulling him without doubt towards the plush new Mosque that stood before him.

Before realising what he was doing, Richard was inspecting the broken door which had been patched with a small square of plywood. While it covered the damage well enough, Richard concluded that it had been a rush job, stuck on loosely with liberal amounts of duct tape. Other than that, there wasn't anything especially revealing about the damage, apparently just another of the hate crimes that plagued the city. There was an unseen element, however, something which drew Richard's attention like nothing had in a long time. It was not the door itself which called to him but a lingering aura. A dark presence that hung in the air like a bitter aftertaste, content to allow others to mask it yet potent enough to defy obscurity. Richard carefully reached out towards the broken lock, feeling there may be something about it that he had overlooked but was stopped and startled backwards as the door was abruptly pulled open.

"I've been awaiting your arrival," came a voice from the hazy black behind the carved door, "but you are not what I would have expected." The haze shifted gently, almost as though the figure behind the darkness was making way for Richard.

"Well..." Richard considered what he could say as he accepted the invitation and stepped tentatively through the doorway. "People tend to change, " he decided diplomatically, feeling it inappropriate to start expressing himself too much, especially given that he shouldn't have been there in the first place.

"This may be true," the Imam replied, pressing the door closed gently, "but your feelings betray you..." His light robe swayed gracefully as he moved around Richard, the rich light filtering through the stained glass casting it in a dozen colours. "Your power comes from your heart...But your heart is conflicted. A two-way street of what you desire and what is right," he stepped forward and looked carefully at Richard. "I feel it would surprise you to know which is which."

Illumination

"I was sent here for a reason, wasn't I?" Richard asked abrasively, uncomfortable with the way the conversation was going, "I don't want your insight, just to know what you know."

"Soon you shall have to face what you seek to avoid..." the Imam continued, even against Richards's requests. "Yourself. Only then can you save that which you would come to love."

Richard gritted his teeth and stared at the Imam, ready to leave if the next thing out of his mouth wasn't what he wanted to hear. "The Illumous," he stated firmly, continuing to gaze coldly at the cleric.

Several seconds passed in silence with the thought of simply walking out growing in Richard's mind. Finally, he snapped his gaze away and was about to go through with it when the Iman suddenly stepped forward and grabbed Richard's arm.

"You can help us," he stated quickly, "and we can help you," he added cryptically.

"So..." Richard tried but was quickly cut off.

"The Illumous," the Imam again added, "the old man is not what he seems. He is the leader of the Dark Seers but he is not even that...He is more. I was entrusted to guide and represent the Seers until they believed us to be worthy again," he sighed and for the first time seemed unsure. "I have obviously failed in this, for those who would protect us have been lost...because of him. Because of the power he now wields."

"Who is he?" asked Richard, beginning to become genuinely intrigued, "what does he want? Why did he even steal the Guardians in the first place?" The questions welled up in his mind as he grappled to understand what a sect of Dark Seers would want with those held to be so pure.

"In the scheme of his plans, they are unimportant."

The Imam hesitated, still unsure that Richard, in his current state, was the right person to burden with the knowledge he would impart. Upon looking into his eyes, however, he could see how deep they went, how the roots of his soul touched the very essence of everything he had sworn to protect. After feeling that, he decided, no-one with such a heart could turn away from their calling.

"The Guardians are merely a ploy to lure the remaining Seers to join with them. Without the symbiotic bond we have with them, my kind becomes disorientated, unable to function without their influence. Some would do anything to get them back. This is exactly what *they* wanted," he flicked his eyes quickly to the heavens. "They wanted to give us a taste of life without them to put us back on the true path. Make sure we wouldn't deviate from it again." The Imam took an unsettled breath and lowered his gaze. "Unfortunately, the Illumous knows this also. They know how many of us will flock to them if they control the Guardians and, given time, even those like myself will not be able to resist their allure... This is why I must pass the task on to you, one who cannot be controlled like us," the Imam turned away and wiped his face slowly, dreading to think about the dark days that may yet come. "I have come to merely glimpse his schemes... No, the Guardians are not important to him and ultimately neither are the Seers. They are simply more strength for his growing army. What he truly wants is a leader. A powerful mind he can corrupt, a vessel to carry the power that would lead his people into a new age. A new age where the shadows from beyond may dominate and everything we know is all but extinct."

"How do you know all this?" Richard asked quickly, suspicious of how he could know so much. "What is it that makes you so much more enlightened than the rest of us?" he asked again, his voice darkening.

The Imam chuckled gently, making Richard cock his head in bemusement. "Surely you realise Lancer sent you to me for a reason?" he turned back to face Richard straight on. "I know because I was there the first time!" he suddenly snapped, his voice shaking. "Only a handful were ever privy to those horrid times, all those centuries ago. Most have passed on now, leaving a young boy who was in the wrong place to keep the memory alive," he took a deep breath and shook his head slightly. "Yes, I know of their plots. It was not of my choosing but it is still my responsibility... They have attempted this before, a long time ago, a rise to power through the corruption of the light. It was only through appealing to our desire for peace that they persist to this day. We were so eager to believe they had been destroyed that all they need do was play to that belief," he looked meaningfully at Richard for a few seconds as if he felt sympathy for a plight he was yet to discover. "The child of two Medians," he announced clearly. "Back then, like now, the product of the union was a Seer...But there was one, a child of great power who could commune with The Other Side. All because his father, albeit for a split second, had once touched the great beyond...Much like yourself, I believe," the Imam added, nodding to Richard as he stood, his heart pounding in his chest, feeling that the tale was going somewhere he would not like. "This power awoke the Illumous and they took the child, bent on corrupting its very soul to serve their purpose. The one who would lead them to the union of worlds. An eternal living afterlife for all on this Earth and beyond...It took everything we had just to stop them but still he lived."

"And the child?" asked Richard, his speech quick and fearful.

The Imam sighed and hung his head. "I'm afraid it was lost to us... The corruption had spread too far."

As Richard felt a large lump swell in his throat and a tear trickle down his cheek, the Imam rose his head again and looked straight at Richard without expression, his eyes unblinking.

"Maybe this time it doesn't have to go that far," he finished clearly and calmly.

All around him silence fell and shock shot up Richard's spine, spreading out across his body making his skin prickle as the realisation fell on him. It forced the air from his lungs and clutched at any other breath he could take for a few seconds.

"She's..." he managed weakly before turning like a flash and running as fast as he could out of the Mosque, knowing how grave the situation had now become to him.

"His name is Earnest Franklin," the Imam added calmly, watching Richard rush from the building. "I feel you'll be wanting to speak with him."

III-III – Messiah

... there has arisen, between us and you, enmity and hatred for ever (...)
-Al-Mumtahana 60:4

I didn't know how to react to this, I didn't even know what to think. No matter what I had been through, nothing could have prepared me for this. It was something I had begun to consider but I never could have imagined it happening in this way. I couldn't help but think on how things would be had I never visited Lancer, had I possessed that much more conviction and then it struck me. For the first time in what seemed to me like an eternity, I was glad for whatever spark of power I had left within me. In an instant, just like I always had all those years ago, I knew what I had to do.

As I ran, a sharp catch of breathlessness struck me deep in my chest and I keeled over on myself, almost falling to the ground. The Imam's words had cast a darkness across my mind, though, haunting me ever more with each step I took closer to home, driving me to break my own body if it meant preventing his words from becoming reality.

The pain struck me again, more intense this time, rising up from the bottom of my lungs, burning through my chest as it rose to tighten around my throat. It felt like this was my punishment, a torment for turning my back on everything I had ever been. Just as I felt that it would never end, I was there, standing before my own home as though I were trespassing in a hostile land. At that moment

I wasn't sure of much but somehow I knew that there was much worse to come.

Quickly twisting the key in the lock, almost snapping it off in the tumblers, Richard forced open the front door, allowing it to smash into the coat rack, shattering the hangers. Before it was able to fall to the ground, Richard was already halfway up the stairs, leaping up two steps at a time.

"Hollie!" he screamed at the top of his voice. "Holle! Are you-"

He burst into the bedroom to find the curtains still drawn and various affects scattered about the floor. In the corner were the remnants of a lamp which had apparently been smashed against the wall, its mangled fabric shade laying amongst the shards of its own porcelain base.

Richard wheezed and coughed uncontrollably, his chest only now beginning to constrict from the exertion. Each breath was a hell in its own right as he tried to force the air into his burning lungs. Trying to ignore the pain, he looked solemnly at the bed. The sheets were screwed up and arranged as though there had been a futile struggle. Richard dared not to think about exactly what happened here but knew he must if he had any chance of making sense of it all.

Reluctantly, he looked closer at the sheets and found small streaks of blood. They led to a larger spatter mark spread over the side of the bed where the sheets had been pulled partially onto the floor. He peered cautiously over the edge of the bed and saw what he had been dreading. On the floor next to the sheet smeared with bloody fingerprints was the heavy security torch which Hollie kept on her bedside cabinet; its end still sticky with damp blood.

Suddenly all the pieces fell together and the sequence of events began to take shape. Unbeknown to Hollie, one or more assailants had gotten into the house and attempted to abduct her, causing a struggle to break out. Obviously, she had proven to be more trouble than the assailants had expected so they had needed to use some considerable force to subdue her. In Richard's mind she had been held down by one of her attackers while another had used the torch to bludgeon her unconscious. It was only then they had been able to unceremoniously carry her away.

Richard cursed under his breath, causing him to cough again. Feeling the sting in his eye and catch in his throat, Richard rubbed his bloodshot eyes until they were sore but it was no good. He couldn't take it; he couldn't allow himself to. The fear, the anger, the sorrow. They all rose up inside him, forcing a reaction he was not entirely accustomed to. Sinking down, he gently sat on the edge of the bed and merely stared out of the doorway on to the dingy landing.

For far longer than he would have liked, Richard simply sat and stared, thinking over what had even happened in the past half hour. How did a simple favour for an old friend turn into this? Would it have even happened had he not gone out? He sighed heavily, still trying to recover his breath but stopped halfway through and realised that there was something amiss about the landing. Something which, in the commotion, he had missed. The short corridor was draped in shadow despite there being more than enough light at this time of day to illuminate it.

Slowly pushing himself up from the bed, Richard stepped out onto the landing carefully. As soon as he did, a chill encompassed him, a presence that dwelled on his thoughts allowing nothing else to cross his mind. Pressed forward by the sense that something was waiting for him, Richard crept closer to what was now the spare room.

After three years he still hadn't found anything to use the room for other than storage. It would seem that something else had, however. As his eyes fixed on the door handle, there was a bizarre, almost vortex-like aura to it, a swirling mist of sorts which seemed to reach out, pulling Richard's hand towards it. Eventually he took the handle tightly and immediately turned it, pushing open the door without a thought about what could be in there.

The long-abandoned room beyond was nothing more than Richard had expected. In the dull, dusty light, choked by the tightly drawn curtains, was a room left exactly as he remembered. There was a desk pushed up against the side wall and a dresser next to it, its surface coated with assorted clutter and a thick layer of dust. Around the room were various other flat pack cabinets and extraneous items from about the house. All of them had been haphazardly placed wherever there was space, stacked one atop another and left to be forgotten. Richard's eyes continued to scan across the room, eventually coming upon the single bed pressed into the corner, the foot facing squarely towards the door. Even after all of this time it remained neatly made in a futile hope that, by some miracle, its owner would one day return to reclaim it.

Richard sighed and gently shook his head, noting how this was the worst possible time to start dwelling on the past. Even so, the memories plagued him, the decision he was still trying to justify to himself. He thought about all the reasons why Medians tried not to get close to people. Of them all, it was the loss that hurt the most. The fact that Medians rarely lived to see old age and the ones which did were changed in ways not worth considering. Richard knew this better than most yet still he made attachments. Deep down he knew how it would end, how it always ended but he also knew that he couldn't bear to be alone.

Hanging his head, Richard's thoughts searched for an answer, an idea of what to do next but his mind was blank, too consumed with fear and anger to formulate a solution. With no other recourse and hopelessly under prepared for the task ahead, Richard turned back towards the doorway but was suddenly stopped as something caught his eye. Looking back across at the dresser, his attention fixed on a pair of ceremonial candles amongst the jumble of items. He watched them carefully as their wicks occasionally flickered as though they were trying to light themselves. At the base of the candlesticks were rounded fragments of pale blue Angelite. It was something, Richard knew, which was said to have the power to amplify a connection with the Other Side. Creeping closer, he looked upon the small shards, as most Medians did, with a degree of caution for it was considered the tool of the detached, ones who could not see beyond the veil. It was certainly not something to be used by those whose auras bathed in the grim light of the border worlds.

Why was it here then? Richard asked himself, inspecting the arrangement closer. Something was trying to get through, he decided. A powerful presence that was not just trying to return to the living realm but break through the border so they may physically interact with the world.

Richard grimaced and grunted at the turn of events, reaching into his pocket and pulling out a silver flick lighter. Against his own better judgement, he jerked open the lighters cap with his thumb. In one smooth movement, he sparked a bright yellow flame to illuminate the grim dullness of the abandoned room. This was neither the time nor place to be dealing with wayward souls but to have them roaming the house would only cause more problems down the line. In truth, this may have simply been a distraction, Richard decided, reaching the lighter towards the sparking wick, but it may have been one he needed.

As soon as the flame touched the parched twine the door slammed closed and the wick instantly erupted into a tall, jet-black flame. It stood upright and motionless with a subtle yet somehow reassuring glow radiating from the invisible halo. Richard raised an eyebrow, impressed at how quickly the presence had opened the portal. Quickly he set the second candle alight and snapped shut the lighter, placing it gently back into his pocket without taking his eyes from the large, eerily still flames.

"Come on, I haven't got time for this," Richard stated firmly to the altar, placing his hands on the dresser and leaning forward heavily. "*She* doesn't have time for this," he added eventually, sinking his head to the dresser's dusty surface, closing his eyes tightly.

"Why else do you think I'm here, Rich?" The voice was familiar and calming to Richard, especially considering the situation, and made his eyes flick back open. "I wouldn't have travelled all this way if I didn't think it was worth it."

Richard lifted his head slowly from the surface again, turning around towards the source of the voice. "How could it be you?" he tried to edge away, pressing himself into the dresser as he did, and looked in petrified disbelief towards the hunched outline sitting on the edge of the bed. "You..." Richard tried again, convincing himself to step slightly forward as the figure raised its head to look directly at him, revealing a face he knew almost better than his own. "Chris?"

Illumination

Through the distortion of concussed reality, whispered voices enshrouded Hollie, tempting her with the promise of substance only to take it away as she drifted in and out of consciousness. In time the befuddling veil began to lift and the voices gained an extra clarity, discarding the unsettling distance they had held from her. They took shape as fixed points around her, moving in conjunction with the echoed steps of their owners. As her mind roused from its muddled slumber, a near intolerable pain swept around from the back of Hollie's head. The sharpness of the pain quickly faded but instead left an intense, unceasing gnawing which washed back and forth through her skull making her wince in pain.

"I see you're back with us, at last..."

The voice was clear yet the meaning of its words still escaped Hollie's clouded mind. She shuffled as much as she dared, trying to bring herself around but only succeeded in reigniting the pain in her head.

"I am so glad you are unharmed," the voice added with increasing clarity.

"Is that what it is?" growled Hollie, her voice slow and slurred. With an effort greater than she was prepared for, she managed to force open an eyelid onto a blurred and painfully bright world. "Not exactly what I'd call unharmed," she finally continued, struggling slightly against rope ties which bound her to a metal chair. She strained to open her eyes again, blinking a few times to clear her vision. After a while she was able to see the elderly man who paced in front of her, dressed in a long white gown.

"You live, do you not?" he asked casually and leaned in closely to look at her face. "Ahh, he will be pleased," the Prior concluded, standing back and rubbing his hands together. "You are exactly what he was hoping for and not too far gone either."

The old man breathed easily through a bright smile and waved a hand loosely, gesturing behind Hollie. In response two moderately built men clad in tight black vests and dark jeans abandoned their positions behind her and moved to exit the room.

"My assailants, I presume?" asked Hollie as she carefully watched the men leave. She inspected the thick metal door, finding a small viewing slat around eye level, before quickly scanning the rest of the cell. There was no window or even any sort of apparent ventilation, just bare, unchanging concrete all about her. The floor too was made up of simple terracotta tiling, unique in no way other than appearing relatively clean and new.

"I do apologise for their... blunt encounter with you. You see, although useful for simple tasks, they do tend to lack the understanding of anything more than a heavy object," he sighed and seemed to lament the situation. "Suffice to say, all they care about is where their next payment is coming from."

"I'm touched by your compassion," Hollie scowled cynically, forcing at the ropes tying her hands again.

"Then again, measures had to be taken given that you would have been most... difficult had you been given the choice to accompany us," he waited for a few seconds, considering the women in front of him. He then smiled gently again and crouched down, forcing Hollie to recoil back as much as the ropes would allow. "I assure you that we mean not to harm you. Quite the opposite, in fact. We would have you as our honoured guest."

"Release me, then," snapped Hollie, once more tugging at the ropes. "Why should I believe you if you keep me like this!" she gritted her teeth and leant forward, staring the old man in the eyes.

"We do this for your own protection... as well as our own," he quickly stood back up and walked around Hollie, out of her sight. "Considering what you bear, any harm which comes to you would be detrimental to our efforts."

"What are you talking about?" growled Hollie but was immediately cut off by her head being forced down as the Prior inspected her wound.

He parted her hair and lightly touched the scabbing sore, making Hollie breath in sharply, hissing at the sudden pain. Once again it washed through her head, making her wince and almost pass out. After a second or two the old man released her, letting her throw her head back and bare her teeth at him, her loose and matted hair falling to cover half of her face.

"You will rest," the old man stated clearly, taking a stance back in front of her. "Soon enough everything will become clear," he abruptly turned and headed to the doorway.

Illumination

"Wait!" shouted Hollie as he stepped through the metal door and slammed it closed from the other side, sliding a bolt into place with a clang. "You can't leave me here like this!" she screamed at the door just as the slit opened sharply and the man's eyes appeared at the opening.

"Rest now. I guarantee you will begin to think much clearer if you do," he slid the shutter back into place and walked off, his footsteps disappearing into the distance.

Hollie closed her eyes tightly and ground her teeth, struggling to cope with the pain The Prior had left her in. She thought about how she had ended up like this, what she could have possibly done to deserve it. Richard had wanted their lives to be normal, just a simple, everyday existence without having to consider anything remotely out of the ordinary. She would be lying if she said she hadn't always wanted the same but she had been scared. Scared of this exact sort of complication, although she never thought it could ever get this bad.

Sitting alone in the cold, empty cell, with no idea why she had been imprisoned in the first place, Hollie came to an unsettling realisation. It was something which she had always known in her heart and a thing, she suspected, Richard must have as well. That it was never possible for Medians to live like everyone else did. That anything bad or other worldly was drawn to them, and them alone, so that everyone else could go about their peaceful lives unfettered.

She looked around the cell once more, the pain in her head starting to fade again, and thought about what Richard had been through. How similar it all must have been, that same fear and anticipation. This, she decided, must have been the way of all Medians. To be tested in fire. To overcome or die. Richard had just about been able to overcome but, at the end of it all, would she? Would she even be the same person? Even if someone eventually came for her, right now, she needed to face this on her own. Like every other Median in their time of trial; she was alone.

The inverted heavens twisted and turned in a world unsure of itself, where life blurred into the obscure and every action was merely an echo of truth. The clouds radiated darkly against the swirling grey of a tormented sky, broken only by the black sun shining a fragmented aurora over the world below. The dark star existed only because it should, a cold reflection of reality, its only reason being that the living realm possessed it so this one must as well.

The large house seemed to exert an excess energy into the ether, breathing as though a living being. It was the thrum in the air of the living world made visible, a shimmering wave radiating darkly out into the void. A beacon to some but to most it was a warning, a symbol of power amongst the ineffectual.

Inside, caught between the skin of two worlds never meant to meet, Richard stood bewildered at the presence of his oldest friend. He was an anomaly, one who should not be, a soul having already moved on to the Other Side, never to return. Yet there he sat. Richard's mind convulsed as he fought his instincts which screamed to purge the invader. He tried to reason that it could all be a mental break as he tried to come to terms with what had happened to Hollie. Despite the unreality of it all, something remained distinctly palpable to Richard, the indefinable sense to see the world beyond dreams.

"Don't be scared, Rich," Chris said softly, "I'm not a malicious spectre and you're not hallucinating either. This is all very much real... Too real if I'm honest."

Richard was frozen for a few seconds, staring at his lost friend. "How?" he finally breathed uneasily.

"It's..." Chris looked around briefly, trying to gather the right words to express himself, "complex," he finally finished, unsure if he should elaborate further. "Look, my time here is short," he added quickly.

"Short?" asked Richard, raising his eyebrows. "You just turn up like this and then say that you can't stay long?" he snapped, still trying to process the situation. "How about a 'Hi, Rich. How's life?'"

Chris smiled shortly, getting to his feet and turning to Richard. "How *is* life?" he asked genuinely.

Richard cocked his head and rolled his eyes, "you know, same old, same old...Tried giving *this* up," he raised his arms to the ghostly

Illumination

atmosphere. "You know, that whole living without hassle from the worlds of intervening existence."

Chris moved towards Richard, trying to avoid startling his old friend. "I know how you feel...I've been watching and all I can say is that you shouldn't give up on this. There is so much you still have to gain...Such wonderful things await you, Rich. You have to believe me."

Richard sighed heavily and turned away briefly before swinging back around and pointing a finger accusingly at Chris. "Believe you? Tell you what. You wanna prove there's something good to be had? Tell me where she is. You say you've been watching so tell me how to save her."

"I can't, Richard-"

"Can't!?" screamed Richard. "You know who she is, right? What she means to me?"

"I do but this is not what I'm here for!" growled Chris, matching Richard's tone and quickly silencing him. "I'm sorry but there are bigger things to worry about. I wouldn't normally even contemplate doing what I've done...Do you realise how many rules I've broken by coming here?" he stopped and waited for Richards' eventual nod. "...So, you know I wouldn't do it just for anything?" he looked sternly at Richard again for a few moments then rubbed his eyes. "Admittedly, it wasn't as hard as it used to be," he added quietly to himself, catching Richard's attention again.

"What happened?"

Chris thought for a while, unsure how much he should divulge and less certain how much of it he was right about. "Cracks are appearing...The Other Side is growing closer to the living world and soon it may even be possible to return from there entirely. I mean, how else do you think I managed to get here and, trust me, if I can do it then you better believe there'll be others..." Chris looked Richard in the eyes and thought about what it had cost to stop the last one. "It'll be on both sides too. That means more like you. More with the power of the Other Side and as the worlds move closer soon enough there will be no divide at all. Think about it. Those with the power of the beyond, able to step between life and death at their own leisure. They'd be a god."

Messiah

Richard sighed, almost in relief despite Chris' warning. "I think I know who you're talking about...These wannabe gods are the bastards who took Hollie..." Richard closed his eyes and tried to control his fears. "They're the ones trying to manipulate the planes...the Illumous...Now I know what they're trying to do, I might be able to stop them," he tried to leave but barely even managed to turn a shoulder before Chris grabbed his arm tightly and pulled him back.

"You don't get it, do you?" Chris barked, throwing his free hand forward in frustration. "I know who the Illumous are and I know that they are nothing compared to what is still coming...They're not causing the cracks, they're just using them. Why do you think they've returned now? Why do you think they believe their 'Messiah' has chosen this, of all times?"

Chris stopped and looked Richard deep in the eyes again but this time it was different. He stared at him with a meaning that went beyond anything to do with the Illumous. In all the years he had known him, Richard had never seen Chris quite like this.

"Do you really think it's a coincidence she got pregnant now?" Chris spoke the words slowly, trying to make them as palatable as possible.

A shudder shot up Richard's spine and his eyes began to well up as, once again, the meaning of Chris' words sank in. What the Imam had insinuated was one thing but hearing it like this was something else.

"They are all connected, Rich. Everything is converging to some final play... But the Illmous aren't it, they're just the buffet for something much worse... I know you're dealing with a lot but you'll need to be ready...For all our sakes."

Richard began shaking his head gently, then with more conviction as he seemed to decide something. "No," he said quietly, "I don't care what comes next. I'm going to get my family back, Chris, and if some whacko cult wants to get in my way, then let them."

"I guess people don't change after all," he let go of Richard's arm and nodded firmly. "I know you want answers... but I think you already know where to find them..."

Illumination

Richard opened the door slightly before turning back to Chris. "Yeah," he said as the candles flickered and reality began to return around him. "I guess I do."

Richard sighed heavily, swinging the door wide open and exiting back out into the living world. With his absence the candles were quickly extinguished by an imperceptible breeze. Just like that the space was back to being a dusty, cluttered storeroom and Chris was gone.

"How are the preparations coming?" asked Earnest absently, gently touching his rejuvenated face as another cloaked figure moved into his auditorium. "I trust they are advancing promptly."

"Indeed, Sire," the man scurried from the mouth of the dark tunnel and across the polished floor to the foot of Earnest's throne. He was the Prior responsible for Hollie's capture although his demeanour was far less brazen as he bowed before his lord. "The holy barer has been located and is now in our..." he considered the word carefully, briefly glancing up to judge Earnest's mood, "...care."

Earnest suddenly sucked in a sharp breath and flicked his eyes down at the disciple, his gaze becoming fixed and piercing. "She is being treated well?"

"Ergh..." the Prior tried in vain, "well enough, Sire," he looked around at the row of perfect sculptures, including the newest, half shattered addition. He knew exactly what they were and would do anything not to join them.

"If I find her harmed in any way..." Earnest started, staring down at the man below him.

"She was...difficult to reason with and the hired hand may have been somewhat overzealous with their force," he started quickly, making sure Earnest did not have the chance to finish his no doubt devious thought, "but I give you my assurance that she has not been permanently harmed. She is resting in her cell-"

"Cell?" Earnest snapped, rising quickly from his chair, making the Prior start back. His motion was so swift that even a few of the guards twitched nervously. "You do realise the importance of our guest, do you not? At this moment there is nothing more vital than what she carries. Therefore, I think both she and I would appreciate it if you did not cage her like an animal!"

"But my lord, she is a dangerous risk and is still extremely volatile-"

"Do you defy me?!" Earnest growled deeply, a black haze briefly shimmering over his face, tingeing his eyes a dull red.

For a moment he hovered over the Prior before calming and stepping down from his throne, taking his follower lightly by the arm. In a flash he silently drew a short dagger from his cloak and smoothly buried it in the Priors stomach.

"Now..." Earnest started gently, pressing on the blade deeper as the Prior clutched at the hilt, "next time I would hope that you utilised your discretion more wisely," he slowly withdrew the dagger, allowing the Prior to curl over in pain, "...and never question me again."

Earnest waved his free hand over the wound and a few black wisps leapt from his palm. They swirled around the bloody lesion, knitting the flesh back together until it appeared as though nothing had occurred.

"I shall deal with her myself," he said finally, placing the blade back beneath his cloak. "You may leave me now..."

The Prior bowed his head nervously, looking down in disbelief at his stomach. Before he could incur any further wrath, he hurried back towards the narrow tunnel, clutching at his stomach all the way.

"When will they learn?"

Earnest stepped around a few drops of blood on the polished floor and sidled over to one of the guards, making him quiver uneasily. He scrutinised the guards' attire for some time as if to revel in the discomfort he was causing. At last, he straightened the guard's robe with a sharp jerk and quickly moved off towards the entrance tunnel, letting the guard sag slightly in relief.

The dank tunnel system was a far cry from the lavish auditorium. Within them there was only a dim lamp light to guide the way, the antique lanterns casting occasional pools of dull orange light across the moss-covered flagstones. Unfettered by the claustrophobic space, Earnest marched past an array of passages, each branching off into the warren of dark tunnels. It was only his intimate knowledge of the labyrinth which prevented him from becoming lost, eventually directing him down a slightly wider tunnel, its walls buttressed with crumbling red brick.

Soon enough it became apparent that this passage was not part of the original tunnel system but had rather been dug through into an area of much more modern design. The damp limestone gave way to breezeblock walls roughly coated in concrete and mortar with the tiled floor looking almost pristine in comparison.

There was only a single guard here, dressed in the same robes as those in the main auditorium. He gave a hurried bow and stood to attention while Earnest inspected the four iron doors which dominated the room. Three had their viewing slits open, revealing empty cells beyond, but the fourth was firmly sealed, making Earnest scoff.

"Show her to me," he stated clearly to the lone guard.

Quickly obliging, the guard quickly bowed again and hurried over to the locked cell, opening it with a speed as though his life may depend on it. Behind it, Earnest found Hollie still tied to the chair, drifting in and out of consciousness as she tried to fight the effects of an untreated concussion. Immediately Earnest rushed in and went about untying her bonds, the thought of her trying to escape not even crossing his mind.

As soon as the ropes binding her arms fell away, Hollie brought up a clenched fist with as much strength as she could muster, trying to strike Earnest cleanly in the chin. Instead, with barely a hint of motion, Earnest managed to catch her arm and bend it back, gazing deeply into her hazy eyes as he did.

"I do not wish to hurt you," said Earnest calmly, continuing to press Hollie's arm back, making her grind her teeth. "You have already suffered far more than I would have liked." He released her wrist, allowing her arm to fall limply at her side.

"You're just like the other guy!" growled Hollie, pressing herself against into the chair as Earnest continued on to untie the remaining ropes lashing her feet together. "Promise to help then leave me tied to a chair to die!" Earnest looked up briefly as if to take what she had said into consideration. "Only he wasn't stupid enough to untie me!"

Again, Hollie struck out once the ropes were loosened, catching Earnest with the fiercest kick her weakened body could allow before making a dash for the door. Her break for freedom was short lived, however, as she found herself faced with the tip of a halberd, the twitchy guard at the other end jabbing it towards her.

"I release you," Earnest said, slowly getting up from the floor and adjusting his robes, "simply so that you may come to trust me…" He stretched out an arm invitingly, offering for Hollie to return to the cell, "but I'm afraid I cannot allow you to leave."

"I don't know who you are or what you want with me but I'm sure as hell never going to trust you!" she snarled and gestured to the stark concrete walls. "You expect that you can break in, assault and kidnap me then expect me to miraculously trust you?" she laughed shortly and looked to the ground in desperation. "What kind of joke do you think this is?"

"I guarantee that from this point on you will be well cared for… Then, soon enough, you will come to realise that your destiny lies with us," he stared at Hollie again while she backed herself against a wall, futilely looking for any sort of escape route. Hanging his head, Earnest rubbed his eye casually and picked something from beneath his nail, rubbing it between his fingers. "Would you accompany me, please?" he asked shortly, reaching out an offering hand.

"Will I hell!" Hollie spat the words at him, moving around to the far side of the cell where she could see the guard at the door, the halberd still braced in his grip.

Earnest withdrew his hand and placed it calmly by his side, taking a step towards Hollie. "Let me put it this way…The alternative is something I think we would both rather avoid."

He gazed at Hollie meaningfully, his eyes shifting in colour, glowing with a dark radiance which hypnotised her into considering his request. After a few seconds Earnest looked around to the guard and nodded to him gently, making him lower his weapon and retake a stance at the tunnel entrance.

"Come with me?" asked Earnest softly, reaching out a hand again.

Illumination

Hollie craned her head to examine the unguarded doorway and considered running again. With a little more thought, she began to consider how she had no idea where she was or even what sort of resistance may stand in her way. Coupled with a not insignificant head wound slowing her down, Hollie concluded that her chances would be slim at best. She was also beginning to fear that her host's patience, while liberal, may not be limitless. After a while, she forced herself to step forward and quickly felt Earnest's hand press against her back, guiding her from the cell. Without thinking she shrugged him away and made sure to keep a step ahead as they exited into the narrow tunnel.

Stepping barefoot onto the damp, mossy stones, Hollie couldn't help but shiver uncontrollably. To an extent she had been sheltered in the prison cell but now the cold breeze whistling through the tunnels whipped up around her, chilling her though the thin linen of her nightwear.

They worked their way through the system of passages, the cool air only seeming to grow stronger as they went. With it came a much fresher scent than the musty air of Hollies captivity, leading them through what seemed to be miles of the cramped tunnels. Every time Hollie began to fall back, she would be met with Earnest's hand again placed uncomfortably on her back, spurring her forwards again. On and on they trudged until they at last arrived at the base of a steep stone staircase nestled at the end of one of the passages.

The ancient steps had been worn down by centuries of use and were dipped in their centres, causing gaps to open where the steps had started to come away from each other. At the top of the staircase was the dull but unmistakable glow of sunshine and the source of the fresh air. It was something Hollie was all too happy to see and set about heading towards before Earnest even had the chance to prompt her further.

As she approached the end of her climb, Hollie was forced to shield her eyes against the brightness of daylight after spending so much time in the gloom below. Stepping out from the open trapdoor, she did her best to look about her new surroundings but found herself instead blinking wildly at the light, unable to see much of anything.

"The change can be somewhat intense," Earnest stated calmly without suffering the same discomfort.

Once more he placed a hand gently on Hollie's shoulder and guided her a few steps, ensuring that she was facing the correct way.

Rubbing her eyes, Hollie managed to look through squinted eyes at a large space with rows upon rows of squat wooden benches placed along its length. To their sides were small stained-glass windows lining the building, leading up to another, much larger window with a mural depicting the Virgin Mary.

"I know this place," whispered Hollie softly. "My mother always made me come here," her mind drifted, thinking of times past and how much had changed. Suddenly her expression dropped and she clenched her fist tightly, cracking her knuckles in the process. "How long have you desecrated this place!?" she snarled, swinging around to face Earnest ferociously. "How dare you!"

"Believe me when I say we chose this place only for its unique qualities. You see, the building happens to be constructed on a nexus of sorts, a place where the membrane between worlds is much thinner than usual," Earnest eyed Hollie knowingly. "You can't tell me you haven't noticed them here...More of them pushing through than anywhere else?" he smiled gently and looked around dismissively at the church. "Say what you want about religion but someone knew what they were doing with this place... Us, however..." he shook his head absently, "we do not care not for the beliefs of this world. Especially not so much as to desecrate them out of malice," he leaned in closely towards Hollie, cocking his head and raising his eyebrows slightly, "unlike some I could mention..." he took a deep breath in and looked over Hollie as if he were staring into her soul. "Such as a certain... associate of yours," Earnest spoke the words with a deep sense of knowing and his eyes hazed over again with that unsettling darkness.

"What do you want from me?" she asked quickly, trying to ignore his last comment. "You didn't abduct me just to insult my taste in friends... no matter how much you seem to be enjoying it," she added, seeing that Earnest took a degree of pleasure in his efforts to shake her confidence.

"Quite," he responded shortly, unwavering in the gaze he held over her. "Indeed, that was not the reason," he finally flicked his eyes away from her and looked about the place, seemingly impressed by its architecture despite having no doubt seen it countless times. "You'll be relieved to know that it is not actually you that I require. Although, you are still of vital importance to our cause...You see, I would have what you carry..."

For the first time Hollie looked upon Earnest with a genuine degree of fear. "Carry?" she asked in an effort to play dumb. "What are you talking about?" she glanced over her empty hands as if to emphasise her point. "I don't *carry* anything," she insisted, slowly realising that Earnests' eyes had drifted over her body and settled on her stomach.

"Come now, we both know that you are the mother of the future," slowly his eyes moved back to meet with Hollies again, "our future..."

"No... You can't-" tried Hollie, unable to shake the hold she suddenly felt Earnest had over her. "You can't know that! You can't!" she screamed at last, clutching her hair tightly in distress.

Earnest moved silently towards her and reached out an inviting hand one final time. "We knew long before you could have. The coming of such a one... It has been ordained for centuries... Truth will be revealed when the boundaries which divide us fall..." Earnest slowly reached out a second hand and raised them both above his head towards the rafters of the church, "and come, he shall, to lead us to our divine purpose. To bridge the worlds and join all as one great whole," the words resonated around the building, strengthening his resolve.

As he spoke Hollie fell to her knees and clawed her fingers through her hair, unable to comprehend what he wanted to do. "You can't...Can't know..." she repeated quietly over and over until she suddenly stopped for a second. "Richard doesn't even know..." she finished before falling completely silent.

Earnest looked down at her and lowered his arms. "Come, my dear. I am quite sure he has made the discovery by now... Although this does pose some amount of complication given that there are now no lengths he will not go in order to have you, and what lay within you, returned to him." Earnest bent down close to Hollie and pushed back a length of hair from her face. "Such power...A pity he will have to perish for our dreams to live. After all, we cannot have our messiah, nor his revered mother... distracted..." he looked firmly at her, "especially not before her tragic death while giving birth..." he smiled shortly and got back to his feet.

Hollie suddenly flicked her eyes up at him and raised her head slowly, grimacing at everything about him. "Do what you want with me..." she scowled furiously, "but I will never allow you to do anything to my child!" she spoke in low, hideously dark tones, peering out menacingly from beneath a matt of fallen hair.

Earnest took a breath in sharply. "Pregnancy is long... Minds can be changed," he noted, confident that this would be the case. "Assuredly, so will yours."

"Go to hell."

III-IV – Illuminatus

So taste ye My Wrath and My Warning

                                                             -Al-Qamar 54:39

*C**hris was right, I did know where to go, not that it made me feel any better about it. It was a place I hadn't been in a very long time, not since I was a young man first stumbling onto the truth of being a Median. I still knew a few people who went there so it wasn't as though I was completely in the dark about the place. It's just that I would have preferred if some of them avoided it altogether. Then again, I guess to stop them would be to deny myself the very same all those years ago. Now, though...things have changed. I had changed and wasn't welcome there at the best of times, let alone after helping to disgrace the Seers. They didn't want ageing Medians with a foot in the Other Side spoiling their fun, reminding them of a mortality which was either too close to too far away for them to care about. All they wanted was a night to forget about whatever plagued their living existence. Unfortunately, tonight would not be one of those nights...*

Richard stood, frozen in the early afternoon sunshine, the warm rays washing over him and casting a deep shadow across a nearby wall. Despite the summer sun, it felt to Richard as though a dark cloud weighed heavily over him, its shade draining what little faith he had left.

He turned to look fixedly at an old metal door set virtually unnoticed within the wall next to him. It was covered in faded graffiti and smeared with decade old rust, perfectly camouflaged in the urban bustle.

Jerking himself around, Richard turned his attention to a small plaque just to the side of the door. With the bright sunlight glaring on the old, corroded copper the wording was near invisible to anyone not aware of it. On the face of it, the black and sickly green muck filling the etched letters only seemed to make them that less legible. Richard knew better, though, for to the right people, the words shined with an unnatural vibrancy, even in the dead of night. Covering the plague from the glare of the sun with his arm, Richard managed to make out the words he remembered from his youth.

ENTER NOT THOSE WHO REFUSE TO SEE

This was the place, Richard thought to himself. The town had changed but this was the same. He turned back to the busy street, only acknowledging the noise of the traffic now it was in view. It all seemed like a dream to him. The people rushing past him, fretting about their simple, everyday lives while something much worse than any of them could contemplate threatened their eternal existence. Rather than pitying them as other Medians might, their frivolous concerns only reminded Richard of why he wanted to be like them. But now he was deeper than ever, daring not to think about what was being asked of him and what would happen if he were to fail. That's why he had come to this place. Even though it felt like an act of wild desperation, Richard knew there was no better place to find out what he needed to know. The Imam had known this as well, the *people* here, he affirmed to himself, knew all there was to know about what transpired between the worlds. They were things that shouldn't be known by any mortal, secrets meant only for the dead. Then again, Richard considered, those who frequented this place usually didn't realise there was a difference. The problem was that they were all night dwellers which meant that, while the sun was up, this place was no more helpful than anywhere else.

Illumination

Richard looked up at the sky and squinted at the deep blue ocean of air, barely a wisp of cloud to spoil the summer sun. Even though it was probably the more sensible course of action, Richard wasn't prepared to wait hours just for the mere chance at learning something. He looked down again and across the street to catch a glimpse of a ghostly figure. It hung, motionless, on the far side of the road, hidden partly in the shade of the railway bridge and shrouded in an ethereal white haze. Before he even managed to fathom the sight, a car rushed by, distracting Richard's glance long enough for the figure to vanish.

For a time, Richard went over the apparition in his head, trying to comprehend what it could mean. Then, in an instant of clarity, it dawned on him who the figure had been and shuddered as Chris' ghostly, echoed voice pierced the fabric of existence itself. It implanted itself in the back of Richard's mind, overpowering the rest of the ever-present voices. In turn they all began to fall silent, the single, overpowering voice of a bygone Median rising above the choir of lost, indistinct muttering.

"Do what you must..." came Chris' forlorn voice through the ether between the worlds.

"Are you following me now?" grunted Richard, shaking his head.

"I'm always watching, Rich."

"Ok, well how about you don't? Either that or tell me something useful!"

"Too much is at stake not to. Even now the planes drift ever closer...More so than even the Illumous realise...You must do all you can to avert this, my friend."

"Why?!" Richard shouted out loud in the middle of the street, drawing the bemused attention of several pedestrians. "You know all I care about is *her*!" he finished in low, almost deluded tones. "Now will you tell me where she is or not!?" he screamed again, turning the heads of several more people, including a pair of community officers.

There was a pause for several seconds, almost to the extent that Richard thought Chris had left him again, before one simple word was pressed against the world into Richard's mind. "No," he stated shortly, making Richard turn harshly and stop short of punching the wall behind him, "I cannot..."

"Cannot or will not?" Richard forced between gritted teeth.

"Cannot!" said Chris again. "Although her presence can be felt, her location is hidden...Even I cannot see her." A disturbing quiet settled in Richard's head as the subtle murmurings of the damned abandoned him altogether. "To find your answers, you must follow what you feel to be true...Do what you must," he at last repeated.

Richard was about to answer but chose against it as he realised that his friend had already left him, sunken back into the depths of the border worlds. This disturbed him more than he cared to admit. It wasn't just that a long dead friend was haunting him but the fact that he was able to do it so readily.

There was always a constant pressure on the living world from those beyond, an eternal struggle to return to the world they knew so well but never had he seen anything like this. Most in the border world were merely imprints, echoes of themselves calling through from the Other Side. Those condemned to the Median Worlds were the ones who had clung too tightly to life, refusing to move on at all costs. Then there were those who had simply gotten lost in the crossing, destined to linger between worlds as a phantom of life. All of them, though, every single one, Richard thought, had taken decades, years upon years of a lost existence to make even a slither of their presence felt again. Except Chris. Here he was, actively influencing the world of the living, pressing through to be far more than just a drone in the recesses of Richard's mind.

Suddenly everything fell into place and, whether he wanted to or not, Richard knew it was time to accept the truth. The things he had been told. They were more than just tasks he could absently attend to in the hopes of returning to some form of comfortable normality. He had been responsible for all of this, done something no living person should have ever done. By touching the Other Side, he had ripped a hole between the planes, cracking the very fabric of the world. A crack the Illumous were all too ready to exploit, tearing it open until all that had ever or would ever be merged into a single, unified reality.

Illumination

Richard gasped, unable to accept his own reasoning. Without him the Illumous would never have had a reason to rear their heads again. Most of all, they wouldn't have needed Hollie.

Stumbling back against the warm brick wall behind him, Richard felt as though he was drifting, lost and alone in an abyss of his own creation. The people who passed him became nothing more than distant, intangible shadows, a cold manifestation of his despairing mind.

While the world became as a dream to him, a wild, terrifying urge suddenly took hold of Richard. Everything he feared, all he had ever run from culminated in this one action, a single gesture of faith which would seal his future.

He distantly glanced up at the busy road in front of him, cars rushing up and down the baking tarmac, barely slowing for even the traffic lights. Without thinking Richard pushed himself away from the wall as another car hurtled along the road and stepped into its path without a second's notice.

With a piercing squeal of braking tyres, the car hit Richard side on, sweeping his legs from beneath him and throwing him across the bonnet. He rolled over the windshield and was launched towards the far side of the street where his body tumbled limply onto the curb, his head cracking against the pavement. Finally, the car ground to a halt some way down the road and fell silent, smoke billowing from its tyres, as a crowd began to quickly gather around Richard. A few tried to provide some sort of aid but, as they always did, most stopped to merely gawk at the spectacle of his broken, prostrate body.

In the midst of fading life and agonising pain, time seemed to slow around Richard. Those around him moved like a memory, as though their actions were only echoes of the distant past. The air around him began to fade, the life in it draining away to a colourless void.

Without fighting the urge, Richard allowed his eyes to fall shut and one last feeling drifted through his mind. It wasn't fear or regret but a simple hope that he could achieve in death what he could not in life. With that his mind fell silent and he was gone.

I didn't know what I was doing. Everything seemed like it was a dream, some terrible nightmare which had finally led me to this. Of course, I had other options, I could have waited for an answer to present itself, get what I needed from the bar. Chris had shown me something, though. By speaking to me as if the borders weren't even there, he had made me realise that there was something far greater at work out here, no matter how much I tried to deny it. It was greater even than my desire to keep Hollie safe... enough to drive me to this.

I had already spent too much time in the Median world. Under normal circumstances even a second there would allow the Other Side to take hold of my living soul and drag it into eternal death. Regardless, I was compelled to take that one last risk and see, even if just for that second, the truth of what I had done.

Richard shuddered and a sharp chill spread throughout his body, the sensation of a nothingness against his skin. His head spun as though he were being tossed around by a world that didn't know what to do with him. Slowly it came to him that he was falling, loosely tumbling through the invisible air of an eternal void. Had the situation been different, Richard would have felt it to be almost freeing. Soon enough, though, he was jerked by an unseen force and lurched uncomfortably as his mind and body fell back together.

He waited for a few seconds, expecting to feel the glacial touch of the Far Side pulling him away. Instead, all he felt was a fierce scratching at the back of his mind, as though something was telling him that nothing was quite as it should have been. Soon he came to realise that there was an almost imperceptible warmth which passed over him every so often. It lingered on him, like a breath on the back of his neck, scrutinising him, knowing he did not belong. Richard dared not move, remaining motionless for some considerable time, refusing even to open his eyes, lest the afterlife finally snatch him away.

The longer he refused to react to this new environment, the more he learnt about it. It occurred to him that he had stopped falling some time ago and was now splayed across a tarmac pavement. He wondered for a second if he had really left the living realm at all but there was something about the ground beneath him which told him otherwise. There was something about it which did not feel entirely real, but then nothing ever did in the desert. Everything was just an image pressed against the world, holding the feigned illusion of reality in lieu of its own. But this was different. Rather than simply mimicking the living world, it was as if the desert were mocking it. It stayed with Richard like a bitter taste he could not spit out, the foulness of it making him feel sick.

Eventually Richard dared to open his eyes slightly, squinting cautiously at a world on its side, but quickly flicked them wide once he saw what was out there. Pressing himself from the ground, Richard gaped in dumbfounded silence as dark images shifted all around him. They were each surrounded by a shimmering, near indiscernible halo of red energy which glowed all that much brighter out of the corner of Richard's eye. The outline translated to the buildings and cars, every one of them with a faint crimson glow which stood atop the deep black aura painting the city.

Richard looked around in an effort to understand what had happened. The desert was a place no-one truly understood but this was something entirely different. Everything he had known, the years he had spent learning of the celestial worlds, it all meant nothing now. The only thing Richard had to rely on anymore was what he put together for himself.

Thinking on what Chris had said, a sort of clarity started to emerge from the chaos of Richard's mind, giving an unsure meaning to what the Median World had become. Was this really what the collision of worlds looked like? A prelude to the Illumous' ultimate goals?

Richard looked about at the varying shades of shifting reality, the subdued hue of buildings a backdrop for the vivid sprites drifting around the street. He watched carefully as they turned and moved like that of any normal person, failing to realise that this is exactly what they were. They were the radiance of a person's life force burning into the fabric of astral space.

Richard looked around again and turned just as one of the sprites stepped through him, continuing along the street like nothing had happened. The encounter left him with that same unnerving warmth as when he had arrived and a disquieting notion dawned on him. It was not simply that each of these absent forms fleeting by was a living person, merely going about their lives. It was more that, somehow, he knew them.

Each one of them projected a sense of their persona into the air, the changed world stripping away the seclusion of their own minds. In a place usually so devoid of it, the vast surge of unfiltered life was enough to overwhelm Richard, the usual chatter which plagued his mind paling next to this constant barrage of thoughts and emotions. What's more was that each of the shades who passed through him briefly entangled with Richard's own awareness, granting him an uncomfortably intimate familiarity with them. It almost felt to him as though, for a moment, he *was* them.

Across the street was a ring of shades, gathered around another who appeared as only a faint, translucent shadow of darkened energy. It took Richard no time in acknowledging that it was him, at least the fading image of his dying body. He turned away quickly, trying not to think about how close he was to the edge of life. It seemed the only thing that kept him from crossing over completely was that the Other Side wanted nothing to do with him now. That, he concluded, was something he could not guarantee would not last.

Turning back out of morbid curiosity, Richard watched the scene as a dread rose up in his chest. Whereas once the dead had haunted this place, briefly traversing it on their way to eternal rest, they had now been ousted, not by some terrible horror of the Abyss but rather the living. He gazed up at the sprawling sky, a turbulent, desolate sea of vibrant, living red against the deathly blacks of the void. Everything about what the desert had become troubled him, he could feel it eating away at his sanity, the knowledge that everything was far beyond what he knew to be real. Richard tried to bury the feeling, fighting himself for some sort of focus or even the real reason he was here in the first place.

In the midst of thought, all the turmoil which had plagued Richard sank into irrelevance as he asked himself why he had done something so extreme. He had done it for Hollie, that much was obvious, but now there was another, someone Richard was willing

Illumination

to go beyond death for. Even still, there was more to it than that. Whether he liked it or not, whatever part of the Other Side which resided within Richard had whispered the answer, guiding him to a place where he could find his family. It was far from the selfless gesture it seemed, however, and was rather an act to preserve whatever balance still existed between the worlds. No matter how he had tried to escape his calling, Richard would be forced to accept that the fate of his family and the worlds beyond were inextricably tied together. To save one would be to save both and to abandon his post now was to forsake all.

Richard swung around quickly as he felt a dull, itching warmth gently caress his back, reaching out towards him like tendrils creeping through the open air. In the distance stood a bright prism that rose high over the buildings in the city. The glowing tower of light shone a vibrant red which brightened to a blinding white towards its centre.

Squinting through the incandescence, Richard was able to make out the shadow of the cathedral's bell tower engulfed within the scarlet citadel. It was a place he knew all too well given how many had tried to return from the border world there. All too quickly, Richard's eyes began to burn and he was forced to tear his gaze away from the blinding spectacle, puzzled by the extent of physical discomfort. Usually, the desert offered nothing but a cold numbness but the fact he could still feel pain, even without a corporeal body, told him just how close the worlds had come.

He considered everything he had seen and felt here, glancing between the spectres again. Questions arose in his mind about how exactly it had all come to pass, how had it happened without anyone noticing? In the end, Richard decided, none of that mattered. The important thing was that he had found what he was looking for. He didn't know if it would lead to Hollie, he didn't even know if he would get the answers to his questions, but he knew that shining citadel was the key. So long as he followed the path laid out for him and renewed his faith in the gifts of a Median then everything would work out. Given all Richard had been through, the flame of faith was a difficult one to rekindle. Regardless, he had been given a chance he couldn't afford to let slip away.

Richard definitely turned back to the prism of light beaming high into the stormy, eerily desolate skies and began to run along the street. Ahead of him awaited the cathedral and something that should never have existed.

None of this was right. I was losing any sense of where I was and soon I would start to forget who I was. The desert ate away at the soul at the best of times but now... Now it was something different. The Median world was colliding with the living plane and already souls were bleeding through. Given a little longer, people would start falling between worlds entirely. In a few months there wouldn't be anything left of either world, just a single, deformed existence where no one lived or died. That was never going to be the end of it, though. The Illumous would always push on towards their ultimate aim. In time, nothing would be the same anymore. They would tear away the divide between worlds and nothing would be left to stop them. Only by seeing it with my own eyes did I understand why it had to end now. That tower of light was a beacon, a message for me and me alone. It was meant to lead me to the Illumous, to show me the truth and make sure I did everything in my power to stop them... It had to end, and I had to be the one to end it.

Earnest followed Hollie closely as he pressed her through yet more of the sunken tunnels, the turns they took seeming to edge further and further away from both the church and the auditorium. Hollie considered where she was being taken, concerned it was somewhere isolated, a place she had less chance of being found. Of course, for all she knew, they could have been going around in circles in that labyrinth, making it impossible for her to map them out let alone anyone else.
As she slowly trudged along, not saying a single word, Hollie played scenarios over in her head, trying to find if there was anything she could have done to avoid her predicament. She knew they wanted both her and the child alive but apart from that she had no guarantees of what would happen to her in the short term. She hoped that Earnest, twisted as he was, would stand by his word and

that no harm would come to her, at least until she was able to escape. His word alone wasn't nearly enough to hedge her bets on, however, and once the child was born, they were off altogether.

Eventually the dark tunnel opened out into another small chamber. This time, rather than bleak concrete walls, the space was clad in pristine whitewashed plaster adorned with an array of paintings and patterned tapestries. Standing out above them all were two large, vertical banners hanging parallel to each other on two opposite walls. They depicted a golden star with pointed, spoke-like arms radiating out from the empty centre, set upon a beige, linen fabric. Spanning the entire floor of the small chamber was a mosaic sporting the same motif. The topmost ray of the golden emblem struck out towards a heavy mahogany door, its top arching high towards the ceiling and its face indented with square panelling. Either side of it stood another pair of guards, completely still and with their halberds poised at their sides.

"Welcome to your new home," Earnest's voice stated from behind, making Hollie jump slightly. "I know you are scared but you will be cared for...for as long as this takes." Earnest's voice carried a foreboding undertone which told Hollie everything she needed to know about his intent. "For now, though, your every need will be tended to," he placed a hand softly on her shoulder and pushed her gently toward the doors, prompting the guards to open it for her.

Before she knew what was happening Hollie was walking towards the open doorway. Inside laid a suite worthy of royalty, a startling difference to the network of tunnels snaking around under the city. There was a king-sized bed placed squarely against the side wall, made up with highly decorative and clearly expensive sheets. To its side was a large bookcase lined with hundreds of tomes as well as a huge selection of films for a flat screen television attached to another wall. In the corner lay another doorway leading to a plush bathroom lined with sparklingly white tiles and golden taps.

The hand pressing on Hollies shoulder grew firmer and finally pressed her into the room. Once she had stepped through the door it was removed and she was left to look around the suite, turning back to Earnest as the guards began to close the doors.

"You will be happy here," said Earnest softly, disappearing behind the doors, "I promise you."

The doors slammed shut, shaking the ground slightly and a lock was loudly turned followed by deadbolts sliding into the ceiling and ground to secure Hollie in the room.

Earnest sighed, lamenting that it had come to this. In his mind she would have come to join them out of her own free will, without the need for imprisonment. Her botched abduction and sheer stubbornness made sure that was never about to happen now.

Eventually he turned to exit the chamber, coming to face another Dark Seer. He was easily as old as Earnest and clearly high up in the hierarchy of the Illumous only, without the benefit of the time defying brutality employed by Earnest, his haggard appearance betrayed his true age. All things considered, though, his movement was quick and nimble for such advanced years.

He turned to Earnest's side and started to walk with him, grimacing slightly. His wrinkles flexed and gently rearranged themselves, the consequence of a full and exotic life taking its toll on a fragile body.

"The process is accelerating," the senior Dark Seer stated firmly, pacing slowly along the dimly lit tunnel without facing Earnest, "the planes are approaching faster than we anticipated."

"It is all within our control," advised Earnest, his voice calm and gentle.

"Soon, I fear it no longer shall be," the old Seers voice wavered, "there is too much power building in this world, I have seen it in the plane of the Medians...He is coming here. For her."

"And, of course, he will fail," added Earnest, still pacing calmly onwards.

Finally, the old man turned, stopping Earnest with an outstretched arm. "The power of the Other Side cannot be contained. Even now it grows within the child...It feeds from it. There can only be one, my lord, that is how it was ordained and that is how it must unfold. If it does not then we will not be able to control it, rather it will control us... Either the father must be removed..." he hesitated before speaking the words but knew they must be said, "or the child must be sacrificed."

Earnest struck out an arm and gripped his apostle around the neck tightly, pressing him against the damp tunnel wall. "You dare suggest such a thing?" he growled, his eyes flashing an eerie, otherworldly crimson as he tightened his grip, dark tendrils beginning to seep from his arm and creep towards his victim. "Nothing is more important than our deliverance at the hands of this *child*!" Earnest grunted and relaxed his grip, acknowledging this one was probably better off left alive, useless, as he was, for any sort of meaningful regeneration. "Know this…" he released the frail man and withdrew his arm, the dark wraiths sinking back into his body as he did, "though you may know what I am, if you dare to question me again then I shall not hesitate to kill you."

"Yes, my lord," the Seer replied weakly, lacking the confidence he had displayed just moments ago.

Earnest nodded firmly and stepped back. "You must know that I am aware of all which occurs in that world of false Seers. As such I shall deal with this interloper as I, and only I, see fit..." Earnest gritted his teeth before pulling his robe firmly back onto his shoulder and storming away back along the tunnel, leaving the Dark Seer to collect what pride he had left and retreat away.

Richard slowed to a jog and hopped down from the curb onto the street, marvelling at the shining beacon ascending high into the air before him. He felt the urge to cough and gasp for breath, his immaterial body believing it was exhausted from running. Richard had to remind himself that it was just that, an urge, yet another illusion conjured by this world to imitate the rules of the living world.

He gazed across the shimmering wall of vibrant scarlet, beyond which stood the warped image of the cathedral. Even with the living world imprinting more than it ever had upon the desert, there was still a distinct absence to the buildings he had passed. It was an ethereal quality which made them all somehow unreal. All but this one. Every weathered sandstone block which made up the cathedral seemed almost too tangible; a hyperrealism of the immaterial.

Suddenly a living echo stepped up behind Richard and carried on into the street, passing through his arm as it went and making him coil away. It stopped a little way into the road and checked in both directions before continuing on through the shimmering red boundary without incident.

Richard's eyes widened and the sense that he had lost all understanding of this place returned. As the echo stepped through the boundary, the wall of light scanned across its form and a living person appeared on the other side. It was a middle-aged man in a suit, carrying a briefcase, presumably on his way home from work. Just a normal, everyday person going about his normal, everyday business and yet here his mere appearance defied all sense. Before Richard could completely appreciate what was going on, the man reached the other side of the street and passed through the far side of the barrier again, cutting its corner. Once more he was unfazed by the experience and continued on along the street, once more nothing but an empty echo.

Richard shook his head and squinted, unsure if what he had just seen was real. It wasn't enough that normal people were being forced against the fabric of the world, stressing it to breaking point, now they were crossing it without even realising. Inside the rift it was neither the Median world nor the living. It didn't even resemble the Border world, if such a thing still even existed.

He slowly moved to the boundary and, rather than hearing it, felt an unsettling hum which only grew more intense the more it was ignored. Richard lifted a hand and gently pressed it against the wall of red light, pushing it through to the other side, making the glowing barrier ripple and shudder as if to reject his presence. Almost instantly he obliged and pulled his hand back, looking it over carefully. Richard clenching his fist softly, the sensation of the subtle breeze and warm afternoon sun of the real world still lingering on his palm. He opened his hand again and shivered, unable to believe what he had felt was real.

Finally, with a deep breath, Richard closed his eyes and stepped through the boundary. For a brief moment, as the searingly bright light washed across his face, Richard's mind was dragged back to the past. For that split second, he saw the lorry screeching towards him, greasy smoke billowing up as its driver tried desperately to swerve away. Then he was apart, watching from afar and unable to stop what was happening. It was a memory he had relived countless times and now, just as before, there was nothing he could do other than watch his parents die.

He pressed even harder against the field in an attempt to escape the memories but he was only met with more resistance in a slow, gruelling battle of will. Richard managed to push himself onwards while the images grew stronger, each of them scratching at his mind, seeking out his darkest memories to taunt him with. His lonely childhood, the turmoil of learning what it was to be a Median and the death he had become numb to over the years.

With a final push, he punched his hand into the open air and experienced one more vision before breaking through entirely, tumbling to the ground on the other side. He clutched his head as a wave of pain swept up through the back of his neck, pushing reasonable thoughts aside in preference of a swelling agony. He felt his stomach turn and a gnawing at his insides as he retched, straining to comprehend how he was able to do such a thing without a physical form. At last, the pain began to ease, allowing the visions to come back to him. He shook his head and tried to forget about the violent transition, focussing instead on the ordeal that was no doubt to come.

Slowly Richard pressed himself to his feet, stumbling slightly while the world around him felt fluid and strangely intangible. The atmosphere spun around Richard, making the simple act of standing far more difficult than it should have been. It was only made worse by that final vision playing over and over in his head, doing its best to distract him. The others were bad enough but this one was worse than them all. It was not enough to merely push it to the back of his mind to be forgotten. Sooner or later, Richard knew he would have to face it but for now it was just another nightmare he didn't have time to indulge.

Finally, he steadied himself enough to take a few tentative steps towards the cathedrals' large, ancient doorway. Cautiously he reached forward and pressed a hand against the old wooden door, making the wood sink inwards with an almost foamy texture.

Eventually, with further persuasion, the frame gave way and a ghostly echo of the door swung quickly open before him. Almost immediately it came to a near dead stop, hanging defiantly in midair, drifting impossibly slowly to an unreachable end. Richard stepped through the narrow gap he had formed as the doorway flickered and shifted against its own nature.

Without warning he was thrown forward by a fleeting gust and managed to turn in time to see the door blink back into its original position, unable to hold the false echo in this fractured reality. He squinted at the door, trying to understand what had happened but all he could focus on was the shrill pain still ringing in his head.

Gritting his teeth, he turned back to the open church, the pain growing again with every move he made. It swelled in his head, feeling as if skull may crack open and once more another barrage of visions passed before his eyes. This time, however, it felt more controlled, as though the images had been chosen rather than being a random manifestation of his mind. They were the souls he had exorcised, those he had sent back to the Other Side and, for each of them he saw, it felt as though a part of himself went with them.

"So much is the same," a voice echoed from the far end of the church hall, taking Richard unawares, struggling through the never-ending array of visions, "and yet there is so much to learn...So much more to experience... My only regret is that, sooner or later, everything must fade into mundanity as the world adapts to even the greatest of changes," the distant voice gave way to approaching footsteps, ominously drawn out across the nave, "as would have you, I trust... Eventually."

Richard grabbed his head as the pain surged again and made him sink to his knees. "What's happening?" he managed to spit through gritted teeth as the footsteps grew closer.

His vision shifted and faltered, glimpses of gathered parishioners seated row upon row in the pews before him. They slowly moved away and drifted in and out of his vision as if they were merging in and out of existence. He grabbed his head again and looked up sharply, quickly glimpsing a shadowy echo of Hollie among the crowd. She moved her hand from her head down to her chest and then from shoulder-to-shoulder mouthing simply 'Amen' before she was gone again.

"To experience such wonders...It is truly a gift, wouldn't you say? To see the past, much as you are able to now..." Suddenly there was a muted silence and the voice appeared right next to Richards's ear, "or even the future..."

The softly spoken words raced into Richard's mind and pressed against his thoughts, imposing their own will upon him without a second thought or care. He looked around a dark, stale room as the words bore into his memories, embedding what they wished him to see.

Without realising anything had changed, Richard became aware of a baby crying, gurgling as though it wasn't entirely sure how to breathe. Slowly turning around, he caught sight of Hollie's limp body upon a steel table, surgical implements scattered all around her. Staring in disbelief at her expressionless face, Richard carefully took her hand and squeezed it, sinking his face towards hers, hoping the truth of this had somehow escaped him.

The baby's distressed cries continued to howl in Richard's ears, forcing him to glance around, a tear falling silently from his eye. At last, he settled his sights on Earnest clutching his newborn tightly to him, the dawn silhouetting any number of Dark Seers behind him. Just as he turned to join his brethren, a wide, haunting grin crept across Earnest's face and a roar of cheers erupted all around him.

With a start, Richard was pulled back, the image racing away into the distance as reality took hold of him again. He watched as dark tendrils withdrew from his head and found Earnest stood over him. The majority of his features were greyed out and a vibrant red aura surrounded the old man but, even without knowing what he looked like in the first place, Richard knew that this was the man he had been told about.

"I feel I must commend you," Earnest said softly, moving away from Richard while the tendrils sank beneath his skin, "your persistence is quite admirable. Especially in a time of such...personal turmoil," he looked over Richard's hunched figure, his mouth trying to form a question. "We have been observing you for quite some time. You see, you became of great importance to us when you blazed across the astral planes. We were particularly interested in what you would create, however. Such a wondrous thing it will be... You should be proud. The unifier of worlds, the bringer of eternal peace."

"Is that what you call it!?" snapped Richard, trying to press himself upright again. "I know what you're trying to do...Don't you understand? Life. Death. It won't mean anything. The dead and the living will become the same thing and that was never meant to happen. You'll pull reality apart!" Richard fell back onto his hands with the effort and looked up at Earnest again, grimacing furiously.

"Your kind enjoys melodrama, doesn't it?" he offered, casually reaching out a hand. "Just think of it though. The glory of a united existence, loved ones together for eternity. Even you, my friend, will live forever with those you have lost standing forever at your side."

For a brief moment Richard was captivated by the thought but quickly remembered why he was there in the first place. "I haven't lost them all yet! Now take me to Hollie!" he growled, finally managing to resist the pain enough to stubbornly get to his feet. "I know what you want from her but, mark my words, you're never going to get it!" he lurched towards Earnest and scowled at him. "You may be able to see me in this place like any other Seer, even play your imaginary games but there's no way in hell you can stop me!"

Earnest sighed and ground his teeth. "I'm afraid that's where you're wrong," he whispered, striking out to grab Richard by the collar and throwing him back down to the ground. "You could have become something great in the new order! A god among men," he snarled the words as he hung over Richard, leaning on his knees to observe the helpless mortal. "I am genuinely saddened that it should come to this. You could have been so much more but, as it stands, you have proven yourself an enemy of the Illumous and a threat to all we would accomplish... As such, I'm afraid your journey has come to its end..."

Earnest pulled the sleeves back on his robe and began reaching a bare hand towards Richard's face, his futile struggles all but ignored as the tendrils began to creep through the air. Again, they darted around Earnest, a living force of their own, wrapping around him until they covered his entire body.

"...and you will finally be at peace."

As he spoke the words, Earnests' body burst into black flame and a dark being emerged from it, connecting with Richard's face. The last thing he saw was the vibrant, scarlet eyes of the other worldly entity as the deepest, coldest terror he had ever felt rushed through his veins. Then there was silence and he felt nothing.

III-V – Static Tension

Wherever you may be, death will overtake you
                                                    -An Nisaa 4:78

From beyond the perplexing darkness came an unsettling throbbing. It came and went, echoing across the shapeless distance as if to beckon any who heard it. No matter how many times it was experienced, no-one would ever truly become accustomed to this vacant and lonely place. Although, neither would they recognise or even remember it when in a lucid state of mind, transient as it was, in its very nature.

With the fleeting grip of that wakeless realm slipping away, Richard began to stir, comfortable in the knowledge that he had somehow fallen away from Earnests' grasp. Even so, the sensation remained with him for some time, the feeling of his living soul, the very essence of life, being ripped from his body.

The throbbing grew gradually louder and took on an abrasive texture which hurt his ears. Accompanying it was an ill-defined melody suggesting it may have been music but all Richard could focus on was the low drone of dozens of people all speaking at once.

Without even fully returning to the waking world, Richard started to formulate what he was going to do. By this point he had worked out where he was and how much time must have passed. It was time he couldn't afford to lose and, out of sheer will, he flicked open his eyes and sat bolt upright. For a moment the room spun violently around Richard, forcing him to wait while his blurred vision cleared

Illumination

and his stomach settled. As he grew more coherent, it became apparent just how loud the music was and made Richard grasp at his ears, gritting his teeth in irritation.

"You're lucky to be alive," a disparaging voice came over the music next to him, "let alone get away with barely a scratch."

"What?" asked Richard weakly, turning quickly to the man.

The movement only made his head spin even more, making him realise just how drained and helpless he really was. He tried to speak again but instead sighed heavily as his mind raced with thoughts of getting away.

"Then again..." the blurred outline of the man said more calmly, "you are the *special* one they all keep on about...Maybe that power really does protect you."

Richard rubbed his eyes and strained at the figure, his shape slowly becoming clearer. "I know you," he mused softly.

"Course you do, Rich...old friends, aren't we?" he sneered. "Long time ago that was, though."

Richard straightened up as much as his wandering balance would allow and tried to focus on this old friend. "Ardal," he acknowledged. "Are you really still running this place? I always thought barman was low, especially for a man of your talents."

Ardal smirked briefly and pushed himself out of a chair next to the cot Richard had been lying on. "It's a living," he said flatly, moving across the small, darkly decorated room, "keeps me out of trouble. The kind that seems to follow you around... Not to mention that I get to meet all sorts of characters...I even know a couple of your friends."

"I don't have any friends," Richard bluntly replied, trying to dismiss the comment.

Ardal turned back to look straight at Richard. "Family then," he clarified shortly. "Don't worry, I didn't mention anything about old business. He isn't even aware I know you. All for the better, wouldn't you say?" he smirked again, this time more for his own benefit rather than Richards. "Kid's got a few stories of his own, I'll say."

"I am aware," said Richard shortly, trying to acknowledge the topic as little as he could.

Static Tension

Ardal took a deep breath in and leaned down to Richard. "No..." he breathed quietly, "you're really not." He leant back again, eyebrows raised as if to encourage Richard to think on how times changed as well as the people with them. "Still, I doubt you stepped in front of a car right outside my place just because you wanted an excuse to catch up..."

"I needed their help," Richard stated quickly, gaining enough strength to add a level of urgency to his voice, "but I got what I wanted...Now I just need to get out of here," he tried to stand up but felt Aardal's hand clamp onto his shoulder and push him back to the cot.

"What's the rush?" he asked casually. "I'm sure you didn't piss off those bastards in the Illumous while you were in the desert or anything?" he slightly raised his hand from Richard's shoulder and cocked his head.

Before Ardal could continue, there was an enormous smash from beyond the side wall, drowning out the thudding music. It was followed by a few more, smaller crashes before the music was cut off entirely, leaving the bar in silence.

"I guess that answers my question."

Looking curiously to the door through to the main bar, Ardal absently pressed Richard down again as he once more tried to get up. "Let me guess..." he cast a loose hand towards Richard, "you got what you needed but it didn't quite go to plan? So not to plan that it literally knocked you back into your skin..." he clasped his hands together and raised an eyebrow.

Richard took a deep breath and looked back to Ardal, occasionally glancing at the door anxiously. "How?" he gawped for a second without a sound escaping his mouth. "How would you know? I barely even know what happened. I mean you don't even have the sight."

"I have made a lot of friends here...These Vespers, they're not like us. They don't even comprehend things like we do, everything's the same to them. Some of them give me titbits now and again such as why some lunatic-" he grimaced at Richard briefly, "dove in front of a car right outside my place..." his deep glare burned into Richard before it was broken with a wry smirk. "They can track you,

you know. The Illumous. Residual ectoplasmic energy, some call it…Basically a trail of breadcrumbs straight back to your body."

"That's why I need to get out of here," growled Richard slowly, leaning forward.

"You see the thing about Vespers," continued Ardal, ignoring Richard, "is that they don't tend to care about anything, not really…Well unless some goons break in and spoil their fun that is…Much like your new buddies just did," he sat back in his chair and took a long breath in. "I wouldn't worry, though, these lads really know how to look after themselves."

Despite the reassurances, Richard continued to shift uneasily, staring at the door. "You don't understand! I know what they are…They-" he thought for a second, his mind struggling to grasp the idea. "I know what *he* is… None of us are safe."

"And *I've* known that for years…" he offered the words with a contemptible nonchalance. "What you really need to realise is that times are changing. The Median World…" he tilted his head back loosely towards the door, an ever-growing set of crashes and screams resonating through its flimsy form, "it doesn't belong to them anymore. The age of the Seers is over. All of this, everything that's happening is for one reason and you just don't seem to get it. The Medians have a legacy that stretches back beyond Seers, Vespers or even me but they've always needed someone to look to; a leader. Back in the day the Seers just took advantage of that and look how everything turned out."

There was a sudden barrage of gunfire from beyond the door and the bar fell silent. Only now did Ardal crane his head around, a modicum of concern creeping into his expression. After a moment more of quiet, he turned back to Richard with a slightly more worrisome demeanour and finally allowed him to stand up.

"The truth is that Medians are capable of so much, even taming the desert if they wanted. Nor do they have to be alone, they never did... they just need someone to guide them…" he gave a long sigh in an effort to compose himself then gave a quick smirk. "Go," he offered simply, tilting his head towards another door which led to the alley, "do what you have to. Make proud those who have fallen in your name and those who still stand with you."

Static Tension

Richard made a break from Ardal and to the outside, briefly glancing back to see him still seated, absently picking at his nails. If Richard didn't know better, he would have believed Ardal had no idea that the Illumous could burst through the door at any second and kill him. He considered speaking again, trying to get him to leave, but he knew the attempt would be futile. Instead, he continued out into the dark and hurried along the damp alley, oblivious to the water dripping onto him from the gantry overhead.

He emerged out into the pouring rain and barely had a chance to step out into the amber light of the street before the boarded-up windows of the bar exploded outwards in a deafening fireball. The explosion jerked Richard violently out into the road and all around him cars swerved and screeched to a halt. For a while he tried to catch his breath, the blast having knocked it clear out of him, and with ringing ears he gazed, weary eyed, at what had happened.

Already the bar had been consumed by fire with flames licking from the blown-out windows, spitting ash into the street. Slowly rising to his feet, Richard stumbled towards the building, dazed and in disbelief that the Illumous would go this far.

A woman suddenly appeared in front of him, urging Richard to stop as she tried to tend to him and it was only now he began to notice just how grazed and burnt his own face was. He looked distantly around at the street strewn with debris as it smouldered in the rain. Finally, he fixed his gaze back to the bar as rubble began to fall from its walls. Then from the corner of his eye, Richard caught a glimpse of a figure partly obscured by the thick black smoke. It was dressed from shoulders to feet in a long black robe and wore a jet-black fedora, tilted in such a way as to obscure its face. Emerging from an alleyway a few buildings along from the bar, the figure seemed to ignore the commotion altogether and fix its attention entirely on Richard. Without hesitation, it raised a handgun and began firing it indiscriminately into the street.

Flinging himself backwards, Richard started to run as fast as he could, weaving in and out of a small crowd fleeing for their own safety. With a few more shots ringing out into the night, the assassin lowered his spent pistol and watched Richard run out of sight.

"He can't run forever," the assassin stated in frustration as another man, dressed in an identical outfit, stepped up beside him.

The second assassin clutched a shotgun tightly and a grin broke out from beneath the brim of his hat. "We know where he's going..."

Huddled in a bus shelter, a couple watched in bemusement as Richard rushed past them, oblivious of the rain lashing against him. Rather than give himself a break to process what had happened, he continued to limp along the deserted street, jogging when his exhausted legs allowed. It wasn't simply that he did not want to stop but more out of fear that the assassins may, at any second, emerge from the darkness. He could barely believe that such a secretive society as the Illumous would resort to the methods he had been on the wrong side of, especially to deal with just one person. He considered if Ardal had been right. Could he really be that important to them? To all Medians?

While Richard trudged on through the freezing rain, the pitch black, starless sky mocking his ever-dwindling options, his mind raced. Earnest had connected with him in the desert, planted memories that were not his own but rather than simply twisting Richard's mind for his own use, he had opened a doorway. As well as the false memories, a flood of information had poured from Earnest's thoughts into Richard's own. The Illumous, their history, all their attempts to tame the Other Side. He knew them all. He even knew of Earnest, the creature he had become upon abandoning his humanity centuries ago and, at last, he learned of himself. It finally came to him why the Illumous wanted him dead, why he and his own child could not exist in the same world together.

The thought struck Richard like a lightning bolt, forcing him to stagger and nearly fall as it forced the breath from his lungs. He stumbled into a dripping hedge and quickly gazed back down the dark street, only illuminated by a few dull, intermittent street lamps. He hung his head and closed his eyes, wishing none of this had happened, wanting only to go back to the relative contentment he had embraced so recently. At last, he opened his eyes and looked back down the street again, knowing that they were still chasing him and wouldn't stop until he was dead. Their master desired control over his child and the longer Richard stayed alive, the more of a threat he was.

Dripping wet and wheezing gently, Richard forced himself up and shook his head. He didn't know how he was going to do it but he was determined to put a stop to the Illumous, no matter what it took. He would make sure that no-one else had to die because of the cursed power that flowed through his veins. He couldn't do it alone, though, and there was only one person left who he thought could help him. The one person Richard still truly trusted and the only Seer amongst the unordained not to have been lost to the ranks of the Illumous.

With a jerk he started off again, running as fast as he could through the howling night. He ran until he could no longer breathe and his legs felt as if they would give way beneath him. The pain surged through every part of him, his entire body straining against every step. Yet still he continued, on through the night, only stopping when he finally arrived at that old and crumbling sandstone chapel that he had once known so well.

Richard stared up at the blackened building, the years of neglect and weathering on show for all to see. The various disfigured gargoyles silently watched Richard from their perches around the high balconies, their features rounded and barely recognisable, mere shadows of their former selves.

Suddenly Richard became aware of the rain pouring down onto him and he rushed across the street into the small alcove concealing the entrance. He reached forward and pressed his hand against the rusted iron but immediately pulled it back, staring at his palm as though some invisible force had burnt it. Slowly he reached out the hand again, pressing it against the cold, damp metal and pushed, feeling nothing of the burn this time. Exposing a gap against the wall, he wedged himself through and forced the door shut again with a muted clang.

Richard examined the empty building and stepped carefully across its cracked tiles, while rain dripped from his hair and coat leaving a trail of small puddles across the ground. No matter how much he tried, he couldn't get used to this place now. Since the Guardians had left it was like something had irreparably changed. The old

Illumination

place had always offered some deep sense of safety, comfort almost, even when there was no reason for it. That was now long gone, taken along with Lancer's pride and position, the same as every other Seer bar only the very highest. Until they redeemed themselves, it was only the most respected of Seers who bore the honour of protecting the Guardians. It was now clear that day of redemption may never come and, after what Ardal had told him, Richard wondered if that wasn't a good thing.

Something else was off, Richard mulled to himself while staring at the bare rafters, the emptiness of it all, the burning door. It was not simply that the place no longer provided the safety it once had but rather that it was actively unsafe.

"It's because it's cursed," said Lancer quietly, his words echoing around the hall as he stepped out from one of the side doorways. "I can see it in you, you're scared. My home frightens you now, makes you feel like you should just turn and run," his thick, Germanic undertones slipped through darkly as he spoke low and suggestively.

"I am scared because I've just been shot at by clichéd Illumous assassins!" growled Richard loudly, firmly stepping forward, shaking another pool of rainwater onto the ground. "Not to mention god only knows what is happening to the Desert!" he carried on angrily, throwing his arm aside, unsure whether to fear for his life or simply be angry at the insanity of the situation. "It's all so messed up," he said, more calmly this time, "the Median World, it's-"

"I know," murmured Lancer, moving around towards Richard. "We all do, the Seers that is. We always have."

Richard bore his teeth and gritted them tightly. "You have? Why in the hell didn't you tell me!? Do you know what I've been through today!?"

"It all happened for a reason," Lancer stated calmly.

"Cut the crap!"

"Everything happens for a reason," Lancer's voice was almost soothing in its composure, despite doing nothing to placate Richard. "You went through this because you had to-" Lancer raised his voice to prevent being spoken over, "it all needed to happen so that you would find the truth and *believe* it... That goes for your own truth, as well." He stopped and took a breath, prepared for a rebuttal but received none. "The others..." he started again softly, "they gave in to the void that remained when the Guardians left. Few remain on the path of light...I am the only common Seer, one not ordained to be pure by the powers beyond..." he sighed again and struggled to continue.

"But... How could it all happen in such a short time?"

"You don't understand," snapped Lancer soberly, "it's been going on for months...Years maybe. When the Guardians left there were those who wanted reform, a different way of thought. They wanted to embrace the beyond rather than simply watch over it...There was chaos and yet some were too distracted to even notice..."

Richard shook his head in defiance. "I needed time, Lancer. I had stuff going on."

"Ah yes, the *regular* life. Please regale me with how that goes as, for some of us, a life such as that is simply not possible."

"Lancer, I-"

"You abandoned us," Lancer swung around and pointed a finger accusingly at Richard. "You abandoned me..." he slowly lowered his arm and took a moment to collect himself.

"I'm sorry..."

"The Illumous' resurgence was seen by some as a calling, delivery from our plights," Lancer continued, ignoring Richard's words. "But it was anything but that. Like everything they do it was a ploy, perfectly timed to exploit us in our time of crisis... Regardless, Seers flocked to them, even ones who saw through their facade. Never has such a thing happened on so large a scale and I fear that, even if we get through this, our caste will not be able to recover."

Lancer lowered his head and took a step into what little light there was where it became apparent his clothes were dirty and torn. It was something Richard had missed before, as if some part of him refused to acknowledge the trials he had clearly been through. As Lancer moved closer, Richard couldn't help but feel wretched. Not only had all of this been because of him but maybe he could have helped to fix it, if only he hadn't been so wrapped up in himself.

"Our time is over... but yours is only just beginning..." Lancer gazed at Richard as though he were the only thing in the world. Eventually he rolled his eyes and turned away, "not the most auspicious of beginnings, I will grant you," he shouted, moving away quickly towards the far end of the chapel. "Your little jaunt to the Desert? *They* think it was my idea, that you're my puppet! In the eyes of the beyond we are all traitors. Not even the ordained get away with it now! We are cursed," he stopped at the far end of the chapel, beneath the large stained-glass window and breathed heavily. "The feeling you get here now? The terror in your gut? That was all you."

Richard tried to form the right words but couldn't find any. He simply watched as Lancer wrestled with what he had become and began to wonder if there was anything the old man still had to offer.

"Where others fought, I hid. Where others embraced the new nature of the Desert, I looked away. Where the others turned their backs on all they had known, all that had kept them safe, I stayed loyal," Lancers words rumbled around the chapel like thunder. "They should know by now that I would die before joining those Dark Seers on their unholy crusade! You hear me!?" he began to scream, staring up at the rafters with his arms thrown wide open. "I would rather die!" he dropped his arms loosely to his sides and looked back down to Richard.

"You think they heard you?" Richard asked weakly, unsure what to make of the spectacle.

"They hear everything," Lancer mumbled, a scowl set firmly on his brow, "they just don't care. The ways set out to protect the worlds now serve only the ones who created them..." he choked on the words and sputtered on his own tongue. "I can no longer follow an edict which would condemn me."

"So, what?" asked Richard forcefully. "You're just going to give up, wither away here?"

Lancer grinned and narrowed his gaze. "You misjudge me. For too long I have been caged by their rules, my hands bound when I could have made a difference. Without them I am free to fight the enemy at our gates and to see what was to remain unseen." Lancer's grin shifted into a demented leer as he considered the possibilities. "I will not do this for the dogmatic powers who seek to control me. No, I will do it for myself and in the name of the souls who had no other choice!"

Static Tension

Richard stepped back, suddenly fearful of his old friend. "You really think they'd let you go rogue like that?"

"Let them try and stop me," he grimaced and turned to stare at the huge, ornate window.

A deep rumbling began to resonate through the building, as though prompted by Lancers words, shaking the chapel's aged foundations. Then, in a shower of pulverised glass, the window imploded into the chapel and a vast swarm of swirling Guardians poured through. Thousands of them swooped through the building and weaved through the high rafters, kicking up a gale as they went.

A gentler smile returned to Lancers lips and he raised his arms to the swarm, knowing they were not there to harm him. In response they plunged towards him, swirling all around Lancer until he could no longer be seen.

Richard stood in awe as the mass of ghostly beings choked the air, enveloping all before them. Soon enough their frenzied motions slowed and their veil rose to reveal Lancer, his eyes glazed over with a bizarre silvery haze. He stood for a few seconds, motionless and silent, before opening his mouth and speaking with a strange otherworldly tone.

"I am one with them," he stated simply. "They heard my words and judged me worthy."

Lancer's eyes glimmered and the Guardians descended again, sweeping around him for a moment before quickly ascending again. They presented a changed man, clean and redressed in a grand ceremonial tunic with his blonde hair slicked back flat against his head.

"I guess they didn't want another yes man," mused Richard, transfixed by the sight. "Just needed to make sure they had the right guy."

"I am reborn," Lancer proclaimed, stepping away from the blown-out window. "Last and final of the ordained."

The Guardians abruptly turned and began flooding out of the window again, leaving Lancers eyes to fade back to their usual blue.

"That was...something," Richard managed to stutter. "Not sure what but it was definitely...something," he took a breath and tried to digest it all. "What now?"

Lancer tried to answer but wasn't entirely certain himself. "I command them now. All of them," he thought for a second and struggled to comprehend the power he had been granted. "They say a Seer's true calling is to know the Aether, the space between worlds, the threads that connect them. Only ordained Seers are said to have this power, though. The ones who have proved themselves."

Richard nodded shortly. "I could be wrong but I'm pretty sure you just did that," he blinked tightly, still trying to decide whether any of it had really happened. "What are you going to do with it?"

"Nothing's changed," said Lancer defiantly. "I'm going to fight the Illumous on my terms..." He looked out of the shattered window as a bolt of lightning tore open the sky, a deafening roar following as if Lancer, himself, had commanded it. "I'm going to end this."

The Prior weaved along the tunnels of the Illumous' subterranean complex, finally emerging into Earnests large auditorium. The sudden light against the pure white walls burnt his eyes slightly after the dark tunnels and yet he forced himself not to blink. He feared what he must to inform Earnest for he knew all too well that his master's wrath was nothing to underestimate. To him, failure was not an option.

Gradually his eyes adjusted to the gleaming walls and forms around him began to take shape. As he looked up to the throne, he saw Earnest pull away from a knelt statue, basking in the vigour of youth as the stolen life seeped into his skin, rejuvenating his form. While the Prior continued to watch uneasily, Earnest waved several guards over to arrange the statue with the others and turned to move towards him.

Shuffling uncomfortably, the Prior tried to quickly straighten his attire as Earnest moved up to him.

"I trust you have news," asked Earnest flatly with a voice much softer and steady than it had before.

Despite their new, youthful appearance, Earnest's eyes sparkled with the knowing of age. Even so, his face was that of someone barely out of their forties, the wrinkles on his ancient skin having been stretched out to seem as if they had never existed. Even his hair was darker, having only a few stray greys scattered here and there

The Prior shifted restlessly, feeling Earnest's power only grew with each rejuvenation and that now was the worst time to give him the news. "Uhh…" he stammered, seeing Earnest's patience already waning, "the Median, my lord…"

"He is dead?" asked Earnest quickly, his newly softened voice failing to provide any comfort.

The Prior choked on his words again, finally spitting them as fast as he could before recoiling away from his master's inevitable fury. "No, Sir."

Earnest gritted his teeth irritably but did not strike forward as the Prior had expected. Rather, his haunting figure hung in the tension filled air for a few more seconds, fixing the Prior in place. Eventually Earnest turned his back to consider the information, giving the Prior a chance to sigh a slow breath of relief. At last Earnest turned back and stared directly at his counterpart.

"No matter…" he said with an unexpected calm, "incompetence was anticipated… I expect we have also been revealed to the world during this escapade?" he gazed at the Prior who gawped wordlessly. "As I thought," he added shortly. "You do realise that it was the misguidance of my subordinates that failed to bring our plan to fruition last time?…Not our enemies. Not a lack of power or leadership but our own short-sightedness…"

The Prior trembled and struggled to keep his breathing under control while Earnest began to pace slowly around him.

"As I said, it doesn't matter. Our enemies have fallen to our will and I expected as much from the Median… I have no doubt that, in time, he will come to us…"

Earnest rounded the Prior and moved towards the long row of statues, inspecting his new addition as the guards heaved it into place.

"Nevertheless…" he offered, his voice filling with a tentative caution as he brushed a hand over the statue's face. Its features were frozen into a stance of terror, capturing the moment of death. "We can wait no longer. Already the child's power grows," he snapped his hand away from the statue and turned back sharply to the Prior who maintained a safe distance away from his superior. "Without the immediate death of the Median, it may even grow out of our control... We must release the power he possesses, begin the cleansing and acquaint this world with the new order." Earnest took a step towards his subordinate and placed a hand on his arm. "Gather the High Seers, bring me the mother. It is time we met our people," he grinned darkly with red lightning flickering across his eyes, "and achieve our destiny."

High in the sky, the air cracked open and thunder roared through the clouds heralding the arrival of the cloaked figures far below. They appeared in the shadows, unnoticed to the general populace but there nonetheless. They watched and waited, ready for the inevitable chaos that would erupt when the border between worlds finally broke down, releasing everything that had been forgotten. They waited to defend their new dominion from the terrible darkness that lurked in the neverworlds, to save the ones who were worthy and slay the ones who were not. At last, after all their manipulation, all of their meddling, they simply had to wait, assured in their supremacy, for the hell that would soon be unleashed.

III-VI – Radiance

All that is on Earth will perish

-Ar-Rahman 55:26

*H*ow did things get like this? How did they get so far out of hand? The Seers, the Illumous... All that I had once known was gone and it was my obsession with leading a normal life which had caused it. What's worse was that I hadn't even realised it... I couldn't shake the feeling that if I had been there for Lancer then it wouldn't have gotten this bad. Deep down I knew it wasn't the case. After all, I was just one person, what help could I have been? Still, if I had just been there then I could have at least said with conviction that I had stood by a friend in their time of need. None of that mattered now, though, and with it only being a matter of time before the Illumous caught up with me, I had to believe that one person could make a difference.

There was a huge rumble of thunder that shuddered the crumbling walls of the chapel. Lancer gazed up at the broken window as the driving rain poured in onto the old mosaic floors, making them glisten in the flashes of lightning. Another rumble shook the building and a fork of lightning tore across the night, prying open the sky for a brief moment. It seemed to spill out an unearthly light, illuminating shadows where there were none before sealing shut again, the tear consumed back into the fabric of the night air.

Illumination

"This is not a normal storm," said Lancer shortly, looking back at Richard, "the membrane between this world and the next is breaking down." He pointed sharply out of the window as another crack opened up in the sky. "That's not just lightning," he stated firmly, the agitation in his voice growing, "they're shatter points. Cracks in the walls of reality."

"And you say I'm dramatic," quipped Richard quietly, prompting Lancer to rush towards him.

"You realise you sped this up, don't you? Merely by going to the Median World and coming back, the power you hold has drawn the planes exponentially closer than they already were...You are as a magnet pulling at the Other Side! You won't go to it so it is coming to you." Lancer shook his head and wondered if he could ever make Richard understand. "What makes things worse is that the growing power in that kid of yours is doing exactly the same!"

Richard looked up at Lancer quickly, gazing curiously at him as he considered how everyone knew about Hollie's pregnancy before him.

"Don't look so surprised," started Lancer casually, "what do you think started all this? Why do you think I sent *you* to the Imam? I called and you came..."

"You knew and you didn't tell me?"

"No Seer can ignore a power like that coming into this world, it's just they knew long before I did. Long before anyone should have been able to know."

"That doesn't answer my question," growled Richard. "Why didn't you tell me?"

"It wasn't my place, I was protecting you, it would have only distracted you. Pick one you can live with," he sighed, feeling that Richard was failing to focus on the important points. "You have to understand that this has been coming ever since you touched the Other Side. A cascade of events leading to right now." Lancer paused to make sure Richard was finally paying attention. "When the Abyss was unleashed onto this world, it just gave the Illumous a way to see through time itself... They saw your son."

"I don't care," Richard breathed, exhausted with the prophecies and visions. "I know what I need to do," he stated firmly, recalling what he had been shown at the Illumous' temple.

"Are you sure?" asked Lancer sombrely. "This isn't going to be some walk in the park, you know."

"It never is...I have to save my family, though."

Richard turned towards the exit and quickly found Lancer at his side. He smiled as they stepped up to the rusted iron door and took hold of the bulky handle.

"Just like old times, eh?" Lancer chuckled as he heaved open the door, the chill of the wet air rushing in to meet them.

"Unfortunately so..."

Richard stepped out into the rain but was swiftly forced back inside by a hail of gunfire, the bullets ricocheting off the walls around him, kicking up a cloud of dust to cover his escape.

"Or not," he finished, cowering behind a wall, clutching a bleeding wound in his shoulder.

Gritting his teeth in pain, Richard slumped against the inside wall while Lancer pressed the iron door back into place.

"No, I don't remember ever being shot at," griped Lancer, flinching every time a bullet hit the outside of the door.

"Well not when I was with you, at least," Richard chuckled slightly, wincing and tightening his grip on the wound as he did.

"You've been shot," Lancer finally noticed, quickly moving to inspect the wound.

"Oh, have I?" asked Richard, swatting him away as he tried to pull open his jacket. "It's fine, it just clipped me. Bloody birdshot." Richard gritted his teeth and pushed away from the wall, doing his best not to cry out as pain surged through his shoulder and blood started to seep through his fingers. "Mind you, I wouldn't have pegged these guys for the loud option," he added just as the gunfire at the door ceased.

"You're pivotal to their whole scheme, Richard, an uncontrolled variable," Lancer stressed the words as much as he was able, holding his hands out wildly. "Freely running around with the kind of power you have; it throws everything into chaos for them... At the

Illumination

moment the only thing they care about is making sure you don't see tomorrow."

Richard pointed a bloody finger accusingly at Lancer, starting forward abruptly. "Look! I'm about sick of everyone going on about this *power* I hold. If I'm so powerful then why the hell can't I do anything with it? Why can't I snap my fingers and help my family!?"

"It's not like that, Richard," Lancer replied calmly and laid a hand on Richard's shaking arm, pressing it down to his side. "It's an essence, the life blood of an existence we're not meant to touch yet. Despite all the precautions and rules laid out eons ago, you have. That, my friend, is the most powerful thing anyone should be able to imagine," he watched as Richard's expression relaxed, the words placating his anxieties for the moment.

"Fine then," Richard conceded at last, "but I'm still going after them, even if I have to go out there and see to every one of those bastards myself."

Lancer smiled widely. "I wouldn't expect anything less... Although I feel just waltzing out there would be foolhardy to say the least," he walked back into the chapel and ushered Richard over. "They've got the front covered but there is another way out. An old parishioners' exit, quick escape from sermons I'd imagine," he started over towards the altar and one of the side doors. "Now I can't guarantee they don't know about this route as well which could make our job somewhat more difficult."

"So much for options," grumbled Richard, looking back over his shoulder as he closely followed Lancer through the door.

"We do have these, of course..."

The room was nothing more than a closet filled with old religious paraphernalia including an old lecterns, robes and candle arbours. There were even portions of old railings and several pews stacked against the walls. Wasting no time, Lancer hurried over to the corner and picked up two stubby, golden candlesticks and gently tossed one to Richard. He fumbled it for a second with his free hand then inspected the grubby brass, eventually turning his gaze back to Lancer with a distinct lack of amusement.

"This? Against guns?"

"Look," stated Lancer flatly, "it's the best I can do, alright? If they're out there then this might just give us some sort of fighting chance." While he spoke, he pulled aside a cloth emblazoned with a large Pentecostal flame to reveal a small wooden doorway leading out to the night beyond.

"Well, I suppose any sort of a chance is better than none at all," Richard murmured, following Lancer to the doorway.

"Alright," Lancer said quietly, taking a hold of the door handle, "here goes nothing."

Lancer pulled at the rusted old handle and pushed the door open, tentatively stepping out into the rain-soaked car park behind the chapel. As he looked around the short barrel of a handgun emerged from around the ajar doorway and a muffled voice ordered him to drop the candlestick. Without a word, Lancer complied and eyed Richard as he was forced to turn away from the doorway to be searched. Waiting until the assailant emerged from behind the door, Richard silently crept out from the storeroom. Without hesitation he heaved the candlestick as hard as he could around the back of the assailant's head, knocking him to the ground.

Lancer looked around cautiously and sighed with relief at the sight of Richard. "See, I told you it would work out," he said flatly, a little rattled by how the situation had panned out.

"Quiet!" hissed Richard, silently closing the door and starting across the car park. "There's more, remember?"

"Yes," came another voice from behind, making them stop mid step, "there are many more of us... Too many for you, I am afraid."

Turning around as slowly as they dared, they both began to raise their hands uneasily, the action causing Richard to grimace with pain. As they turned, they just managed to catch a glimpse of another figure behind the Illumous agent. It picked up the candle stick Lancer had dropped and clubbed the agent across the head, setting him on the ground alongside his partner.

"You can't be left alone for five minutes, can you?" came the familiar voice as it dropped the candle stick with a loud clang.

Richard and Lancer lowered their hands slowly and looked down to the bodies then back up at who had saved them, not quite believing who it was.

Illumination

"Now are we going to do this or not?" asked Ardal irritably, shaking what rain he could from his mack, "cos someone's gotta pay for my bar!"

The sky continued to twist and contort, the membrane of the world cracking like fault lines in the air. They showered the world below with an other worldly light as the planes were pulled inexorably together, the jagged edges of distant realities tearing open a universe of unknowns. The shimmering maws opening all across the city whispered truths and fables from times long past. At the same time as forgotten memories of the ancient dead found physical form in a strange land, the living became but an illusion, a trivial story as they were swallowed up by time. So too, the others came. Those trapped between worlds; scourge of the desert, horrors of the Abyss.

Each time a life vanished, however, or an entity of the between became flesh, the Illumous were there to contain and, moreover, control. They would harness the power of the crossings, tame the process to their own liking and yet it was happening too quickly. The dead became manifest and began to overwhelm their handlers, roaming the streets with neither knowledge of nor regard for the beings they now existed alongside. They possessed only one drive, to preserve the new life they had been granted at all costs. It wasn't much but with thousands of misplaced entities all with the same goal, it was enough to throw the Illumous into chaos, casting their ancient and meticulously laid plans into disarray.

Richard strode ahead, leading his companions towards the Illumous' temple. It was the focal point of the celestial collision he had seen in the desert but also the way to Hollie. All around them, through the sheet like rain, the air pulsated and sparked as the tears in reality descended to ground level. The long streets now held only the manifested and cloaked members of the Illumous trying desperately to control them, each as oblivious to the three as each other.

"They're losing control," shouted Lancer over the pouring rain and cracking lightning, "it won't be long now, we have to hurry."

"Don't you think we know that?" asked Ardal angrily, "if we get hit by one of those damned cracks then I think it'll be a pretty obvious sign that we were too late!"

"You're alive," stated Richard suddenly as he continued to stride toward the cathedral, his shoulder having become numb enough to ignore. "How?" he finally asked, the notion of Ardal surviving the bar explosion at last dawning on him.

"I have my ways," replied Ardal cryptically, "you know that."

"I don't know anything" snapped Richard as they stepped up to the large cathedral doors. "Not of you," he growled while Lancer pressed open the doors and peered inside. "I never have."

"It's clear but they know we're here," Lancer warned, "there'll be any number of those bastards on us in no time. We need to keep moving!"

"I'll stay, hold them off," tried Ardal, turning dismissively away from Richard.

"The hell you will!" Richard grabbed Ardals arm and pulled him back to face him. "You always managed to divide my attention so I could never see what you really were…"

"How's your arm?" Ardal asked casually, eying Richard's bloody shoulder meaningfully.

Lancer laid a hand on Richards' back. "Really, we need to go," he looked up at a row of white clad figures emerging from the rain.

"He's right…You've run out of time," Ardal rested his hand on Richards and slowly peeled it away from his arm. "Some things are meant to wait," he lowered the hand and gently released it, smirking slightly as Richard was pulled away into the building and the door was slammed shut behind them. "I have been waiting too long," muttered Ardal blithely, turning to the figures bearing down on him.

"What the hell was that all about!?" snarled Lancer, pushing Richard in towards the centre of the nave. "We're in an unfathomable amount of danger and you seem to be trying as hard as you can to alienate one of our few allies!"

Richard breathed heavily and started over towards the trap door. "I'm sorry, it's just that there are too many questions… about everything. The time I've had without all *this*, without being a Median…It's made me think. There are more things in heaven and

Earth than we could even imagine, let alone achieve, and that's to say nothing of whatever's beyond that."

"So?" asked Lancer with agitation.

"So why does it all seem to happen to me? Even before I crossed over and got this... power, things just always seemed to happen to me and *he* was one of them." Richard pointed back at the door with his injured arm and grabbed at his shoulder for the effort. "He was always there," he forced through clenched teeth, "he's never changed, never even seemed to age... He's not what he seems, Lancer. He knows things, I can feel it."

Richard heaved at the hatch, struggling to pull it open with a single arm but was quickly joined by Lancer, helping him to swing the trapdoor over onto the stone floor.

"Tell you what, you two can have a nice sit down and talk it out some time," started Lancer sarcastically. "Only can we make sure it's not when we're all at risk of living with a perpetual lack of death for all eternity!"

Lancer pushed Richard harshly towards the opening in the ground, prompting him to start down the steep, slippery steps. With a final look around the cathedral and a quick glance back towards the door, Lancer followed him, pulling the trapdoor tightly closed behind him.

Deep below the city's foundations, beneath pipelines and sewers, carved from the living bedrock was the Illumous' auditorium. Its grand stature remained peaceful and silent, far from the chaos consuming the streets above. In its centre stood Earnest, tall and motionless, encircled by seven of the highest elders of the Illumous' order. Each of them whispered a chant to themselves, murmuring the words over and over.

Where guards had once been posted around the edge of the chamber, there were now only the statues of Earnest's fallen benefactors. They stood as silent witnesses to a ritual too hallowed for the eyes of mere sentries.

The encircled elders continued their chant as Earnest suddenly looked up to the entrance into the chamber. From beyond there was the distinct sound of footsteps stumbling through the labyrinthine darkness. A sickly smile slowly spread across his face as silhouettes started to materialise from the dank darkness and he knew his time was drawing near.

"Get your hands off of me!" screamed Hollie as she emerged from the tunnel with the Prior pushing her along roughly, his hand clamped firmly around her arm. They stopped short of the circle of Seers and Hollie managed to shake herself free. "You! What the hell do you want with me now?" she snapped, pointing fiercely towards Earnest.

Earnest slowly raised his arm and flicked back a finger, ushering the Prior to bring her closer. "Circumstances have changed, my dear. I'm afraid even I underestimated the pureness of the aether running through you...or the persistence of your...." he thought for a second, "companion, for that matter."

"Richard?" breathed Hollie weakly, "what have you done to him?" she growled again while the Prior pushed her into the circle and forced her to her knees.

"*We* have done nothing to him," Earnest casually offered, stepping around her. "It is, in fact, what *he* has done to you," he stared deeply at her as she tried to avoid his gaze. "If it were not for him crossing the planes and drawing the worlds together faster than even we could achieve, then we would not need to take this action. You see, given that our intended leader is hardly able to guide us into this new world which so rapidly approaches, a replacement is required. One who must, I fear, take the power you carry within you..." Earnest struck a hand forward and grasped Hollie by the head, digging his fingers into her skull. "That leader will be me."

"What is this place?" muttered Richard irritably, fumbling along the damp walls.

"A maze carved out over a thousand years," Lancer said with almost reverence, "dug to fit whatever role they needed."

Richard scoffed. "What, did they get contractors in or something?"

"The Illumous hasn't always been a small cult of fanatics," explained Lancer calmly. "Long ago they were a thriving community, respected as seekers of truth. That was until it was known how corrupting that truth could be..." he trudged carefully along the tunnel, admiring the effort that went into it. "They always liked their seclusion. The tunnels always helped to keep their enemies confused and at arm's length."

"Then what bloody chance do we have?" Richard snapped, stopping dead in his tracks. "This is just another one of those things I could have really done with knowing about!"

"We'll find our way," Lancer offered with confidence, "there's no need to fear."

"Care to explain how?"

Lancer turned around and stepped back towards Richard. "There is a part of you down here. The power that you would deny is the very same which courses through your child. It calls to itself and, as it draws the Other Side ever closer to us now, it will draw you to Hollie."

Richard was silent for a moment, contemplating the idea. "How?"

"You must open yourself to the power, accept it. Only then will you control it." Lancer placed a hand across Richards eyes and held onto his arm. "Listen... Look past the now, beyond the voices of your mind and into the beyond..."

At first there was nothing but fear, his own dread which had been with him since finding that Hollie was missing. Doing his best to push that aside, Richard found something else, a part of himself that had been usurped by something familiar but also altogether alien. The more he focussed on it, the clearer it became, growing within his mind until he was awash with it. Suddenly it was as though his eyes had been opened and he saw everything. There were the cracks in the sky far above him, the warren of tunnels ahead and, in the distance, a beacon which pulled at him, drawing him in like a magnet.

Pulling Lancers hand away from his face, Richard stared along the dim tunnel which had seemed so bright only seconds earlier. "It worked..." he mouthed in astonishment, "I know where they are..."

As he pressed his fingers into Hollie's face, a dark cloud began rising from the ground around Earnest, spiralling around his limbs and engulfing his entire body. Suddenly seven shadowy arms struck out from the centre of the circle into each of the Dark Seers, twisting around them and squeezing what life they still had out of them.

"I must give thanks to him," came Earnest's voice, now gravelly and distorted behind the dark clouds, "this was not to be my destiny until the child's power matured." From the cloud an entity of pure malice and hate pressed forward. Its bright crimson eyes were set against a ghostly, jet-black face which seemed to endlessly melt upon itself, a fluid cascade of darkness. "But now that the essence of the Other Side is within my grasp, this world shall die and I will rule over an eternity of unceasing death!"

The tendrils swirled around the room and swallowed the circle of Seers as the entity rose up high into the air, feeding on the lives of those below. Suddenly it turned sharply, powdery trails of inky black hanging in the air behind it, and watched as Richard and Lancer rushed into the chamber.

"That's..." Richard stammered upon laying eyes on the towering creature, "that's not what I signed up for," he managed to say, edging backwards as Lancer sidled in front of him. "What the hell is that thing?"

Lancer moved slowly forward, drawn now by the inexorable curiosity of something he believed to be extinct. "It can't be," he whispered as the huge bulk heaved and stared down at him, "you can't exist."

"I can..." a shady, haunting voice boomed around the walls, before finally settling painfully upon Lancer, "but you won't!"

Another tendril shot out from the main mass of the entity and crashed down to the ground just as Lancer dove out of the way, scrambling to his feet and pushing Richard back into the tunnel.

"Care to let me in on things?" Richard said quickly, pushing up from the damp ground. "*What is it?*"

"A Lurker," Lancer wheezed shortly, "an evil that is meant to be extinct."

There was another crash as the Lurkers arm slammed to the ground again, shaking the tunnel and showering the two with dust and shards of stone.

"The Illumous," Lancer started apprehensively, "they're a collection of misguided Seers, nothing this strong. The Lurkers were meant to have been wiped out centuries ago, banished to the Other Side."

Illumination

Richard grabbed Lancer by his shirt and pulled at him. "What is it, really?" Richard asked through gritted teeth, "where is that Illumous bastard?"

"That's him," Lancer replied simply, "that's his true form... He must have needed to replenish his life force before he could manifest..." he looked between the statues positioned around the Lurkers colossal form and cradled his head heavily as he realised how Earnest had done it. "Those poor people... but that still wouldn't have been enough... unless..." he broke free of Richard, nearly pushing him to the ground and stared at the creature in horror. "He wants the power for himself."

"To hell with this!" Richard snapped darting back towards the auditorium only to be pulled back sharply as another arm struck the ground. "I have to stop him!" snarled Richard, thrashing against Lancer's grip.

"No, Richard. Don't you realise what that is? It's a Guardian, only everything opposite to what we know. Like Seers become Guardians when pass on, Lurkers are what become of truly Dark Seers. I don't mean these fallen Seers; I mean the kind of corrupt being that hasn't had a kind thought in its life. A creature evil enough to do that!" he pointed past Richard towards the statues. "It takes a lot to make a Lurker and once it exists, it's near impossible to stop," he lowered his arm and looked again at the monstrous beast. "Guardians pool power into a collective, share that power for the benefit and protection of Mortals... Lurkers are unwilling, incapable even, of doing that. Instead, they feed on the power and anything else that gets in their way. Mortals, Seers, Guardians... even other Lurkers..."

"They didn't go extinct, did they?" asked Richard simply, slowly coming to grasp the truth Lancer had feared.

Lancer shook his head sombrely. "I don't think so, at least not in the way we thought."

"It doesn't matter," Richard said firmly, looking Lancer in the eye. "I can't let him do this to her."

"I know," Lancer replied quietly, "but look at what he's capable of," he gestured to the statues again, "I'm not going to let that happen to you. I think I'm the only one who can stop him now," he added with conviction.

Richard squinted at Lancer as if trying to unravel an enigma. "The Guardians?" he asked finally.

Lancer softly laid a hand on Richard's shoulder and nodded gently. "They trust me…"

Without another word or resistance from Richard, Lancer turned and strode, unafraid to set right every sin the Seers had ever committed.

Rising up at Lancers approach, the Lurker withdrew from the circle of Seers, revealing seven stone remnants, each more contoured and disfigured than the next. In the centre laid Hollie, unconscious but alive, having been spared from the fate of the others. Above her drifted what Earnest had become, smaller now and no larger than a man, but no less powerful. It bore a passing resemblance to the spectral profile of a Guardian only it was jet black and shimmered with the eerie dark light of a place beyond knowing. Without any distinction, its limbless body merged into a stubby head and a pair of bright red eyes stared out from deep within the murky soot.

"Heretic," the Lurker screeched into Lancer's mind. "I would have the Median watch. Bring him to me and you may yet take a place at my side."

"No," Lancer stated firmly, staring fixedly at the creature above him.

The Lurker gave a terrible cackle which shook the chamber and stabbed at Lancers ears. "You have no dominance here! You are weak, your kind is gone!" the dark being drifted down and inspected Lancer closely. "You have fallen from *their* favour and have no way to stop me!"

Lancer gazed up into the Lurkers haunting red eyes. "My people may have fallen to your seduction but for as long as I draw breath the light will live on."

"Then you will die and that light will be extinguished!"

In a movement quicker than the eye could see, the Lurker darted towards Lancer, its eyes burning with crimson fury. With a movement just as swift, Lancer held up an outstretched hand, halting the creature mere inches away from him. For a second the Lurker hung there, restrained by some invisible force as a roaring began to resonate around the auditorium. Then, out from the tunnel, emerged thousands of Guardians which encircled the Lurker and pulled at its shadowy form, trying to rip it from the living world.

"The light *will* remain," Lancer repeated peacefully as he watched Guardians tear the Lurker apart.

"But you will still die!" screamed the Lurker defiantly in Lancer's head, forcing him to his knees as Richard emerged from the tunnel to help him.

Without warning, the Lurker attacked one last time, throwing out a tendril which knocked Richard away before quickly wrapping itself around Lancer and tossing him against the arched ceiling. For a few long moments, Lancer fell through the air while the Guardians pulled the Lurker back and finished their work. By the time he hit the ground, the spinning mass of Guardians had already started to dissipate, the violent winds they had brought with them fading as quickly as they had come. Eventually the last of the Guardians dwindled to nothing and the Lurker was gone.

In the silence of the auditorium, the air seemed to whisper with a lingering voice, a will beyond Earnest or any of the Dark Seers. "In time..." it said shortly, struggling to hold on as long as it could, "my will be done..."

For some time, the three laid motionless amongst the statues, a strange quiet creeping from the chamber and out into the city. It touched the fallen Seers, bringing with it a dismay and the knowledge that they had failed.

Eventually Richard began to stir and sat up, looking around at the desolate chamber. Immediately his eyes fell on Hollie and yet his attention was innately drawn to Lancer. Hurrying over to his side, Richard could see that both of his legs were bent back, shattered from the fall, and that there was a pool of blood seeping from his head onto the cracked tiled floor.

"Lancer!" he shouted, grabbing his arm and shaking him gently. "Come on, not like this!"

Lancer's eyes opened a little and he tried to raise his head, looking uneasily up at Richard. "It's over?" he asked weakly.

Richard nodded slowly. "Yes, it's over...He's gone."

Lancer sighed gently and tilted his head back into the pool of blood. "Then I can go in peace."

"No, Lancer! You can't, I won't let you...This-" he waved vaguely over Lancers wounds, "this is nothing, you'll be fine."

Lancer suddenly grabbed Richard's hand and squeezed it tightly. "It's alright, Richard... I found redemption...and now it's my time," he smiled as much as he could and squeezed again. "Remember what'll happen to me? It's alright...I'll be alright... so should you," he looked into Richard's eyes one last time and slowly their shine drained away as his hand went limp.

As a tear ran down his face, Richard laid Lancer's hand across his chest and got to his feet. For a time, he hung his head and mumbled a few words in an effort to ease Lancer's soul into its next life. Eventually he turned and set his eyes on Hollie who was still sprawled out in the middle of the stone circle. Immediately he bolted over to her and dropped down to his knees, pressing his fingers against her neck to find a pulse. Just before finding one, her eyes opened and looked up to him peacefully.

"It's gone," she whispered. "The power he wanted. He got it and took it back with him."

"Are you alright?" asked Richard quickly, "the baby?"

"We're alright but that essence... I can feel the hollow without it..." she sat up and looked around. "We're alright," she repeated, trying to assure herself of the fact. "At least we will be," she looked around again and found Lancer. "No..." she gasped in horror, "he can't be..." she added, hurrying over to his body.

For an unfelt time, they hung over Lancer, trying to comprehend the meaning of it all. The meaning of his passing and the meaning of their own lives. No one knew exactly what happened to Seers when they died. They became Guardians, that much was understood but beyond that it was a mystery. Where did they go when not servicing the living? What did they even experience? This was still one of the great mysteries that even Medians couldn't fathom and with no more Seers, it was unlikely they would ever find out. What's more was that, for the first time in untold years, Medians were on their own, free to unlock their potential or descend into chaos.

Illumination

At last, they decided that there was no meaning and sometimes it was all as senseless as it seemed. Even their own salvation and the ultimate redemption of the Seer legacy tasted bitter in the light of what was lost. It was at this point they turned, unspeaking and left, allowing the devastated hall and those in it to rest eternally.

Stepping from the cathedral into the damp dawn, the air clear and fresh after the storms, Richard and Hollie watched as the sun began to creep over the sprawl of houses stretching to the horizon. Richard looked down at the unconscious agents about the doorway, then up and around for Ardal. As he suspected, Ardal was already long gone, taking with him the answers Richard desired. For now, it made little difference for Richard was simply content that they had escaped with their lives. There would come a time, however, when he would need those answers and, at that time, he knew that Ardal would be there.

"Harmless now," stated Richard quietly, looking between what was left of the Illumous, "them and any like them will soon find that everything they fought for is gone..." he took a deep breath of the cold morning air, gazing around again. "They'll have to find their own way now... Although I'm not sure many will be able to live with themselves after all of this."

"So, what now?" asked Hollie, turning to Richard.

"The tears will heal, the cracks between worlds will close... Things might be weird for a while but the planes should go back to normal now the imbalance of power is gone. Reality has a way of recovering like that..." he smiled for a second. "Life goes on."

Richard thought for a second about what he had said and debated whether to continue. At last, he decided against it, knowing that the moment was too fragile already. Even so, Hollie noticed something in his eyes, that hidden fear of something terrible. She opened her mouth to speak but there were no words. Instead, she simply reached over and slipped her hand into his, grasping it tightly as they both watched the city shine with the dawning sun.

When I was a child, I remember being told that there were things beyond both knowledge and control. Today I experienced both. The nature of everything I knew had changed forever and I had lost a dear friend. Now, more than ever, I should have wanted to turn away from everything I was meant to be, everything everyone wanted me to be but instead I finally knew why I couldn't. I had a responsibility to protect this world, to protect those in it from everything that lurks in the beyond. At times I may even have to protect it from itself. With this insight I accepted once and for all who I was and what I had to do for I knew what was coming. That familiar shade in a place so distant...

As it always did, life indeed went on, the mayhem of fractured reality falling into a memory that was all too easily forgotten. Naturally people changed to accommodate the new and the lost but no matter what happened the world kept on spinning. Each day passed as it always had, uncaring of the events that it harboured.

Sometimes the past crept up on Richard, the silence when he visited Lancer's memorial made sure of that, yet the sound of his newborn son soon put it to rest again. He had a reason to focus on the future now, a reason to let go of the tumultuous memories he had clung on to for so long. When he looked at his family, Richard felt contentment like he had never experienced and yet, try as he might, there was a foreboding he could not shake. The Illumous had shown him terrible things in their warped mockery of the Median world; visions of the end and eternal shadow. They had shown him his own death and the terror it would herald.

He tried to tell himself that they had all been ploys by the Illumous, attempts to keep him away, mere visions that weren't even worth dwelling on. The night told him something different, though. Just as he entered the realm between waking and sleep, the words would come. They drifted across the void and echoed in Richard's mind, silencing all other voices.

"I shall be born again."

Printed in Great Britain
by Amazon